"*Foretold* is a thrilling read! Cassandra is the kind of heroine that I've longed for, the kind that proves there can be no courage without fear and no heroism without determination. Lumani's debut expertly weaves a tale of grief and love, hope and betrayal that will grip you from page one and leave you begging for more."

-Greta Kelly
Author of *The Frozen Crown*

"*Foretold* is a riveting story of a young girl grappling with her own mind, and through the darkness of her emotions, learning her inner truths. Lumani delivers a must-read, with a heroine whose journey to personal growth rivals her fantastical journey in pure magic."

-Amber Rae
Author of *Choose Wonder over Worry*

"With an action-packed story, complex and unique magic, and charming, deeply human characters, *Foretold* is an incredible debut [with] heart-wrenchingly beautiful and realistic depictions of struggles with OCD, anxiety, and grief."

-Anya Leigh Josephs
Author of *Queen of All*

Runner-up for the 2021 Maxy Award
for Young Adult Literature

Publisher's Note:

If you enjoy this novel, please leave a positive rating and/or review on Goodreads, Amazon, or other similar websites to let other readers know. Reviews work! Support your favorite authors.

THE SCRYERS
BOOK ONE

FORETOLD

VIOLET LUMANI

Uproar Books

1419 PLYMOUTH DRIVE, NASHVILLE, TN 37027

FORETOLD

Published by Uproar Books, LLC.

Cover art by Shayne Leighton.

ISBN 978-1-949671-21-6

First paperback edition.

To Emirson, Evalina & Brendon
for filling each day with magic

To my mom and dad
for always telling me I could do anything
(except the stuff they disapproved of)

And to Nicky
forever missed even though
he voted me off the island

1

Today is a good day.

And on the heels of that thought, as if summoned by it, its shadow follows—the image of my father lying in a pool of blood, the victim of a break-in occurring right before I get home. It's a whisper of an impression but enough to kick it off: a familiar, inky sensation spilling down my spine and snaking out, growing in power and urgency. My fingers twitch. I reflexively ball them into fists.

Please. Not in front of the school. A strangled cry rips its way up through me, but I wrestle it to a tortured squeak.

I pick at my peeling nail polish and draw in June-warmed air heavy with the scents of honey-roasted nuts and sweating garbage bags. It's hard to ignore the avalanche of jostling elbows pouring out of the school around me, but I try as I slowly move down the steps and through the gates to the sidewalk.

Focus on that. Focus, Cass. One. Two. Three. Four. I am in charge.

Mrs. O's rust-red bodega awning calls out to me from across the street, and I lock onto it with all the intensity of a heat-seeking missile. I'll pop in to visit her before heading home. It's a Friday so Dad will order lasagna from the Italian place around the block; he'll pretend he made it, and I'll pretend to believe.

A perfectly predictable plan. I almost feel normal.

Good. Focus on the lasagna. Five. Six. This compulsion is not me.

I dig my nails deeper into my palms and fight the urge, pleading with myself. It becomes harder to see the world around me, to focus on anything but overcoming this. *Make it to ten. Make it to ten.*

Seven. It does not rule me.

Eight...

I leap over a spider's web of a sidewalk crack to a "safe" patch of pavement and rap my knuckles on the street lamppost five times. I'm too mortified to look up and see the confusion on the faces of those around me—or worse, pity—so I pull off the flyer taped to the post.

Maybe they'll think I'm super into... I glance down at the paper. "*Hot* Yoga—Naked Yoga Classes for Beginners."

"Summer plans all set, huh?" one of the senior boys asks. His friends snicker. *Awesome.*

The light changes and people stream around me, some grumbling as I stand rooted in the middle of their path. After all, they have places to be. I do, too. But right now I need to wait.

The inky feeling has abandoned my spine and pooled in my limbs, leaving them leaden. Steely skyscrapers loom like gray giants, pressing down on me. The intersection light is about to turn again and the crossing crowds slow to a trickle, but I can't move. *Oh God, what is this? This is new.*

"Atypical," Dr. Ward called my OCD and its various manifestations. Not exactly a word sixteen-year-old girls want associated with them, unless a cute boy is saying, "It's *atypical* how gorgeous she is."

This feeling, though, like an invisible python's squeeze, holding me in place, choking all thought from me until only animal panic remains... this is *off*, even for me. The idling cars at the intersection accelerate into a blurred river of metallic sound. A group gathering on the sidewalk presses closer, and I fight for control as my heart beats a runaway staccato against my ribcage. *You're okay, you're okay, you're okay, okay, okay.*

I shouldn't be surprised. My OCD triggers are usually dark, intrusive thoughts, but my compulsions... some people have to run through predictable rituals to feel like everything will be okay, but although I've got a few favorites, mine are random. Washing, repeating, picking, whatever—the need to go along with twisted impulses, and the crushing certainty that noncompliance spells disaster. The thoughts, *the worry*, always hover in the background, but it's been a while since I've had to fight off such a fierce urge to bust out an OCD ritual. I'd even fooled myself into believing I'd mastered them.

Move, I beg my worn tennis shoes, blinking back tears. I summon up Dr. Ward's exercises as the light turns for a second time. Or third? I've been standing here for an eternity, I know that. *I guess I live here now*, I think, swallowing a hysterical laugh. Humanity parts around me like the Red Sea.

My eyes dart around as I seek out assistance, a lifeline, but no one makes eye contact in this city if they can avoid it. A blue-black glint of hair from across the street catches my eye, and then the boy beneath the hair looks up at me. His eyes are bright blue. I can tell, even from a distance. They draw me in until everything narrows to those two sapphire points. In that moment I can smell the tang of

3

his skin, the place where his shoulder meets his neck. My fingertips tingle, but not with a new OCD compulsion—with remembered touches.

I know him. How?

His surprised expression gives way to a slow, sweet smile I feel deep in my chest. *Oh my God.* I glance behind me, but sure enough: it's me he's looking at.

And suddenly that panicked, glued-in-place feeling melts away, like I've stepped into a shower. I exhale the lungful of air I was holding in and experimentally lift my foot off the ground. I'm loose, and I *need* to move—closer to him.

Maybe my body knew I was waiting for him, for this moment, before I did. My cheeks warm, and the corners of my lips twitch upward in a shy answer to his smile. I can feel myself blushing. He points to himself and to me with eyebrows raised in question, asking if he should come over. I shrug in what I hope is believable disinterest, and my heart leaps when his smile widens. I've never felt this before, this soaring...

He moves to make his way toward me, taking a step—

Screeching tires. Horns. Screams. My mouth works once, twice, but no sounds emerge. I hear a keening wail in the distance, and it's a second before I realize I'm the source. I tremble violently, staring stupidly.

The driver steps out of his car and shouts as he peers at the crumpled figure in the street. His hands pull at his hair in despair as he paces around, unsure of what he should do next. I clutch blindly for the streetlamp again, bile rising in my throat.

"Are you alright?" a woman asks.

Chaos. Strangers, good Samaritans, run to help the boy, but he's gone. I know it, I can feel it, and the loss claws at my gut. I've just watched a boy die, skidded across the pavement. Dark spots dance in front of my eyes. Is this what fainting feels like?

I focus on the woman with a herculean effort.

"Do you want to sit?" She sounds worried. Her white blonde hair waves around her shoulders like a flag of surrender.

Am I okay? *No.* I look out onto the street and...

No accident. No boy.

An urban orchestra. Horns sound in the distance. People chatter, laugh. Cars once again idle at the red light, engines quietly purring.

I sink down hard on the curb, panting. *Not real. Not like Mom.*

"Can I call someone for you? Do you need an ambulance?"

I lick my lips and swallow with an effort. "I'm fine, thanks. Just a little dizzy. I..." I swing my gaze around, trying to acclimate to where I am. The school behind me, Mrs. O's across the street. The crosswalk on Dryshore and Third. Me? Cass. Cassie. Cassandra Morai. The roar in my ears recedes, slowly. My heartbeat settles into a steadier rhythm.

"Is she having a stroke?" a girl I recognize from school asks, more eager for gossip than my well-being.

"I think she's going to throw up," another girl offers eagerly.

I'm attracting a crowd. That, finally, penetrates my confused fog, and I leap to my feet. "I'm good. I just skipped lunch today and I'm feeling lightheaded." Shaking off the crushing misery is difficult, but embarrassment is a great motivator. I concentrate on my breathing the way Dr. Ward always encourages. She'll be pleased to know, despite all my resistance, that I really do pay attention. For some reason the thought almost triggers another bout of hysterical laughter, but I clamp my jaw shut as best I can.

It wasn't real.

But my mind whispers back: *You've been wrong before.*

2

"Go home, Cassandra," Mrs. Otero says.

"Rude! I came here specifically to visit you and you're kicking me out?" My eyes stray to the shop window and the offending street beyond.

"You came here to eat my popsicles and hide from whatever is bothering you. I see right through you, little one."

Mrs. O can only see shadows due to an accident from her youth, but she still knows everything going on in her cramped little store. I toss the ice pop stick in the trash and leap off my countertop perch to grab a broom. The shop is spotless, but I'm no freeloader.

"You're always asking me to stick around, and now you want me to go. Got it," I mumble.

Mrs. O shakes her head, her henna-orange hair barely budging with the movement, and attempts to pull her kind, matronly face into a disapproving expression. Her softly rounded cheeks and fleshy chin make it impossible. "You know I love having you here. But what do we say about the ostrich?"

I pull a face and dutifully repeat, "'An ostrich can hide, but its problems will wait.' You know ostriches don't really hide their heads in the sand, right? They're rotating their eggs when they do that."

"Always with the random facts and the fancy words. Well, since you're so smart, you know even a flawed saying can hold true. Confront your problems, drag them into the light. They grow in the dark."

I sweep and say nothing.

"I know you can hear me." Mrs. O places one hand on her plump waist. "You should be out doing something fun, with friends your own age." She walks off toward her back office.

I roll my eyes. Friends my age? "I would if there were any."

"Learn to forgive, Cassandra," Mrs. O calls.

This isn't the first time she's thrown that bit of advice out there, and it won't be the last. I sigh, abandon the broom, and wheel a hand truck loaded with boxes over to the shelves in the middle of the store. I set an empty box down at my feet and drop an expired can of peaches into it. Expired peas soon join them with a satisfying bang.

Grief is contagious. Or, at least, that's how my friends acted when Mom died. Like it'd invade their perfect little lives if they were subjected to my pain for too long. I remember hearing them, the ones that didn't immediately dry up like a dying vine, wondering when I'd "get over it"—as if a mourning grace period I wasn't aware of had expired. I pick up a can of beets and slam it into the box. Maybe misery has a shelf life. Who knew?

I snort. *Forgive?* I walk the box of expired cans to the back office. "Hey, do you smell skunk? Mrs. O!"

There, sitting in her office chair with a joint suspended on the way to her mouth, is Mrs. Otero. "It's for my glaucoma."

"You don't have glaucoma! You're blind."

She grins. "Oh, yeah."

I shake my head, some of my anxiety leaching away. "You're the worst influence ever."

"No, just human. And you have a beautiful smile." She holds up a hand to stop me from speaking. "I can hear the smile in your voice, and I can tell it's beautiful. You should smile more often, Cassandra! Laugh! What do I always say?"

"An ostrich can—"

"You know what I mean."

"Fake it until you make it." I laugh.

Mrs. O nods wisely, as if I've just confirmed she holds the keys to the universe. "Smile long enough and your mind will catch up."

"You've been spending too much time reading the greeting cards on the counter, Yoda," I say.

"I have no idea what cards I have."

She knows exactly what cards she has. I set down the box and march back to the shelves, tearing into the new shipment of cans. Mrs. O shuffles behind me and puts a sturdy, warm hand on my shoulder. She doesn't say a word, just pats twice and hands me cans to organize.

That's how it started with us: a sorrowful look and a pat on the shoulder at my mom's funeral. Then, later, she'd share anecdotes about my mom when I'd pop in for a gallon of milk. I eventually stopped making up errands and accepted we'd become friends. There was something in the way she reached out when I was at my lowest, when I was gathering all of the broken bits of me and trying to glue them back together into who I used to be, that told me she had experienced loss, too. There's a stink to those of us who have. A dirty, secret compassion, I think.

That boy... as comforting as Mrs. O's presence is, I can't kick this feeling, like the last of the light in the world has been snuffed out. The big ball of misery in the center of my chest swells. No good. I don't want to stress out Dad, so I need to put my game face on.

"I won't pry, but I have an ear with your name on it when you're ready. You know that," Mrs. O says, moving behind the counter again.

I hesitate and briefly debate telling her about today. After my mom passed, I told a few friends about the things I'd seen and felt before she fell ill—a vision of her collapsing and the sense that something terrible was going to happen. The reactions I got, chock full of pity, humoring me, flash through my mind. After my OCD diagnosis, those same people assured me it had just been my catastrophic thinking, the fuel that feeds my obsessive-compulsive actions. Mrs. O is different, but even she has a limit for the amount of nuttiness she can tolerate.

I circle the counter and give her a quick hug. "I know. Thank you." She squeezes me back and smooths my hair behind my ear. The door chime sounds before I can take my leave.

"Hello, Mrs. Otero!" A sandy-haired man in an ill-fitting gray suit maneuvers his girth through the doorframe. Mrs. O stiffens as he slides his briefcase onto the counter and busies himself with the latches. "Good to see you again. I wanted to drop the paperwork off personally. Prepared in braille for your convenience. I think you'll be pleased with the city's offer."

"I recall telling you that you're not welcome here. Please leave," Mrs. O says with an alarming wobble to her voice. I step closer to her and glare at the stranger in solidarity.

The man hands over the documents anyway. Despite her clear

anger, Mrs. O runs her fingers over the pages quickly, and her face pales. "Generous? You call this generous? This is robbery. I've been here for seventy-four years. My father worked like a dog until he had enough to buy the building and open this store. You're not only taking away my livelihood, you're taking my home! And for what? To make a rich man richer?" Mrs. O's voice crests on a tidal wave of pain, and her hand shakes as she sets the papers down. I take another step closer to her, willing her to take comfort in me the way I always have in her. "How is this legal?"

"Ma'am, I feel for you. I promise that I do. But with all due respect, I don't have to defend the city's plans for this lot. I'm just doing my job here. What you do, where you go, or how you use the restitution offered..." He shrugged. "That's all on you. Retain counsel and formally push back if you want, but it doesn't take a crystal ball to work out how this will end." He pulls out a hand-kerchief and wipes his brow before noticing me for the first time. His smile fades when I fail to return it.

Mrs. O looks deflated and close to tears. "Please leave," she whispers.

The man picks up a candy bar and places a large bill on the counter. "Keep the change." He leaves, a sad silence trailing in his wake.

I watch the expressions dance across Mrs. O's face. "Who was that?"

Mrs. O jerks, as if she'd forgotten I'm still in the room. "Life isn't always fair, Cassandra. You've already learned that lesson well. We're always at the mercy of forces more powerful than us." She raises her downcast rheumy eyes. "The city is going to take this place, and I'll be forced to move."

"They can't do that!" I've never heard her sound so defeated. This is Mrs. Never-Let-Anything-Keep-You-Down-Otero. She always has an answer. Always has advice.

My panicked tone breathes some life into her. Mrs. O straightens and visibly pulls herself together. "Don't fret, dear. I'm sure everything will be okay."

I leave the store, unconvinced.

MY STREET AND THE ONES SURROUNDING IT HAVE THE feel of a cozy neighborhood tucked into the middle of an enormous city. Proud old brownstones line both sides of the street, their stone staircases bowing in warm welcome, and most everyone knows everyone else. A few neighbors greet me as I pass and I half-heartedly wave back, kicking at a coupon for a free psychic reading on the ground, my mind fixated on the moment I can finally close my eyes on this day. Mr. Williams stops hosing down the sidewalk in front of his building long enough for me to pass. I mumble a quick thanks and hurry along.

The brownstone attached to ours has been under heavy construction for the past year. It was my favorite even before the restoration effort, but now I'm positively obsessed. It's one of those little pockets of the city that feels plucked out of a history book. It's four stories of gleaming white stone, gracefully arching glossy black windows, intricately carved balconies. Mrs. O told me the entire building is for the owner's family, unusual for our block; most brownstones are like mine, subdivided into apartments.

Though I've never been inside, this building gives me a feeling

I can't explain, like a tickle in the back of my mind. Sometimes I picture myself curled up on a comfy sofa in an elegant room with a book and a cup of tea. I close my eyes to capture that feeling, letting it wash away the worry burning holes through me. When I open them, the beady black pearl eyes of a crow are trained on me. It's perched an arm's length away, on the wrought iron fence in front of the building.

I scream. I can't help it. The bird flaps its wings and shuffles along the fence, cocking its head to watch me. I can almost smell it from here: wind and musk and fear. Maybe the fear is me.

The crow watches me closely as I edge away and dash up the brick steps leading to my building, almost tripping as I take them two at a time. I fumble with my keys and look down, but the crow is gone. To my left, though, in the doorway to the brownstone I love, someone is stepping outside. I feel at once as if my stomach has dropped down to my feet. I'm going to barf all over the steps.

No.

He smiles at me—a boy who is all dark hair and blue eyes, who has my body quivering and my heart breaking. It's a miracle I'm still standing.

The most beautiful dead boy in the world is looking over at me for the second time today.

3

I remember hearing a pilot on TV once describe a cloudless, vivid sky as "severe" blue. This boy's eyes are bluer than that. They're even bluer than they looked from across the street earlier today.

I catch myself. There was no "earlier today."

"You alright?" he asks.

"What?"

"I know I've been pushing furniture around for an hour, but I don't look that bad, do I?" His hair reflects the almost-summer sunshine, and those bright eyes brim with humor.

I grimace, not sure what he saw in my expression. "No, you look good. I mean, sorry, I was thinking of something else." My face flames.

He throws one hip onto the stone rail by his door and grins wryly, a gut punch of even white teeth. "Ah. Okay. Colin," he says, gesturing toward himself.

"Cassandra," I rasp in response.

"Pretty name. Nice to meet you. You're literally the first person

I've met in the neighborhood." He smiles, radiating an open friend-liness, and I resist the urge to lean over my stoop's railing to bask in its warmth.

His nose must have been broken once, but was set in a way that doesn't take away from his looks; it keeps what could've otherwise been a too-flawless face grounded in reality. That perfectly imperfect nose is set above a firm chin split by a slight indentation. He's all tall, rumpled sweatpants'ed adorableness.

He tries to get a conversation going, like a dog walker pulling along a reluctant hound, and I answer on autopilot. Or at least I must, since the exchange continues. All I can think of is how surreal this is, and how comfortable he feels to me. Familiar, like my favorite sweater.

"What do you guys do for fun around here?" he asks.

"'You guys?'" I look around questioningly, surprising myself and probably him with the sudden upspring of playfulness. He has that effect on me.

"Nice." He gives me a lazy smirk.

I peer up at him from under my eyelashes, forcing some words past the squeal blocking the exit to my throat. "I don't know. Most kids hit the park. Otherwise, they scatter like cockroaches in the light, all over the city. Working or whatever."

"Okay, so that covers everyone but you. What do *you* do?"

"I'm like veal. I kind of hang around in the dark and—"

He lets out a bark of laughter. "Fun fact, veal is why I'm a vegetarian."

"I've never had it," I say, and smile as he earnestly fills me in on all his veal-related objections and love of animals.

I used to be like this: happy to meet new people, playful. It's been so long that I nearly forgot what it was like. The thought brings me back to reality. Back to when I watched my mother die. Twice. I turn, shove the key in the lock, and stammer, "It was nice meeting you. I'll see you around."

I rush through the door and up the stairs, ignoring his startled look with a pang. I can't have any part of this beautiful dead boy— even if he happens to be alive for now.

"HOPE YOU'RE HUNGRY. I MADE LASAGNA," DAD CALLS out from the kitchen.

I hang my coat, trying with all my might to ignore that the red fringe on the long hall rug is mussed directly in front of the kitchen door. I shake out my hands and roll my head to stretch my neck like an athlete before a race. I will *not* fix that fringe.

"Smells good," I respond, pushing thoughts of the boy, of *Colin*, down deep. A quick peek into the trash on my way into the kitchen confirms that Dad forgot to hide the take-out containers again.

"You're late. And on your last day, too! Thought you'd run out of that building like it was on fire," Dad says as he drops a kiss on my forehead. *No, just running away from birds and dead boys.*

"Sorry, stopped by Mrs. O's," I say, inhaling the steamy Giuseppe's Ristorante goodness and grabbing silverware to set the table.

Friday night dinners are an intricately choreographed dance. I sit and wait as Dad scoops lasagna onto our two plates, watching as he fights with a stubborn strand of gooey mozzarella cheese. He's almost always forced to use the kitchen scissors to cut that cheesy thread, and when he does, he will turn to me, cock an eyebrow, and say, "My apologies, ma'am." It's so dumb, and even though it's ten-year-old boy humor, I laugh every time.

Within seconds I am stuffing my face with much-needed comfort food across the small wooden table from him.

"How was your day? Breaking hearts and taking names, or what?" Dad asks.

I snort. The way he talks sometimes, it's like he's got a carnival mirror image of me in mind. Except the carnival mirror version is the real me, a distorted mess of a person agonizing over a hall rug fringe.

"Yeah, I got married like three times on the way here," I say. Colin, lying in the street, flashes through my mind. I shove him and his ghostly accident out of my head, but my eyes drift to the doorway and that mussed rug fringe instead.

It happens once, twice, three times, back and forth, *thoughts of Colin, eyes on the rug*, like a psychotic seesaw I can't stop. Like I have to choose to concentrate on one or the other.

I fight it. With OCD, the more you can think about an urge without giving in, the less control that impulse has over you. Supposedly.

"Married! And you didn't have me walk you down the aisle?" Dad tsks, ripping off a hunk of bread. "So, no boyfriend, just a few husbands. What about Christine and Lara? Are they dating yet?"

"Each other? Or boys? The answer to both is no."

"Cute."

I shrug and don't volunteer that I haven't talked to my former best friends in ages. I have no idea what they do or don't do anymore. They could be madly in love with each other, for all I know.

"When your mom was your age, she had a bunch of suitors. You know, a lot like Odysseus's wife."

I latch onto our game, ignoring the part about Mom. I can only touch my tongue to one sore tooth at a time. "Penelope. First guess, correct answer. Twelve points," I say in response, our board game of Trivinometry having spilled over into regular conversations a couple of years back.

Dad smiles. "You're so confident you're scoring yourself now?"

"Yup. Speaking of faithful, too bad this monarch didn't feel the same. He had a bunch of wives. Even executed two of them."

"Henry VIII," Dad answers automatically.

"First guess, correct. Twelve points. Okay, but if you count his annulments, how many wives did he technically have?"

"Four. No, wait. Two. He had four annulments."

"First guess, wrong. Second guess, correct. Three points for you, nine for me, plus your twelve stolen from the first part. Twenty-one for me."

"My, oh my, the student becomes the teacher." Dad tries to salute me with his fork, but a string of mozzarella connecting that fork to his plate prevents it. He glances down and mutters, "They use too much cheese."

"They?" I grin.

"I. I use too much cheese. So, if you won't dish on boys, at least tell me about your day."

I take a long drink of water. Dad laughs at my obvious dodge. What do I even say? *There's this boy I'm crushing on, but he's probably going to croak because I hallucinated his death.* Dad's got enough on his plate with me. He doesn't need more to keep him up at night.

When I don't answer, Dad says, "Come on, Cass. Give me something."

And suddenly, with a flash of brilliance, I realize there *is* something I can share. "Mrs. O might have to move." I fill him in on her exchange with the man from the city as we stand and clean up the remnants of our dinner. I wait for Dad to roll up his shirt sleeves before handing him a plate.

"That's a real shame. She *is* this neighborhood. Such a toxic application of a policy meant to help people," he says, scrubbing at the dish. "It's interesting, actually. The concept of eminent domain has been around since the 1600s. The Dutch—"

I groan and Dad chuckles.

"Sorry, I'm a history professor. We can't help ourselves."

We migrate to our overstuffed sofa and lose ourselves in TV. Dad retrieves the Trivinometry box from the bookcase and re-parks himself near my feet as he sets up the board.

"Real game?" he asks.

I nod.

"It's funny to think this started out as a way of helping you with school, and now it's a weekly crushing defeat for you."

"You won two in a row. Relax, Dad."

"I'll relax when I'm crowned Trivinometry Master of the Universe for the third week in a row."

"Is this how old people trash talk?" I ask, reaching for an orange to peel.

Dad smiles. "Remember how your mom used to decimate us both?"

"Yeah," I say, quietly. Weird how her death is now my very own B.C. and A.D. split in time.

"Alright, I'll start." Dad grabs a card. "The word is 'octothorpe.'"

"Octo is eight, and thorpe... isn't that a small village? So... eight villages? That can't be right." I think for a minute, then sigh. "Fine, I give up."

"Kids these days might know the octothorpe symbol as a 'hashtag.' Your twelve points are mine. Read 'em and weep," Dad crows as he grabs the pencil and marks his score on the little game pad.

I sit up, hand him half of my peeled orange, and pluck a card. "You're going down."

A knock sounds at the door, and Dad moves to answer it. "It's probably 4D. He wants to borrow that new Queen Boudicca bio." Daryl, our down-the-hall neighbor from apartment 4D, uses Dad like a personal library—to Dad's delight. "One sec," Dad says, and rushes off to answer the door, book in hand.

"Jeffrey! You don't look a day over ancient," a woman says. If I hadn't already recognized that voice, the commingled scents of expensive, excessively floral French perfume and stale cigarettes would've tipped me off. Aunt Bree has come to visit. "Security in this building is lax, you know. A drug fiend let me in, no questions asked."

"Well, if you'd let us know you were coming, I would have made Cassie stand down there in her red jacket and doorman's cap. You know we own a telephone, right?"

Dad enters the room and rolls his eyes, his sister hot on his heels. I stand to greet her.

"Look at you!" she says, inspecting me. "You've grown like a beanstalk. How long has it been?"

"Two years," I respond. Two years, nine months, seventeen days. Since the day we buried Mom.

She beckons, and I allow her to kiss the air somewhere near my ear. She drapes herself on our flea market living room chair and sets down her handbag, Cleopatra lounging on a beaten-up pleather throne. I drop back onto the sofa across from her.

Aunt Bree is one of those people so pretty their presence alone can make you feel completely inadequate—and her attitude basically lets you know she agrees you are, in fact, a lesser being. Perfect features, silky, obedient dark hair that always curls the way it should, and cat-like mercurial eyes that flash green one moment and brown the next. Dad and I have the same hazel eyes, and they're my favorite feature—except when I see them reflected in Bree's face.

"So, I'm back from Italy... obviously." Aunt Bree spreads her arms in a "voila" gesture.

"And you left your phone on the plane?" Dad suggests.

"Oh, let it go, Jeff. You always loved surprises. And I've missed you two! Especially you, young lady. You were all knees and bangs before, but I can work with this. I bought you something." She studies me a moment before pulling a small glittery box out of her purse and putting it on the table. "Go ahead. Open it."

I glance at Dad and reach over, pulling at the ribbons and the lid. I hold up a thick gold bangle.

"It was *very* expensive," Aunt Bree offers.

"Thanks." I set it on the table.

"You're welcome. Us girls should do something. Maybe a spa day! We can fix your hair then, too."

I hate that my hand automatically reaches up to touch my hair. There isn't much to it. It's long, plain, light brown—sun-streaked if I spend enough time outside—and usually in a ponytail. Another insecurity added to the pile. Awesome.

"It'll pull double duty since highlights also prevent lice," she adds.

"That's not even remotely true. And Cass doesn't have lice." A muscle in Dad's jaw flexes and his right eyelid twitches. He gives me a tight smile.

Aunt Bree reaches into her handbag again and pulls out a cigarette and lighter. She sparks up and leans back, exhaling toward the ceiling as if in relief. I look between Dad and Bree and back again. He and his sister may look alike enough to pass for twins, but they're complete opposites when it comes to anything else.

"You can't smoke in here, Bree," Dad says.

"You breathe in worse walking down the street, Jeffrey." She turns and ignores him. "So, what's new and exciting? Two years is a lot of ground to cover." I open my mouth to respond, but Bree's certainly not done talking. "Me, I've been on a recruiting mission for work the past year. All over creation." She leans forward and shields her mouth from Dad with the hand holding the cigarette. "I'll share the R-rated stories when *someone* isn't around."

"Aubrey," Dad says warningly.

"Fine, PG-13."

Dad shakes his head, and I choke back a reluctant laugh.

"Anyway, *Cassandra*." She says my name like someone searching for a word that's finally come to them. "You're nearly a woman! How exciting! If you need advice on anything—boys, clothes, shaving legs... That last one you might be on your own for, actually. You take after your mother, bless her soul. But, other than that, if you need anything at *all*, I am completely here for you. Every girl needs a mother."

My brief amusement goes up in smoke. "I have a mother."

"I was a wreck for ages after she left us, by the way. Awful." She shudders delicately. "We shouldn't dwell on the past. Always look to the future. Haven't I always said that, Jeff? You can't do a thing to change the past, but the future is simply paved with possibilities." She studies me and then delivers an exaggerated wink.

I think my eyelid is starting to twitch, too.

"My point is you need someone. A woman's influence. You're... what now? Fourteen years old? It's a delicate age. Periods. Relationships. Off to high school. I remember those days," she says.

My face goes hot. "I'm sixteen. Almost seventeen."

Aunt Bree waves a dismissive hand, cigarette smoke snaking over her head. "You'll be thankful you look so young when you're older, trust me."

"You mean when I'm as old as you, Aunt Bree?" I catch Dad's surprised grin before he smooths a hand over his mouth to wipe it away.

Aunt Bree's smile falters, but then she titters. "Looking young at any age is a blessing, of course."

Dad leans forward with his elbows resting on his knees and his fingers intertwined as if in prayer. Probably praying for the strength not to grab her by the back of her expensive tailored dress and toss her out a window. "Why are you here, Aubrey?"

"What kind of question is that? I can't visit my brother and niece?"

"You can, but you don't. So what do you want?"

"So dramatic. Somewhere, a stage is missing its star," she laughs. "I've been abroad working, Jeff! I'm here now, and I thought it'd be good for Cassandra to spend some time with the *one* female figure in her life." She looks down at the Trivinometry board. "I didn't realize how dire the need was."

Dad shakes his head. "No."

"Shouldn't you let her make that decision for herself? I'm worried about her."

Dad crosses his arms. "Your sudden concern for Cass is touching, but it's still no."

It's annoying to be talked about as if I'm not literally four feet from them.

Aunt Bree crushes out her cigarette on the second-grade pottery gift I made for my mom and immediately lights up again, turning to me. "How would you feel about coming to work with me, sweetheart? A fun summer internship!"

"Aubrey," Dad warns.

"I think I'm good, thanks."

Dad's dark look must finally register, because Aunt Bree stands and gathers up her things. "Fine, we can discuss another time. I need to get going, anyway." She gives Dad a loaded look before saying, "She needs a woman in her life, Jeff. If not me, then maybe that girl-friend of yours?" With a bat of her eyelashes and a swish of pricey silk, she disappears through the doorway before Dad can react.

My heart stops.

The front door opens and closes a second later. Then silence.

"Always pleasant when she comes to visit, isn't it?" Dad says dryly, before closing his eyes and sighing. He looks older, somehow, when he opens them. "I wanted to find the right time to tell you." He swallows hard. "I'm sorry you had to hear about it from Bree, of all people."

"Okay."

"You're upset."

"No." I'm not lying. I don't know how to label the churning in my chest, but "upset" doesn't cover it.

"Honestly, Cass, it's... I wasn't looking, but I... You might like her."

Even though he's still sitting here with me, he's suddenly a million miles away. I've lost something precious. I can't place what, but I know it by the hollow burn inside me. I pluck apart the napkin in my hands.

"I love you. You are the most important person in my life. Now and always. You know that, right?"

"Yeah."

"If you ask me to end it, I will. I don't want you feeling—"

"No." I could never ask him to do that. I want him happy, even if the thought of this woman makes me want to climb under my blankets and bawl. "It's..." I force in a breath. "It's fine." I don't want to know anything about this woman, and yet I hear myself ask, "How long?"

"I've known her for a while, but we've only been seeing each other for a couple of months."

"Okay."

"You are my number one priority, Cass, I promise you. Lasagna and Trivinometry Fridays. Bookstore Sundays. All of it. This doesn't change anything."

It changes everything. "It's okay. You deserve..." I reach for something for to say, anything really. Bree's question pops into my head. "I've been thinking about maybe getting a summer job, anyway, so it's no big deal if you spend time with—"

"Oh, honey... you don't know how happy I am to hear you're open to getting out there... meeting people, forcing yourself out of your shell—" He pauses. "So long as that job isn't with Bree."

I shake my head with a halfhearted smile.

"You know, I kicked around the idea of this one college prep summer camp upstate that your guidance counselor was hot about, but it was way out of our price range, and I wasn't even sure you... Anyway, I really think getting out will do you a world of good, Cass." He hesitates. "And maybe when you're ready, I can introduce you to Eleanor."

A name makes her real.

"Want to finish this game? I know you're a big, bad *fourteen year old* now, but..."

"I'm actually kind of tired, Dad. Aunt Bree takes a lot out of a person. Raincheck?"

He nods slowly. I ignore the lick of guilt his deflated expression sparks and stand to give him a quick peck on the cheek.

I straighten the rug fringe on the way to my room.

4

Job hunts blow, especially if you're scared you'll do something nutty to tip off a potential employer that you have a broken brain. Dad would get on my case if he heard me talking about my condition that way, but I don't really feel like being kind to myself at the moment.

"I don't understand why I can't work here," I say to Mrs. O, for the tenth time. "I'll work for free."

"I could never let you do that," Mrs. O responds.

"But you always say you need help."

"Yes, but I mean *mental* help." Mrs. O grins. "Besides, working somewhere else will be good for you. Forces you to be brave. Try something new. Fake it until you make it, little one."

I groan and push myself off the counter, spinning my little stool around. I bombed my interview at the bookshop by repeating my answers five times—it always has to be five times—and blew off my next two interviews after that. So I've basically resigned myself to the fact that I'll never find a job.

Mrs. O busies herself with her inventory, asking me to read off the packing list before I carry a box into the store's back office. Her desk is piled high with all sorts of files, order forms, and dented cans of food, but a bright yellow paper with the word "WARNING" stands out. I don't want to be nosy, but I can't help myself. I tug at the yellow paper and glance back to make sure Mrs. O isn't near.

"NOTICE TO VACATE. TO ALL OCCUPANTS: A Writ of Possession, Cause # 079-370782-2877 has been issued ordering eviction from this property. You and your belongings will be removed, if you have not vacated the premises on or before..."

The words swim. I wipe my eyes. She has to leave by the end of the summer. *What am I going to do?*

I put the paper back. My chest aches. I picture the awful things that might happen to Mrs. O if she's forced out. *What if she falls and she's all alone? What if she can't afford a new place and has to live on the streets?* A flash of lightning travels up my neck and crackles along my scalp. I'm standing in a dirt lot, the remnants of rusted rebar and concrete pushed by bulldozers to my right and a metal crane overhead. The noise is deafening. Mrs. O stands off to the side near a plywood fence, talking to a man in a black suit and hardhat. Tears stream down her face.

I blink and I'm back in Mrs. O's office, shaking and drinking in air as fast as I can suck it down. It's a minute before I can calm myself enough to walk to the front of the store. I try to control the tremor in my voice as I make an excuse to leave.

What is wrong with me? Why is this happening? My OCD catastrophizing always feels real to my body, but it's always been *thoughts.* I've never been confused about what I was *seeing.* Until now.

"Break your momma's back!" a man catcalls from the adjacent construction site. I shoot him a dirty look. It hits me what he meant a moment later—I've been jumping over sidewalk cracks like a lunatic. Absentmindedly giving in to urges is... not good.

I purposely step on every single crack after that, fighting the nausea and dread it brings. At least I'm pretty confident it's not going to hurt my mom. I'm a sweaty mess by the time I reach my building. Fighting yourself with every single step is exhausting.

IT'S TOO HOT IN THE APARTMENT, EVEN WITH AIR conditioning, and so the blacktopped roof, which radiates the day's absorbed heat, is nearly unbearable. I shift on my folding chair and stare at the night sky. At least the wide-open expanse above helps a bit with my claustrophobic helplessness. This sadness is just a sucking mud, dragging me down.

"Hey, Cinderella."

My head whips up and I glimpse Colin's silhouette in the dark. *Just because it happened with Mom doesn't mean it'll happen with him... and even if it does, he's a stranger. It's not like it'll affect...*

Of course it would affect me.

"Unless you turn into a pumpkin at midnight, you don't have to bolt." Colin's voice rings out again when I don't respond.

"Sorry," I say softly.

"What for?" He steps into a spot of light, and my eyes drink him in with a thirst I didn't know I was capable of.

"For the other day." *For what might happen to you.*

All of the brownstones on this block are attached to one another. My rooftop and his are only separated by a short, thigh-high wall. Colin walks over to his side of the wall and gives me a wry sideways glance as he leans forward to rest his elbows on the building's ledge. "If I accept your apology, does that mean we get to start over?"

His presence is a warm blanket after a trudge through an endless December. I want to bury myself against his chest and dive for the door leading to my stairwell all at once. "Okay."

"Alright, starting over." He clears his throat. "Hi there. I'm Colin." He reaches out and I stand, hesitating a second, embarrassed by what repeated washings have done to my hands: the red, scaly patches; the swollen, chapped knuckles; skin that wouldn't look out of place on a seventy year old. We shake, his warm palm sliding against mine, and my breath hitches as I pull away.

"Pretty smooth opening line, huh? Nothing that would send a girl running away, right?"

I smile slightly. "I'm Cinderella, but my friends call me Cindy."

Colin grins broadly and shoves his hands into his pockets. He turns to look out at the sea of flickering city lights and I wrestle my giddy, fluttering heart into submission. "You forgot to leave behind a glass slipper."

"Squirrel fur," I correct.

"Okay, I'll bite. What?"

"It wasn't glass, it was squirrel fur. Charles Perrault, the guy who wrote the version of Cinderella we know, jacked a medieval version of the story, and the word for squirrel fur in French sounded a lot like the word for glass and..."

Colin laughs. "Yeah, I'm gonna go ahead and say Charlie

improved the story. If you'd left behind a squirrel fur slipper, I'd have Cinderella'd it in the opposite direction."

If I were a normal person, with normal problems, this boy, the canopy of stars above us, the muted city sounds would inspire a million school-notebook daydream doodles of "Mrs. Cassandra..."

"What's your last name?"

"Random. Why? Want to know what to put in the police report?"

"Exactly."

"It's Clay. Colin Clay. How about you?"

"Morai. Are you... are you liking it here so far?"

"Well, when I'm not terrorizing girls I just met with my thoughts on veal, sure." He glances at me and scrunches his nose, his lips quirking.

I shake my head. "It had nothing to do with that."

"Oh, so it was just me?" He mimes a shot to the heart and staggers back a few steps.

I bite back a smile and we settle into a companionable silence. As my eyes roam his profile, it strikes me that it feels like familiar terrain, even though I barely know him. "You miss home?"

"I'd probably miss home if we stuck around anywhere long enough for me to have one. My dad moves around a lot because of his job." He pushes off from the ledge, turns around, and leans back. "He bought this place instead of renting, though. You might be stuck with me, neighbor."

"The horror," I say. His laugh feels like a sunrise.

"Ouch. Maybe I should go back to Prague. It's beautiful there, and the girls don't wear squirrel." He chuckles at my mock stony look, and then his eyes light up. "Wait. What's that shirt? Oh, no way!" He gestures toward my worn concert tee, salvaged from

Mom's stuff before Dad packed everything away. "I'm obsessed with the Atomic Dons!"

"Whoa. They're an old band. I didn't think anyone knew them."

"Yeah, well, you'd be surprised what you'll find in random record shops in Latvia," he says. "'Spindle Rock' was my anthem two years back. That summer I was all William Faulkner quotes and Atomic Dons lyrics. Constantly. Dark. I drove my tutor nuts."

"You like Faulkner?" I ask, more shocked that he knows who that is than by his choice of music. "For someone so cheerful, you have a pretty depressing taste in authors."

"That's because I'm deep and complex." At my expression, he frowns. "I'm trying to appear mysterious, and you're blowing it for me."

I straighten my face. "I'm sorry. Go ahead. I'm just impressed that you read! Half the people at school only read whatever's on their phones."

"No, the moment's gone," he grumbles. "And yes, I read. Byproduct of traveling a lot. Books don't need Wi-Fi."

"Yeah, that's why I like writing."

"You write? What kind of stuff?"

I cringe, wondering what possessed me to volunteer that info. "Nothing. It's stupid." I haven't written since my mom died.

"I bet it's great. Bust it out! Or is it like nonfiction 'dear diary' type stuff?" he asks.

"I'm not having this conversation."

"Dear diary, today I met this boy Colin Clay—"

I blush clear to my roots. "The only way you'll ever read anything I've written is if I'm somehow incapacitated and you steal one of my notebooks."

"Then you'll never see one of my drawings," he retorts.

"What do you draw?"

"You'll never know."

"Oh, it's like that?"

"Most of what I do is motivated by spite." He shrugs.

"Then you'd *love* the Spite House. Have you seen it yet?" I ask eagerly, turning to face him more fully.

"I know what the words in that sentence mean individually, but I have no clue what they're doing all together like that."

"The Spite House! There's this tiny house this guy built back in the 1800s. The city was buying up land to build the park, and they tried to get this guy's tiny patch. He was annoyed by their low offer so he refused to sell and built a sliver of a house on it instead. It was some kind of legal loophole to keep the land, out of spite. It's still there, right in the middle of the park."

"Okay, I *haven't* seen the Spite House, but now I feel like I need to see it *immediately*. You'll have to take me for a tour."

"Yeah, sure," I breathe. Once upon a time I was a person, but now I am a puddle.

"So besides doing some light reading in the pitch dark, what were you doing up here?" He gestures to the colossal book on the ledge in front of me.

I shield the cover from his view. There's no easy way to explain a book called *Anxiety, Obsession, and Control: OCD and its Rarer Manifestations,* so I pretend it's a book on constellations. I'm not a good liar. "Looking at the stars. Or trying to, anyway. Light pollution makes it hard. You?"

He glances behind him. "Want to come over to this side? It's not much, but we have cushy chairs. Easier on the neck."

In answer, I throw a leg over the divider wall.

I follow him to a sitting area flanked by a number of large potted plants where two inviting lounge chairs with plush cushions await. Colin stretches his long frame out on one, his hands pillowing his head, and I take the one next to his, sitting cross-legged because even with a foot's distance between us I can't lie down next to him.

"Alright. Lay some knowledge on me," he says.

I swallow, thinking quickly. "See that semicircle?" I point toward a patch of stars. "That's Corona Borealis. In Greek mythology, it's the crown Princess Ariadne wears when she marries Dionysus after being abandoned on an island by the hero Theseus."

"Not much of a hero if he went around abandoning princesses," Colin observes. "That's what's in your book?"

"No, I... er..."

"Squirrel fur shoes, the Spite House, and now sad Greek princesses? Do you read encyclopedias for fun or something? Oh, wow. Your face. You don't, do you?" Colin laughs. "If I get up and grab your book off the ledge, is that what it'll be?" He feints getting up, and I grab at his arm. He looks down at my hand and smiles, lying back. I release him with a blush.

"I... I like knowing things," I say with a self-conscious tug at my shirt. He doesn't need to know about weekly Trivinometry matches or how long I sat reading my mom's old encyclopedia set in her closet after she died. Mindlessly. Compulsively. Like I'd find the answer to *why* in there. I wrap a string from a frayed edge of my shirt around my finger. "I like facts."

"I like that you like knowing things," Colin says in a gentle voice. "You know, I've never been able to make out how people looked up at the night sky and saw crabs or fish or whatever in the stars.

Or how people believe that it has any impact on our lives." He looks over at me. "I hope I didn't insult you again. I figured you were a budding astronomer with that book... You're not a horoscope lunatic, are you?"

Something I read earlier in my book comes to mind. "Maybe they drew pictures in the sky to try and make sense of the unknown. Maybe they thought it impacted their lives because..."

"Because?"

"Because it made them feel like they had some control."

He looks contemplative, then stands abruptly and pushes his chair over with his foot until it's touching my own. He lies back down, and I'm keenly aware of how close he is. It's as if his body is pulsing in the darkness next to mine, a boy-sized heartbeat. "Well, if they could draw crabs and fish in the sky, we can draw you."

"Crabs and fish and me. Flattering. Okay, let's see what you've got."

Colin laughs and points up. "Look there." He sketches out a shape with his finger.

"I don't see it."

He sits up and grabs my hand, pointing my index finger toward the sky, which means my stomach erupts into a beautiful mess. His warm hand holding mine and his upper body leaning into me send wave after wave of electric, chaotic *feeling* rioting through me. My breath locomotives out of me in shallow huffs. *What is he—* He tips his head close to mine, sending my stomach tumbling over itself further, and traces my finger from star to star. "Now do you see it? Constellation Cass."

I nod my head slowly, and my lips curve at the whimsical nonsense. "That looked like a big circle. You just called me fat?"

Colin turns his head and looks at me. "This is why we can't have nice things, Cass." His desert dry tone makes me laugh. "The stars are not cool with body shaming." He smiles warmly, still holding my hand as he lowers both our arms.

I go still.

Panic. The hamster wheel of anxiety roars to life inside me. *The door to the roof. Did I prop it open? I'm locked out here.* This is bad. Very, very bad. The need to go back and *fix things, touch something, the handle, five times* claws its way up my insides. *Oh God. Count. Make it to ten. Count.*

He releases my hand and looks back at the sky. My heart jackhammers against my ribs. The impulse passes eventually, but I'm drained. I close my eyes and mentally lash myself. Why can't I be *normal?*

Colin looks over at me again and gives me a crooked grin. I try not to picture his broken body lying on blistering asphalt.

5

I scrape the bottom of my sneaker against the subway step with a grimace: a psychic reading coupon and a wad of gum are stuck on good. *It's okay, okay, okay, okay, okay.* I climb out of the Timbits Waterway subway station after I've dislodged them, eagerly anticipating breathing untainted oxygen again. The relief doesn't last.

The sky has taken on a reddish cast and darkened under threatening clouds. The street is mobbed. Chanting picketers flow around me like a river around a boulder. The press of hundreds of bodies amplifies the humidity. A low rumble sounds. I mistake it for thunder until I hear a bullhorn-amplified voice:

"Hey, hey, ho, ho! Jon Clay has got to go!"

The protesters repeat it in a roar.

I push my way to the front of the Rise and Grind Café and press through the crush inside, dodging picket signs and their caffeinated owners passionately arguing politics.

A girl at the counter with a nose ring and blue apron rolls her eyes when I tell her I'm there to interview. "We filled that spot last week," she says over the noise. She gestures to a guy in a matching apron whose upper lip can't restrain his jutting two front teeth. "I don't know who called you, but I'm the manager and it wasn't me."

I decline her offer of a free drink and leave, pulling out my cell to call back whoever lured me out here. The out-of-service message is easy to hear despite the crowds. The air takes on an electric hum, and a creeping prickle of unease moves down the back of my neck.

A scream sounds, followed by others, and suddenly the steady stream of protesters becomes a torrent. Someone shouts "bomb!" I don't need to hear more. I run like a scared animal, all sweat, instinct, and terror. I crash through crowds, blindly pushing, my heart thudding. Thunder rumbles and the heavens open up, dousing everyone in sheets of cold gray rain. My mind supplies an explosion of body parts behind me that, blessedly, doesn't come in reality.

A hot dog cart is upended, sending scalding meat water everywhere. I veer to the right, down a narrow side street, wiping rain from my eyes and leaving the heaving, straining masses and their now muted cries behind me.

I spill onto a cobblestone stretch of road and slow, bending and sucking in shallow breaths, practically tasting the damp decay of the sluggish river nearby.

I fall, but the crowd doesn't realize. I'm trampled.

The police think I did it. I look suspicious. I—

Stop.

I straighten and give my head a vigorous shake, peering through the silver mist around me sent up by the rain-cooled cobblestones.

It's an older, quieter part of town here, a vestige of the city's quaint fishing days. The bite of the pelting rain finally registers, and I press myself into the meager shelter that a window's overhang provides. There are no sidewalks, and the aging red-brick buildings sit right at the road's edge—just wide enough for a single car to pass through with care—lending the place a claustrophobic feel. If a car were to drive down this road—

I glance up the way I came, weighing the danger of rejoining the crush of panicked protesters against staying in the dubious sanctuary of this narrow, oppressive deathtrap of a road.

Aunt Bree is standing in a gated alleyway tucked between two buildings, directly diagonal from where I'm shivering, watching me. She draws on her cigarette and shifts her hold on her umbrella. A manila folder is tucked under her arm, and above her swings a small black iron sign with the words "Theban Group" laser-cut out in blocky letters.

I cross the street slowly. "What..."

"What am I doing here? Waiting for you," she says with a Cheshire cat grin.

"But... I don't understand."

Aunt Bree tosses her cigarette onto the ground and turns on her heel, gliding away on a precarious pair of stilettos. "Chatting in a monsoon is less than ideal. Come with me."

I follow her through the gate dazedly and down the alley, side-stepping a puddle of mustard-colored nastiness the rain is intent on splattering everywhere. We reach a scarred wooden door, and Bree tugs it open to lead me into a lobby that calls to mind my dentist's office: cramped though free of clutter, and neat but leached of all color and personality. It's so boring that it's put the guard behind the check-in desk to sleep.

"What do you mean, you were waiting for me?" I ask.

"I went through a good amount of effort to get you here," Aunt

Bree says, as if that explains anything. She folds up her umbrella and tosses it near the door.

The rain has soaked through my clothes and drenched my shoes. I blink away droplets from my lashes. "That doesn't make any sense."

"Dominoes, Cassandra."

"The pizza place?

"Yes, I orchestrated your being here via fattening cardboard covered in cheese," Bree says. Then she lets out a long, slow sigh. "I set up a series of dominoes and watched as they tipped over in exactly the way I wanted. One by one."

I struggle to digest what she's saying. A question suddenly crystalizes. "Were you the one who called about the job at the coffee shop?"

She shakes her head, her smile sympathetic, as if I'm being hopelessly dense.

We've reached the ancient snoring man seated at the reception desk, eyebrows hanging heavy over his eyes. His arms are crossed over his large belly and his head is bent forward, a down-on-his-luck Santa Claus. Aunt Bree tosses the manila folder onto the counter.

"Stack sounds thin, Ms. Morai. Your guest is missing an MV-77, I'd say," the man rumbles, his sleep-thickened voice echoing. He cracks open his eyes. "Looks thin, too."

"Noted, Theodore. Now, if you don't mind?" Aunt Bree picks up the file.

"One, three, seven today," he says.

Aunt Bree circles the desk without another word. I glance back at Theodore. "Thank you," I offer uncertainly.

Theodore smiles. "You're very welcome, young lady," he says.

"Good luck to you." He's back to snoring by the time I catch up to Aunt Bree.

We've entered a room full of soul-suckingly dreary cubicles. Phones ring in the distance, and flickering florescent ceiling lights stretch back deep into the room, casting everything in a faintly greenish tone. I have no idea what is going on or what we're doing here, but my upset suddenly has an outlet in Aunt Bree.

"I'm not going anywhere until you tell me what is going on," I call out as she picks her way down an aisle.

Aunt Bree turns and rolls her eyes. "I'm trying to help you, but you're making it hard."

"I don't need your help."

"Really? Everything is fabulous for you, then? No unexplained intuitions or strange dreams? Instincts about what might happen next?" She pauses and eyes me up and down. "Clearly no instincts about what not to wear, but none of the rest rings a bell?"

I tremble. It's an unpleasant feeling being wet, but that's not why it feels like an ice-cold finger is sliding down my back. *How does she know?*

"Let me ask you a question: How would you like to have some control over your life? Real control. Be more than a pathetic feather in a tornado. Please don't make that face, Cassandra, it will give you wrinkles. I'm not trying to offend you. Most people live like you, stumbling around waiting for things to happen to them. I, on the other hand... I manifest my own destiny." She smiles and takes a step toward me. "You're either a queen or a pawn in this world. I am very much a queen." She raises her eyebrows and lifts one shoulder in a very continental shrug. "Even if none of what I've said applies, you *are* looking for something to do this summer, aren't you? At the very least, this will get you out of the house while your father is busy with that girlfriend of his."

I wince, and then hesitate for just a second, her words caressing my mind seductively. I don't know how I ended up standing across the street from her earlier, and I'm pretty sure I don't believe she orchestrated *everything* that had landed me there, but... "Dad doesn't want me working with you," I say, because I can't think of anything else.

She smirks. "Jeff is already planning on sending you here. He just doesn't know it yet."

I eye her suspiciously and heft my backpack higher on my shoulder. "Why are you doing this? Why me? Why now?"

"Oh, Cassandra. You simply weren't ready before. But I've always cared about your future."

I snort.

"There's a pleasant sound. Come with me, please. There's someone I want you to meet." Bree continues along and I force myself to follow, peeking into the cubicles as we pass. Family photos, cat calendars, stuffed animals... random pops of personality dot the walls and surfaces of the desks, as if to remind the people working in them that there is still life on the outside, that they aren't corporate Russian nesting dolls—people stuck in a beige box, in a beige room, in a beige building, in a beige world. And Aunt Bree wants me to rot here all summer.

We approach a bank of three elevators on the far side of the room and enter the one in the center. The doors close behind us with a worrisome grinding sound, and Bree presses the buttons for the first, third, and seventh floors, followed by the button for the alarm.

"What are you doing?" I ask.

"The combination changes every day," she says by way of explanation, her meaning opaque as ever.

Before I can ask, the metal panel behind me—the one I thought was a solid elevator wall—slides open. I turn around and gasp.

6

I t's as if someone set fire to a rainbow.

I trail Aunt Bree into a cavernous space topped by a stained glass dome. Brilliant morning rays filter through the colored glass to illuminate a place alive with noise and movement and *life*. I try not to gawk, but when Aunt Bree isn't looking, I crane my neck as far back as it'll go to stare up at that ceiling.

"How is this... what...?" I can't spit out a coherent question. My head is on a swivel. It was raining outside not five minutes ago, and here it doesn't look like there's a single cloud in the sky beyond the dome.

There are three vaulted halls branching off this area like bent tines of a fork, the rough stone walls speckled with windows and doorways giving it the feel of an indoor city. In front of us, crowds mill about dozens of vibrantly colored caravans and carts dotting the expanse.

"This is Rhodes Rotunda. Your one-stop shop for food, supplies... tetanus. It's where most people your age tend to congregate, so I expect you'll probably take most of your meals here. It's... popular," Aunt Bree says.

Aunt Bree expertly weaves her way through the cart-made alleyways, avoiding the zigging and zagging patrons with ease. I swim against a current of humanity after her, my gaping making it impossible to dodge the merchants hawking food and random bric-a-brac.

"How is this place so huge? Why?"

Bree smiles. "We don't use it *all*. Room to grow. We take what we're given."

She hasn't answered my question, and I hate riddles. Before I can tell her, a man jostles me with his shoulder as he passes.

"Give her back her wallet, Marko," Aunt Bree says, barely pausing. "She keeps her money in her shoe anyway."

I frown after her, wondering how she landed on that info, and turn to the man.

"Sorry, Miss Aubrey. Is a habit," the man calls out in a thickly accented voice. He gives me an apologetic puppy dog look from behind long, dark eyelashes. "I am working on quitting," he says, handing me back my X-Men velcro wallet. It was buried in my backpack and carried for luck since Mom bought it for me. I yank my backpack around to my front, shoving my wallet back in the bag. When I look up, he is dancing away behind a cart loaded with knives, and Aunt Bree is gone. I scan the unfamiliar faces, the jarring chaos around me, and the mammoth space around me immediately seems to contract, squeezing down on me. A burst of panic sets me to running. The colors blur around me. *You're okay, okay, okay, okay, okay.*

I spot her between a cart selling silk hangings and another selling bleach-white bones.

"We'll get your registration finalized, and then you'll meet with

45

Martin Pict. He'll serve as your mentor," Aunt Bree says as I nearly careen into her back.

I draw a shuddery breath. It takes a few before I can trust myself to say anything. "What exactly do you do here?"

"Insurance. Risk management." Bree looks back at me and winks.

I stare after her. "*What?*"

"Oy!" A toadstool of a woman points at me and Aunt Bree. The object of her shout, a pretty girl a little older than me rushes over with a tray strapped to her shoulders.

"Breakfast meat pies!" the girl says. My mouth waters as the savory smells of garlic and onions and mystery meat waft over and set my stomach growling.

Aunt Bree catches my wistful look. "Magpie meat pies are more butter than anything else. A second on the lips, a year on the hips." She soldiers on, refusing to pie-gaze with me.

"There's *magpie* in those?" I ask, horrified.

"The magpies aren't in the pies. *We're* the Magpies," the girl gestures to all of the rickety caravans and their vendors peddling goods. "You want one or what?"

I decline and race after Aunt Bree with only a tiny longing glance back over my shoulder. "Do you expect me to believe you sell insurance here?"

"Yes. We can see the future, darling. What else do you think we'd do to make money?"

My pulse quickens. I mentally ease my toe into the insanity of her comment. "Win the lotto?" I offer, carefully.

Bree chuckles drily. "That'd be nice and inconspicuous, wouldn't it?"

"You're not serious," I insist, waiting for the moment my gullibility become a punchline. The rimshot never comes.

A portly little man ahead of us holds a large crystal orb over his head. It reflects the dome's rainbow glow in brilliant flashes. "Crystal balls! Made from the finest imported Egyptian crystal. Clearest crystal for the clearest visions of the future or your money back!" His reedy mustache twitches with every syllable. "No inclusions, no imperfections, no problems!"

I whip an incredulous look at Aunt Bree, who is eyeing me with amusement. She shrugs. "I told you, everyone here is a scryer. Like you."

Like me.

A woolly mammoth of a man at a candle cart pulls on an oven mitt and pours melted candle wax into a bowl of water. "According to this, he isn't cheating," he says. The morose woman next to him bends to look at the side of the bowl, her worry giving way to joy as she observes the floating wax shapes. She claps in delight. I don't get to see her expression when the man adds, "Course, this doesn't mean he won't," because a willowy woman is tugging at my arm as we pass, trying to draw me to her cart of wooden sticks.

I apologetically decline her wares and shake my head. It takes me a beat to understand why my cheeks ache; my smile is face-splitting. I can't help it. "Who are they? The Magpies?"

"A lawless bunch of mediocre scryers we tolerate because they provide a service," Aunt Bree says with a sigh. "Every Theban Group location has some, but we've been blessed with a critical mass thanks to Jordan's bleeding heart; some nonsense about respecting the old ways while moving to the new, as if there's something worth preserving in *this*." Bree's movements give away her growing irritation as she warms to her subject. "We opened a new satellite location last year, and within a week a batch of these vagabonds made their way in, like mice, pressing through cracks, and..." At my look she adds, "Magpies are Magpies no matter where you encounter them. Whether they're born in the outside world or in here, whether you run into them at a county fair, or in their strange little camp, they're all the same—they've all suckled at the same anarchist teet." Bree pins an approaching Magpie with a severe look, and the poor man almost trips over his own feet to scramble away. "You forget how *annoying* the Magpie camps are when you've been traveling. I need to talk to Jordan about creating an executive entrance. So much to do."

Beyond the caravans, there is a clearing, and my eyes don't know where to look first. An animated man is entertaining his four friends near a fountain, a huge mechanical sphere ringed by motorized zodiac symbols leaping and looping through jets of shooting water. The man wildly waves a meat pie as his appreciative audience laughs. Cawing birds swoop and dive through the fountain's spouting water. A notebook-toting group chases the birds around the hall, copiously taking notes.

"Did you catch the asymmetrical flight pattern, Nalan?" a woman near me with a slick of dark hair asks her companion.

"Got it. Notice the choice of perch? Like Ms. Fenice said," the man responds, his eyes owl-large behind his eyeglasses.

"What are they doing?" I ask Aunt Bree.

"Ornithomancy," she responds dismissively, which as far as I'm concerned, explains nothing.

Aunt Bree leads me past guards dressed in hunter green uniforms carrying mean-looking guns, and a circular desk of more guards buzzing like hornets. A frisson of disquiet passes through me at the sight. Bree notices.

"Can't be too careful."

We head down the long hall directly beyond the guard station. I stare up at the arching glass ceiling, up at the windows, at the doors in the stone walls around us. And then, without warning or even the semblance of a transition between the two spaces, we're walking down a sparse concrete hallway. I look back, goggling at the bright city-space behind us, then at the austere path ahead of us. This entire place is strangely cobbled together, like patchworking took up architecture as a hobby.

A metal door with a tin-can shine sits at the end of the hall. An intercom panel to the right features a single red button, and a small engraved sign above simply reads, "Scryer Services."

Aunt Bree presses the button. After a beep, a nasal voice says, "Records, please." A metal slot slides opens in the center of the door, and Aunt Bree slips paperwork apparently belonging to me through. "Step on the mark and face forward." Aunt Bree ushers me onto a red X on the floor. A flash goes off, and a badge with my surprised expression slips through the slot. I pick it up. It reads: *Theban Group, Cassandra Claire Morai, Initiate.*

"Photogenic, aren't we?" Aunt Bree says in amusement.

A thick stack of papers is pushed through the slot. "You're missing the MV-77 form. Please complete and return no later than the morning of Orientation. Goodbye."

I shove the form and badge into my backpack, lightheaded with thoughts of Alice and her looking glass, and race to catch up to my white rabbit, her heels already clapping into the opulent space to the left of the Scryer Services door. It wouldn't have looked out of place in a medieval castle, with its hanging velvet banners and stone gargoyles—except for this row of weird copper bird cages set into the wall. One of the cages opens as we approach; elevators, I realize, as Bree enters, holding the door for me. She presses a button, and I examine her in dismay as she pulls a thin, long, silver device from her pocket, scrolling through it with her index finger. I'm pretty sure I look like an electrified rat, but her hair is somehow perfect despite the humidity and the rain. It's ridiculous. This whole thing—this whole place—is ridiculous.

Maybe there's a gas leak and I'm hallucinating all of this. That's got to be it. The alternative would mean... My wet shoes squish uncomfortably, confirming this is very much real life.

It hits me like a lightning strike to the head: this is real. My visions are real. I have abilities. I can see the frigging future! Oh. My. God. The implications rush at me all at once, and I suddenly feel very, very dizzy.

I can see the future. Which means my... oh. Oh no. My Colin vision is real. I pick at the skin of my thumb.

"You said you control things. Your destiny. How? You can change the stuff you see?"

"Your training will fill you in on all of that," Aunt Bree says.

"There's training?"

"Yes."

"What is it like?" I ask.

"You'll see."

"Where did our abilities come from? How did you know I had any? What happens after training? Can you tell me *something?*"

Aunt Bree pockets her device and stares. "Relax, Cassandra. You'll learn more during Orientation."

I tap my foot and bite at my thumbnail. *"Relax?* You should know that I can't exactly relax since you're the one who can apparently tell the future here."

Aunt Bree laughs. "We're not omniscient, Cassandra. We see snippets of the future, not everything. Although that's changing with Jordan's work. He is..." She pauses with a faraway look, unlike any I've ever seen from her. "A genius. There's no other word for it."

"Jordan?" It's the second time she's mentioned that name.

"Jordan Welborne, our CEO. He—" The elevator door opens, and Aunt Bree turns her attention to the endless corridor of doors curving dizzyingly in front of us. She smiles at me as she steps out, and it has the feel of someone sun-frying an ant under a magnifying glass. "You're late for your meeting with Martin. You'll love him. He's nurturing."

She leads me to a pair of odd doors directly across from one another; they would have been startling on their own, but they're doubly so because they're flanked by loads of completely uninteresting ones. The door to my left is covered with dozens and dozens of keyholes, some small and dainty, others huge and ornate. The door opposite looks like the rest in the hall, except it's an appalling, retina-searing pink. Aunt Bree gestures toward the pink door, and I raise a fist to knock.

"I'm okay. Okay. Okay. Okay. Okay," I whisper. Five times. I know it doesn't *really* help anything, that it's temporary relief. I know it's giving OCD a win. But this urge doubles as a pep talk, and I can live with that right now.

"Enter," a voice says from beyond the pink wood. I look at Aunt Bree, but she's already walking back toward the elevator.

"Where are you going?"

"I'm not a babysitter, Cassandra. Meet with Martin, and I'll be back to escort you out."

Breathe. You're okay, okay, okay, okay, okay. I bite at my thumbnail and push open the door, nearly knocking down a teetering stack of books leaning against the wall. I reach out a hand to steady them. It's as if a library has exploded. Books. Papers. Pamphlets. Folios. The room even has that musty library smell. A few paces away, next to the stack I managed to keep upright, a small avalanche of books fans out across the floor from its original heap. I pray it was like that before I entered and gingerly step over the literary land mines.

An enormous window overlooking the river and the rain-sodden landscape beyond takes up the back wall, and the light it lets in illuminates streams of dust in the air. Groaning shelves full of curiosities and texts line the three other walls. A rolling ladder rests up against one, co-opted due to lack of space, brittle leaflets stretched over every rung.

It's back to raining again? And... if the river is there, and we entered through that alleyway, this place must take up a good chunk of the waterfront... but even if it takes up the *entire* waterfront, that Rotunda was immense... and based on how much walking we just did... The logistics of it all hurts my head. I'm assuming that there's some sort of magic at play here, but I'm only just wrapping my head around the fortune telling of it all. I don't really want to get too far in the weeds with obscuring the laws of physics.

I think I can see a hint of a desk under the mountain of texts in the center of the room. The mountain speaks in the booming voice of an angry man. "So, you're the nepotistic waste of time I'm supposed to vet. You're late. Punctuality, in spite of what your generation might think, is not a cute relic of the past."

I hear what I think is the squeak of a chair longing for oil being pushed back. "I'm sorry? I didn't even know this place existed."

"Was that an apology or a question?"

"What?"

"Are you hard of hearing, too?" A slight man with a big bark and salt and pepper hair rounds the desk. He firms his jutting chin and narrows his flinty eyes behind his spectacles. "You said 'sorry?'" He pitches the second syllable of the word higher. "So, was that a question, or was that an apology?"

"It was an... apology?"

Disapproval is Mt. Rushmore'd into every line of his face, like the emotion was carved there and left to weather the elements for generations. "Sit. *There.*" He gestures to a small alcove to the right of his desk, where two faded blue seats and a small wooden side table are positioned under a porthole-like window.

I hesitate, pushing the hanging skeleton of an alligator-like creature out of the way before moving to the alcove.

He seats himself on the chair opposite mine and leans back, his hands folded across his paunch. "I am Martin Pict. You will address me as Mr. Pict. I have never served as a mentor because I have never wanted to, and I do not want to now. But since your insufferable aunt is Jordan Welborne's Lackey-in-Chief, I've been commanded to assume the position."

I'm going to kill Aunt Bree. *You'll love him. He's nurturing.* The worst.

"Let's start with the basics. In order to be accepted as a Theban initiate, I need to know the precise number of visions you've had and the nature of same. Begin."

I open my mouth and close it. "Um... when you say visions...?"

He waves a hand airily. "Visions. Scrying. Divination, premonitions, second sight, prophecy, whatever you want to call it. How. Many. Times. Have. You. Had. A. Vision." He sits back and studies me.

"Um..."

"Do you begin every sentence with 'um'? Dreadful." His diction is strangely precise, as if every word has been carved out of his mouth with a scalpel. "You have an unfortunate habit of keeping people waiting. I'd like an answer sometime today." Mr. Pict picks up a thick book next to his chair and flips a few pages with sharp flicks of his wrist.

"I've had two? Or three, actually," I respond tentatively. He looks up from the book on his lap, and his expression makes me want to run away.

You're okay, you're okay, you're okay, okay, okay.

"Asking or telling?"

"I'm telling." I try to sound as firm as possible.

"Two or three. Quite underwhelming. What medium or manner did you use to scry?"

"Medium?"

Pict's face takes on a look of pinched disapproval. More disapproval than before, anyway. "Like pulling teeth. Did you use a mirror? Water? The stars? A crystal ball? See it in a dream?" He raises his voice. "Deduce it from the blasted animal entrails of a sacrificial beast?"

"Oh. Then... no medium? All those times I just saw it. While awake. I was crossing the street last week, and I saw this guy die right in front of me. Only it didn't really happen. I ended up meeting him later, and he's alive." I hold my breath and wait. When Pict says nothing, I offer unhelpfully, "His name is Colin." As if *that's* the piece of information that'll seal the deal.

The silence stretches.

"Right." Mr. Pict slams the large tome on his lap shut and sets it on the table. "I once had a vision like that. Of a young girl dying."

My stomach clenches. "Did she? Die, I mean?"

"That remains to be seen. But she seems to be laboring under the misapprehension that I suffer fools lightly. Please know that I am many things, Ms. Morai, but patient is not one of them. Perhaps you think that you are amusing; if so, allow me to disabuse you of that notion. I do not find you entertaining. I do not find my current predicament entertaining. Life in general may be a theater of the absurd, but scrying is deadly serious." He glares at me. "Novices *do not* scry without a medium to channel their skills. If you are able to sufficiently hone your abilities during Theban's initiate training, if you complete the Coil Walk and achieve Oracle status, then and only then *might* you do so."

Pict stands, marches to his desk, and returns with a folder, my name boldly printed across the front. "You require my approval to attend orientation, and I would not lose an ounce of sleep ending your career before it begins, exalted lineage be damned. Have I made myself clear?"

I sit in miserable and confused silence.

"I asked you a question, Ms. Morai."

"Ye—yes." My voice sounds cracked and dry. I try to swallow but nothing slides down.

"Asking or telling?"

"Telling," I say through gritted teeth.

"So, let's begin yet *again*. What medium, Ms. Morai, did you use to achieve your two, *or three*, visions?" His voice has taken on a mocking quality.

"I didn't use a medium." My voice quavers, but I try and keep it strong and clear.

"You are dismissed," Pict says.

I didn't think that I could feel more depressed than I was the day I saw Colin die, but to be given hope—that I can *have some control*—only to have it snatched away is almost more than I can take. I feel my murky depths welling up and spilling out.

One, two, three... I'm in control.

I pick at the skin of my thumb, ripping at a rough piece of skin until it stings, reopening a cut that was healing so that blood blooms in my nail bed. This feeling and these urges are always stalking, waiting in the dark ready to pounce, and right now it feels like they're going to win.

Four.

"Don't make me repeat myself yet again," he says.

"Please, Mr. Pict, I can learn. I..."

Five.

A loud thud nearly startles me out of my seat. Pict has tossed the thick book from the table onto the floor in front of me. *The Iliad and The Odyssey* now rests at my feet.

Pict leans back and crosses his arms. "The Theban Group is a venerable organization founded to protect scryers from persecution and exploitation and allow them to nurture their abilities. It has since morphed into a vulgar for-profit corporation, but that is neither here nor there. The point remains that we do not allow imposters or liars into our midst. Sortes Homericae, Ms. Morai. Bibliomancy is the fastest way to parse through this mess. If you have any abilities at all, even low-level ones, Homer will pick them up."

I grab the book and clench my teeth, waiting.

Six. Seven. This urge does not rule me.

"Concentrate. Clear your mind until nothing exists but you and the weight of that text on your lap."

I try, but my head is awash with renegade thoughts. *Eight...* I stare at Pict.

"If you're not going to take this seriously, Ms. Morai, we can end this charade now."

"I'm sorry, I'm just having trouble—"

"If you must think of something, think about the absence of everything."

What does that even mean? *You're okay, okay, okay, okay, okay. Nine.* I inhale deeply. *Ten.*

"After you have cleared your mind, you will hold the book so that the spine rests on your lap and allow it to fall open to a random page. You'll then repeat the following, 'Do I have any scrying abilities?' After you ask the question, you will place your finger on the page and trail it in slowly widening circles until your instincts tell you to stop. You'll then read the line to me. If you come up with nonsense, I'll know you're a fraud." He stretches his lips into a semblance of a smile. It's more alarming than his dislike. "We'll determine here and now if you can ever be more than *this*." He waves his hand in my direction.

His words upset my mind's precariously loaded apple cart, spilling out worries and self-soothing thoughts apace: He doesn't dust often. It's fine, only a little dust. In my lungs. *Stop. One. Two. Three.* I didn't even ask to be here. *Four. Five.* Bree ambushed me with all of this. I need to run and find the closest faucet. *Six*. I need this. For Colin. Remember your ERP therapy. I can bear this exposure. I won't act on my compulsion. I can have real control if I make this work. *Seven*...

By the time I reach ten, my breathing has settled and I've convinced myself of the rightness of this path. The promise of real control holds OCD's demands at bay.

"Do I have any scrying abilities?" I ask.

I place my finger on the page and begin to trace invisible swirls, concentrating on the friction of the page on my index finger. It's smooth as my finger glides along, as if following an invisible road in my mind. Suddenly, I feel a tug, as if I'm being willed to stop. I look up, startled.

"Read the line aloud," Pict says.

I squint at the dense text on the page where my finger stalled. "O thou, whose certain eye foresees / The fix'd events of fate's remote decrees."

His expression is inscrutable, and he says nothing for a moment. Then, "We may have *some* ability to work with."

My heart leaps with a joy so intense I must glow with it. I'm suddenly bursting with goodwill for this awful man.

Pict pulls out a small gilt mirror from inside his suit jacket. "Take this and tell me what you see."

I set the book next to me, wipe my clammy palm on my pants, and accept the mirror's handle. It's warm to the touch from resting against Pict's body. I look into it, but the only thing I see are a set of huge mossy eyes and an ominous red spot on my forehead that may or may not be the makings of a zit. Judging from the dull throbbing I'm suddenly aware of, signs are pointing more to yes.

"It looks like black squiggles. Oh, and spots. They're falling. Is this—is this a vision?"

"Black squig—oh, for the love of... *No,* those are eye floaters. Your aunt will be happy to hear you'll make a delightful ophthalmologist."

I take my gaze back to the mirror again and try to clear my head. I see Colin in my mind's eye, my mental compulsions wrestling with the rest of my thoughts, but I push him back, determined or desperate. The strain of it... The pressure in my head builds until it seems I'm in danger of venting it via my eyes bursting from my head. My reflection in the mirror shows a face ablaze and glistening with sweat. *Please cooperate, brain.*

I start to feel a tingling in my temples, like the beginnings of a headache.

As I stare into my reflection, a drowsy darkness slowly spreads inward from my peripheral vision. Like smoke, it fills everything up until my sight is reduced to pinpoints. They linger long enough that I think this is it, the height of the vision, when the pinpoints begin to recede and whispered voices sound in my ears, slippery little hints of sound that come and go so quickly I can't grab hold of one long enough to understand. I feel a little flicker of fear as the voices start in one ear and move to the other, circling and building like fluid until they become a cacophony. Dark shapes begin materializing out of the thick fog in front of me, but like the sounds, I can't make them out.

Suddenly, one low voice, much closer than the others and accompanied by the overpowering scent of flowers, rasps, "A red blessing approaches. Look to the glass. Death comes quickly and respects no one." The vague black shapes begin to bubble and ooze before sliding down in red streams. "Death comes quickly and respects—"

"What did you say?" The mirror is yanked from my hand, and the fog quickly lifts. I blink. Pict is peering at me. "I asked you a question."

"I didn't say anything," I say. The space behind my eyes throbs. Pict sets the mirror down. "'Death comes quickly and respects no one,'" he says, leaning forward. "That's what you said, Ms. Morai."

"Oh," I respond dumbly. I try to shake off the haze hanging heavy in my mind, the throbbing of a faraway headache growing closer. Pict is giving me a strange look, and I fidget as he stares. "Was that... was that a vision? What does that mean?"

Pict ignores my question. "You are to report to Orientation in two weeks. Scryer Services will have a training schedule for you at that time, which will include our one-on-one supplemental training sessions." He shuffles through the pile of books next to him and pulls a few worn texts from the stack. "I expect you to familiarize yourself with the principles outlined in these by the time we next meet. And so we are clear, if I am to serve as your mentor, you will eat, breathe, and sleep scrying. You will not lie about your abilities or lack thereof. You will not keep anything from me. Is that understood?"

I accept the book. "Yes, sir."

"Asking or telling, Ms. Morai?"

I have no idea.

7

A unt Bree is apparently too busy to see me out of Theban
Group herself, but her extremely efficient assistant Martha
is waiting for me when I leave Pict's office, blinking her wide-set
frog eyes and wearing an expensive but ill-fitting outfit that looks
like a Bree cast-off.

"So... you can see the future?" I ask her as she leads the way.

She darts me a glance, quick as you can say *ribbit*, and nods.
"I wouldn't be here if I couldn't."

"How'd you end up working for my aunt?"

She makes a noncommittal sound in response. Martha's
expression is hard to read, but I'm guessing maybe she wasn't so hot
for this job.

"Does everyone work here after training?" I ask while we wait
for the elevator.

"Most," she says, pressing the button for the bird cage elevator
another few times.

"What about school though?"

She gives me a strange look and leaps to enter the elevator when it arrives. When the doors close, she mumbles, "Don't know why anyone would ever go back to school when they've been handed this opportunity."

I guess most people ditch regular school after training? Aunt Bree's definitely smoking something if she thinks her professor brother wouldn't flip his gourd if I dropped out of school.

Martha leads me back the way Bree brought me at a brisk pace— or tries for a brisk pace at least. My rubbernecking on the way out, especially in the Rotunda, no doubt slows our progress, irritating her. I hold my follow-up questions until we're trudging back through the beige cubicle room.

"So pretty much everyone works here. Do they all live here, too?"

"Most live here or at one of the dozen smaller satellite offices we have around the world. Some choose not to," she says.

"Do people actually sell insurance here? These guys are scryers?" I gesture to the cubicles.

Her sigh is infused with the frustration of a thousand kindergarten teachers. "Yes. And yes." I get the sense she doesn't want to tell me too much. Maybe scared of saying something to freak me out. God knows what Aunt Bree told her about me.

Theodore waves as we pass his desk. I give him one in return.

There is a car Martha arranged for me waiting out front, and she seems to relish packing me in it and slamming the door behind me.

The ride home is a quick one. I let myself into my apartment, still woozy and, if I'm being honest, mentally treading water as I replay everything I heard today. If not for the weight of the books Mr. Pict gave me dragging down my bag, I'd suspect I'd had a nervous break.

Dad is already home as I toe off my shoes. He grins like a nutjob, waving some papers at me. I smile warily, wondering what the intent look in his mossy-hazel eyes means.

"Don't be mad."

"Mad?" I say, walking to my room and dropping my bag just inside the door.

"I told you about the college prep summer program upstate? The one that costs a boatload of money?"

"Yeah?" I tamp down my suspicions. There is no way...

"I called your guidance counselor up and told her it was too rich for our blood, and she insisted she call the camp and see if anything can be done. Scholarship spots or anything. Before you say anything, it was a longshot and I didn't think it'd go anywhere, so there was no point in getting your hopes up. Or, you know, your anxiety up. And even if it did, I figured we could just turn it down if you really didn't want to go. But then you said you were thinking of a job and... well, Ms. Kelly scored you a spot. Whatever your school pays that woman is really not enough. This place is really elite, Cass. I mean look at this."

I accept the glossy brochure and sit heavily, Bree's words floating back to me: *He's already planning on sending you here. He just doesn't know it yet.*

Dad is oohing and ahhing as he points out the imaginary upstate retreat's best features over my shoulder, but it barely registers. Martha is crazy good at creating official-looking documents, complete with instructions for how parents can send off their "camp kids" and a *Frequently Asked Questions* doc tucked into the brochure. Transportation is included, Dad points out. Will they really arrange a bus load of kids to go to fake camp with me? Aunt Bree does seem the type to take her lies seriously, I guess.

Dad mistakes my reaction. "You don't have to—"

"No, no. This is... this is cool, Dad. I'm pumped."

For just a moment, my belief in Aunt Bree's abilities, in what I saw today, wavers. I almost laugh out loud at the thought of me disembarking from a bus at a normal camp and demanding to be taken to the fortune telling stuff. But no... the timing is too suspect, and as insane as today was, it was definitely not all in my head. How on Earth did they rope my guidance counselor into all of this? Did Ms. Kelly even know she was being played?

Dad smiles at me, and I stretch my dry lips into an answering approximation of one. Then he heads to his room and parks himself at his desk to finish up some work stuff, and my ears pick up soft humming coming from his open door. My poor father is so excited for me that it's enough to set my eyes watering with guilt. I feel like a dishonest douchebag.

I wander into my kitchen and open the fridge, peering in as if some comfort food will have miraculously appeared in the twenty minutes since last I looked. Why couldn't I develop chocolate conjuring abilities alongside the scrying? I pause, marveling at that thought: me, a scryer. I grab a blueberry yogurt and spoon and plop down on the couch, but I don't have the energy to look for the TV remote so I just sit and stare. Somewhere in one of our plaster walls, an old pipe gurgles and clicks. Dad's humming has stopped. It's too quiet.

I lean back, licking my spoon and wondering again at Aunt Bree's dominoes, leading me to Theban, getting Dad to send me to a camp without him knowing. I'm going to study mother-frigging *magic*. I huff out a laughing breath in wonder and launch myself off the sofa. I should be working on that MV-77 form or studying Pict's books.

I ditch my yogurt and jet to my room to grab my bag, frowning when I see a familiar orange coupon resting on my floor. I must have missed it when I opened my bedroom door earlier. *"Madame Grey's Psychic Readings. Good for one FREE reading,"* it reads.

Maybe I tracked it in on my shoe? The thought skeeves me. Those frigging things are everywhere lately. I pick the coupon up gingerly and toss it—after all, it's not like I need to go to a psychic to see the future anymore—then detour to the bathroom to scrub the crap out of my hands for a long while.

Maybe I should read on the roof. Where I might see Colin. Which is totally *not* the reason for wanting to study on the roof, but kind of completely is.

I towel off my hands and grab for my bag before I head upstairs. My excitement at diving into the texts or maybe seeing Colin is dimmed only by thoughts of my contaminated bedroom. Only a cleansing fire would be enough to sanitize the space or to knock the thought that I tracked garbage into my room out of my head.

Speaking of fires, there's a fancy new warning sign on the door to the roof claiming an alarm will sound if the door is opened, but I know the owner's way too cheap to have alarms installed. Honestly, I'm convinced that even the sprinklers in the halls are fake.

The rain stopped before I left Theban Group, and the ground and the folding chairs have more or less dried, but a sweet post-downpour earthy smell lingers in the air here. It takes me back to summer walks with my mom in the park. The memory bites, flaying my scarred heart. Petrichor... that's what the smell is called. The Trivinometry word comes to me, and I blame Colin's garden-like patio for amplifying the scent.

At the reminder of Colin's existence, I look around nervously.

No sign of him, so I walk over to the ledge and loiter there like a full-on weirdo. He would spot me instantly if he were to come out. I drag my folding chair so it faces his lushly green patio area and prop my feet up on the knee wall, pretending to read. After I've glanced at his door for the hundredth time, it becomes obvious Colin won't be making an appearance today, which means that it's safe to tuck into my reading. But first...

I pull my phone out and search for whatever I can dig up on Theban Group. The first hit is for the company's website.

It's so... normal. Like a digital version of that beige room with the cubicles. Insurance rate quotes. Commercial policies. Words and more words.

I click out and scroll through the search results. A few news articles on glittering fundraising galas and do-gooder work. Aunt Bree is in one of the shots, smiling her cat-got-the-cream smile up at a man the caption identifies as the Prime Minister of Greece. The story gives her title as the Head of Theban Group Foundation, the philanthropic arm of Theban Group, and identifies her as instrumental to helping alleviate a migrant crisis. Another picture shows her and some random gray-heads posing with a group of refugee girls in school uniforms.

Bree? Really? My aunt is the head of a global charity? Doing things like saving migrants? I guess her whole thing about helping me wasn't bogus.

Wikipedia gives me some more on the company. All of it boring and nice and impossible to reconcile with what I saw today. I click around, drawn deeper and deeper into off-topic hyperlinks until I'm reading about the ancient city-state of Thebes and its myths about Heracles and Oedipus.

I set aside my phone and pull out the first book Pict gave me, skimming through odds and ends outlining the origins of Theban Group... and holy crap, this is nothing like that Wikipedia entry. Here, there is no mention of business subsidiaries or acquisitions or Wall Street; instead, it's all about protection for scryers who were hunted, persecuted, stuck as royal pets throughout the centuries— real "off with his head" type stuff. The trivia geek in me sighs with glee before the thought occurs that my own ancestors may have faced these horrors.

My eyes race over page after page, and I gnaw at my lip, not noticing until it stings. I stop, and once my concentration-tick has been mastered, I flip ahead and come across a section on something called the "Agon"—I guess a sort of ancient Olympics for scrying— and I pause, a footnote catching my eye.

"It is often described as having a cool and beckoning zephyr's kiss that lures the unsuspecting in to investigate. Scryers have had a symbiotic relationship with the Celidon Coil for millennia, some saying the one's abilities could not exist without the other's, but that relationship is not without its struggles. The Celidon Coil is a place of power and protection for scryers precisely because it is a danger to outsiders. A controlled introduction of a scryer to the Coil environment during the Agon is necessary to neutralize the extreme danger the Coil would otherwise pose."

I leaf through the remaining pages before setting it down, resolving to pour over every word later. A smile pulls at my stinging lip as I pick up another book. I'm going to learn how to do all of this.

I'm a part of this. If I were the type to squeal, that's how I'd describe the noise I just made. But I'm not a squealer. At least that's what I tell myself as I shimmy in my seat and crack the hefty sucker open.

Good lord. It's like a chemistry textbook, except instead of stoichiometry and moles and oxidation, I'm reading about the Canon of Thought Singularity. It should be fascinating—it's the how-to's of magic, for God's sake—but they could bottle *Twardowski's Principia: Principles and Techniques of Applied Scrying* as a cure for insomnia.

After I've blinked myself awake for the fifteenth time, I toss the book back in my bag and grab my MV-77 form and a pen, determined to recapture that feeling of elation.

"Have you visited Mount Parnassus in the last twelve months?" "Have you ever been arrested for divination-related fraud?" "Indicate the date of your last incidence of déjà vu." The hell kind of questions are these?

"It looks like you just took every expression your face can make out for a test drive," Colin calls out.

I freeze and scan his patio, but don't see him until he moves. "You were hiding behind the potted plants? That's not creepy or anything."

"I wasn't hiding. Well, not from you anyway. I was reading. Like you." He approaches the little dividing wall and holds up the Stephen King novel *Under the Dome*.

"Oh, I know that one. Aliens planted the dome, right?"

Colin looks briefly stunned before flipping through to the end of his book. "Ugh, come on!" he groans with a laugh and tosses the book behind him.

I blush. "I'm sorry! Your fault for skulking around in shrubbery."

"Clays do not skulk, thank you very much. We prowl mostly, and some lurk. There was an uncle once-removed who crept once, but we don't talk about him."

I laugh, left giddy by my belly's flip-flopping and the rush of heat that washes over me when I look at him. Some of what I read about the Coil could just as easily have been about Colin. His smile, his summer sky eyes... all of him. He has a happy gravity, a draw that pulls me in. Everything is brighter and lighter when he's around, like changing a channel and living in high definition for the first time.

"Synonyms won't save you, skulker," I say.

He grins. "I think your punishment for spoiling my book, and my punishment for not-skulking, should be a visit to see the Spite House. Together." He looks away. "If you're free."

It's funny how, before Mom died, my heart was a thing that beat in my chest to keep me alive. It wasn't until Mom shattered it that I realized how much it could feel. And now... with Colin so awkwardly sweet and asking me—me—to hang out, I'm realizing my heart can feel more than pain. It is currently spasming and spinning with an insane rush of delicious joy.

"I mean, it's cool if you—"

"When?"

His blue eyes swing back. "Now?"

"Okay."

"Yeah?" he asks.

I nod and hold back a smile. "Sure." I stand and back up toward the door to the stairs, my bag of books pressed against my chest. "I have to drop these in my apartment first, but... yeah. Let's meet downstairs in a few." I nod again for good measure because I'm not sure what else to do. And I flee, because that's something I'm good at. I race down the stairs, through the door to my floor, down the hall and through my front door, *definitely* squealing all the way to my room.

8

Today is a good day. And I don't even have to convince myself of it too hard, though I'm wiped from a morning spent having the reality I'd lived in all my life torn away from me and replaced with an entirely new one.

On the way to the park, we talk music—and at one point we both bust out the lyrics to one of the more obscure Atomic Dons songs at the same time. I blush and break off, but still, I'd bet my life he was the teensiest bit impressed.

Plus, it's sunny out, I'm having a decent hair day, and hey, it helps to know I'm not insane—I can see the frigging *future*.

I look over at Colin, his hands in his pockets as he strolls along next to me. He catches me looking and smiles. *The future*. The thought is suddenly a cloud blotting out the sun. My excitement dims, and my sense of self-preservation kicks in. What am I doing? What if I can't save him?

"There's no way seeing the future is better than flying," Colin says, his question about wished-for superhero powers having devolved into a debate.

"You want to fly? Have you ever driven anywhere outside the city? Ever seen how many bugs end up squashed on the windshield? Picture that, only on your face," I counter.

"Ever heard of a helmet?"

"Yes, you'd look like the sickest superhero ever in your safety helmet," I say. Colin laughs. "Plus, what about breathing? You can't fly too high or you won't be able to breathe. Which means you've got to stick to lower altitudes and duck birds and power lines and buildings or whatever. The logistics are a nightmare."

"Yeah, yeah. But seeing the future is lame unless you can actually *do something* about it," he counters.

Please let there be something I can do to help him. Save him. Save him. Save him. Save him. Save him. Save him.

A ball rolls in front of us with a mop of a dog in hot pursuit. The dog notices us and pauses, forgetting the ball entirely. It trots over to investigate and sniffs my leg, brushing up against me, tongue lolling in its mouth and tail wagging. Colin picks up the ball and buries his hand in the dog's off-white gnarls of fur, giving it a little scratch behind the ears. He throws the ball back toward the dog's owner, and it darts off in chase.

It looked dirty. Fleas. Colin has... we're...

Stop it.

The fleas are...

Stop it.

Colin glances at me, unaware I have diagnosed us both as terminally ill with bubonic plague in the space it took him to throw a ball. He slaps at his arm. "I can't believe I let you drag me out here. The mosquitos are no joke. Where's this Spite House?"

"Almost there." I take a breath, talking myself off the ledge.

You're okay, okay, okay, okay, okay. I've been happy, yes, but mental illness isn't a spigot you can turn off just because things are going your way for once. "And you're the one who demanded I take you as punishment for skulking, remember?"

"Lurking, not skulking. And that was before I knew it meant being eaten alive."

"Right." I force a smile and point ahead of us. "Thar she blows."

A tiny slice of a house juts pugnaciously out of its tree-covered surroundings a little up the path, its optimistic butterscotch color completely at odds with its confrontational origins. It's two stories tall, but so narrow a person with a decent wingspan standing with arms outstretched in front of it could reach almost end-to-end.

"Ha! The little window has shutters!" Colin says, picking up his pace as we approach. "This is insane! Some dude really built this for spite?"

"Yep, Jacob Hollingsworth built it in the early 1800s. There aren't any windows along the sides of it because it was wedged between the neighboring houses. Those houses are long gone, but this thing is still around." I lean down and pluck the pant leg that brushed the dog away from my skin. *You're okay, okay, okay, okay, okay.*

"So good ol' Jacob won. Last man standing," Colin muses.

"Wait until you see the back."

I bite at my thumb until it bleeds. *Enough. You're not contaminated. This is false control.* We circle the house. Colin laughs out loud. "A balcony on the second floor. This guy wasn't messing around. Can we go in?"

I hold up a key. "Not usually, but my dad helped restore this place." Having a history professor for a father comes in handy sometimes.

We walk back around to the front, and I open the door. It's like walking into a wall of heat. The stale air, humidity, and dust create a nasal cocktail that sets me off on a coughing fit. I wave my hand to clear the air in front of me and only make it worse. I'm going to die. This dust—

Colin follows me in and pats me on the back. "You okay?"

I nod weakly, and he seems to accept that answer, looking around gleefully.

"It's like a real little house! Did the guy actually live here?"

"Yeah," I croak. "He had to. It was the only way he could build it."

He puts a foot on the first step of a tight staircase hugging a wall. "Why didn't the city take it? They can do that, right?"

I pause, the sour taste in my mouth not entirely due to dust and coughing. "Eminent domain. Yeah, they can take stuff. I'm not sure why they didn't. Maybe it was grandfathered in or something. And the guy lived so long that the house became a curiosity after he died, so then they couldn't get rid of it."

"You coming?" Colin asks, looking back as he climbs up the stairs.

I follow him up, the stairs creaking ominously with each of our footfalls. I worry about the integrity of the wood and picture myself falling through, but Colin doesn't seem at all bothered. At the top is a small room with a window behind us and a narrow bed, a small chest of drawers, and an opening to the balcony in front of us. Colin looks around, his hands on his hips.

"Okay, so... I love this place. Let's move in."

I laugh, which dissolves into a coughing fit again. "I'm going to hack up a lung. Can you love it from the balcony? There's like twenty inches of dust in here."

Colin lifts the latch to the balcony door, the hinges shockingly silent and well oiled. I knock on the door frame on my way out, five light taps, soothing the beat inside my head. We step out on the slight platform, and I gratefully gulp the fresh air as we look out at the park. The scenery is a little different from this vantage point, and the balcony looks sound enough that I can actually enjoy our surroundings.

"Not a bad view. It's so pretty out here," I say.

"Yeah," Colin responds.

I glance up at him. He's looking at me, his mouth open like he wants to say something. He turns toward me, his chest brushing my arm, his warm breath caressing my cheek. "Hey, Cass?"

"Yep?" I'm suddenly super aware every inch of my body. Of his.

"I'm..." He leans closer, gently pressing me to turn toward him. A full body flush moves through me. I part my lips.

It's only a small creak, but it's enough to turbocharge my anxiety.

"We need to get inside. This balcony isn't safe." I rush into the dusty bedroom, breathing heavily, my emotions a jumble of fear and mortification and disappointment.

Colin follows me in, looking sheepish.

I'm so dumb. I try to crowd out the images of collapsing wood, broken limbs, jagged impalements.

Count your steps. Five hundred fifty-five sounds right. Walk, doesn't matter where, walk until you count off five hundred fifty-five steps. It'll feel better.

Counting steps won't help.

"What were you saying out there?" I ask, seventy percent sure I interrupted a kiss. I swallow, trying to claw myself back to that moment.

"Oh. Nothing... I'm just glad I met you. Happy we're... friends, or whatever. We moved around so much, I haven't had a ton."

"Oh." *Friends.* It's such a *nice* thing to say. I don't have many—any. It's really sweet. So nice. So bland. So... awful. Did I just friend-zone myself? Or did I misread what happened out on the balcony? I want the Spite House to collapse and swallow me whole. I choke it all down, ashamed by my selfish reaction and semi-grimace, hoping it passes for a smile. "Me too. Happy that we're friends, I mean." I give him a soft punch to the arm. "Pal."

"Hey! Violence is not cool! Be civilized and retaliate by building a spite house or something."

I force a laugh.

I'd promised to introduce Colin to Mrs. O after the Spite House, so instead of getting to wallow in my misery at home, I lead my *pal* out of the park and toward her bodega. I look down and notice one of those free psychic reading coupons at our feet. Then another. Then more. I look ahead. It looks like they were dropped out of a plane like WWII propaganda. I swallow a whimper and look across the street, then back at Colin. Something feels wrong.

Colin notices the coupons, too. "Ooooh! Fortune teller?" He leans down and pops up clutching two coupons. "Come on! The place is over there. Let's go!" He tugs at my arm.

"No! I don't want... that place is... let's just go to Mrs. O's," I say, pulling back.

"It'll be fun!" he says. He drops my arm and jogs across the street, daring cars to hit him and sending my heart shooting up my throat on a geyser of fear. He's at the door and pulling it open by the time I reach him.

The bell jangles as we step inside, and I scan the room while moving closer to Colin. Our blood splatter would match the color scheme perfectly. The window is covered by heavy red curtains, and the shabby furniture, illuminated by ruby Christmas lights and fake flickering candles, looks like something out of my nana's old house. Every seatback is covered by a crocheted brown, red, and orange throw blanket. A deck of tarot cards is fanned out on a round table in the center of the space.

The walls are covered in clichéd mystical symbols "borrowed" from other cultures. A prominent sign hangs by the door releasing Madame Grey and her associates from any liability and advising that fortunes read are strictly for entertainment. I count to calm myself.

A woman enters the room through a bead curtain hanging in a doorway. She's a pocket-sized lioness in a leotard, her thick waist ringed by a colorful sash and her mussed hair piled high on her head like the morning after prom. A hunger for business or money or something else claws its way past her thick layer of cosmetics as she spots us, until her elated grin melts away everything except the kindness in her dark-rimmed eyes. I straighten a bit, breathing again.

"Hi! We have these things that say the first reading is free?" Colin asks, holding up the coupons.

"That's right," the lioness says, in this breathy train-whistle voice. She clasps her hands and blinks up at us. "I'm so happy you came. *So* happy!"

"Are you Madame Grey?" I ask, instead of asking what I really want: *Are you going to kill us?*

"No, no, I'm Narisa. Please! Sit, sit." She ushers us to the table, pulling on our arms until we drop down onto the chairs. "We'll start with you," she says to Colin, grabbing his hand, studying it.

She leans over it close and then bends back, peering at it from as far as her seat will allow. "Okay. Confirmed, then. Confirmed."

"What's confirmed?" I ask.

"You don't know?" she asks with a look of puzzlement.

"I—" I look at Colin.

"No, we don't know. What do you see?" Colin asks, a wry expression on his face. I think *he thinks* this is just theatrics. I'm not at all sure that it is.

We're okay. We're okay. Okay. Okay. Okay.

"Better the cards tell you. The cards will tell," Narisa says, scooping up the tarot cards in one smooth move. She shuffles them with casino dealer flare and then holds the cards out for Colin to cut.

"So, is there, like, a special school you go to, to learn all this?" Colin asks as he watches the woman.

She looks up at me while she answers him, a small smile on her lips. "There is. But *this*..." She shuffles again, drawing her hands apart, the cards flying from one palm to the other. "This, I learned on the internet. Lots to learn on the internet."

Colin laughs, but the woman has her eyes closed, her hands hovering over the deck of cards as she concentrates and silently mouths some words. She fans out the deck and then asks Colin to select three cards.

She flips the first over. A man crawls over a dune. "Eight of Sands in the past position... you've been searching, seeking, never finding. A journeyman, that's you."

"Well, my dad is a diplomat, so..."

Narisa flips over the second card. "Three of Spirals, present position. Pain and grief. Oh, so heartsick." She rests her hand on her bosom and gives Colin a pained look.

She flips over the last card, a disturbing one of a man lying in a pool of blood, a number of sharp hook-like things jutting from his back. "Dear, dear... Ten of Thorns in the future position," the woman breathes. "Confirmed. Disaster baked into the path you're on. You're in danger."

Colin beams. "Oh, yeah? Awesome."

The woman pulls a crystal ball out from under the table and sets it down in front of her. "This is serious, young man. I can't tell exactly, but..." The woman gazes into the crystal ball, her eyelids growing heavier and heavier until they're barely open. "I see movement, but not a trip... This is... activity. You moving. Movement all around you. Rushing. Blurs. Crossing—"

"Crossing the street," I blurt. Colin and the woman start and stare at me. I add, "I mean, I'm guessing. You jaywalked like a suicidal stuntman before. You need to be careful."

Colin rolls his eyes.

"Come. Come. The last part of your reading is through here." The woman stands and reaches out a hand to Colin. I start to stand, but she says, "You wait there. I'll be right back. Right back."

"No, we need to stay togeth—"

"It's cool, Cass," Colin says with a devilish grin. "Don't you care I'm in danger? I need to get a karma tune-up or whatever." He pauses and whispers, "Scared?"

"No reason to be scared. No reason at all," the woman tuts. "All friends here. That's the truth. All friends."

The woman stabs me. My hands press to my gut. Blood spills over them. I scream. She leaves me there to bleed out. Dad finds my body. He cries. He's alone now. Coupons for free psychic readings are stuffed into my mouth.

I'm okay. I'm okay. I'm okay. I'm okay. I'm okay.

But now there's a new thought playing around in my head: *Compulsion or vision?*

I concentrate on counting and breathing, so much so it takes me a second to realize there's someone standing near the beaded doorway. The woman is about my mother's age when she passed away and looks like someone who'd try to sell you on a regimen of granola and sunshine to treat a broken leg... except for her unnerving pale blue eyes. She pulls off the blue scarf covering her white hair.

My blood screams through my veins. I push my chair back, launching to my feet, keeping my eyes on hers. "You were at the school! That day when I saw Colin die! Who are you? What do you... why—" All the questions I want to ask tumble over one another like a stampeding crowd.

She holds up a hand. "Narisa told you we mean no harm. It's the truth. There's no reason to be scared, Cassandra."

"How do you know my—"

"You'd be surprised at how much we know," she says. "I'll explain. Please sit, and I'll answer all of your questions." She sits at the table, and when I remain standing, she adds again, "Please."

I ease back into the seat across from her, though my feet tingle with the urge to run. I press my hands down onto my thighs to keep from knocking on the table.

The woman reaches for the cards Narisa abandoned and shuffles. "I'm Madame Grey. And what I want is to help you. Cut the cards." She places the deck in front of me.

I try to force whatever scrying abilities I have into telling me something, anything, about this woman, but I get no flashes or impressions beyond the violent imagery my OCD is whipping up.

I fight to keep the images from implanting themselves in my brain. From germinating and growing. I count.

"I don't want a reading. I want to know what's going on." I'm proud of the false steadiness of my voice, even as I glance at the beaded curtain, picturing the little lioness drugging Colin, chopping him up.

"Theban Group is not what you think." Madame Grey sets the cards aside and leans in, a strand of white blonde hair falling in front of one ice chip eye. "You don't know what they're doing. What they're capable of."

I swallow my surprise. "What do you mean?"

"The less you know, the better. For now. For your own safety," she says. She pulls a small glass oval from her pocket and pushes it across the table. It's a translucent eye with a piercing blue iris. "Please, Cassandra, we need you to take this. Bring it with you to Theban Group. Carry it at all times."

"But what do you think Theban Group is doing?"

"I am telling you, for your own—"

I stand. "Colin! We need to go!"

"I can help you save that boy's life. I saw what happens to him, too. He's not the only one in danger. You need to tread carefully."

"I don't need you to save Colin. Or me."

She stands and sets the glass eye on my side of the table. "Please take that with you. It's a powerful protective amulet. Evil eye."

"Colin!"

Colin appears in the doorway, followed by Narisa.

"You know where to find me when you change your mind," Madame Grey says, a weary cast to her features.

I back away from the table, leaving the eye where Madame Grey set it, and practically drag Colin out the door. "You look shook. Your reading tell you your cat is gonna die or something?" Colin teases.

I ignore his jokes and press the anxiety down deep inside me, along with the Spite House disappointment and all the rest of life's upsets. Colin jogs off when we get to Mrs. O's, saying he needs to grab something before he goes in.

"There's my girl! Find a job yet, little one?" Mrs. O asks from behind the counter as the door chime announces my entrance. I'll never know how she knows it's me who's done the entering, though.

"Yeah. Figured I'd give being a senator a try. I leave for D.C. next week."

"Senator Morai does have a nice ring to it." Mrs. O busies herself with counting the money in her register with the help of a currency reading device. It vibrates with the introduction of each new bill. "Seriously, though."

"Yeah, I'm..." Learning how to hopefully save you and Colin, and take control of my life, and not to be afraid anymore, and... lie, apparently. "Going to a summer camp instead."

"That's wonderful! You'll have so much fun. I'm happy to see you putting yourself out there."

"Yeah." I shuffle nervously.

"Out with it, little ostrich," Mrs. O says.

"I told you, ostriches don't—"

"Yes, eggs. I know. Don't try and change the subject."

"There's a boy I want to introduce you to. He'll be here any second and... Oh my God, stop smiling like that! Don't smile like that when he's here. He'll know..."

"Know what?" Mrs. O asks.

"I don't know... that you have the wrong idea about him."

"I didn't make the broth. I only tasted it."

"I don't know what that means, but you need to cool it with the Yoda stuff. Oh no. This is him. Okay. Act normal."

"I've never heard you so flustered," she says.

"Colin! Hi!" My voice is too high and I try not to wince.

He smiles warmly and comes up to my side by the counter. "Hey, Cass. You didn't tell me your younger sister worked here." He brandishes a surprise sunflower. "This is for you, ma'am."

Mrs. O laughs in delight. She reaches out, and Colin places it in her hand.

"Such a cornball." I shake my head.

"A charming cornball, though? Maybe? Did it work, Mrs. O?"

"Oh yes, I'm charmed to within an inch of my life. But you, young man, have me at a disadvantage. You know who I am, but I don't know you."

"This is Colin," I say, at the same time Colin says, "Colin. Cassie's friend."

"I didn't know Cassie had a friend named Colin. It's a pleasure meeting you."

"She didn't mention me?" he asks.

"I wrote a book report about you. She probably hasn't gotten around to grading it yet," I say.

"I bet it was dark and mysterious and Faulkner-esque," Colin says.

I snort, and Mrs. O smiles.

"I think my mom said she was in here not too long ago? Katherine Clay?"

"Ah, you're the diplomat's son! I hope your mother comes and visits again soon. It's been lonely ever since *someone* started their job hunt. I sit here all by my lonesome, praying a nice young gentleman will wander in to reach a certain box on the top shelf in my office. The one over my desk. It's back that way." Mrs. O points.

"I'm your gentleman. No problem at all." Colin flexes, and I laugh in spite of myself. "You laughing at my muscles isn't offensive at all." He whistles on his way to the office.

"What box do you need?" I ask Mrs. O.

"Fool's errand to get a moment alone with you. To let you know I approve, little one. He's a prism for your light. Fun, open, playful. He's good for you."

"I told you, he doesn't like me like that," I whisper.

"I notice you didn't say you don't like him like that."

"Hey, there's a few boxes back here. Which one am I supposed to be grabbing?" Colin's voice sounds from the office.

"The one labeled 'batteries,' dear," Mrs. O responds.

"Is there a box of batteries back there?" I ask. I know her too well.

"Nope!" Mrs. O crows cheerfully. "And deny all you like, but that boy likes you. And you like him. And it warms my old heart more than you know." Mrs. O reaches out her hand, and I put my hand in hers. She lifts it to her lips.

"I love you. You're wrong, but I love you," I say.

"I'm blind, not *blind*. You'll have to come back for some girl talk when you don't have your young man with you. I'll fill you in on the signs you're missing. When you lose your sight, everything else is heightened, you know."

"Neat. Didn't realize that included becoming a barometer for crushes. What's going on with the guy from the city, by the way? With the eminent domain stuff?"

Mrs. O sighs and pulls her hand out of mine. "I told you not to worry about that."

"I know you did. But I do. So what's happening?"

"Hey, I'm not seeing a box with that label up here," Colin calls out.

"My mistake, dear. I'll have to place an order," Mrs. O calls back. She sits back on her stool behind the counter and pats the one next to hers. I walk around and sit. "I am appealing, which should buy us a little bit more time, but I probably won't be able to stop it. They want a nice, shiny supermarket here, and a ton of apartments, and they want them now. Doesn't matter that I don't have a mortgage on this place and I've always been on time with my taxes."

"No wonder people build Spite Houses," I mutter. "What would stop it? Like, is it the lawyer? Is it the judge?"

"What does it matter? It won't happen anyway."

"Humor me! Please. What would stop it?"

"Maybe if the developer pulled out of the project? Then the city wouldn't have any reason to take the place."

"Who's the developer?" I ask.

Mrs. O gestures at a paper on the shelf under the register. "Some bigshot. Tautamo Associates."

I mentally file that information away and hop up as Colin approaches, leaning forward and dusting his thick dark hair with his hands until it's endearingly disheveled. "It's really dusty on those top shelves. If you want, I can come back one day and help clean up and organize. It's too high up for you to be messing with."

"Aren't you sweet? I would love the company. Especially now that your Cassie here has abandoned me for this *camp* she's going to..."

"I have not abandoned you. And didn't you say you wouldn't accept free help?"

"I said I wouldn't give you a full-time job when I couldn't pay you. I love the occasional helping hand. Especially when it's from sweet young men who bring me flowers and pretend to think I'm your younger sister."

"See, Cass? I don't chase all the ladies away," Colin says.

"Just the smart ones."

Mrs. O and Colin chuckle, and I wrap her up in a big hug. She throws an arm around me and returns it briefly.

"Have fun, you two. Go get into some trouble. This one plays it much too safe." Mrs. O gestures toward me.

"I promise to be a terrible influence," Colin says.

I grab the paper with the developer's information and shove it in the waistband of my jeans while they're distracting each other.

"She's really great," Colin says, once we've left.

"Yeah, she is."

He steps off the curb while we wait at a crosswalk, and I yank his arm to pull him back onto the sidewalk. *He slips, falling in front of a car. Ambulances. I'm the one to talk to his mother. His father. Telling them he's dead. His mother screams.*

"The fortune teller said to be careful with streets!" I say.

"Yeah, yeah," he says with a laugh. "You're really lucky, by the way."

"What?"

"Mrs. O. You're really lucky to have her."

"Oh. Yeah. She sucks down weed like a frat guy, and she likes tormenting me with advice, but she really is amazing."

A moment passes and the light turns. I stick close to Colin, warily looking around as we cross the street. Colin nudges me with his shoulder. "Wonder how many boxes I'll have to pull down from shelves before she adopts me."

"I'm pretty sure you're already in."

He reaches my stoop and turns to me with a serious expression. "You didn't mention you're going to camp. When's that happening?"

"I leave in a couple of weeks."

"Oh... okay. I guess we'll have to hang out every day until you leave, then." His eyes are midnight velvet as they scan my face, and I desperately want to spin the moment into a fairy tale. Instead, I puff out a laugh that I hope sounds authentic.

"Right. Sounds good. I better get inside now, though. My dad's probably home."

"I'll see you tomorrow. And I'll sketch out our joint custody agreement," Colin calls out. At my confused glance back, he adds, "For Mrs. O."

I shake my head and let myself in my building.

That night I dream of Mrs. O's tormentor, pale-eyed nutjobs, and boys who don't want to kiss me.

9

"You can take that with you," Colin says, pointing at the book I'm holding. Faulkner's *A Fable*. "It'll give you something to read on the bus tomorrow. How long's the drive to camp?"

"Sweet, thanks," I say, ignoring his question and the reminder that I'm headed into the virtual unknown tomorrow.

I've bombarded Aunt Bree with text messages, and she—chock full of encouragement but citing how busy she is—looped in Martha to give me hard-fought drips of intel that haven't exactly helped with my comfort levels.

Will there be other people training with me?

Yes.

There's a place for me to live there?

Dorms.

Do I need to share the dorm with a roommate? (This one had me especially worried.)

No.

Is the training just classes and stuff? Like school?

Yes.

What happens if I suck at this scrying stuff?

...

I hug my knees up to my chest as I flip through the book Colin's offered up. It's not just worry about tomorrow that has me shaking, though. The central air in Colin's house has his bedroom meat-locker cold.

Colin notices me shiver, of course, and he hops up and ducks into his walk-in closet—a luxury in this city—and reappears, balling up a maroon sweatshirt that he tosses at me like a missile. I block it with the book, laughing.

He wasn't kidding about hanging out every day. We've been inseparable, and when we're not together, I stare into space thinking about him.

He drops down to sit across from me on his rug, his lashes hiding those rich blue eyes that usually take center stage on his face. I greedily drink in the black of his hair and the angles of his face. "I'm going to miss you, you know," he says with a lopsided smile.

My heart lurches. "What?"

He plucks the book from my hands and examines it. "When you're at camp. It's going to suck around here."

I pull his sweatshirt on over my head to cover my expression. "I'm going to miss you, too." *Unfair.* He shouldn't say things like that when I'm about to expire from unrequited love.

When it's time for me to leave, he gives me a lingering hug and I wrap my arms around him tightly, my thoughts keeping time with his beating heart.

I'm going to save you. I'm going to save you. Save you. Save you. Save you.

He releases me and moves to kiss my cheek, catching the corner of my mouth when I turn. I blush and stammer. He flushes and apologizes, his expression inscrutable.

When I climb the knee-wall and open the door to my building, I turn to take a mental picture of him, ruffled dark hair, hands in his pockets, solemn eyes. I wave and close the roof door behind me, feeling as if my chest were used as a punching bag. I touch my fingers to the corner of my lips and burrow my face into the neck of his sweatshirt. It smells like him.

I pad back to my apartment slowly. *It's okay. You'll be back for your birthday.* Dad insisted he be able to pick me up for my birthday, and whoever answered the "camp" hotline graciously said they would bus me back for that. Martha is good.

The front door opens five minutes after I enter. "Where's our lasagna, chef?" I call out.

"Damn it! I'm so sorry, Cass. I knew I forgot something," Dad says. "Let's make it pizza Friday instead? Giuseppe's cut their delivery driver." He sets down his messenger bag. "Unless you really want it for your last night at home?"

The world has spun off its axis. "No, it's cool. Pizza. Sure. I'll call up Sal's and order a pie, I guess."

"And garlic knots."

Breathe! It's okay. "And garlic knots. Trivinometry will be extra fragrant tonight."

Dad sits next to me with a sigh. "Can we scrap Trivinometry and just hang out tonight? The revisions for my manuscript were due today, and the university is breathing down my neck. Then Eleanor stopped by to say hi, but she ended up staying so long I didn't finish my edits, and I lost track of time. It's been a mess of a day. Not to mention my baby is leaving me tomorrow."

"Yeah... of course."

It's okay, okay, okay, okay, okay.

Just over half an hour later, the pizza I'm not hungry for is sliding down my throat like gravel. It gives me crazy heartburn. Odd, though: that pizza heartburn is still there in the morning.

IT SEEMS FITTING THAT MY FAKE PICK-UP FOR FAKE CAMP would be in front of my school, feet away from the place I watched Colin die. It's a good reminder why I'm doing all this, too, since my feet are longing for a good escape. I gnaw at my lip and pick at the skin of my thumb.

"Remember your sunscreen! And if you need anything, you call me, okay?" Dad rests his hands on my shoulders.

"No cell phones allowed, remember?" I mutter.

"They said there's a computer lab with phones you can sign up for. And of course in an emergency—"

The driver of the bus parked in front of the school pokes her head out. "Sorry to break it up, but we're on a schedule. Bags are stowed and we're waiting on you."

Dad pulls me in for a bear hug, and I hug him back fiercely. "You go out there and slay dragons, okay? Even the ones in there." He points at my head, his eyes damp. "I love you."

"I love you, too." My voice catches.

I run over to the bus before I call it all off and confess everything. My dad and I haven't been apart since Mom...

The doors close behind me, and the driver smiles. "Tell your aunt I was convincing, yeah?"

I nod and take the empty first seat, staring down at Dad through the window. *It's going to be okay. Okay. Okay. Okay. Okay.* I pick at the duct tape on the seat. We're pulling away when I see Mrs. O has rushed over, white cane in hand, and is talking to Dad. I stand, but we're moving too fast now. I watch them until we take our first turn, until I can't see them anymore.

I sit down hard.

"Don't stress. You'll see your parents super soon," a voice says from the seat across from me.

I wipe at my eyes self-consciously. The girl is a stick of dynamite topped with a crop of corkscrew curls that bounce and pop with every movement. "That wasn't my mom," I say.

She shifts, turning toward me fully, tucking a foot under her. "I thought maybe your dad was into old ladies. It's cool either way. Love doesn't care about numbers. That's why I'm going to marry Jordan Welborne. Have you ever seen him? He's so gorg." She smiles with her whole face, her wide mouth vying for dominance with her large, dancing gray eyes. "You're Cassandra Morai, right? That's a mouthful. Cass-an-dra. Serious. Do you go by Cassie? Yes? Cool if I call you Cassie?"

"Sure."

"Cool, cool. I'm Regan. You look my age. How old are you? Your aunt is like a big deal with a capital 'D,' if you know what I mean. Even if I didn't know anything about her, you can tell. It's her whole vibe, you know? I'm pretty good at picking up what people put down. That's how I know you and I are going to get along."

I don't know how to respond, but it feels as though a whirlwind has picked me up and tossed me miles away. Before my mom passed, I would've been friends with someone like her. Now, though...

she's interrupted my cry, and my body feels the lack of that release keenly. I just want to rest my head on the cool glass of the window and weep quietly, but the chattering is making that tough.

"We were all waiting for our dorm assignments," she continues, waving her hand in the air to indicate everyone on the bus, "and your aunt told a bunch of us to take a ride on a bus to pick up her niece, and we all filed onto this thing like nice little sheep. 'Keep your mouths shut, and if anyone talks to you, pretend you're off to summer camp.'" She mimics Aunt Bree with scary accuracy. "It's hard for me to keep my mouth shut when I'm excited though."

I shift to look behind me, really registering the others for the first time. There are about twelve people behind us, an even sprinkling of guys and girls around our age, their conversations blending into a gentle murmur. I'd almost think I was on a city bus with the mix of ethnicities and the ratio of kids wearing gear I can't afford to those who look just the opposite. "Is... are you all training with me?" I ask the girl, Regan, curiosity briefly winning out over my misery.

"Oh yeah, all of us and then some. I think I heard someone say there are twenty-four initiates this year. What's the deal with the whole camp thing? Why'd we have to pick you up?"

"My dad doesn't know about Theban Group."

"Makes sense, then! Yusef over there?" She points to a boy a few rows behind us, and he gives me a nod hello when I turn to look. "His granddad is the only scryer in his family, and no one else knows anything about it. He convinced everyone to send Yusef to what they think is a regular boarding school."

"I flew in today," Yusef says in a melodic, accented voice.

"From hella far away, too. I thought there was a satellite office near you," Regan says to him. To me she says, "Your aunt recruited us all. I heard she hit up like six continents."

"There is a satellite. But here is better. Headquarters is the center of it all." Yusef smiles.

I smile politely at the boy, then turn to look out the window, watching a shabby Spiderman-outfitted man pose for pictures with some tourists.

"You know, *Fortnight Foresight* did a whole spread on your aunt in their latest issue," Regan says, drawing my attention back to her. She says it loud, and I glance around, hoping the others don't think I'm a snob for my connection with Bree... worrying this girl's friendliness is because of that connection.

She digs into her bag and hands me a glossy magazine. The cover is dominated by an image of Aunt Bree from the shoulders up in a pool. Her gorgeous face is damp and flawless, and her dark hair is pulled back tight. Her cat-like eyes stare coldly beneath the cover line: *Aubrey Morai. Theban Group's Hottest Oracle Reveals All.*

"I'm not really close with my aunt," I say in a voice that carries.

She shrugs, easing my worry over that second concern, as least. "This was a really good article, too." Regan points at a smaller cover line. *Breakup Blues. Get Over Him & Get Your Visions Back On Track.* "Like, even if you aren't dealing with a breakup, it has some amazeballs tips on clearing your mind."

I flip through the magazine, the reality of what I'm going to Theban Group to do, to learn, hitting me again. "Do you mind if I borrow this?"

"Go for it. I have a ton of back issues at the dorm, too, that you can borrow. I collect them. Re-read them constantly. My mom always calls *Fortnight Foresight* a tabloid rag, but honestly, it's the best way to keep up with what's happening in the scrying world."

"What's happening in the scrying world," I repeat. Regan takes it for a question.

"Oh, you know, some old predictions came true recently, and there were a few new biggies announced, but those'll take a hot second to happen so who knows. There was an article on new scrying techniques in this issue, too... I mean, yeah, there's some Oracle gossip in there too, but it's *not* a tabloid."

"Ah. Right. Your mom is a scryer?" I ask.

"Nah. Her mom was, though, so she knows all about it. Skips a generation in my mom's family, and only girls get the gift. My dad's side was just him and some rando ancestor further up the family tree."

"How did you find about this place? Did your family tell—"

"Uhm... I've legit always known about this place. My mom's side of the family, back when my grandma was young, moved into the big HQ for a job her dad got here. That was like a gabillion years ago. But since my mom isn't a scryer, I didn't grow up on-site. I've been inside, though, back when I was a baby, but I don't remember it at all. My mom says my Dad brought me here to show me off..." She trails off.

I open my bag to stash Regan's magazine with a smile of thanks.

"Ugh, is that the MV-77?" she asks, pointing to the paperwork poking out of my bag. "How'd you do with it? Disaster. I binge ate an entire box of chocolates after filling it out."

I glance down and push the form back in. "Good, I hope. Lot of weird questions."

"Weird with a capital 'W,' for sure."

I debate asking the question I've been kicking around. I couldn't find anything in Pict's books about it, but I worry how my ignorance will be received by this girl. Will she laugh at me? She seems the type to laugh at everything, but maybe not maliciously?

"Can I ask a dumb question?"

"I live for dumb questions."

"Okay. Where do our..." I lower my voice. "Abilities, or whatever, come from?" I pause, a cringe waiting in the wings of my blank expression. She doesn't laugh, though.

"My grandma always said it was *a gift from the gods*, and all that," she says, affecting a booming deity-like voice. "Mom says my dad always called it a curse. I don't know. I read a pretty cool article on this stuff a while back in *Fortnight Foresight*—see, not a tabloid rag, *Mom*. It had some panel of scryer scientists. Most of them said it was maybe hypersensitive instincts or something. That people's brains are forever filling in blanks all day long, in the background, in the subconscious, but *our* brains just go the extra mile and let us see things in our conscious mind, or fragments of things, or whatever. Some other lady disagreed and said she thinks it's actually something about our tie to the Coil instead... or something. I can't remember. But whatever, the others all laughed at her, anyhow." She shrugs and grins. "Whatever it is, we're so badass, I can't even stand it."

We pull up to Theban Group's blink-and-you'll-miss-it entrance, and everyone rushes to disembark into the brick alleyway. The bus driver assures me she'll see my bags in, and Regan hooks an arm under my own, pulling me along. "You have a badge, right? God, your pic looks like mine. Deer in the headlights. It's ridic they don't give you any warning. Look, I'm a hot mess in mine, too."

Theodore, the sleepy Santa, checks all badges and gives us the combination to the elevator. As I pass his desk, he winks one heavily-browed eye. "Nice to see you again, Ms. Morai. Seven-eight-two today."

We file through the cubicle room, with Regan whispering she'd rather die than take a job in this area of Theban Group, and the first batch of our group passes into the elevator. I look around as the doors close behind them and we wait our turn.

"How do the jobs get assigned?"

"The Agon. There's tests and stuff," Regan says.

The elevator doors open, and the rest of us file in. One of the boys waves me in. He smiles, calling even more attention to the wispy and pitiful collection of hair strewn across his upper lip. "After you, princess. Thanks for the colossal time suck."

I grimace, and Regan rolls her eyes. "Shut up, Dill. Just enter the code," she says.

He punches in the code, and the back panel of the elevator door opens on the stained glass-domed expanse.

"Isn't this the coolest? This is the friggin coolest," Regan says. "This is ours now!"

Friggin coolest doesn't even begin to cover it. The boy's verbal jab fades to the farthest corner of my mind as I lift my face to that jewel-hued dome. *It was real. This was real.* I shake my head and laugh out loud, Regan joining me. My eyes feel as if they've grown three times their size just to take it all in once more, and my hummingbird heartbeat is out of control as we move through the colorful caravans, Regan pointing out all the retail therapy targets she plans on hitting.

We emerge from the caravan crush a few moments later, and a gaunt drill sergeant of a woman approaches from beyond the fountain, the light rotunda crowd parting for her. She's followed closely by a heavily armed guard.

"Hey, what's the deal with the guys in green?" I ask Regan as we slow to a halt, watching the woman approach.

"Oh, the security guys? Not everyone loves peeps who can see the future. Wasn't too long ago they were motherflipping burning us at stakes," Regan says cheerfully.

The woman nears. Her dark pantsuit is crisply pressed, and she has a face like a hairless cat topped by an iron-colored helmet of hair. The sharp edges of that bob saw at the dark hollows beneath her cheekbones as she moves.

"Come with me, if you please," she says. "I know not all of you have settled into your dorms yet due to a minor inconvenience—" Here she stares directly at me. "—but Orientation is about to begin. You can address your housing after your mentor meetings. If you still need a room assignment, you can visit Scryer Services then. We'll have it sorted for you."

She turns on her heel and stomps away. We shuffle after her.

"That's Agatha Triggs," Regan whispers. "She's Welborne's right hand. *Fortnight Foresight* did a profile on her last year. I have that issue upstairs if you want to read up." Regan proceeds to recite everything she can recall from said article as we trail Triggs and the others farther into the guts of a building that doesn't make any sense.

I only got a taste of it on my last visit, and that was with the sands of shock thrown in my eyes. A second viewing doesn't make it any less disorienting. My surroundings are definitely weirder as we walk deeper into the building. Different styles, architectural details, and time periods are knitted together thoughtlessly, as if the original building swallowed up its neighbors with every expansion. Modern museum-like expanses give way to cramped, damp cellars, which in turn open to a vast library. We pass through the library into a cave-like space. I'm about to point out that the distance between us and our group has grown a good amount when Regan squeals, stopping me in my tracks.

"Oooh, this has to be... Yes! This is the Momentorium!" Regan shouts. "I read about this place!"

"Momentorium?"

Beyond the point where the rough cave walls end, a long red gallery begins, stretching ahead of us. Pedestals topped with glass display cases, lit from within, line both sides of the crimson rug running the length of the hall. Framed mirrors in every size, material, and shape hang haphazardly on every bare spot of the high walls and even on the ceiling, giving the place the feeling of a majestic but eerie funhouse. Our steps slow as we take it all in.

Regan races into the center of the room as the last of our group departs the other end, and she peers at the contents of the glass box atop one of the pedestals; a small charm dangles from a chain and glints as it catches the light. "Holy crap. *This* is the pendulum Godfrey Royce used to scry out the European start of the Black Death in the 1300s!"

"How do you know that?" I gaze at her in admiration.

She smiles cheekily. "There's a sign."

I peer in closer. "Oh, he died right after this prediction."

"Yeah, of the Black Death," Regan says.

I nod and bite back a smile. She notices.

"Funny, right? Just because you see the train coming doesn't mean you can get out of the way." She roams farther into the echoing gallery, leaving me to chew on that.

"Ogham staves!" Regan says, pointing at some underwhelming notched sticks. "Altan Dar used them to predict Caesar's sacking of Alexandria!" She pinballs from display to display, exclaiming over anything that captures her attention. "This is the mirror Detective Niyati Patel used when she was hunting that serial killer. The dude who was mounting heads on his walls? She was such a badass."

"Should I be worried you're so into disease, war, and serial killers?" I ask, attempting to joke as I trail after her.

"Oh. My. God. Come quick!" Regan wildly waves me over. I look into the display, and dramatically lit up is... a dog-eared copy of a small furniture catalog. "I'm totally fangirling out." She wriggles her hands at the wrists and jumps up and down. "*This* is what Tuck Bryson used to predict the script that got him his award for Best Director!"

"Okay..."

"I know what you're thinking, bibliomancy isn't the sexiest way to scry, but he makes it look sooooo good," Regan says with a huge sigh.

She has no clue what I was thinking, since I've never heard of Tuck Bryson. She must see something in my expression, though, because she grimaces. "Do I sound like a lunatic? You must think I'm mental. It's just... this place!" She wheels around, arms wide. "I've dreamt of being here for years. Years and years and years. I count crystal balls instead of sheep when I sleep. I've read legit everything I can get my hands on about scrying. About Theban. Every scryer biography. Studied the Oracles like a psycho ex-girlfriend. Everything on the rituals, on the craft. My dad used to yell at me when he'd catch me reading them under the blankets with a flashlight, but I didn't care. I wanted to be... *this*! This is everything," she says fiercely, as her eyes mist. She laughs and wipes at them self-consciously.

I awkwardly pat her arm, simultaneously wanting to erase her embarrassment and understanding the feeling of wanting to be someone else. Someone better.

"I know, I'm a tool. I was even super sure I'd marry Bastian Welborne someday." At my look, she says, "Welborne. Like Sebastian Welborne? *The* Sebastian Welborne? Jordan Welborne's so-hot-your-teeth-sweat son. You don't know who that is?"

I open my mouth and close it, shrugging helplessly.

"You are *so* lucky you met me." Regan laughs, no trace of tears to be found now. She once again links arms with me and pulls me along. "Strap in, chickadee. Your education is about to begin."

10

Enormous windows drench the Orientation reception room in sunshine. I stand on my toes to see if I can spot Regan at one of the elaborate buffet tables or among the laughing faces that pass, but the riptide of the mingling crowds separated us not long after we entered. *It's fine. You don't really know her, so you don't need her.*

I return my attention to the small group of big personalities I've washed up on the fringes of like driftwood.

"You okay?" the girl closest to me—Tessa—asks. She reminds me of a sunflower, with her short yellow-blonde hair and all the inches she has on me height-wise. And she's outwardly super confident when eyes are on her. But I notice her shoulders keep rolling forward slightly, as if that self-conscious hunch is her real natural state. She gives me a kind smile with a mouth full of braces.

I blow out a breath and smooth a hand down my black tee and pants, wishing I had dressed up... or down... or differently. Or just that I was different. "Yeah, just... this is..." I widen my eyes, and Tessa understands immediately.

She looks around us and then whispers, "I've had nightmares every day for ages, worrying I'll do something to mess this up." The girl next to her draws her attention, and Tessa squeezes my arm in support before turning.

Here and there, I try to double-dutch my way into their conversation, but mainly I just contribute well placed nods and half-smiles—nothing to draw too much attention. I've mastered melting into my surroundings over the years. Only thing tripping me up right now are the askew veggie platters on the table near the door. I've straightened them twice now, but people keep bumping them out of place.

This worry is not real. You do not need to straighten those dumb platters. They won't make a difference. Get a hold of yourself.

No one knows me here. No one knows what I used to be like or what I've become. No one knows about my stupid urges. I can reinvent myself, create my own mythology... take the training wheels off of Mrs. O's "fake it until you make it" theory and pretend I'm a confident, bubbly... I would excuse myself from the group, but no one is paying attention to me anyway, so I just march to the table and push the offending platters into place.

Dad didn't want me with Aunt Bree. He thinks I'm at a camp. What if he finds out? Why didn't he want me with her? A thought occurs, one that should have long before now: does he know about this scrying thing? How do I ask him without letting him know I directly disobeyed him? And who the hell is Madame Grey anyway? What was she hinting at about Theban Group? It's too late to turn back now. Or maybe not? This place is so far outside my comfort zone I can barely see it from here, but it's technically only a handful of subway stops from my house. I need, suddenly and fiercely, to get out.

No. I'm here to help Colin, his sweet smile in the moonlight. I'm here to help Mrs. O, to save her place. *You're doing this for them, you coward. Fake it until you make it.*

"Is this stuff that good?" a boy asks. I back away from the platters, glad he's mistaken me for a glutton instead of pinning down what I was really doing. I give a small pursed smile, hoping it'll pass for an answer.

He has a collection of perfectly fine features—smooth warm brown skin, broad forehead, straight nose, eyes the color of weak tea—but combined they give him a kind of social camouflage I'm almost jealous of. He's wiry, but not so much it's super noticeable, and he's wearing jeans and a faded canary polo shirt, a color that also helps the eye skip over him like a stone on water. He hesitates, clearly as comfortable starting conversations as I am, and runs a hand over his short sable hair before saying, "Sorry, I wasn't groaking you. Just saw you came back a third time."

"Groaking?"

"Ah, yeah... my great-grandma lived with us, so sometimes my vocab can be extra special," he stammers. "It means, like, staring at someone eating and... you're Cassie Morai, right? I was on the bus your aunt sent." He points to the badge strung around his neck. "I'm Noah."

"I'm kind of obsessed with a board game where 'extra special vocab' words come in handy. You'll have to toss a few my way," I say, trying to set him at ease even though I'm barely there myself.

I tell him about Trivinometry and we exchange pleasantries, the dance of two gawky souls in an unfamiliar place robotically latching onto a point of intersection in one another. I took for granted how easy it was gelling with Regan, since she handled the heavy lifting. I look around, wondering where my social grease went.

"Oh my God, there you are! If I had to spend a second more with those awful guys, I'd die." Regan rushes up to us, her face flushed with excitement and pure drama. She launches into a hug. I stiffen before hugging her back with the teensiest amount of relief. "They're not *all* awful, probably. The guys, I mean. But you know what they say—you are who you stay with. I try not to be judgy, but if they're hanging around with Griffin, then they must be idiots too." She gestures toward a group of boys posted up by a shrimp display boasting a Poseidon ice sculpture. I only recognize Dill by what Regan called his pedophile 'stache. I have no clue which one might be the offensive Griffin or what he's done to rile Regan up.

"Regan, this is..." I turn, but Noah has melted away, no hint of pale canary yellow in the crowd to betray where he went.

"Could he be any more gorgeous?" Regan asks. I look over, baffled by her Griffin-change-of-heart, before realizing that she's fixated on someone in the complete opposite direction.

"Who?"

"*That* snack, my friend, is Sebastian Welborne."

There are about twenty people in the direction she's pointing, but I know instantly which one is Sebastian. He's leaning his shoulder against a doorway, his legs and arms crossed nonchalantly but his green eyes, chips of sharpened sea glass, are watching, waiting. I know he's a little older than me from Regan's gossip, but he seems even older surrounded by that giggling gaggle.

Sebastian dips his head to listen to what one of the girls next to him is saying, and the guy to her left shoots eye daggers at her for the crime of capturing Sebastian's notice for a split second. There are five of them there, gladiators fighting for a haughty king's eye, armed with biting quips they blurt out while anxiously watching Sebastian for his reactions; I can tell in the way their laughter erupts and dies almost as quickly. There's even an outer ring of hangers-on whose constant glances tell a tale of longing for the right opening in the conversation, or just for the courage, to penetrate that inner circle.

Gross. All of it.

I mean, I get the physical appeal, I guess. He's solidly built, with shortly cropped dark blond hair. And despite his obvious arrogance, he has a mouth that makes you think of first kisses. I probably shouldn't notice, but his arm muscles bunch up nicely under his blue button down. But since my mom died, I've had a lot of time to watch people at school. Guys like him... okay, there are no guys like him at my school, but all of the popular boys have that same obnoxious "worship me" energy. And the desperation radiating off of the ones fawning over him? All for the crumbs of someone's attention? Seen that before, too. So sad.

Regan lets out an exaggerated sigh and slumps back against me. "He's *divine*. Swoon-worthy. Completely awful with girls, but I'd let him be awful to me any day of the week." I learned during Regan's random fact-dump that she devours romance novels. It shows.

"No one's worth being treated badly."

"It's not that he's mean or anything. It's more... he's got a reput-tion. Never had a long-term thing. But girls don't believe him when he says he's not interested in anything serious, I guess."

Does the guy catch Regan staring? No. To my everlasting mortifi-cation, he looks up as *I'm* eyeing one of his muscular legs, outlined brilliantly thanks to his casual stance and revealed by a shuffle in his entourage. He raises a single perfect eyebrow, and I try not to twitch self-consciously or blush a permanent shade of red as he looks me up and down.

Instead, I mimic Aunt Bree, minus her essential nasty Bree-ness, and force myself to return his gaze when he finishes his inspection, raising my own eyebrow in response. I can reinvent myself here, and the new Cassandra Morai is calm, confident, and collected. I turn away and immediately ruin the effect, tripping over my own feet. *Stupid* tight shoes. Only a moron would wear new ones today.

Swallowing an embarrassed groan, a glance back confirms that Sebastian noticed. His eyes mock me, and the corners of his lips twitch to reveal a hint of roguish dimple in his right cheek. I glare back, but it's impossible to control my full body shiver. He is trouble—for someone else though. I have Colin, *kind Colin,* whose gentle teasing invites me to participate in the joke instead of suggesting I am one. Keeping him alive is more than enough trouble for me.

"Wait, why is Bastian legit full-on staring at you?" Regan exclaims. I close my eyes and pray her loud voice hasn't carried. "Call the paramedics, I need resuscitation." She lets out a giddy giggle and grabs my arm. "According to the rumor I just started, you guys are totally dating, engaged to be married, making babies. We need to bottle up your pheromones."

Thankfully a gong sounds, loud enough to nearly vibrate the teeth out of my mouth, calling us into the auditorium. I practically flee through an entrance Sebastian isn't guarding, Regan still clinging to my arm.

The room is painted gold and black, with a stage set at the bottom of the room like a sun, its aisles radiating up and out like beams of light. We drop into the seats an usher indicates, and I spot Aunt Bree settling into the front row alongside a few other power suit types. She spots me and gives me a slight smile when I raise a hand in greeting. Sebastian Welborne follows the direction of her gaze and spots me as well. He says something to Bree as he takes the seat next to hers, and I hear her throaty laugh.

An inferno consumes the auditorium, and I am trampled during the stampede to safety.

The stupid thought trips through my mind. I look around, taking note of the exits. For my anxiety's sake, I'm happy my seat is in the aisle, even though I realize the likelihood of fire is nonsense. I shush Regan's loud Sebastian-related declarations as the lights fade. The room falls completely silent except for the occasional cough or sniffle or rustle of clothing. The quiet stretches.

"Everyone, please give a warm welcome to our CEO, Jordan Welborne!" a woman's voice calls out over the speakers.

A spotlight punctures the dark. It trains on a man standing in the doorway behind us, and everyone turns in unison like rolling thunder.

"Good morning, Theban Group!" he says.

The room erupts in applause, and the man grins and waves, the spotlight following him as he bounds down the steps with a coltish energy I'd expect from someone way younger. He's a lanky man with a long, angular, horsey face, a bit older than my dad, and dressed entirely in black. He greets Aunt Bree and the others when he reaches the bottom of the room before moving to the center of the stage.

"Thank you!" He bows extravagantly, eating up the crowd's adulation, then gestures for the cheering audience to settle down.

"Oh, enough now, hush or it'll all go to my head. Now... who is ready to make history?" The crowd roars its approval, and the man's smile gleams in the light. He holds up a hand again, waiting until everyone falls silent.

"The philosopher Søren Kierkegaard once wrote, 'The most painful state of being is remembering the future... *particularly* the one you'll never have.' That sounds like something a scryer might say, doesn't it?" He speaks in a cultured voice that sounds like warm silk pulled over gravel.

"Well, I've gathered you all here, including our twenty-four new initiates who will forgive me for coopting their orientation—" He presses his palms together and gives a slight bow in our direction. "—and those of you watching remotely, my Theban Group family, to tell you those futures Søren worried over? They're not so far from reach after all."

He lets the crowd's hush linger. Then the nothingness behind him suddenly bursts to life, three giant screens showcasing images of torture, death, and chaos, music swelling in time with the horrors shown. I turn my head away from the awful visuals, fuel for my OCD-ravaged imagination, and my heart thumps. The images dissolve into licks of flames. They rise up behind Welborne, casting him in an orange glow. I wonder, if Aunt Bree knew me even a little better, whether or not she'd have warned me.

"Theban Group is our social compact, our commitment to keeping each other safe. We came together thousands of years ago for protection, to hide. And I know that for some of you in this room, if you had it your way, Theban Group would *only* be this, still.

"But to those critics I would argue, why hide behind walls when you can control what's being built beyond them?

"Yes, our coming together made us stronger, in the way there is strength in numbers, but even as our refuge grew in size and sophistication, with multiple satellite chapters around the globe, we were still *weak*. Powerless. Even though we could huddle behind Theban Group walls, we couldn't *do* anything about our foes, or about the things we foresaw.

"Now the traditionalists out there are undoubtedly objecting to this right now in their minds. I can almost hear the stern talking-to they long to give me: 'Scryers could always make minor tweaks to the things we foresaw, Welborne. We have our scrycasting, our rituals.'

"Yes, but what of everything else, my friends?" Footage of earthquakes, volcanic eruptions, troops marching, firing squads once again dart across the screens at Welborne's back. The images are gone before I can react. I glance at Regan. Her expression is rapt.

"Foresee the outcome of a great battle? A plague? Shame, nothing to be done about it, move along. Live with the dread and wait for it to come. We were forced to mourn the futures we wanted, *the futures we could never have*."

The musical cacophony fades into sentimental violins, and a black-and-white portrait of an older man appears on the screen. His features look blasted from a slab of granite.

Welborne continues, "My father knew we were better than that. And he realized there was a way to benefit from what was, essentially, a curse. A way to turn it around. To protect our own—to hide, yes, but also take control. I'm talking, ladies and gentlemen, about *money*. Father recognized that wealth is power, and so he proposed to the Grimoire Council that Theban Group start a business. No reading palms at fairs for us. We would provide insurance to those whom we knew would never need it. Simple. Elegant. Some of you have argued it is dishonest—the ones I respect most are those who have said so to my face." Welborne grins at this, and a few people chuckle. "But even those naysayers can't deny that the money we've made has allowed us to influence the world around us for the better, *and* made us all safer than we've ever been."

Tender music sounds, accompanied by images of smiling faces that belong on the second half of a commercial about feeding the poor for the cost of a cup of coffee.

"Plague?" Welborne says. "We fund medical research and life-saving medicines before an outbreak to minimize the carnage. Food in times of famine, water in times of drought. We support politicians we know will bring about positive change. We've finally been able to use our abilities to *do something!*"

There are some hoots from the crowd, clapping.

Welborne paces. "But it's not enough. What about us? The scryers making all that happen. We've done so much good with the money we've made. Don't *we* deserve more? Maybe those codgers forever grumbling about taking care of our own have a point?"

"We're getting a raise!" someone shouts from crowd. Laughter erupts, and Welborne chuckles.

"Better." The screen behind him goes black, and the music dissolves into tinny futuristic sounds.

"We were able to profit from our insurance endeavor because my father's engineers spent countless hours examining past omens and visions, pairing them with historic events until they hit upon an algorithm that allowed us to chart out the little events that lead up to larger ones—to map pockets of the future out like a puzzle. That technology required a great deal of computing power. In fact, it required a supercomputer that took up the entire three basement-level floors of this building. But I'm pleased to announce that, thanks to some bloody brilliant breakthroughs on our part, we've been able to take all that tech and streamline it for individual consumption."

The image of a thin, slowly rotating device flashes, catching the light as it goes. It looks like someone poured silver into a smart-phone mold. In fact, it could almost pass for a rejected smartphone prototype, longer and thinner than my iPhone but metallic gray all over. It's the same device Aunt Bree was messing with in the lift on the way to my meeting with Pict.

"Announcing—the ICARUSS!" Welborne crows to the approving crowd's cheers. "If you struggle with brevity as much as me, you can call it by its full name—the Intelligent Communication Apparatus for Rituals and Understanding Second Sight." Hoots sound, and Welborne holds up a hand. "Wait now—you'll want to pay special attention to this. The ICARUSS will not only allow you to do all that my father needed three floors of supercomputers to accomplish. It will not only allow you to decode your visions and omens faster than ever before. It will also provide you with precise instructions for *scrycasting rituals to change the future!*"

The device on the screens stops rotating, and the silver front melts away to reveal a pair of white flapping wings on a black background. The wings dissolve a second later to reveal dense paragraphs of words and diagrams.

The room explodes into thunderous applause. It echoes in my chest as the hard ball of fear living inside me quakes and goes supernova in a blast of exhilaration. It's an optimistic Big Bang, and I can hardly contain it. *No more fear? Stop Mrs. O's move? Save Colin? Save Colin. Save Colin. Save Colin. Save Colin.*

"Outrageous!" a man shouts. The cheering quiets and the room becomes a mess of whispers as the man, older by the look of him, storms up an aisle to bust through one of the metal exit doors at the front of the room.

"Traditionalists," Welborne says with a smile, undeterred. "They hate change. But make no mistake, change is coming. After today, *everything* changes. After today, money isn't the only way we can influence our lives and the world around us. After today, we have real power."

I scan the room to see if any more *traditionalists* are shaking their heads, ready to storm out, but I see only eager faces.

"No more combing through arcane texts for rituals, or mourning those futures we want but cannot have," Welborne continues. "There are restrictions, of course—you'll learn more about those later from my friend Sidney Ford in your Scrycasting course—but you'll be able to change the future more than ever before, *easier* than ever before." He starts to move up and down the stage again, loping faster as his words pick up in volume and urgency. "You have helped this company become what it is. You are responsible for all the good we have put out into the world. You deserve something for yourselves. We have all needed, or wanted, or *lost*. Seize control of your lives!" The cheers reach a fever pitch, and the room reverberates with the force of it. He raises his voice to be heard. "I am Jordan Welborne. And I welcome you all to *your* future."

WELBORNE ROCKSTARS HIS WAY OFF THE STAGE AND UP the aisle toward the doors behind us, shaking hands and waving.

Regan is hanging over me, desperately trying to get his attention. When he gets to my row, he reaches out to shake her hand briefly and touches my shoulder. He smiles down at me and barely pauses in his progress to the door, but the warm weight of that hand lingers long after he moves on.

"I'm never washing this hand. I could die right now and be happy," Regan says.

Agatha Triggs marches out onto the stage, looking like a posh scarecrow, and clears her throat into the microphone clipped to her collar. "Another round of applause for Mr. Welborne," she says in a monotone. She tucks her clipboard under her arm and claps like someone who studied clapping in a book once, before adjusting her thick blue-framed glasses and consulting her notes.

"Alright now. Please. A few housekeeping matters. Directly following this assembly in—" Triggs pulls a silver pocket watch attached to a chain from her gray jacket pocket, glances at it, and snaps it shut. "—less than one minute, we will begin distributing ICARUSS devices in the room just outside the doors here—" My pulse leaps, then immediately plummets as she continues. "—to all *but our new initiates*. The latter group will be issued an ICARUSS by Sidney Ford during his Scrycasting course. For now, all initiates must go off and visit with their mentors. This evening's welcome festivities will be held in the Astromancy Lab. I understand we have some *interesting* entertainment lined up for your enjoyment." Her tone makes it sound like the entertainment will be watching mold grow. She once again pulls her watch from her jacket and clicks it shut with a snap. "Time is up. Off you all go."

The lights are turned on, and everyone gathers up their belongings and files outside. I glance down at the front row but can't see

Aunt Bree or Sebastian in the crowd. Regan hugs her folder to her middle as we leave the auditorium, squeezing her eyes shut with a rapturous expression.

"My mentor is Sidney Ford. I'm so excited! *Fortnight Foresight* said he took over for Linda Fenice in Scrycasting when he joined the org, and he's crushing it. Fenice was more old school, you know? I'm positive he's going to rock."

I feel a twinge of envy hearing the excitement in her voice.

"What's wrong?" Regan asks, noticing my expression.

For a second, my default setting of the last few years kicks in, and I immediately clam up. It's been ages since I've discussed my feelings or fears with anyone besides Mrs. O, but Regan looks genuinely concerned and nothing about any of this is normal. I hesitate a second before confessing I've met my mentor before.

"Does he suck? Who is it? Maybe I've heard of him," she says.

"His name is Mr. Pict, and he's like a walking, talking root canal."

Regan's jaw drops. "Shut. Up. Shut up! You do *not* have Martin Pict as your mentor."

"Yeah."

"Cassie, he's a legend! Like, *beyond* legend. He's an expert in every kind of scrying under the sun. He's pulled down some of the biggest visions in recent history, and he's *never* taken on an initiate! How did you manage to score him? I'm blown away! First Bastian eye bangs you from across a room, and now you're being mentored by scryer royalty. I'm *so* jealous." She charges through the auditorium doors into the hall, throwing her hands up.

I sigh. "You shouldn't be. He's not nice."

A voice behind us interrupts. "Don't feel bad. He's mean because his family died in a car crash a long time ago. Kids, wife, everyone. Even his dog in the back. Pict was driving."

"What?" I turn, frozen with horrified pity and mortification over bashing my poor, evidently grieving mentor. A husky boy is grinning back at me puckishly, his expression completely at odds with what he just said. With his lightly bronzed skin and mischievous smile, he's probably what some would consider baby cute, if they like that yo-bro type. But I'm immediately wary. He reminds me of the guys at school who are forever shouting nonsense from the top bleacher at our assemblies. He's about my age and height, and his clothes are rumpled as if from a fresh bout of rough-housing.

He lowers his voice to a loud whisper and leans his dark head toward us. "They say he's wracked with guilt because it was his fault. Pulled his wife out of the wreckage, and she died in his arms."

"Pict's whole family died. Did you hear that?" a woman whispers to her friend as she passes us. "No wonder he's so... you know. That's so sad."

"How did I not know this?" her friend responds.

"Is that true?" Regan demands. "I've never heard anything like that about Pict, and I've read *everything*."

The boy waits until the crowd around us thins out before answering, his brown eyes twinkling. "Not even a little bit. But oh man, by the end of the week, everyone at Theban will have heard it. Besides Pict, anyway."

"You're a sociopath." Regan turns to me and hisses, "This is Griffin."

"Oh, come on, dude smells like mothballs and moldy books, and he's never met a person he hasn't pissed off. He called me a 'gollumpus' earlier. What kind of person uses insults you have to look up in a dictionary? Who the hell knows what a gollumpus is?"

"It's a big clumsy oaf," I answer.

"That was supposed to be rhetorical." He blinks. "Whatever. No harm, no foul. Now everyone he's ever been mean to will feel a little better about themselves, thinking he was only being a douche because of some horrible tragedy. And they'll treat him extra nice from now on because they feel bad for him. Which will confuse and probably annoy him. Which is hilarious. It's all good."

"Literally you're the worst," Regan says.

"I don't think you know what the word 'literally' means. Maybe ask your human dictionary friend."

"I know what it means," Regan seethes.

"You're upset because I asked if you ever come up for air when you were telling a story earlier. That was me being concerned for your health!"

Regan turns her nose up and pretends to remove a speck of something from her top.

Griffin laughs. "We're going to end up married, and this will be our cute little 'how we met' story. I already saw it in a vision."

"I'd rather die," she says.

"I saw that, too." He laughs again and nods to someone calling his name. A few guys from the group I saw him standing with earlier are shouting out to him. "Gotta run. Nice meeting you, Dictionary. Hey, for short I could call you Dic—"

"My name is Cassie."

"Less fun. See you, Remus."

"*Regan!*"

His silly grin flashes again, and he jogs off to catch up to his friends. Regan glares after him, her eyes narrowed to the point I'm surprised she can see.

"He wasn't telling the truth about the marrying thing...?" I ask.

"No." Regan sniffs. "He's not my type. I like humans."

I laugh in spite of myself.

"Besides," she continues, trudging ahead, "I already told you I'm going to marry Jordan Welborne. Since you're Sebastian Welborne catnip, and you're totally going to marry him, I'll be your mother-in-law."

I roll my eyes. "I'm not. And even if I were, I'm not interested."

"How is that possible? Oh my God, you already have a boyfriend, don't you?"

"No, I don't have a boyfriend." I feel myself blushing.

"You're lying! Look at your face! You can't see your face. You're holding out on me. Dish *immediately*. I need details. What's he like? Is he cute? What's his name? Does he have a brother? A hotter, richer brother?"

I can't help it. I laugh again. "Alright! There's a boy..." Regan's eyes light up, so I hurry to finish. "But he's not my boyfriend. He's my neighbor. His name is Colin."

The name alone sends Regan into raptures. "Colin is such a cute name! Colin." Regan does that with names: runs them over her tongue, savoring and testing. "I approve." A girl directs us to one of the copper cage elevators. We enter. "Can you hit the button, Cassie?"

I hesitate, imagining thousands of fingers touching that little round white cesspool. *Who cleans them? Does anyone ever think to?* Before it becomes weird, I force myself to press it with a knuckle. The doors slam shut and the lift speeds upward.

I don't want to see Pict again. Another interaction with him is more than I can deal with right now. I pull at my contaminated knuckle. *It's spreading like gangrene from my knuckle up through the rest of my index finger. It's moved to the rest of my hand.* I grit my teeth. Come *on.* Not now. Not now. Not in front of a maybe-new-friend. I grip my bag tightly to keep from doing anything stupid.

"So *spill.* Tell me every—Cassie, are you okay? Your face went *white.*"

The doors open on the same dizzying floor Aunt Bree brought me to, and I force myself to step off the elevator. I quickly wipe my brow on my arm.

"Are you okay?" Regan repeats. "I swear, I thought there might be something off about that smoked salmon platter. Oh no, am *I* okay?"

"I'm fine. This day has been a lot and... just stressing about seeing Pict again." *You're okay, okay, okay, okay, okay.*

Regan smiles reassuringly. "It'll be great, Cassie. Really. Mentors are there to help. He decided you had what it takes to be here. Now that you're officially a Theban initiate, I'm sure it'll be better." She looks down at her paper and pauses in front of a door. "This is me. Wish me luck!" She gives me a quick half-hug and knocks a rhythmic beat on the wood.

"Come in," a man's voice calls, and Regan opens the door to blaring classical music. She steps inside and excitedly waves at me she closes the door behind her.

"It'll be fine!" she says before she shuts it entirely.

I drag myself to Pict's pink door and bite at my thumbnail before working up the courage to knock. When I hear him call out, I open the door, carefully this time.

Pict is standing in the center of the room holding a paper. He waves it at me. "I'm reviewing your training schedule for the Agon, Ms. Morai. Rituals. They have you down for Astromancy and Geomancy. Good, good. Salt-Seeing. Fine. Nua. Hmm, okay. Du Lac for Hydromancy. Yes." He stiffens. "Palmistry. They still teach that rot?" He holds out the paper, and I accept it. "It is a solid curriculum. Between your coursework and the work we'll engage in here, you'll be well prepared.

I open my mouth, hesitate.

"Out with it."

"It's... this is a lot. I guess I'm still trying to process it all."

"All you need to know at the moment is that scrying is akin to a muscle, albeit one made of mystical energy instead of tissue and powered by the arcane rather than biochemicals. Abilities must be rigorously exercised. That is what your training here is designed to do."

"But with that ICARUSS thing, isn't scrying—" I almost feel ridiculous saying the word. "—supposed to be easier now?"

Pict glowers at me. At least, I think he does. It's a matter of a quarter-inch dip of his already forever-scowling brows.

"Welborne's bloody toy does not enhance abilities. It speeds interpretation times and conjures up rituals for changes to the future. If you are a weak scryer, you'll produce scarce wood for that particular hearth. Further, when you receive your own device, you are never to bring it to my chambers, is that understood? Others can leverage that crutch. You will train the way scryers have since time immemorial, reading your own omens and signs."

I stare at the ground—even more uncomfortable than before— a stand-in for his dislike of the device and Welborne's tech. There are others who think like Pict here, I guess. The old man who bolted from the assembly and Welborne's mocking comments when he left come to mind. Welborne's speech was a little confrontational, too, when I think about it. I shake my head. No. I'm not going to scratch at this gold coin until I hit imaginary iron.

"Now then, on to your studies." Pict shepherds me to the alcove. "Did you read this?" He gestures to a book, identical to the one he gave me a few weeks back, on the end table between us as we take our seats. Oh no. *Twardowski.*

"Yes."

"Good. Tell me, what are the Four Tenets of Foretelling?

"I think... there was... focus..."

"Yes?"

I reach and open the book, only to have it slammed shut, nipping my fingertips. Pict is leaning forward, glaring at me.

"I don't exactly remember..."

"F.A.T.E. Focus, ability, tool, environment. What is the Canon of Thought Singularity?"

"Something with explosions? I... I don't know." I read every other book he gave me, some more than once. I read *everything* I could find on the internet. But Twardowski was just so damn tinder-dry, and... there was a lot of sighing over Colin keeping me busy the past few weeks, too, if I'm being honest. And in fairness, I didn't realize I'd be getting a pop quiz on day one.

"'The more densely you repress thought, the more violent the explosion of prophesy.' Stop playing with your hair. What about the best resource for interpreting omen symbolism since we will decidedly *not* be using Welborne's silver claptrap? Recite for me the Principles of Premonition?"

"I don't..."

"You don't know. Funny that. This is your first warning, Ms. Morai. I may have been given a lame horse for my first race, but you will not embarrass me. You've wasted my time enough for one day. Goodbye." Pict abruptly gestures for me to leave. I fidget in my seat, then stand, sending a heavy pile of books to my left toppling over like a tsunami of words.

Pict looks at the mess dispassionately and then back at me. "Shall I draw you a map to guide you out of my office, Ms. Morai? Or would you neglect to study that as well?"

I'm proud the tears don't come until I've closed the pink door behind me.

11

"What do you think?" Regan asks, loitering in the doorway to my dorm room. She's positively beaming.

"It's... nice?" I say, taking in my depressingly Spartan home for the summer.

"Think about what you wish it looked like."

I scrunch my brow.

"Seriously! Think about what you wish it looked like. Humor me."

I turn back to the bare walls and bland furniture, and mentally picture a place I'd much rather be at the moment. The walls ripple. "Did you see that?"

Regan laughs. "Of course I did. Come on, concentrate. Really picture it."

I do what she says, and when I open my eyes, I'm standing back in my bedroom at home. I grab at Regan's arm, warily eying my white writer's desk—complete with its blue spill of nail polish— tucked up against my bed. "What is this?"

Regan laughs.

I run to the desk and pull open drawers. Everything is the same. Even the industrial-sized bag of M&Ms that Mrs. O gave me a few weeks back is in my bottom drawer. I pull it out.

"Oh, don't eat those. I mean you'll feel full, but it's not real. The second you leave the dorms, it'll be like you didn't eat at all. They told us to avoid picturing food or drinks here because peeps can get confused. I heard one guy last year ended up on fluids because he was barely eating outside the stuff he imagined, and his body wasn't getting any nutrients."

I drop the bag of candy in my drawer and run my hands over my face. What is happening?

"Is this your bedroom at home? I did something from *Marrying the Melancholy Marquis*. Ever read it? The heroine had this sick cabin on a ship." She pulls me down the hall to her room, which does, in fact, look like the captain's cabin of an eighteenth-century ship. Or at least what I guess one might look like. "Look out my window!"

I move farther into her room and stare out the little porthole window. At the gentle swells of an ocean. "How?" I say. It emerges as a squeak.

"You've heard of the Celidon Coil, right?"

"I read about it. Pict mentioned it, too. Like a labyrinth somewhere deep inside this place. And we need to walk through it at the end of our training?"

"Yep!" Regan chirps. "My grandma said it's so intense to walk through because the Coil absorbs and reflects back thoughts and memories and worries. And not just your own thoughts, either. It's got, like, thousands of years of scryer brainbox insanity to draw on." She leans forward, like someone about to tell a campfire ghost story, and blows a curl away from her mouth. "Only, the Coil isn't as deep inside this place as you think. It's *here*. The dorms, the halls downstairs—you noticed the halls on the way to Orientation looked all trippy? It's because they were ripped away from the Coil when the Grims beat it back to stabilize some space for Theban Group to operate. Everything downstairs is frozen in whatever the Coil was reflecting a second before the Grims pushed it back. Kind of like stuff left close to shore at low tide."

"Grims...?"

"Grimoire Council. That's what everyone calls the scryer leadership."

I can't sustain drinking from this firehose of information. "That sounds..." I hold up a hand, trying to process it all.

Regan grins. "Literally insane, I know. But you're here to learn how to *see the future*. Is it that crazy if the building you're in is basically a mind-reading chameleon jungle?"

"Yes. It is." I give her a wry look and then straighten, alarmed. "Wait. If the Coil reflects back fears and our dorms are—"

"Oh God, no! No negative thoughts can be reflected here, and there are other rules. Can't even frigging picture alcohol or money or any other fun stuff. The dorms are technically semi-culled from the Coil, but the Grims did a binding ritual to let us play around a bit. The halls are all static, though. I heard there are places in the Coil that are stable, too. You can tell because anything that's changeable does that ripplely-pulse thingy."

As if on cue, an almost imperceptible shiver runs up the walls of her captain's cabin around us. She makes a face that says, *See?*

I nod, satisfied—for now. Of course, who knows what my mind will do with that information the next time I spiral?

We head off to the Rhodes Rotunda for supplies, and Regan shares more of her Grandma's mix of gossip and lore about the Coil along the way—about it allegedly growing from a seed planted by the Grims whenever they settle in a new location ("Old scryer mystical stuff handed down for like a gabillion generations. They say the seeds come from a vine that sprouted out of the grave of the very first Oracle, or maybe a tree that grew in the dark of Daedalus's labyrinth.") and the whole Theban Group building growing out of one of those seeds ("They, like, slap a façade around the thing and move in"), with the Coil forever tunneling farther down like roots ("I wonder how far the Coil reaches now. I heard Theban Group's had to abandon places when they lose control of it. But, like, without any scryers to draw energy from, it eventually shrivels up and dies—not pretty though"). It all sounds like a grandma-spun yarn. But at this point, who knows?

The kaleidoscopic light of the Rhodes Rotunda's dome illuminates a mob; lunch and Magpie trading are apparently competitive sports. Regan runs off to talk to another initiate, and I look down at my shopping list for my classes. My stomach grumbles. I wasn't planning on braving the meat pie line, but I end up following my nose like a bloodhound for savory, buttery goodness and queue up.

The boy in front of me turns and reveals a familiar face. "They're fresh off the griddle," Noah says. Ah, my fellow big-word lover and awkward Orientation conversationalist. He's changed into a light green sweatshirt and a blue and white baseball cap devoid of any logos or marks; nothing to proclaim team fandom or anything interesting. Much like the boy and his narrow, everyman face.

"You ninja'd away during the reception," I attempt to joke.

He smiles, looking a little abashed. "No, your friend is just a one-woman distraction."

I laugh. "Yeah, that's Regan."

We place our orders and wait silently for our pies until the Magpie woman hands Noah two tall paper cups. He hands one to me. Startled, I accept.

"Ginger cider. It's the best. This is my fourth today." His small grin reveals a shy and endearing sweetness. "They say not to drink too much or you'll be feeling pretty crapulous later, but I feel..." He looks sheepish. "That's another great-grandma word. I'm going to shut up now."

"It's a good word," I say, looking down at the cup with interest. I take a sip. It's surprisingly refreshing, a cool fizz that curls around my tongue. "It's really good! Thank you."

He beams, and the same warmth I felt on my way here with Regan, like hot chocolate on a snowy day, spreads through me again. That feeling of finding your people. That even though I'm a puzzle piece from a completely different box, I've miraculously wedged myself into a picture I don't belong in but refuse to give up.

The Magpie hands over Noah's meat pies. He holds up his cup, and I tap mine against his. "Cheers," he says. "See you later, Cassie."

I thank him again and sloppily scarf my food the second his back is turned. Aunt Bree's "year on the hips" speech only gives me a momentary unease as I move to wash my hands in the fountain.

Stuffed and satisfied, I approach the rest of the colorful Magpie caravans. I silently thank Aunt Bree's assistant Martha for the heads-up that I should bring things to barter with as I shop around, reminding myself of where I am since it all has the feel of a weird pop-up Christmas market in July.

First stop is a denim-blue wagon dripping in winking crystal pendulums that catch the light as they dance on the ends of their strings. I trade a bunch of dented canned goods from Mrs. O's shop for an onyx unicorn horn-shaped pendulum. The little boy working the wagon strings it through a long black braided cord for me, and I tie it around my neck. It's a testament to how weird I am that Mrs. O only warned me of the dangers of botulism when I asked for the cans the other day, not even questioning why I might want them.

An old pair of sneakers scores me a rune-casting board, and a candy cane candle gets me a pouch of hand-whittled stones. At another cart, a smuggled bottle of whiskey from Dad's liquor cabinet gets me a ceremonial scrycasting bone-handled dagger.

I move on, checking items off my list before coming to a sunshine-yellow wagon laden with mirrors and topped by a green and white canopy. A short, flame-haired man with an equally red pointed goatee is lecturing a taciturn no-necked man.

"You're hammered! Foxed! Cocked! Smashed! Three sheets to the wind! I could go on. I received a thesaurus for my birthday. Who gives somebody a thesaurus? Pendragon, cheap bugger. If it wasn't a re-gift, it will be soon, that's for sure. Pendragon's turned me into a crap gift giver! Anyway, you're drunk is the point, and you've traded away one of our most valuable mirrors for a tortoise and some leaves."

"Her name is Betsy," the other man says.

"Heavens. What has that to do with anything? You aren't to drink on the job. Or if you do, you need to make sure it's in moderation. I'm not big on rules, you know, but for the love of Pete—"

"Who's Pete?" the no-necked man asks.

I laugh. The man with the red hair scowls at me. "Hi," I say tentatively. "Is now a bad time or...?"

"Of course it is, but why should we let that get in the way of business? What's your name? You look like you could use a mirror, and I don't mean that as an insult. I just sell them. Or maybe I could interest you in a tortoise?" The no-necked man slinks off, taking the distraction I've created as an opening to flee.

"Just the—"

"Maybe some mugwort and elderberry jam? Enhance your scrying ability before the Agon. No? Alright. How about a toadstone ring? Detect poison, protect your home from burning, help with bowel obstructions?"

"Just a mirror, thanks."

"Are you sure?" He glances around and whispers, "Something more illicit? One of the last known pairs of adderstone glasses? Holes crafted by venomous snakes of their own free will! *Guaranteed* no scrying manipulation went into their making."

"Just a mirror. *Please.*"

"Well, have it your way. If you show me what you have to trade with, I can tell you what mirrors fall in your budget." He smiles, flashing a gold tooth and looking like a landlocked pirate.

I rummage around in my bag, but I'm fresh out of things to trade. The bangle Bree gave me as a gift catches the light from my wrist. No sentimental tug to Bree's gift surfaces. "This bracelet." I hand it off to him.

"Gold... appears... yes, the maker's stamp is right here. Wonderful! Scryer-forged in Lethe water. *Very* expensive. This will get you anything on this cart, and then some."

I grin and eagerly survey the stock. A small silver mirror catches my eye. Its handle is a carving of a hunched man holding the mirror up on his back; the pained expression on his sculpted little face speaks to me. "I'll take this one."

"Ah, my friend Atlas. Talk about work stress, holding the world up on his shoulders. Good choice. What else would you like?"

"He's holding the heavens up, actually, not the world," I correct. I'm a trivia nerd. I know it, but I can't help it. It's the one thing I'm good at. "And that's all, thanks."

He pulls at his beard. "That's an uneven trade. Do you know what Magpies are known for?"

I inch away. "Collecting weird stuff and making meat pies?"

He frowns. "Well, yes. But we're also known for even trades!"

"Okay, then... you can owe me? Or whatever. I have to get to this intern welcome party now though."

He brings himself up as tall as he can muster. His earring dances from his lobe. "A favor! Excellent idea. I, Bacchy Liddell, will owe you... what's your name?"

"Cassie. Cassandra. Morai. Sorry, I *really* need to get to the party."

"Cassandra Morai. I, Bacchy Liddell, will owe you, Cassie of the Cuff, one favor." The man grabs a goblet from the cart and sloshes some red liquid into it. He spits into it and holds the goblet out to me. "Spit, then we drink."

I rear back. "What? No. Why?"

"Sacred agreements require sacred—"

"Diseases? I'm not spitting in it, and I'm definitely not drinking from it." He moves the cup closer and opens his mouth to say something. The thought of his germs released from the prison of his mouth and floating freely in that cup... "I'm not. *I'm not.* I'm not.

I'm not. I'm not," I quake. I didn't mean to give in. I pick at the flayed skin of my thumb.

Bacchy slowly sets the cup back on the cart and holds up a hand. "No need to get upset. Silly way to seal a deal. Technically, I'm supposed to use red wine, but I never touch the stuff anymore. Two years sober. This is some god-awful bitter plumberry concoction. Before wine, they used to use *blood!* Imagine that! Talk about disease. Handshake instead?" He holds out his hand.

I lift my hand tentatively, then pull it back quickly, hiding it behind my bag.

"How about we forget the handshake and have a very formal, very serious, nod? No touching. People nod at each other all the time. I've never been able to pull off a serious nod, but I'm willing to cultivate the talent. Let's give it a go. Ready?"

I huff out a timorous breath and give him a serious nod and a small smile. He nods back.

"Now, then! I, Bacchy Liddell, owe you, Cassie of the Cuff, one favor, to be redeemed at a time and place of your choosing. It cannot include the killing or maiming of another person or animal. Little disclaimer there. This contract shall only be null and void in the case of one or both of our deaths. When you're ready to redeem, you'll find me here or in our camp; ask about, someone'll point you to where we rest our heads. Even trade, *to be continued.*"

"Thank you," I say, with a voice that barely wavers.

"It's simply what's owed."

"I mean for being kind."

"Never you mind that. As I said, been on the wagon for two years. Tells you I know a thing or two about troubles, right? Now, are you sure I can't interest you in this tortoise? Goes by the name of Betsy..."

I MISS MY DAD. I MISS COLIN. I MISS MRS. O. I WANT MY BED. But I couldn't find Regan at the Rotunda, and now I'm positive I'm going in the wrong direction. I stop and rub at my eyes. The stone cathedral-like path to my left looks identical to the one on my right, and both have a weird summoning feeling that reminds me of the Coil description from Pict's book. I plant my hands on my hips.

"Fuck!" I shout.

I turn around, then yelp. I'm not alone.

Sebastian Welborne frowns and arches a brow.

"Sorry. I don't curse," I stammer.

"Must've been the fucking wind, then." He studies me, the expression on his handsome face unreadable.

"No. I mean, I know I *did*, but I don't usually—"

"The Astromancy lab is down that way," he says, gesturing the way I came.

I give him a blank look.

"For the initiate party?" he offers.

"I'm not going to the party. I'm looking for my dorm."

"No party?" He furrows his brow and crosses his arms. "You'll miss out on all the drinking and embarrassing hookups."

"Sounds awesome."

The dimple in his cheek makes a reluctant appearance and disappears just as quickly. It's a siren's call, making you want to chase it when it retreats. Making you want to do or say anything to bring it back out to play. But then his expressionless shell reappears as he drawls, "I wasn't planning on playing Theseus today, but initiates shouldn't wander alone."

"Oh, so you weren't just following me around?" I quip. I blame his frigging dimple.

His mask doesn't crack. "No."

My cheeks heat. "You mean Ariadne, by the way. Theseus would've never gotten out of the labyrinth without her." I think of Constellation Cass, wishing myself back to that moment. Back to Colin, teasing colors out of my faint light like a prism.

Sebastian narrows his green eyes. "Why do you know that?"

"Why do you know the part about Theseus, but *not* know that?"

There is an appraising light in his eyes when he says, "Come on. We'll shortcut through the Coil."

"I read the Coil's not safe until initiates walk it during the Agon."

He shrugs. "It's not safe until after the Agon if you're alone. You're safe enough with an escort. But if you're scared..."

The Coil. *What if...* I try and stamp out my intrusive thoughts. I want my room, and the growing boredom in this boy's eyes irks me. It can't be that bad if he's so blasé about it. "Which way do we go?"

"Either way. You have to hold my hand, though." At my skeptical look, he says, "You think I'm so hard up I corner initiates to try and cop a feel of their sweaty palms?"

I slowly lift my hand and slide it into his—after wiping it dry on my pants.

"Don't let go," he says. "And don't move backwards once we're in. Understand?" He pulls me along into the shadowed hall, and I gasp at the sensation of plunging into cold water despite being bone dry. It takes a few seconds for the shock to dissipate. "Crossing in and out of the Coil is like that."

"Thanks for the warning," I mutter.

He jerks at my hand. "Clear your mind."

My steps are halting, reluctant. It's as if someone has filled my skull with magnets, and all around us are their opposites tugging at the ones inside my head. The walls here swell and crest, changing in waves, solidifying into an arching red brick tunnel. Sebastian barrels into it, threading us through the blinding dark. I hear him breathing, and I trot along to keep near. The hand holding mine is warm, even if his attitude is frosty, and it feels weirdly intimate, the two of us touching in this close space.

A hand brushes my face tenderly, startling me. *Sebastian?* Another hand. I open my mouth to protest, but a whisper of a palm grabs for my free arm. *Four* hands on me now, touching. More. I yelp. Sebastian tightens his grip, but I can't see him.

"Don't pull back. You're the one doing it. Control your thoughts. The Coil is using your energy against us. Visualize your dorm."

Oh God. What is this? More whispered touches stroke my hands, my arms, my legs. My throat works, and I force myself to keep putting one foot in front of the other, to ignore the pounding of my pulse in my ears. I close my eyes since it's no darker behind my lids than it is in this space. I think of my dorm. I imagine myself there. When I open my eyes, ghostly blue lines appear in front of me, moving, shaping into a watery map before evaporating.

I blink rapidly. "What was that? I saw something. It was like a blue—"

"Blueprint?" he says, sounding genuinely surprised. "Not bad." The backhanded praise sounds wrung from him, and it's a balm after the meeting with Pict.

The Coil washes the tunnel away, leaving just the red brick walkway and strangely translucent bleached brick walls at our sides. Light shines down from somewhere in the high flung ceiling.

I grab for the leash to my thoughts, struggling to forget about those hands in the dark, to stop worrying the tunnel will be replaced with worse, as I command my heartbeat to settle back into a normal rhythm. I'm okay, okay, okay, okay, okay. "What was that in there?" I ask. My voice shakes more than I thought it would. "Why can't you go backwards?"

"You can, but there's a price for it. But scryers should only ever look forward anyway." Sebastian keeps his eyes focused on the path ahead. The space around us hasn't pulsed since the tunnel dissolved around us. A static patch of Coil. Stable, I realize, remembering Regan's words.

"Have you ever tried it? What's the price?" I sound like I've been running.

"It's different for everyone. And the cost to me or anyone else isn't for you to know. All you need to understand is that it can be dangerous and you shouldn't do it."

He leads me up some brick steps, and I feel that cold wash again. Suddenly, it's like someone turned up the oxygen. I can breathe easier, move with less of an effort. I didn't realize I was struggling to do either. We stride down a narrow hall silently.

"Did I interrupt anything important?" I ask, finally, when I've reined myself in. "You were going somewhere before you Ariadne'd me here."

His look tells me all that I need to know. Or I think it does anyway. I don't ask him to expound. There's an ick feeling to knowing I interrupted his visit to some random someone's room though.

"Oh." My cheeks are hot. The quiet grows up between us again.

"I don't know your name," he says, like someone reciting facts from a textbook instead of asking a question.

"Cassie."

"Cassie. Short for Cassandra? A scryer named Cassandra," he muses. "If you know your myths..."

"Yeah, I know how the myth goes." I spent last night staring at the backs of my eyelids, worrying my name was an omen of something terrible.

"You can let go of my hand now."

I blush and yank my hand away from his, noticing with no little relief we've come to the tiled white hall housing my dorm. A few people have decorated their doors. I spot Tessa's construction paper cutouts and the colorful ribbons Regan tied to her knob and realize my own door is a few blissful steps away.

"This one is me." I rush ahead and wrench open my door, eager to shut him and everything that isn't my pseudo-bedroom-from-home out. "Thanks for the help."

He gives a short nod and rubs at the back of his neck, drawing his shirt tight across his chest. I avert my eyes, refusing to stare. "I'm Sebastian, by the way," he says.

"I know." I grasp the handle of my door.

His eyebrows rocket up in surprise. "Been asking around about me?" My eyes snap to his mocking green ones.

The door clicks shut on that deadly dimple. I stare at my reflection in the mirror hanging on the back of my door and groan.

12

The gauzy blue and green silk hangings of Constance du Lac's classroom undulate in the flickering candlelight, giving the bewildering impression that I've been transported to the bottom of a clear, exotic sea. Which would be just as believable as my current situation, I guess.

I shift on my floor pillow and shake my head, still not quite digesting this is all real. But at least I'm not in the denial I was this morning. In my defense though, how could I not think it was all a dream? Waking up in my bedroom from home? Turning over and seeing my star projector night light on my desk... the quote pinned to the top of my corkboard ("The only courage that matters is the kind that gets you from one moment to the next." ~Mignon McLaughlin)? With the sheer insanity of this supremely weird and wonderful place... a place that *trains people to see and control the future*, I'd have worried about my sanity if I didn't wake up and question it all. It took the combined confusion over discovering a bathroom where my closet back home usually is, paired with a quick, disbelieving peek into the hallway, for the events of yesterday to all come rushing back.

The other initiates, like me, are seated in a circle, cross-legged among the heaps of plump turquoise pillows strewn about. Noah gives me a little wave from my twelve o'clock, and I smile in return until my eyes slide past his to connect with our class prefect's... Sebastian. I hate myself for blushing before I look away.

Regan told me each class would have a prefect assigned to help the instructors with whatever they might need. And at breakfast Tessa, whose room is next door to Regan's, informed me that those spots are all filled by the top-performing Agon grads from the past year. But what I just learned, to my abject misery, is that prefects rotate between classes and meeting times, and on top of that, they're constantly swapping schedules amongst themselves, too. So I get to contend with the anxiety of seeing Sebastian *whenever* and *wherever* without warning.

Whatever. I don't know why he sets me on edge, but I don't care what he thinks of me. If he even thinks of me at all. There wasn't a hint of recognition in his eyes when he saw me today, only what I'm quickly learning is his usual aloof vigilance. And, of course, there's also the matter of the girl with the waist-length blonde hair currently being bustled out the door by our instructor. She snuck in to try and PDA it out with Sebastian while our class was settling down. He let her get a few kisses in, but I'd swear he almost looked grateful when du Lac came over to put an end to the shenanigans. Was the blonde the one he was off to visit last night?

It's fine. I have Colin. I wish I had worn his sweatshirt to ward off this chill, but I cheesily want to preserve his scent for as long as I can. I miss him. Him and his quick-to-smile lips and that adorable nose—which I now know he broke at the age of ten after trying to peddle his bike wearing his dad's huge shoes. Colin with his arms around me, his accidental kiss. Saying it's going to suck when I leave for camp...

"Hydromancy comes in many forms, as vast and varied as the sea," du Lac says in a melodic, whisper-soft voice, having closed the door on the protesting blonde with decided force. Theban's hydromancy instructor barely makes a sound as she moves around the room, her blue chiffon dress and curtain of long hair floating behind her. "Water is the most basic of all scrying methods. It was the first reflective surface we had, after all."

"You know there was booze, too?" Regan whispers to me, picking up her pre-class diatribe about my decision to skip the Orientation party.

"Forced fun," Griffin whispers from the pillow next to her. He struggles to pull his left foot onto his right knee. "You didn't miss anything. Except Regis giving me dirty looks over a glass of wine for two hours."

"Don't flatter yourself. I didn't even see you there."

"Sure you didn't."

"Get a room," the girl on the other side of Griffin hisses.

"Water is also the most mysterious, the most mercurial," du Lac continues. "It's elemental. We've worked to harness that power, to make ourselves into vessels worthy of receiving the messages the waters and our abilities wish to bring to us. We've cleansed our minds, readying them to be filled."

"The only thing I want to be filled with is a meat pie. I'm legit starving," Regan whispers.

"Regan, please," du Lac says.

"Yeah, Regan. Please," Griffin says.

"Shut up." Regan glares at Griffin.

"None of that. Negative energy builds and destroys like a tsunami. You'll need to exert control over your emotions for the Agon and beyond," du Lac tuts. "Now, I want you all to stand and pick up your water witching rods."

We each pick up our Y-shaped hazel rods and grasp them the way du Lac demonstrates, with each hand clutching one of the Y's ascending branches and its thick stem pointed outward. Du Lac moves to the long edge of the class, its mirrored mosaic wall shimmering like a mermaid's tail. A long trough runs the length of the wall, and above it, tucked amidst the haphazardly placed glittering shards, a dozen golden faucets are lined up like a Roman legion. Du Lac turns an ornate handle and tugs on a lever, and a steady drip appears from one of those faucets. The she flips a switch and the room is filled with the sound of rainfall, although every other faucet remains dry.

"I want you all to close your eyes, spin around, and concentrate on finding the dripping water. The drip will move periodically from one spout to another. You need to clear your minds and use your witching rod to find the spout. Begin."

Giggling and grumbles sound as kids run into each other with their witching wands. I clutch the edges of my rod and close my eyes, spinning and feeling like a dunce.

Drip.

Drip.

This room feels damp.

Drip.

It didn't look like they put a ton into maintenance. How much mold is hiding here?

Drip.

Maybe black mold. Cancer-causing mold.

Drip.

Mom's tumor wasn't from mold. It wasn't from anything. Nothing to blame except cancer itself. And fate.

Drip.

Fate... Oh God, how long until Colin—

"If you're thinking about anything other than the drip, you'll need to try harder. A hydromantic vessel needs to be scrubbed, rinsed, purified," du Lac says.

"That drip has me ready to piss my pants," Griffin announces. I open my eyes to discover I'm nosing around the wall opposite the one I should be. Du Lac frowns at Griffin and waves him off. He runs off in search of a restroom, and I close my eyes again with a sigh.

I listen for the real drip hiding amidst the recorded ones and tuck away the concern that so much of being a scryer hinges on controlling your mind. If I could've controlled my mind, I would've done it a long time ago, but my brain always swings from thought to thought like a demented monkey in a tree of rotting branches. I give up and use my time to mentally replay my interactions with Colin instead. I add new scenes, things I wish would have happened. I'm funnier. Prettier. More charming. He is *all* about me. He leans over in the moonlight and—

"Cassie!" Regan shoves me.

"What?" I look over the room, taking in the rest of the class filing out.

"I was the first to find the drip," Regan announces proudly. "And du Lac said we can leave early. You're crazy good at the concentration thing but terrible at finding water. You've been stuck in this corner for ages."

I look around for our instructor, sure her eyes are burning holes in me with her disapproval. "Where did she go?"

"Du Lac?" Regan shrugs and jabs her thumb at a door on the back wall. "In the back room with somebody. She stuck her head out to tell us class was dismissed, then shut the door. You seriously didn't hear any of that?"

I march for the exit. Noah is close behind us, and I grab at him to make an introduction to Regan, desperate for a subject change.

"I didn't notice you on the bus," she says to him when we reach the hall. "Noah. No...ah." Regan rolls the name on her tongue. I can't tell what she thinks about him or his name, but Noah's thoughts about her are writ large on his face.

"Ray... gun," he says in response, quietly teasing, his worshipful gaze married to her profile.

Regan smiles and drills him with questions as we shuffle toward our next class, until I slam to a stop, realizing I've forgotten my bag on du Lac's floor. *Crap.* Regan offers to walk back with me—and Noah, of course, immediately volunteers to be our escort, maneuvering so that Regan's the meat in our hallway-march-sandwich.

I push open the class door.

"One word from me and everything you've been working on comes crashing down." The usually flowy, supremely calm du Lac is in a fury. We can't see her or the object of her ire, presumably the squirmy man, because they're still in the back room, although the door is now open.

Regan's eyes widen. "Holy meltdown, Batman. What did she say about negativity tsunamis?"

"Constance, please," the man murmurs. "Don't talk like that. Someone might hear."

I tiptoe to my bag, still resting next to the pillow I was seated on. I can see the man's profile now: he's handsome but gangly, with a shock of floppy hair that looks like it's never met a comb it didn't hate.

"I don't care if the world hears. I'll say what I like when I like. And someone like *you* doesn't leave someone like *me*."

"Okay, then let's pretend you ended things, and we'll part as friends. It's over either way. I love her."

Crack. Her handprint, an angry red mark on the man's cheek, is visible even from here.

"On that note, I think we're done here. For good," she says.

That sets me in motion. I rush toward the exit, waving at Noah and Regan to hurry before me. We shoot down the hall and around a corner, panting.

I press my cheek to the cold stone of the wall, and Regan peeks back around the corner. "No one there. He's either still in the room or bounced out of there in a hurry."

"Who are we spying on?" Griffin whispers from behind us.

Regan and I shriek. Noah manfully swallows his own shout.

"What are you doing here?" Regan demands.

"I was headed back to class."

"It's over. Du Lac let us out," Noah says.

"How long does it take you to pee?" Regan glances back around the corner nervously. The hall is still empty.

"I don't like to rush things. So, who were you watching?" Griffin asks.

"Du Lac just broke up with a guy and slapped him," I say.

"Cassie!" Regan cries.

"What? He asked."

"Relax, Nancy Drew. I won't tell anyone you're a stalker. Besides, it's not that interesting anyway. Isn't she married to the dude who teaches Palmistry? She's probably just fighting with her husband."

"It was a guy with wild hair. He had a scar running down his cheek here." I trace my finger down my cheek from right below my eye to my chin.

"Holy shit. That's Ford! Isn't that your mentor?" Griffin asks Regan, his eyes dancing with glee. "Scandal!"

"Seriously, you're like herpes. Go. Away," Regan says.

"Regan, did you recognize him?" I ask.

"Know a lot about herpes?" Griffin asks with a smile.

"I know enough about you and your friends to know you're like an annoying disease."

"Regan," I say.

"Herpes is one letter away from heroes," Griffin says.

"Alright, come on, guys," Noah says.

Regan rolls her eyes and turns to me. "I didn't see him," she mutters. "He came in when our eyes were closed."

"But I did," I say. "If he had that scar..."

"Oh, Sid," Griffin says in a high falsetto, pressing his hands to his cheeks with a dreamy expression. "Daddy issues, much?"

Regan flushes magenta, her eyes welling for a second. "Shut it, Griffin."

"I wonder what she meant about spilling the beans," Noah muses.

Griffin's face positively lights up. "What, what? This keeps getting better," he beams, ignoring the gathering storm clouds on Regan's face. "What's good ole Sid up to?"

"He's not up to anything," Regan says hotly.

"You met him when? You don't know him from a hole in the wall," Griffin says.

Regan glares at him and takes a deep breath before turning to me and Noah, hooking her arms through ours and pulling us along to our next class.

Griffin trails behind us, whistling.

OUR RITUALS AND SCRYCASTING CLASSROOM, WITH ITS singed Bunsen burners lining the sideboard and its walls covered in charts, could be mistaken for a darker, smaller version of my sophomore-year chemistry classroom. But only if you pretend the posters are of periodic tables instead of scrycasting spells.

"Thank God we get a break from that douche," Regan says, as we settle into our lab partner-style seats. Griffin's scheduled Rituals class is on a different day than ours, something Regan has been celebrating since we parted ways. "You'll get to meet Sid without Griffin. He's amazing. Seriously. He's like Griffin on opposite day." Regan warms up to her topic, advocating for him like I'm a judge to be swayed during sentencing. It sounds like she's trying to convince herself of something.

The man who ambles into the room is, without a doubt, the same one I saw getting slapped by du Lac. The faded scar running down his cheek is starkly white against his flushed face. Regan, all energy a moment before, suddenly looks away, avoiding eye contact.

Noah, seated in front of us, turns expectantly.

"That's him," I whisper.

"Hi, everyone. I'm Sid Ford. Sidney, if you're my grandmother, but to everyone else... I may teach ceremony but I don't stand on it, so you can all call me Sid." Regan's mentor has a rumpled, nutty professor quality, with deep crinkles around his eyes and an easy smile. He walks over to an antique cabinet and throws the carved doors open, the top half of him disappearing inside as he hunts for something deep within. I wince at the sound of glass breaking.

Ford emerges from the cupboard a little dustier but sporting a triumphant grin and clutching an Ebenezer Scrooge-ish silver candlestick holder, a long tapered black candle, and a sharp pair of shears. He sets them down on the first table in our row and strikes a match on the bottom of his shoe to light the candle. It sputters before catching.

"Your life is a collection of moments. Some happy, some sad, some mundane, some exciting. History is also a collection of moments. And so is the future."

Ford grabs the scissors on the desk with one hand, a tuft of his unruly hair with the other, and saws through a clump. Regan inhales sharply next to me. He closes his eyes and begins moving his lips wordlessly, and when his lids open, for a frightening second only the whites of his eyes show. It's only after his retinas reappear that I realize I've put little half-moon nail marks into the soft black coating on our desktop. I loosen my grip and cover my nose when Ford holds his hair over the candle; the overpowering smell of burnt hair and rotten eggs fills the room. My eyes water and burn. The flame sparks, spits. There's a hum in my ears, like when someone has turned on a TV nearby.

"Take a look at the back of the room, guys," Ford says finally. We all turn.

Wait.

A moment later, a large mirror, taking up a good portion of the back wall, shatters as if struck, startling all ten people in our class into jumping. A huge crack spreads slowly, creeping, the sound echoing.

"Magic," someone breathes.

"Seven years bad luck for me, huh?" Ford says. I turn back to him. He's grinning. "Did someone call it magic? That's exactly what people thought when they'd see scryers do things like this. They'd mimic what they saw, trying to replicate it, giving birth to fun little superstitions. I guess the ability to make something you want happen—it is a kind of magic, isn't it? That's what scrycasting allows us to do. If you think of all of those moments that make up the future as a series of dominoes yet to fall, scrycasting is what we do to influence *how* they fall. Or if they fall at all.

"Now, what I did there with the mirror is something we've always been able to do: exert direct influence on one small future change. Bigger changes are tougher to pull off, more complex. Anything really big *was* out of reach. Even our oldest and most comprehensive spell books weren't much help. With this thing, though..." Ford picks up an ICARUSS device from his desk.

One of Griffin's friends, a boy named Dill who sports the most pitiful collection of facial hair ever assembled, snorts. "If I want to become a billionaire, I can make it happen with that thing?"

"You becoming a billionaire is a little too disruptive," Ford says with the air of someone who's heard that question a few too many times. "It's too big a change and would cause a lot of potential ripples in the futures of everyone around you. You've heard of the Butterfly Effect? It's nonsense." Ford turns to the board and draws a chalk butterfly, a series of mathematical formulas, and a tilting palm tree. He turns and claps his hands together in a cloud of chalk dust. "The tiny atmospheric disturbances caused by a butterfly's flapping wings would level off before they can put a dent in anything as complex as weather patterns. That's what our rituals are like right now—a butterfly's wing flaps. As individuals, even as a company, there's only so much we can change directly. That's why we've tried to help make this company a ton of money, so that management can go out there and do all of the good we wish we could arm wrestle into existence. The ICARUSS, though, is like a butterfly relay race. It lets us extend the impact of those wing flaps."

Ford holds his ICARUSS in his left hand and rests his right hand on the surface. "To pull up a ritual I want, I need to channel my energy through this thing," he says, closing his eyes. The device makes a little sound, and Ford removes his right hand and stares down at it. "Okay, I've got it."

He rushes back to his cupboard and pulls out a bunch of items, which he mixes, muttering to himself. He writes something down on a few slips of paper and sprinkles his mixed concoction onto them before folding them up. One he drops into a jar of liquid, and the other he buries in a jar of dirt. He burns a few herbs, waving the smoke into his face using a white feather and inhaling deeply. Then he puffs up his cheeks, holding his breath, and stares down at his wristwatch. Finally, he releases the breath and says, "Alright! Let's see this in action."

A bird flies through the open window a beat later. It takes a turn around the class and settles on a beaker. When the bird tires of that perch and lifts off, the beaker teeters. A boy sitting closest to it grabs at it, catching the glass before it falls to the ground. He sets it back on the shelf and sits, tipping a book off his desk in the process and launching a pencil, missile-like, into the air. Ford catches the pencil and tucks it behind one ear.

"Butterfly relay race," he says with a smile. "I wanted that pencil. I got that pencil."

Everyone begins speaking at the same time, firing questions at Ford. He holds up his hand. "Yes, you were technically part of the ritual, Dinesh. Everyone, hang onto your questions for later. I want you all to give these a try first." He grabs a basket and begins handing out ICARUSS devices to each of us.

I palm mine, and up close it's a light-as-air slip of silver, a little thinner, narrower, and longer than my cell phone. I see my reflection in the device but there doesn't seem to be a screen. I touch my thumb to the center of my device, and the silver melts away, dissolving like draining mercury into a home screen. A jolt of euphoria shoots through me, strong and pure. *This is how I save Colin.*

"Scrycasting rituals can be used to try and bring in visions you want information on, or to manipulate future events, but all of the above require a sacrifice. Write that down. Every. Single. Ritual. Requires. A. Sacrifice," Ford announces over the muted conversations. I pull out my notebook and record it.

He continues, "The sacrifices can be minimal—a skipped heartbeat, an exhale, your energy—or they can be great. Years off your life, even! Your sacrifices will be subjective and proportionate to your requests, but make sure that you're clear about what you plan on giving up or the ritual might decide for you.

"I only asked for a tiny future change before: the mirror in my classroom cracking. Not much of an impact on anyone. Well, except maybe the accounting department since they'll have to replace it. So I only had to sacrifice a small thing, right? As you can tell, I care a great deal for my hair, so it was a big deal." He wryly gestures to the brown Einsteinian mess on his head. "Yeah, it's okay, laugh it up. When I wanted Dinesh's pencil, I had to sacrifice the air I breathe for a period of time. *My* air, though. If *my* ritual in ICARUSS calls for a pinky finger, it's not going to go a long way if I take *his* finger, will it? Someone I just met?" Ford picks up the kid in the front row's pinky and holds his scissors to it. The boy quickly snatches his hand back to safety.

I lean back in my seat, a frown knitting my brow. What does it take to save a life? What will I give up to save Colin?

"The bigger your request, the bigger the sacrifice and... write this down, too... the more involved the ritual will be. More steps, or more ingredients. You saw that with the pencil. That's because you may need to change a bunch of little events leading up to what you *really* want to change. To get that pencil, I had to lure the bird in, and upset Dinesh. And the last piece of the puzzle: you need to be able to block out everything around you and visualize what you want to occur. It's almost like lying to yourself. You need to picture what you want so well you almost believe that your vision of the future already happened. Now, team up. I want you guys to give this a try," Ford says. "Pick something simple."

I hold my ICARUSS the way Ford did and visualize what I want to happen. I visualize it over and over in my mind's eye until the device makes a sound and a pair of silver-feathered wings appears on the screen, coming together and apart as if in flight, then dissolving into an outline of a short ritual.

I make a note of what I need in the way of supplies, and Regan goes and gathers them for us from the cabinet. Noah is fetching for his team, and they chat while they wait in line at the cabinet. She's still smiling at something he said when she returns with our stuff, spreading it all out in front of us.

I close my eyes, sacrificing my sight for a time for my ritual, and concentrate, whispering the words on my device's screen to myself until I can recite them with conviction. An electric current runs along my fingers and up my arms. The hum is back in my ears.

A breeze gusts through the open doorway, slamming the door shut and putting out every candle flame in the room.

"Oh em gee! Was that you?" Regan shouts over the complaining of the others, whose experiments I've interrupted.

I laugh. "Yes!"

Ford walks over. "Very nice job! You aimed for something small, you gave an appropriate sacrifice, and you made it happen. Very, very good work. What's your name?"

"Cassie Morai."

"Morai! I should have known. You resemble Aubrey, you know? In appearance and talent both. When Welborne was training us on the ICARUSS a couple of months back, she was a complete natural. Must run in the family."

I blush, unused to praise. Or positive attention. Or not being a screw-up. "Thank you."

Ford smiles at Regan and turns, unconsciously rubbing his scruff-covered cheek. It's the one I watched du Lac slap, although the angry red handprint is no longer visible.

"Sid, what would it take to make someone love you? Like, if they were *married*?" Regan narrows her eyes, watchful for his expression.

Ford stills and turns, looking from Regan to me and back again. Noah has turned in his seat to watch. "Well," he says, in a measured tone, "love is off limits. You can only lead a horse to water, you can't make it drink. So you can put yourself in that person's path, but there is no controlling love. It's like a flower springing up through sidewalk cracks. A spot of beauty that can grow even in unexpected places."

"What's up with red blessings?" Dill asks.

I start. *The red blessing approaches.* I haven't thought of the phrase since the day I scried it in Pict's office before I joined Theban, but the memory of the swirling despair that accompanied the message sets my body to trembling.

"Red blessing?" I force myself to ask.

"Necromancy," Noah volunteers. "I'm not into it or anything. I just like reading about that stuff." He throws a worried look at Regan, trying to read her reaction.

"That's right, Noah—" Ford says.

"Like controlling corpses?" I ask, cutting him off.

"No, that's movie stuff," Noah says. "It's actually murdering someone for scryer gain. A blood sacrifice. A red blessing is an offering of human blood. A body's worth—"

"It's dark, that's what's up with it," Ford interjects, steering us away from the gory details. "The things we can scry, the things we can influence, have limits. And... well, yeah, if you take a life, you shortcut your way through some of those. But it's a trade. The life you take isn't the only sacrifice you make when you're messing with forces like that, right? Scryers rely on energy to feed our abilities. You tango with dark forces and it strips you of your light."

"So, if you engage in necromancy, you can lose your ability to scry?" Noah asks.

I have to wonder: would I give up these new abilities, this world, these friends, all of it, to save Colin? *Yes,* I think. *Yes, I would.* But the answer comes slower than I thought it would, more hesitant. *Yes. Yes. Yes.*

Ford is opening his mouth to respond when Regan lifts up a pair of scissors and lops off a big hunk of her hair. I'm stunned, considering how much stock she puts into appearance. Noah full on gasps. Even Ford looks a little taken aback.

Regan closes her eyes, repeating the words of her ritual and opening them, holding her hair over the flame. The springy dark corkscrew curls fold in on themselves in threads of burning orange and red.

We wait.

Ford looks at Regan sympathetically and squats next to her chair. "You are beyond talented. Don't let this discourage you. We'll work on it during office hours."

We go around the room, a few people explaining what they asked for, what they sacrificed, and sharing whether or not they got what they wanted; silly things like getting the bird in the room to land on their shoulder. Like Regan, lots of people weren't able to accomplish their goals. I'm feeling puffed up, peacock proud. I tapped into an unknown well of power inside me and made something happen! I'm going to save Colin, I know it. I want to pinch myself to make sure I'm not dreaming.

Before long, we're packing up our bags, brand-new ICARUSS devices in hand, and heading out to our next class. The class across from ours lets out at the same time, and Griffin sidles up to us immediately. Pict follows Griffin out of the same door, a dour expression on his face as always.

"I didn't think training to see the future could be so boring," Griffin moans.

Pict's frown deepens, clearly overhearing. His eyes land on me a second before he weaves around us and stomps off. I silently curse Griffin for making me guilty by association in my advisor's eyes.

"Mathmatiks may kill me before I'm done with it. Or I'll end up killing Pict. Either way, at least it'll be over. If I had to hear one more thing about Pythagoras, I was going to... Hey, nice haircut, Rhesus. Had an accident in class?"

Regan remains uncharacteristically silent, refusing to take the bait. Griffin is still looking at her when he walks smack into one of the life-sized gargoyle statues jutting from the corridor's walls. One second he's next to me and the next he's flat on his back, a look of shock on his face and a red welt on his forehead. The contents of his bag are scattered around him.

Dill and another of their friends help wrench him up. Griffin rubs his head.

Regan marches on, a satisfied grin on her face. "Sacrifice worth it."

13

Regan is on the floor of my dorm, painting her toes a hot pink. Noah is leaning back in my desk chair. He lifts his hand to the ray of late morning sun beaming through my window and stares at his neon orange nails. I watch him blow on them from my bed.

"I can't believe Noah let me paint his nails, but you won't."

I glance at my rough hands and go in for a diversion. "I still don't know why you bother since the color disappears the second you hit the elevators."

Regan extends her foot and wiggles her toes. "Temporarily cute is still cute."

Noah laughs and I smile, returning my attention to the stack of *Fortnight Foresight* back issues Regan let me borrow. I flip through haphazardly.

"It's fugacious," Noah says, touching his nails to see if the polish has dried.

"Is that like *fugly*?"

"Good great-grandma word," I say, turning another page. "Means fleeting. Comes from a Latin word meaning *to flee...*"

"Cassie, my great-grandma would've *loved* you," Noah crows.

I grin, and an article on the Coil tugs at my attention. "Hey, guys... the Coil—this whole thing—" I gesture around us at my Coil-illusion room. "It's a little different than seeing and messing with the future. You ever think about that?"

"Yeah, but it's all the mind, isn't it?" Noah says. "Only difference is what the environment allows. Outside the Coil—out in the world—we can only see or sense the future and *maybe* influence it. In here, we can just project what we're thinking on the world around us in the Coil and these semi-Coil spaces. All still coming from your head though, right?"

I nod, and I ponder his words all the way to the Rotunda after they decline to join me for a meeting with my aunt.

I don't think I'll ever get used to the Rotunda or the way it feels each time I clap eyes on it—like something has bloomed in the murky depths of my chest and is reaching out for that ceiling's radiance. Or maybe it isn't the ceiling. It might be the geeked-out glee of overhearing snippets of scryer conversations. Or both. Whatever it is, over the past week this space more than any other at Theban Group has filled me with awe. And that's saying a lot.

I spot Aunt Bree before she notices me, and for a brief, cowardly moment, I consider ducking behind the Magpie cart where I'm waiting in line. The auburn hidden in her dark hair comes alive in the Rotunda dome-light. She's wearing a breezy belted sundress adorned with a collection of accessories I wouldn't have thought to assemble. But then again, I wasn't born effortlessly chic. The way her lip curls as an initiate darts across her path reminds me, unnecessarily, that the rose has thorns.

"There you are. I should've checked the meat pie line first." Aunt

Bree smiles as she approaches. There isn't any reproach or mockery in her tone, but I immediately know it's an insult. Or... do I? Maybe I'm not being fair to her. Sure, she says rude things with a laugh so she can pretend it was just a grand joke when you take offense, and she has an arrogant air that makes you want to smack her just to knock her off that pedestal she's put herself on. But she's also the reason I even have a shot at saving Colin. She's the reason I know I'm not losing my mind.

"They're good," I say, tentatively. "I got two. Want one?"

She waves the offer away and indicates I should join her at one of the bistro tables near the fountain. I grab my steaming pies in their wax paper jackets and stamp after her, juggling to keep from burning my fingers. "I wanted to check up on you now that you're finishing your first week," Aunt Bree says when I sit across from her. "I've been very busy, which I'm sorry about." She purses her lips into a moue of regret. "But I heard good things about your Rituals class in particular. How are you acclimating?"

"Good, I guess. I miss Dad, but I'm making some friends. I've got an ECC appointment to talk to Dad later today. First one." I shrug and unwrap one of my pies, bringing it to my mouth and sinking my teeth into it defiantly. Aunt Bree doesn't react.

"If you need me to pull strings to get you more frequent ECC appointments, let me know."

That'd make me super popular with everyone here, hopping to the front of the line. But even still, I so want to tell her yes.

"There are benefits to being my niece. You'll want to—"

"Ms. Morai! Haven't seen you in a couple weeks. How'd you sneak past me?" Theodore, the front desk Santa, asks, clutching his own pair of pies and staring at Aunt Bree.

"Maybe I caught you mid-nap?" Aunt Bree says, saccharine sweet. "Or on a snack break?"

"No one gets the drop on me, Ms. Morai. And the logs don't show you comin' in during Kren's watch..." He starts taking down one of his pies with the skill of a lion devouring a gazelle and chews thoughtfully.

Aunt Bree sighs when it becomes obvious he isn't moving away. "Jordan approved an executive entrance. It isn't common knowledge, and I'd like to keep it that way. Understood?"

Theodore straightens. "Of course." He turns his attention to me. "Other Ms. Morai. I see you discovered the meat pies!"

I ignore whatever Aunt Bree mumbles and smile. "Cassie. Yeah, my favorite pair of jeans wishes I hadn't, but I'm glad I did."

Theodore grunts out a laugh and finishes his second. "Now that I've taken care of my own girlish figure, I'd better get back to my desk. Don't be a stranger now, Cassie." He grins and heads off.

Aunt Bree stares at his retreating figure and then down at my own second pie on the table. "You do know Theban has a gym?"

"HIYA, CASS!"

I blink back tears, and the antiseptic pale green walls of the ECC—Theban Group's External Communications Center—swim in front of me. "Hi, Dad," I say thickly.

Theban Group's ban on personal phones and internet has been killing me, and not just because I'm used to having my phone in my hand every second of the day. Yes, the policy is because they make for too big a distraction, and I get that, but it's been a week since

I've heard Dad's voice. It's the longest I've ever gone. Seven painful days of waiting for my ECC appointment. I didn't appreciate how painful the wait was until I heard that gentle timbre on the other end of the line.

"How's it going at camp? What've you been up to?"

"Oh, you know, camp stuff. It's okay," I say, the lie goring its way down my tongue before tumbling off.

"You checking for ticks every day?"

"Yes! I said I would. How's it been having the place to yourself?"

"Well, I miss you, Cass. But to be honest, I'm loving all the left-over lasagna. Didn't realize how much of it you pack away."

"Yeah, yeah," I say, hiccuping out a laugh. "I miss you, too."

"Oh, sorry. Hang on a sec." A woman's voice murmurs something in the background on Dad's side.

"Who's that?" I ask. I pick at the healing skin of my thumb.

I hear him talking to someone before he answers. "Sorry about that. Er... Eleanor is here. I burned our dinner and... takeout to the rescue. It just got here."

I stare at the wall in front of me, my mind supplying images of that faceless woman sitting on my mom's side of the couch. "Oh. Well, go eat, then. I just wanted to say hi. I'll give you a call again when I get a chance. Lots going on here. Have fun."

"Cass..."

"Yeah?"

"I love you," Dad says.

I swallow. "Yeah. Me too. Bye, Dad."

I hang up before he can say anything more, and I open my email on the computer in front of me, angrily clicking around. *Who even uses email anymore? Old people.* And me, apparently. My upset reluctantly fades when I see a name that makes my heart bounce around my ribcage like a puppy in a gift box.

I open Colin's email, and the smile that splits my face is nearly painful.

Dear Cassie,

How's camp? Got to be better than jail, which is where you're headed after committing the unforgivable crime of stealing my favorite sweatshirt. You thought you could bat your pretty eyes and I'd forget all about it, didn't you? Well, you're right, but now that you've been gone for a week, your spell has worn off, and I am *livid*. I suggest you rush back. Not because I miss you. I just want that sweatshirt.

Sincerely,
Colin Jon Clay, III

P.S. Mrs. O says hi.

Below Colin's note is a picture of me behind bars. He's doctored a snap he took of our waffle outing last week. I'm mid-chew and look ridiculous.

I fire back a response, pretending to be a lawyer representing Cassie Morai, unjustly accused of stealing, and race back to my room to throw on his sweatshirt, inhaling deeply to capture the faint whiff of the coconut body wash he steals from his mom's shower and, under it, *him*. I flop onto my bed with my Pict homework, grinning like mad, and try not to let the delicious thought that Colin misses me distract me too much.

14

"**W**ell, well, if it isn't the old albatross herself." Pict's voice echoes off the walls of the corridor outside his office.

Linda Fenice, owner of the door of a million locks, and my ornithomancy instructor—or "bird brain," if you're asking Aunt Bree—levels Pict with a look of disgust before returning her attention to unlocking her door. "Charm, charm everywhere, and not a drop in you, eh, Martin?"

Pict smiles coldly. "Speaking of charming, is that bird excrement on your shoulder, Fenice?"

"Another Band-Aid, Marty? Burying your head in a book has some occupational hazards, doesn't it? Chief among them an absolute lack of friends. Oh dear, you probably don't know what those are, do you?" She clucks her tongue in sympathy. "I'll save you a trip to the bookshelf. Friends are—"

"Ms. Morai, before you stands Ms. Fenice, the one person in the building who might be less talented than yourself."

Fenice laughs. "Your mentee is in my class. Lovely girl with a great deal of raw talent." She finishes with her locks, opens her door, and turns back toward me. "If you ever need a shoulder to cry on, dear—and we know with this lummox there will definitely be a need—I'm across the hall." She gives me a kindly look and glares at Pict before closing her door with a teeth-rattling slam.

Pict turns to me with a furious look. "An extra hour of reading tonight in Vassago's *Pyromancy*." He falls back into his office and slams his pink door behind him.

Awesome. Now I'm even punished when other people piss Pict off. Hilariously, I was just thinking about how relatively mellow he's been the past few days.

I stifle a yawn. It's been a long day, and with a late-afternoon Palmistry class followed by a mirror scrying night lab, it's not over yet.

I run my fingers over the walls of the hall on my way to class, marveling at how the different spaces are so perfectly spliced into one another, from jagged stone to wood paneling to Moroccan tile to wall hangings. I don't usually enjoy silences, since my mind always fills them with worries, but here... Theban is so much larger than the number of scryers here could possibly need, so everywhere outside the dorms, the Rotunda, or the class halls, always has this waiting quiet. But it's different than the empty quiets I dislike. This quiet is heavy. A bated breath come to life.

Regan greets me as I take my seat in Palmistry and rests her chin in her upturned palms. "He is so beyond," she says, staring at our instructor.

I stifle a yawn. "Beyond what?"

"Anything."

James du Lac, Theban's Palmistry instructor and Constance du Lac's husband, brushes his shock of shoe-polish-black hair back off his brow. His bone structure hints at extreme good looks in his youth, and tanned aging skin suggesting summers spent in the sun and winters in tanning beds. He's nice enough, but I can't bring myself to care all that much about palm reading. How would that help me save Colin?

"Pair up, kids, and spread out. Plenty of space here. You want to find a nice, quiet spot where you can concentrate on each other," Mr. du Lac says. "We've studied all the practical stuff this week, and now we execute. You're going to take your partner's dominant hand, palm up, into your own hands. Cradle it, like this." The girl whose hand he has taken into his own blushes. He isn't flirtatious in any way, but somehow every word out of his mouth feels like the start of a romance.

The class fans out, pushing desks together and settling into groups. A hush falls over the room, white noise only interrupted by the occasional laugh or a comment by our instructor.

"Palmistry is still forbidden in some parts. It's too personal. Too focused. Too intimate," he says. "When you scry, you don't know what you'll come back with, who it might relate to, or what it will reveal. With the palm, you know that everything you uncover is going to be about that one person in front of you. And—this is the kick in the head—it's the only scrying method that lets you see the future *and* the past."

"Come on, Cassie. Give me your hand. I want to impress my new husband," Regan says.

"What about Welborne?"

"Old news. James is a total Clooney. Besides, he's a wounded baby bird who needs to be nurtured. He's going to need comforting when he finds out his wife is a basic skank."

"Unless they're already broken up. Or he knows and doesn't care. What about Noah? He's awesome."

Regan's blush is practically purple. "He's young."

"He's our age."

"Guys our age are so immature. I guess he's kind of got an old soul thing going for him, though. Maybe because of his great-grandma always being around? We were hanging earlier and he said 'trousers' and—"

"You guys hung out without me?"

"Well, yeah, but like... ew! Don't get any ideas."

I laugh and wipe my sweaty palm on my knee before placing it in Regan's awaiting outstretched hand.

"Oh no! What happened to your hand?"

I blanch and try to pull it back as people look over at us. She holds tight. "I... I don't... It's nothing."

"Nothing?" She lowers her voice and looks down at my hand, leaning closer. "Cassie, these red patches aren't nothing. And your... Is that dried blood on your nail? Have you had it looked at?"

The pity in her voice sparks my temper. I place my other mess of a hand onto the table. "There's nothing to have looked at. I did it to myself." The confusion on her face and the naked caring leeches the anger from me. I'm left saddened my illness always has to crash the party. I swallow, force myself to look into her eyes. "From washing. And picking. I have OCD."

"Oh. Oh, Cassie..."

"It's not cute like being neat or quirky or neurotic. It's like... my doctor told me everyone has weird passing thoughts like, 'What if I push this guy in front of this subway car?' or, 'Should I jump off this balcony?' or, 'What if my dad dies?' But most people just get skeeved, recognize it's dumb, and move on. I'm the same, except for the moving on part. For people like me, the thought gets *stuck*, like water in your ear after a swim. I'll fixate on the violent details. The meaning. *Why did I think that? Would I do that? What does it mean? How would I feel?* And even though I know it's not real, my body doesn't realize it's not actually happening."

I inhale heavily. "A couple of weeks ago, a dirty dog brushed up against me and I was sure I was going to die. Like, a logical part of me knew it wasn't true, but the rest of me—my lungs, my heart, my entire body—was positive I was toast." I keep my eyes on my hands. Those raw, dry, cracked things. "And when I get like that, when the water is stuck in my ear, I can't get it out without *doing* something. All sorts of things, like washing or saying something five times or touching something. I'm a mess."

Regan's lips twist and she covers my hands with her own. "Cassie! This is your Big Bad. Sometimes you win and sometimes it does, but... these are battle scars. You're a total badass!"

I snort out a laugh and brush at my eye. "Whatever."

"I'm serious! You're totally Cassandra, Warrior Princess."

"It's easy to say, but you don't know—"

"Yeah, I don't know exactly what you're going through. I'm not trying to blow it off or pretend I do. But I get living with fear and..."

I wince. I've triggered something in her. I watch as she wrestles with it.

"You can't see my battle scars, but they're there." She swallows. "My dad abandoned me and my mom."

"Oh, Regan. I'm so sorry."

"Don't be. He didn't care? Well, I don't either. I'm a survivor. And now I'm a scryer. I got a raw deal, but I'll see the next one coming a mile away, and not only because I can see the friggin' future. Plus, others have it worse. We have this opportunity. We're going to *rock* this opportunity. And if we weren't sitting here in my future husband's class and it wouldn't look totally weird, I would totally hug you."

I laugh and blink away the mist in my eyes. I turn my palms up, and Regan places her hands on mine. I give them a squeeze.

"So, what have you learned over here?" Mr. du Lac asks as he approaches our little nook.

Regan responds immediately. "That Cassie is a badass."

"Not sure how you got that from her palm," Mr. du Lac says slowly. "Let's take a look at yours and see what we're working with first." He smiles at Regan and takes her hand. "So, this mound is..."

"Apollo Mount. It signifies a sunny disposition," Regan says.

"That's right. You must be a charming young lady."

"Oh, I am." Regan flutters her eyelashes. I laugh.

"And this dip here, next to your first Mars Mount? Menelaus Valley. Hard time forgiving, but an old hurt... you'll have a chance to... here, where your head line, destiny line, and life line intersect and form this letter? Approaching a decision. A major life decision. This is your heart line. It leads..."

"Wherever you like," Regan breathes.

He sets her hand down and gives it a pat. "Why don't we see what's happening with your friend's palm? Show me what you got from it."

"Sure," Regan says. I present my palm to her awaiting hand. "Okay, so. Hm... the lifeline is frayed here, and the Mercury line jabs into the fate line. That means..." She hesitates and looks up at Mr. du Lac.

His gaze sharpens as he takes my hand himself. "Suffering in your past, tentacles into the present," he says quietly, tracing his hand from my middle finger down to the middle of my palm. He winces. "So young, and so much pain." He whispers so faintly I barely make him out. "But I can't... nothing is set in stone except your past. Usually there are... see here? Your life and fate lines are open-ended. He rubs his thumb over the bump between my index finger and thumb. "Sacrifice." He lifts my hand and peers at it from another angle. "And love. See this here? These parallel lines?" I pull my hand back and stare up at his tanned face. He looks pained. "Your palm isn't giving up its secrets without a fight, kid. Unusual."

When we've packed up and Regan has assured me her wedding to James is off, she adds, "Honestly, Palmistry is a joke. You said it yourself."

"I didn't say that. I told you Pict said that."

"Even better! He's an expert."

"It's fine, Regan."

"No, it's not. I don't want you running off and OCD'ing the crap out of your hands some more."

I laugh. "Very sensitive to my condition, thanks. Not really how it works, either."

Regan eyes me warily. "You're shockingly calm about the 'never seen a palm like this' spookfest."

I laugh again, but it isn't a pretty sound. "For someone with my condition, you mean?"

"No! Anyone would be wigging out."

"Honestly, you're overreacting. I didn't really need Mr. du Lac to tell me I'm a freak. Besides, hearing the open-ended stuff was actually pretty comforting because I know what's coming. That's why I'm here."

"That's why we're all here."

"No." I hesitate. Sharing feels like a trust fall. "It's Colin... I told you about him, remember?" I tell Regan about Colin's death, about that day in front of the school. About my mom. I spare no detail.

"*Cassie*. What the hell? Why didn't you tell me?"

"I don't know. Pict didn't believe me when I tried, and I figured... Anyway, I'm telling you now."

"Well, I'm going to help you. Don't worry, Colin isn't going anywhere. And Mrs. O, who sounds *fantabulous* by the way, isn't going anywhere, either. We'll figure it all out."

"Regan..." My throat spasms.

"Yeah, I know. Best friends. Also? I guarantee you Colin lurves you. And if he doesn't, that means he only gets with uggos and you can do better." She pauses and changes the subject. "You know how you saw things with your mom and Colin? That only happens with tons of practice. That doesn't make you a freak! You're amazeballs, with a capital 'A.' Battle scar Beyoncé."

"Yeah, yeah. I really feel 'amazeballs,'" I say dryly.

Griffin notices us and rushes over, ignoring Regan's audible groan. "You guys see the Agon Coil Walk team assignments? Triggs put them up in the common room."

"I requested you, Cassie," Regan says. "Hope my team doesn't suck."

A smile creeps slowly across Griffin's face.

"No." Regan opens her mouth and screams, theatrical and full-throated. Students and teachers around us stop to stare.

I'm about to reach over and put my hand over her mouth when

something pulls me back—fingers, grasping fingers, hot and tight, around my throat—ripping my own scream from me.

"Help!" it screeches.

I twist it in front of me, pushing at its throat as it holds onto mine. Not a thing. A girl—filthy, skin-and-bones, clawing at me. I shriek again, trying desperately to push her away.

"Help me!" the girl wails.

Griffin and Regan pull at her. She releases me and drops to the ground in fetal position, long matted black hair obscuring her face as she moans and whispers to herself.

A guard in a green jumpsuit pushes through a few onlookers. "Back up! Clear out, everyone!" He brushes by Regan and kneels in front of the girl, pressing a hand to her forehead to smooth back her hair. She flinches. "Samara Trefoil. That's your name, right?"

"No names. No games. Don't play with your food," the girl says in a sing-song voice.

Regan grabs my hand and squeezes. I squeeze back, transfixed. The girl launches herself at the guard, grasping at his shoulders to try and remain upright. He hefts her into his arms, and she goes limp.

"Who is she?" Griffin asks the guard as he moves past us. "What happened to her?"

The guard doesn't respond.

"What was that?" I ask. I begin counting, trying to make it to ten. Regan shakes her head helplessly.

When we enter the Mirror Scrying Lab's moonlit expansive terrace, we're a great deal more somber than when we left our Palmistry class. The night's heavy heat is interrupted by the occasional brackish breeze. I walk over to the stone railing and peek down at the darkly glinting river behind Theban Group.

"I wasn't thinking of jumping," I say, catching the worried question in Regan's eyes. I mean it, too. I'm more worried about the scratches on my neck becoming infected, despite the vigorous scrubbing I gave them in the bathroom on the way to the lab.

Regan nods and greets Noah, pointedly moving in the opposite direction of Griffin, the shared Samara Trefoil trauma not enough to solidify a truce.

Who is Samara Trefoil?

The memory of Madame Grey's warning about Theban Group slides through my mind like a ghost, sending a shudder of disquiet through me.

I pull my mirror out of my bag and set it alongside everyone else's on terrace railing as class launches into full swing. Thessaly Nua, our mirror scrying instructor, nods absently at a latecomer—Sebastian—as he enters. We haven't exchanged a word since he escorted me to my dorm, though I see him at least once a day. Awareness crackles throughout my nerve endings as he circles our group, coming to a stop behind me. My reaction irritates me. For some reason he throws me off, upsets my equilibrium.

"Samara Trefoil. What happened?" he murmurs from close behind me, quietly so as not to disrupt Nua's lecture.

"No, I'm Cassandra Morai," I quip.

He steps up so that he's standing next to me and gives me a serious look. He isn't the tallest person in our group, but somehow he looms larger than everyone else.

I sigh. "She jumped out at me and a guard took her away. I'm okay. Sweet of you to care, but don't sweat it."

"I'm a prefect for the initiate class. It's kind of my job to sweat it."

I flush. "I'm good, thanks."

He gives me an inscrutable look and moves to the outskirts of the class. I watch his golden head as he walks away and wonder if he thinks I was being cold as a ploy. The tidal pull of his looks and his position as Jordan Welborne's son is strong, and most people are happy to wreck themselves on his reef. I've watched as a few of my classmates tried the cold shoulder in an attempt to stand apart from the nerd herd and catch his eye. He stares through them with the same obvious disinterest he shows the ones who fawn over him.

It's not a ploy for me, though. I'm awkward enough as it is around normal people, let alone arrogant golden gods. I close my eyes to call up an image of Colin. Comfortable Colin who soothes me instead of throwing my mind onto a giant hyperdrive hamster wheel. I picture him standing in front of me on a very different balcony, his blue eyes trained on my lips. Slowly leaning in until the Spite House's creaks freaked me out. His scent that day: sun and grass and coconut soap.

"Make sure you always... ah, I've lost my train of thought! Where was I?" Ms. Nua lisps, her thick fringe of bangs swinging and pointy chin twitching as she shakes her head.

"Safe scrying," Tessa volunteers, her braces glinting in the moonlight as she smiles.

"Thank you, Tessa! That's right. You wouldn't operate heavy machinery without an eye toward safety, and Scrying is no different. Proper care for your tools is *crucial*. Size and shape don't matter, but the lunar charge you select for your mirror will impact your visions significantly."

"Good thing for you, Griffin! Size doesn't matter," Regan announces. A few kids chuckle.

"I practice safe Scrying with your mom," Griffin responds.

"As you should." Nua nods. "Tonight, we'll be charging your mirrors with this *gorgeous* waxing gibbous moon. The waxing gibbous charge is fantastic for picking up positive visions, happy things! It'll last you about a week, depending on how much you use it. You'll retrieve your mirrors in the morning, and your homework for next class is to Scry something delightful. Yes? Is there a question?"

"Can you charge a mirror with the sun?" a girl with a long plait down her back asks.

"An excellent question, Helen. Sunlight generates too much heat. It's too harsh, so it bounces off. Lunar light is cooler, so it melts into the glass. Yes? You in the back."

"What about dark mirror scrying?" a heavyset boy, Joe, asks.

Nua hesitates. "That's not something we'll be covering. Dark mirror scrying is not permitted at Theban. Yes?"

The same boy points to one of the mirrors on the table. "But this mirror is black."

"Ah!" Nua brightens. "That's an *obsidian* mirror, not a *dark* mirror. Dark mirror scrying has nothing to do with the mirror's color. It has to do with the light, or lack thereof, that you use to charge your mirror... and that... hm. I... I've lost the thread. What were we talking about?"

"Dark mirror scrying," Griffin prompts.

"Oh yes, thank you." Nua warms to her topic. "Any mirror charged with the dark of an eclipse can become a dark mirror. The Gloaming Moon eclipse set for next week is an especially potent one—Magnitude Five! One hundred and three minutes of totality! We won't see another Gloaming Moon for at least seven years."

"Thessaly," Sebastian interjects, warning in his tone.

"So... er... you... that mirror is not a dark mirror is the point. Obsidian mirrors are a matter of preference. Yes."

I glance over at Regan and Noah. Noah puffs out his cheeks and Regan raises her eyebrows in response, her eyes huge fascinated saucers. She scribbles something in her notebook.

"If you're the forgetful type, you'll want to stay away from other lunar charges and stick with *full* moon charges—they're good workhorse charges that last a full month," Nua says. "Gets the job done, but visions aren't as specialized or nuanced. Now that you've set your mirrors out to capture this waxing gibbous charge, let's pick up a pre-charged mirror here on this table and you all try and figure out what kind of charge your mystery mirror has."

"What, like a blind taste test?" Dill asks, as we each select a mirror.

"Not just taste. You'll need to pay attention to what you taste, smell, feel—all of your senses are in play. Not so much with full moons, but certainly with the other phases. Let's see if you can tell the difference between them."

"Oh! Ms. Nua, I'm getting something!" Griffin shouts before anyone has an opportunity to even make an attempt to scry. "There's this really ruggedly handsome guy staring back at me from this mirror." Clearly, Samara Trefoil is no longer weighing on Griffin's mind the way she is mine.

"Your mirror must be broken," Regan says. "That or your eyes."

Griffin turns with a grin. "My eyes work fine, Ronald."

I stare into my mirror, trying to clear my mind. The scratches on my neck are barely visible. The inevitable infection hasn't reached the surface yet. The germs are still feasting and multiplying underneath my skin. They'll trigger a lymphatic reaction soon, leading to redness, swelling, itching as my body tries to fight them off. It won't be enough to stop the infection, though. How long has it been since I got a tetanus shot?

I look around. I can't concentrate. Pict's tutoring, Dr. Ward's exercises—nothing helps. There's too much ricocheting through my mind. Regan looks like she's in the beginning throes of a trance. I make eye contact with a few others who look like they're having a tough time. How am I supposed to walk the Coil if I can't control my thoughts? How am I going to save Colin?

"I'm not getting anything," Joe says, pushing his hair out of his eyes in frustration.

"I wanted you to try. I don't expect everyone to succeed. Full moon-charged mirrors are easier to handle. The other phases take some getting used to. Sometimes you get a nibble on the line and other times..." She looks befuddled for a second. "Other times you... that is... what was I going on about?"

"Fishing," the boy says.

"Right, thank you!" But Nua doesn't seem inclined to elaborate any further.

"Man, your mentor is a fruit loop," Griffin whispers to Tessa. She ignores him. "Ms. Nua, can you tell us more about dark mirrors?"

"I haven't told you anything at all about dark mirrors, so I can hardly tell you *more*, Griffin."

"Right." Griffin looks over at Tessa. "Like I said. Fruit loop."

"Can you stop being so disruptive?" she hisses.

"Lighten up. She'll forget anything I did five minutes later, anyway."

"I'm not Legacy like you and your dumbass friends. You had a family and a community to coach you up. Everything here's new to me. I want to learn. You might not care, but I do."

"Whoa, relax. It's... are you *crying*?" Griffin looks horrified.

Tessa slaps her mirror down on the table and rushes off the terrace, back inside the building.

"Griffin, you're a complete waste-of-space-asshole. Grow up," Regan shouts, running off after Tessa.

Sebastian nods to Nua and halts Noah's pursuit of Regan, then goes rushing off after them himself. Of course he does. *It's kind of my job to sweat it.*

Griffin looks like he just caught a punch. He glances around and locks onto me. "She really thinks I'm...? I thought that was our thing..."

I shrug. Noah shakes his head.

"No, seriously. I know I mess around, but I thought we were having fun," Griffin insists.

"I think you're an asshole," Noah offers.

"Please stop using that word," Nua interjects.

"Your great-grandma teach you that word?" Griffin sneers.

"She sure did. Best used when someone chases away two girls in tears."

"Shut it," Griffin says, wholly without heat. He stares down at his mirror.

Regan and Tessa return sometime later, Tessa's eyes noticeably red. They both ignore Griffin. Sebastian doesn't return.

With no more interruptions, Nua lets us give it one more try.

A few manage to scry out minor visions, casting their lines out into the future and pulling in minnows.

I end up with a waning moon-charged mirror, according to Nua. I don't get much from it, though. Nothing to help with Colin, or explain what my red blessing vision from Pict's office was about, or even just to tell me what happened to Samara Trefoil. No, instead I have a vision of Theodore from the front desk smiling over a cupcake. Not exactly an earth-shattering revelation.

I look over at Griffin, who's glumly staring out across the river. It looks like he finally realized, as Noah so finely put it, that he's an asshole. If so, I think he got the biggest reveal of the class.

15

Button Field, a large Coil-culled courtyard in the center of Theban Group, has gone from feeling like a vast grass ocean to a tiny bathtub, packed to the gills with picnicking scryers attempting to beat the heat. Between the Frisbee playing and sun worshipping, you'd be forgiven for forgetting where we are. Regan has set our blanket out on one of the only spaces left open, the incline leading up to the ring of knotty pines sitting sentry around the basin-shaped park.

I look down at my ICARUSS again and blow my bangs out of my eyes. I have no idea if the spell I've located to help Mrs. O will work, but I've resolved to give it a try tonight. Colin, though... this stupid thing hasn't kicked back a ritual that can help him yet. Closest I've gotten is something to change traffic patterns, and another spell to ward against a broken leg. I hold the ICARUSS in my hand and concentrate again, begging my scryer energy to reel something in that can save him. Colin's emailed video from earlier today runs through my mind. It began with the camera trained on his face as he walked, his smile mischievous and his blue eyes twinkling.

"Hey, Cass! So, while you're over there playing capture the flag or whatever, check out the laugh-a-minute you're missing here." The camera angle turns so a neatly organized shelf of boxes comes into view. "Oh yeah, that's right. Mrs. O's dusty shelf is now unrecognizable. And look at her desk!" He pans over an equally tidy desk, then turns the camera to Mrs. O, who is approaching the office. "Mrs. O, for the cameras please, can you tell Cass how much fun we're having?"

Mrs. O shakes her head. "Cassandra, he's as ridiculous as you. Ninety degrees outside, gorgeous day, and he's in here organizing my office. I'm going to have to pack it all up soon enough anyway, you strange—"

"You're supposed to stick to the script!" Colin yells. Mrs. O gives him a look of tolerant affection, a smile playing about her lips. Colin's mimics Mrs. O's voice, moving the camera as if she's speaking, and her smile widens. "Oh, Cass, this dear boy and I have been having loads of fun in your absence. Why, just yesterday he was juggling a few cans and sent sardine juice everywhere. Wasn't that just the cat's meow?"

Mrs. O laughs. "You're lucky you're such a card or I'd toss you out of here. We miss you, Cassandra. I hope you're having fun, little one."

The camera turns back to Colin. "What she said."

A palm-sized crystal ball rolls alongside my leg, knocking me out of my reverie. Noah sits up from his spot on the blanket. "Sorry about that!"

I roll it back over to him and he lies back down, throwing the ball into the air again. I notice, not for the first time, that he and Regan keep exchanging little loaded glances, and she brushed her hand against his when she thought no one was looking. They think they're slick, but even Griffin caught that one.

My ICARUSS makes a sound, and I eagerly watch the moving icon of wings on the screen until a ritual appears... *Becoming a Crossing Guard.* I set my device down and rub a hand over my face in frustration.

"That's not right!" Regan says. She glares at Griffin, who grins back at her. "People aren't toys, and Triggs said no more scrycasting pranks."

Griffin claws at the loose dirt next to our blanket, digging a small hole, and drops in a sprinkling of herbs. "Relax. We're supposed to be practicing for the Agon, right? Button Field Billiards is how I practice. Okay... red shirt guy with the football over to the duffle bag girl," Griffin says. He spits onto the herbs, buries the whole thing, and whispers something over the hole. He wipes his hand on the blanket, squinting at his red-shirted victim. The guy runs to catch a football, leaping, and landing right in front of the duffle bag Griffin mentioned.

"Almost, Griff," Noah says.

"Patience, young Skywalker."

The guy takes a step back and catches his foot in the bag's strap. He flails as he falls backwards onto a blanket belonging to a pretty girl I've seen in the halls from time to time. The guy jumps up, apologizing, and she smiles, setting down her book, murmuring something reassuring by the looks of it. It isn't more than a few seconds before they're both smiling and settling in for a chat.

"See? That wasn't so bad. I made a love connection, probably," Griffin says.

"What did you sacrifice for that?" I ask.

"Minute off the end of my life." Griffin shrugs when Noah gives him an incredulous look.

"Besides the fact the sacrifice is insane, you had no idea they'd like each other," Regan responds.

"I did. That girl kept eyeballing that dude. I got him to notice her. Bam, love connection." Griffin fires an imaginary arrow, doing his best Cupid.

"Say they do end up together. Maybe there was someone better for her than that guy. Maybe there was somebody better for him. Maybe their lives would have been better before you messed with things you don't understand. They're not puppets," Regan fumes.

"They're perfect for each other. I'm a keen observer of the human condition, Renée."

"Observe this human condition." Regan gives a one-finger salute. "And the name thing is getting old. Work on new material."

"Just because—"

"You guys are like Pict and Ms. Fenice," I interject, driven by my ICARUSS frustration and my fear. If a fall over a backpack cost Griffin a minute of life... I still have no idea what *saving* a life will cost me.

A red blessing approaches. Look to the glass.

"I was reading about that blue moon Ms. Nua mentioned in class. Gloaming Moon. The one next Friday?" Noah murmurs, probably to cut the tension. "Pretty neat. *Scryer's Almanac* says—"

"If we're Pict and Fenice, you two are douchey gameshow contestant blue-hairs," Griffin interjects.

"Can you loan me your *Almanac*?" I ask, letting Noah know I stand in solidarity with other trivia nerds. "I've run through Regan's magazines and need something new."

Noah nods, a smile shining through his light brown eyes.

Regan picks up her Agon study guide. "Let's just get this over with. 'Individual exams before the Coil Walk are designed to measure how well an initiate understands scryer history and theory,'" she reads, "and gauges if one can scry using different tools and methodology. They include a mix of written questions, oral presentations, and some live demonstrations." She groans. "Ugh. Public speaking is the *worst*."

"Is it? Somewhere a starving kid is crying for you," Griffin says.

"Knock it off, Griff! Leave her alone," Noah says, raising his voice.

"I don't need you to fight my battles," Regan snaps. She swallows and softens her tone. "But thank you." Noah puffs up and leans back against the tree.

"Alright, so that covers the exams," Regan continues, flipping ahead in the book to where she's inserted a sticky note. "Then comes the Coil Walk. We go in as a group and we *walk* the thing to try and get to the Laurel Plain. It's at its mildest during the Agon. That's why it's tough but not impossible. Closer you get, better your grade."

"Even still, it's not easy," Griffin says. "If it were, everyone'd be an Oracle. Most people have to hunker down and wait to be fished out by the rescue crews. And my mom told me that when she walked the Coil for the first time, three initiates from her year died. Guess somebody in the group had a mental problem and the Coil fed off that. *Three people gone*, all because of the nightmare in one dude's mind."

Regan looks struck. She gives me a pained look, and I inwardly quake. *I'm okay, I'm okay, okay, okay, okay.*

"I heard that's what happened to Samara Trefoil." Noah makes a face. "Most initiates were pretty much out before whatever was in her head popped off."

There's no way I can walk the Coil. Not now, not if something like that can happen. I've got to escape. I've got to run, get home, get far away.

But not yet.

Milk your training for whatever you can, help Mrs. O, save Colin, and then leave this place far behind.

The thought brings a pang. I've started to finally feel like I belong somewhere. If... *when* I leave, my friendship with Regan will be over.

But that's not what you're here for. I found a ritual to help Mrs. O. Now, I need to figure out how to save Colin.

And what you'll need to sacrifice to make it happen, my mind whispers.

I pluck the guide from Regan's numb fingers and flip through it, hurrying beyond this subject. "According to this, the Coil Walk will push scryers and their abilities to their limits. Most scryers will not reach the Laurel Plain—" Griffin nods and gestures in an I-told-you-so way. "—but those who do will be anointed Oracles. All scryers, regardless of whether they reach the Laurel Plain, may use the Coil to shortcut to any place within Theban Group with relatively little risk of danger after the Agon. Footnote here says that the 'controlled introduction of scryer Initiates to the Coil works to limit or suppress the Coil's immune system response so that scryers may later traverse the Coil. This inoculation is only possible during the Agon.'"

Griffin peers at the book over my shoulder. "What the hell is that?"

"Minotaur," I say. "Mythological half-man, half-bull. If the Coil sucks up what people are afraid of, then I guess it'd draw on what each generation fears."

"Each generation? I'm so scared." Griffin rolls his eyes. "What's it going to give *us*? Bad online dating and global warming? The movie *CATS*?"

"It stores fears, too," Noah adds. "Once something's brought to life in the Coil, it stays there, becomes real. Mr. Khalid told me during our mentor meeting last week that there's a full-on ecosystem in the Coil. Predators and prey, this whole fear-fueled food chain."

"What about that?" Griffin whistles, still peering at the book's illustrations. "Is that a pit filled with spikes? Dude, that's some Indiana Jones shit. Well, Reggie here is a loon, so we're already screwed."

"Maybe *you're* screwed. *We* will be fine," Regan says. She gives me a firm look, willing me to believe, then looks over to Noah. Noah winks at her, and she responds with a small smile.

"What's up with your eye, man?" Griffin says, squinting at Noah.

Noah flushes. "We'll have to stay together, try and control our thoughts, and scry our way through," Noah says firmly, looking downright sunburned. "We're the first class to use the ICARUSS, so we'll have our abilities, each other, and some help."

"And if anyone falls behind, the rest of you have to remember that you can't go back," I say.

"What do you mean 'the rest of *you*?'" Regan asks, eyes narrowed.

"Us. The rest of us," I say. I pick at my thumb.

"Alright, so let's practice," Griffin says. He rummages through our bag of supplies and makes to toss a mirror at Noah.

Noah holds up the tiny crystal ball in his hands. "I'm good with this," he says. He kneels next to me. "Here, Cassie. Let me help you with that." He takes the sticks I've gathered and waves away the matches I hold out, briskly rubbing the sticks together to efficiently build a small fire.

"That was really cool," I say, blowing on the little flame the way he shows me and ignoring the creeping gloom inside me.

Noah shrugs. "No big deal. I was a Scout. Troop 137! Merit badges and all that." Regan looks over at him with interest. Uniforms are her weakness. Even Scout ones, I guess.

Noah and Griffin busy themselves with their crystal balls while Regan reaches for the bag, pulls out a few things, and begins messing with her mirror. I examine the smoke from my fire, reading the flames licking the air and interpreting the crackling sounds. The air around us smells like summer pines and smoke.

"I can build a fire in two seconds, but I'm still not the best at calling on visions." Noah says. "They come when they feel like it."

"Here, try it this way." Regan settles next to Noah and reaches for the ball in his hand. Noah inhales sharply as she leans against him.

Griffin frowns, watching them. "We're supposed to be scrying, not making out."

Noah widens his eyes and gives his head a little shake as if to say, *What the hell.* Griffin goes back to his crystal ball, a frown still etched onto his brow.

"Maybe we should try to bring on visions of danger? I mean, that's what we're going to be looking for in the Coil," Regan says, pressing a dark curl behind her ear.

"Good idea!" Noah says, with a little too much enthusiasm.

If only Colin's feelings were that easy to read. Does he *miss* miss me, or is it like a friend? I squelch the lick of envy and concentrate on being happy for my friends instead.

Regan gives Noah pointers on technique. I tip my water bottle to snuff out my fire, then dump the rest into a small palm-sized copper bowl, along with a dribbling of oil. Scrying the patterns in the rainbow oil slick reveals just as much as the smoke: nothing. I pull my pendulum from around my neck and dangle it over the liquid. When tuning fork-like vibrations ring through my core, I gently blow on the horn-shaped onyx crystal to set it swaying, willing the air from my lungs to lead me to knowledge. The pendulum swings, slowly at first, then picking up momentum until it begins tapping symbols on the lip of the copper bowl. I sketch out each symbol on a pad and consult my ICARUSS to translate the message.

The meaning behind the string of symbols strikes like a hot poker. "Red blessing approaches," I whisper.

Regan and Noah look up at me sharply. I grab for the book I stashed in my bag and with shaking fingers ask a question to verify my scried message. I let the text fall open and run my fingers in circles, waiting for the pull to stop. I read aloud:

"*Death twitches my ear* / '*Live,*' *he says*... / '*I'm coming.*'"

"Well, that sounds like confirmation to me," Griffin says. "Okay, so necromancy, I guess. Now what? Who is it? Who the hell is sacrificing *a person*? When is it? How do we narrow it down?"

Regan looks up from her mirror, her face ashen. "It's Sid. I saw him. Alone in the dark, scared. I don't know what's going to happen, but it's happening *now*."

"Mr. Ford? Where was he?" I ask.

Regan shakes her head.

"We should tell someone. Fast. Maybe they can find him. Help him."

Noah shoves his stuff into his bag and leaps to his feet. "Are you guys coming?"

We race along after him, entering Theban Group's halls, an electric knowledge crackling along my bones. *The red blessing approaches. Look to the glass.*

Griffin flags down a guard. "Hi, yeah, listen, we just had a vision or two about Sid Ford and—"

"Record it in your ICARUSS." The guard yawns as he starts to walk away.

"But it's life and—" Noah calls out.

"There isn't time!" Regan cries. "It's *close,* I have this feeling. Don't you feel it, too? It's happening now!" She turns her huge gray eyes on me. I always have that feeling; it'd be weirder if I didn't feel like everything was about to fall apart.

"Follow me. I know where he is," Griffin says.

We chase after him, following his twisting and turning path—until the feeling of being doused in cold water hits me. Regan gasps.

We're in the Coil.

"Stop!" I shout, blind terror coursing through me. "We've crossed into the Coil. No one try to go backwards. Sebastian told me it's really bad."

The space around us is barren and gray, like the inside of a meat locker scrubbed of carcasses. I can see my breath when I exhale.

"We don't have a scryer escort," I say. "We're not supposed to be here. If this place is bad during the Agon, it's—" I can't bring myself to finish the sentence. I try and clear my thoughts.

Don't think of the time with Sebastian. The hands, hands everywhere, touching, gripping...

We hear a muffled sound. Then another. It comes from all around us, echoing off the metal walls. Griffin and Noah instinctively press closer, their shoulders pressed to mine and Regan's as we huddle together.

"What touched me?" Regan whispers.

"Clear your thoughts, everybody," Noah says.

That is my fault. Stop thinking of it. There are no hands. No hands gripping, pulling, ripping. No hands. No hands. No hands. Hands. Hands.

"What the fuck!" Griffin shouts, touching his cheek, his hand coming away bloody. "What just did that?"

"Everyone, it's okay. It's okay. Clear your thoughts," Noah says again, his tone even. Calm. He takes Regan's hand and pulls it to his chest, placing it over his heart. "It's okay," he repeats to her. He turns and gives me a reassuring look. "We'll be okay. Okay?"

He said it five times. My breathing evens out. It's a sign. I'm taking it as—my OCD is taking it as a sign.

Griffin stares down at the crystal in his hand. "I thought Sid was here. I could've sworn he was..."

I pull out my ICARUSS, sandwiching it between my hands and begging it to spit back a ritual to help find a missing person. It takes a half a second before it sounds and the wings on the screen dissolve into a spell. I whisper the chant and concentrate on Ford, picturing his distinguishing features—the scar on his cheek, his nutty professor dark hair, Regan's extreme affection for him—holding my breath and waiting for a pull in the direction we should take.

"I think it's this way," I say. We press on, farther in but more cautious now, listening, waiting. Some spaces remain steady and others ripple violently like a magician flipping a tablecloth, changing in a blink.

"It's like the dorms," Regan says quietly, "but faster."

"Like a mind-reading chameleon jungle?" I ask. She gives me a small smile.

The walls around us now appear to be made of heavily packed earth and exposed root systems, thick branching arms and fine hair-like tangles lining the surfaces. We reach a crossroads, each way shrouded in darkness. I pull a book from my bag.

"Hope that's a Robert Frost poem you're reading," Noah says with a stark laugh.

"Left," I say. "I think."

Griffin pulls a flashlight from his pack and we shuffle on, reaching a curving staircase that calls to mind the inside of an upside-down lighthouse. Left with nowhere else to go without retreating, we begin to descend, spiraling deeper and deeper. I touch my hands to the walls on either side of me and wrench them back. The surfaces are soft, damp. Griffin's flashlight reveals a white fuzz coating everything, a kind of subterranean moss; the splashing of our careful footfalls in the puddles underfoot are muffled by it. We reach the bottom, and Regan shrieks.

The light from Griffin's flashlight bounces off of an enormous mirror planted in the center of the broad room. Sid Ford kneels in front of it—a lightning-shaped black blade pressed to his throat. A black-shrouded figure is holding the blade, the vicious serrated edge poised to tear through the tender flesh of his neck.

"Stop!" Regan screams.

The figure peers at us, a horrible ghoulish white skeletal mask obscuring its face. The dark cloak almost makes it look like it's a floating disembodied head. The figure shifts, lifting the blade an inch or so away from Ford's neck. Griffin takes a step forward, wielding his little flashlight.

"Leave him alone!" He waves the flashlight back and forth like a lightsaber. It would be comical if the situation wasn't so fraught.

The skeleton-faced figure hesitates and breaks off into a run, robe floating behind it until it disappears into the dark depths of the Coil.

Ford wobbles on his knees, as if swaying to music we can't hear, his face contorted in pain.

"Sid! Sid, are you okay?" Regan asks. We approach and she sets a hand on his shoulder. At her touch, Ford convulses and drops to the ground, writhing like a beached fish.

"Help him!" Regan turns to us wildly. Noah reaches down and flips Ford onto his back. Ford's eyes are rolled back in his head. His tongue lolls out of his mouth. The walls around us ripple wildly, snapping to hospital walls and back again.

Griffin grabs Ford around the arms, hefting him up against his chest. He whispers something over and over, holding Ford until the quaking stops. Ford pulls away and starts retching. I grimace and look away.

"What did you do?" Noah asks Griffin.

"I told him he was alright. I *willed* him to be alright." Griffin shrugs. Regan is staring at Griffin in a way I've never seen from her. He shrugs again and self-consciously clears his throat. "We shouldn't be in here. We need to get out. Now."

"Here, I'll get his feet and you get his arms," Noah says. They try to lift Ford but only manage a foot or so before he drops back to the ground.

"He's heavy, man," Griffin says.

"Lift with your knees," Noah says. "It's not that bad."

Griffin grunts as he hefts Ford up. "Pretty sure muscle memory is my problem. I've never had muscles, so they have no memory."

Ford moans, startling Noah and Griffin into dropping him again. He lands with a splash in a puddle partially of his own making.

"Watch it!" Regan scolds, rushing to Ford's side. "Sid. It's me, Regan. Can you hear me?"

He moans again, as if in extreme pain, then opens eyes wild with fear. "No. It won't work. You need—"

"You're safe, Sid, it's us. You're okay." Regan smooths the shock of messy hair back from his forehead. Ford blinks, awareness dawning. The scar on his face is bone white.

"What's happening? Where are we?"

"You were attacked," I tell him when he looks over at the rest of us.

"Do you remember anything?" Regan asks.

Ford stands with an effort, waving away Noah's offer of help. He looks ahead. "We're in the Coil? You came in here without help? Before the Agon? You could have been—how did you find me?" He sways and Regan catches him under the arm. "Thank you. All of you. Let me get us out of here."

Ford closes his eyes. When he opens them, we follow his lead, hand in hand.

The space around us continues to change, this time in small, almost imperceptible ways. We do have a scryer escort now, after all.

"It's just up here. Blank your thoughts and follow close behind," Ford says.

I look up at him. There's a sadness fixed to his expression that I recognize. I remember it on Dad's face after Mom died, and I see it in the mirror every day.

A tremendous, bone-weary loss: he's in mourning.

16

I f heaven has a waiting room, it looks like this.

I'm sitting on a Clorox white chair in a room full of blindingly snowy walls. On the glass table in front of me is an alabaster vase of perfect white calla lilies. Everything is bright, and clean, and orderly.

Griffin leans forward and presses one thumb to the clear glass, leaving behind a fat fingerprint. He smiles in satisfaction and waggles his eyebrows at me. I'm torn between smiling back and hunting for Windex. Instead, I reach over and grab a tissue, handing it to him. "You've got dried blood on your cheek."

Agatha Triggs, Welborne's wire-thin assistant, appears, her spine as rigid as a bow the second before its arrow is loosed. "You can wash up after your meeting. Come with me." She stalks away, and we file behind her down a glass-lined hall of bustling offices and workspaces.

"This is like a zoo for rich people," Griffin says, eyeing a few well-dressed Oracles seated around a conference room table as we pass. Noah swallows a laugh. We're all wiped, but infected with a kind of triumphant euphoria. We saved a man's life.

"Very amusing, Mr. Eden," Triggs says, as we reach the end of the hall. Her face, framed by that iron-colored helmet of hair, is so smooth and unlined it looks like she's never found anything remotely amusing in her life. She opens the door. "In you go."

The office is large and bright, all steel and glass and swaths of whites and reds. Sebastian is seated across a desk from his father.

"What matters is what you think—" Sebastian is saying. He notices us and falls silent, leaning back in his chair.

Jordan Welborne smiles his large-toothed smile at us and stands. "Regan, Cassandra, Griffin, and Noah, right? Sebastian, did you want to stay, too?" Welborne's gaze is filled with fatherly warmth.

I miss my dad.

"No. Thank you. I've got things to take care of." Sebastian stands and gives me a sideways glance as he departs, pausing only to prop the door open for Aunt Bree as she enters. She's dressed in a red so vivid she looks like a bloodstain even in a room full of crimsons.

Triggs leads us all to a sitting area. After we've all found our chairs, Welborne says, "I hear you four have had an ordeal."

Bree has claimed the seat next to his. She raises a brow at me. "My niece is full of surprises."

"Sidney Ford would not be here today if not for your bravery. From the bottom of our hearts, we want to thank you," Welborne says.

"Did you guys catch the freakshow who tried to take him out?" Griffin asks.

"No, but I'm not surprised. The Coil produces all manner of creatures. For our protection, of course. It should be safe for scryers who have completed the Agon, but nothing is ever certain."

"Creatures?" I ask. "I thought it was a person."

Every head in the room whips toward me.

"What gave you that impression?" Welborne asks, frowning. "And the rest of you? What did you think?" he asks.

"It looked like a skeleton-faced nightmare ready to slice into a dude's throat. That's what I thought," Griffin says. Noah nods.

"Well, whatever it was, it's gone now. Sid is safe," Aunt Bree says. "If you can't tell us anything else—"

"Red blessing!" I interject. "I—I scryed some stuff about a red blessing. Twice. Once before orientation and again right before we saved Ford. A red blessing is a human sacrifice for a scryer ritual, right? That's what my visions were about?"

Aunt Bree freezes and looks to Welborne. His brow knits further and he rubs his lantern jaw.

"Why didn't you bring this up before today?" Triggs asks, pawing through her ICARUSS. "There is *nothing* in the ICARUSS mainframe about any red blessing visions by anyone. What else are you withholding?"

"It may have been a woman," Regan blurts, clearly thinking of du Lac. "I'm not sure, but... it was a feeling."

"This is outrageous. I apologize, Mr. Welborne. I will personally handle their re-interrogation," Triggs says.

Griffin groans. "We sat through the Spanish inquisition with that girl at the front desk already."

"It's okay, Agatha." Welborne laughs. "I'll go and interview Sid myself when he's had a chance to rest. They've sedated him. If there is more to this story, I'll find out when he wakes. Sound good?" He smiles at us. "Now for the fun part. As a thank you for saving an instructor, and using your scrying abilities to do it to boot, we are exempting you from the individual Agon assessments."

"Sick!" Griffin crows.

"It is indeed. First time Theban Group has ever done so as far back as I can trace. I do hope this token shows how appreciative we are. You'll still need to walk the Coil as a team, of course—I'd exempt you from even that if I could, but your venture into it today wasn't enough to render the Coil safe for you. And, anyway, you'll want your shot at becoming an Oracle. Based on how well you performed as a group getting to Sid's side, I'm sure it won't be an issue for you." He stands, and we follow suit. "Now! I'd better get back to running this place, and you'd better get back to your studies." He shakes our hands with a smile.

When he walks off toward his desk, Triggs bustles us toward the door.

"They're not taking this seriously," Regan whispers, reading my mind. "The red blessing stuff... any of it. If it was a person—if it was du Lac—Sid is still in danger."

"We'll protect him," Noah says, reaching out to comfort Regan. Griffin rolls his eyes and trudges forward.

Aunt Bree follows us out and looks me up and down, taking in my appearance for the first time. She shudders delicately and pulls me aside. I wave Regan on.

"Did you leave anything else out? Anything at all? Details you might deem unimportant may be critical," she says. "Did he say anything?"

"No, he was out of it. He didn't—" I stop, frowning.

"What?"

"I was going to say he didn't say anything, but he did. In the Coil. After that thing ran away, he was scared and said something like, 'It won't work.'"

Aunt Bree frowns. "Poor Sidney," she whispers, looking truly saddened. It's the most potent flash of humanity I've ever seen out of her. I feel bad for her. She gazes sightlessly at Welborne's office glass door, rubbing her lip unconsciously with her thumb, before straightening. "Your search history on the ICARUSS has raised a red flag."

"My search—wait, you're *spying* on me?"

"Cassandra, don't be naïve. If you're using an organization's device, always assume someone is watching your communications. *Anything* life and death gets flagged at Theban. Now, why don't you explain so that I can smooth over the situation?"

"There's nothing to explain."

"Are you trying to protect Sidney? Is that why you're searching for that ritual?"

"No. It had nothing to do with him. I was looking up ways to try and help someone else."

"Who? And to do what, exactly?"

"Live. I'm trying to save someone's life. I saw them die in a vision. It's not Ford."

Aunt Bree peers at me suspiciously. Then her expression clears. "You can't," she says simply.

I fist my hands. "What do you mean?"

"I mean that you can't save someone destined to die."

"I have to!"

"No, Cassandra. This isn't me assuming, correctly, that you lack the ability. This isn't your 'believe in yourself and prove Aunt Bree wrong' moment of truth. There is no way that you can avert a foreseen death. It's too big a change. Leave it alone."

"We saved Ford," I say.

"You didn't see a vision of him *dying*, you sensed danger, a blood sacrifice. There's a difference."

"There has to be a way!" I take a step back, blood thundering in my ears.

"There isn't." She shrugs.

"And I wondered why Dad can't stand you." My chest constricts. *There has to be something.*

"And here I thought we were getting on these days. But oh, I've missed you! The surly teenage attitude, the facial expressions sure to help that cabbage patch of premature wrinkles along... you're so predictable, Cassandra. My best advice, not that you asked for it? Make your peace with this. There's nothing you can do." She smiles. I wonder if it makes me a bad person that I'm happy to see she has lipstick on her teeth.

I force myself to keep it in, to not let it show. The hurt. The dread. The rising urge to knock five times.

When Aunt Bree reenters Welborne's office and saunters toward his desk, I give in to all three.

MRS. O.

I have the ritual to try and save her building. I have the things I need for the ritual. I've only scrycasted for small things, and I've been scared to try it before now, but I have to give it a go sooner or later. If I can't stop Mrs. O's move, there's no way I can save Colin. And I'm still trying for that, Aunt Bree be damned.

I pull a basket loaded with ritual supplies out from under my bed. It's a weird collection of things, mostly stuff Bacchy gathered for me, like evaporated seawater salt, rope from a stubborn mule's lead, and wormwood leaves. There's also the picture of the developer that I pulled off the internet, and the letter with his contact info I swiped from Mrs. O. A second basket joins the first, loaded with more odds and ends. Bacchy told me the jar of tiny pink eggs would've never hatched into birds, but I still feel awful about having to smash them.

I wipe my damp palms on my pants before scrolling through the instructions on my ICARUSS and try not to let my usual crazy thinking intrude while I mix up the ingredients I need.

First, purification. I move to my bathroom and fill up the tub with cold water. I'm a pro at cleansing rituals, but that's not something to be proud of. I look down at my hands with a sigh and sprinkle a few of the herbs onto the water. The smell reminds me of damp leaves revealed by a snow melt.

I strip and step into the tub, immediately plunging below the water and holding my breath as I mentally tick off the time my ICARUSS specified. My lungs burn and my body shakes from the cold, but I hold the line until I hit that number. When I burst up from the water and wipe the rivulets from my eyes and face, my teeth chatter so hard I'm shocked my jaw doesn't break. I throw on a robe and pad barefoot back into my room, leaving a trail of wet footprints behind me.

One liberally poured salt circle, burnt pile of herbs and twigs, and incantation later, and I'm ready for the sacrifice. This one calls for blood. *Super.* At least it isn't a red blessing's worth.

I cut five strips of fabric from the shirt Mrs. O bought me for Christmas last year and set them aside. Then I take my ritual knife and inhale deeply.

Now or never.

I hiss against the pain as I draw the blade down one finger to the place where it meets my palm. A scarlet line follows the blade's path, the blood beading quickly. It's a superficial cut, but one that has me picturing all sorts of Coil germs invading into my body. I wrap a strip of the shirt around my wounded finger like a maypole and repeat the slicing and wrapping with my other four fingers.

When my blood has saturated the strips, I remove them and tie them together with the rope to bind Mrs. O to me. Then I drop it all into a little pan.

"With this blood / I will arrange / My required future change," I say in a strong, steady voice. "Bind her here / Bind her near / Remove the obstacle we fear."

I light a match and toss it on top of the pan; the five blood-damp strips catch right away, flaring a lime green color and reeking of decaying roadkill and heavy rainfall. I grab the smoking pan's handle and rush it to my open window, placing it on the sill and waving the smoke outside.

The printout of Mrs. O's tormenter—the developer—is added to the pile, along with the letter I stole from her. It catches and sparks purple. I imagine Mrs. O's developer dropping his bid for her property. I picture his eminent domain case going away. I envision it over and over so many times, each time identical to the last, that when I open my eyes, I can't tell if I'm remembering something that's already happened.

The flame goes out suddenly, like a birthday candle in a windstorm. I grab for a washcloth and press it to my throbbing hand, staring out at the silent street of my neighborhood from home.

And I hope.

17

〜

A dragonfly as big as my forearm flits in front of me. It hovers for a moment, massive eye reflecting the street light I'm standing under, before it zips away into the churning, swirling dark. Another halo of light appears ahead of me, and the dragonfly waits, its beating wings an aquamarine blur.

I follow, with dread but unable to resist, from one street light to another as they flick on ahead and extinguish behind me. No going back.

Suddenly, the light that next pierces the night is at the top of a long staircase. I climb, but the dragonfly is gone by the time I reach the top. The door in front of me creaks open, like every horror movie ever made.

I'm in an entryway I've never been in before, but there is something familiar about this place. I run my fingers over a delicate hall table. A vase of fragrant black orchids sits in the center. To its right is a bowl of rotting oranges.

My stomach rumbles. Naturally, I move to the kitchen. A plate piled high calls to me, but as I approach, it blows away, crumbling to dust. I grab at a loaf of bread next to the plate, but it squeezes through my hands like wet sand.

Humming—a gentle, soft sound, vaguely like a lullaby—is coming from somewhere in the house. I head back the way I came and climb the stairs, higher and higher still, until I reach an open door and step through.

It feels as though the whole of the universe is curving around me, a canopy of light punching through dark, galactic swirls all rotating at a dizzying speed.

The humming again. I climb over a small barrier to my right, and there, in the pale light, is my mother.

I reach out to her. Her hair is longer than I've seen it. It flows around her like a shroud. Her humming stops.

"Cassie." Her voice is music. I rush to her and she enfolds me in her arms. It is quiet there. It shuts out the light.

"Time to choose," she whispers, pulling away. She lifts her hands, and in her outstretched left palm is a fistful of grapes, in her right a lush red fruit resembling a plum. I grab for the strange plum eagerly, my teeth piercing the firm skin, the thick ripe juices coating my tongue. It tastes of iron. I drop it, gagging, and look down at my hands. They're stained red.

She smiles with my mother's mouth, a sad smile, but it's not her, and she parts her curtain of hair to reveal a dripping chest cavity, ribs splayed like a butterfly's wings, the center devoid of its heart. "I'd give my heart for you. What will you give for him?" she whispers.

I stumble back. The juices bubble up, blood, pouring past my lips, running down my neck. My teeth begin crumbling in my mouth, and my hands fly up, trying to keep them from falling out.

"Easy! You're okay. It's a dream. It's not real," I dimly hear a *familiar voice say.*

"Just because it's a dream doesn't mean it's not real," a second voice says.

"Not helping, Nox," the first voice says dryly.

———

MY EYES FLY OPEN. I SHRIEK AND CLAW AND KICK. I'M pressed against a strong chest. A pair of arms tighten around me, holding me.

"That's not my mom! It's not her," I sob.

"I know. It's okay." A hand moves in soothing small circles on my back. He whispers comforting nonsensical words and phrases in my ear as my sobs ease into sniffles. A few shuttering breaths and all is quiet.

Disoriented, I grimace and swallow to wash way the iron taste lingering in my mouth. And for the first time, I wonder whose embrace I'm in. I don't even remember why I'm being held in the first place.

I take a breath. He smells like fresh linen and sneaking out after dark. I look up.

"You smell good," I say, and clap a hand over my mouth.

Sebastian's dimple flashes. "You, too."

I hear unkind laughter and realize my entire Babylonian Dream Scrying class is now awake and staring at me. I quickly push apart from Sebastian and comb a hand through my sleep-ruffled hair.

How did I end up in his arms? I look around, then down at my cot and scratchy green blankets. I remember anointing myself with oils the way Luke Nox showed us. I glance over at our swarthy instructor and down at my hand. I remember writing out Colin's name in ash on my palm after burning my dream questions... the images from my dream come rushing back to me. My eyes sting. Noah and Regan have rushed over and planted themselves on my cot like guards, Regan at my head and Noah at my feet. I wave away their concerns, but my eyes well again.

"How about I take her out so she can compose herself?" I hear Sebastian say.

"Yes, sounds like an excellent idea. Next time I lunch with your father, I'll be sure to tell him you're an ideal prefect." Luke claps his hands and turns. "Everyone else, please record anything from your dreams you can remember. Hurry now, before you forget! We'll spend the rest of the class analyzing the symbolism."

I glance around at my busily writing classmates and avoid making eye contact with the few remaining gawkers.

"Can I... can I wash my face... and stuff first?" I ask Sebastian.

"Of course," he says, firmly but still gently.

My cheeks burn. I grab my bag and run off to the restroom to make myself as presentable as possible. Sebastian is waiting for me when I emerge, and I glance back and catch the huge grin and thumbs up Regan gives me. At least one of us is over my episode.

"Don't forget, I'm stopping by your room later for *some tea*," she calls.

I follow Sebastian out. What do you say after completely flipping out in front of someone? And after waking up on his lap? I pick at my thumb. "I'm sorry about..."

"Don't apologize."

"I'm pretty sure I hit you," I insist.

"I'm pretty sure you did, too."

There's a red mark high on his cheekbone, right under his eye, that I think I'm responsible for. I wilt inside.

Sebastian sees something in my expression and pulls me along. My hand feels small in his. "There are a couple of people you should meet." He turns down a tight pathway and pushes open a heavy metal door. I don't examine why I don't mind holding his hand too closely.

Every head in the cafeteria-like space swivels, except the one belonging to the dead animal lying on the stainless steel table. A heavily scowling man has his arms elbow deep in the animal's stomach, his thick arm hair glistening with fluids I'd rather not think about.

"How many times, Sebastian? How many times, I ask?"

"Vencel." Sebastian's tone is firm but conciliatory. "I thought Haruspicy only met on Tuesdays. It won't happen again."

"Nem. You say this before, but you still treat this place as your playground." He pulls his arms out of the carcass and props one on his smocked hips, the other picking up and brandishing a large butcher's knife. A few of the students standing around the table, looking like residents observing a surgeon at work, wisely move out of his way as he takes a step toward us. "You keep it up and you be on this table instead of Aneska."

"You named that thing before you killed it?" one slightly green-looking girl asks in a small voice.

"Nem! I did not kill this animal. Management crybabies worry about animal feelings! Sacrifice is bad now. Bah! This—" He gestures to the animal in disgust. "—this animal die of natural causes."

Sebastian tilts his head toward the exit across the room. Still holding my hand, he pulls me along, moving slowly to avoid attracting Vencel's notice again.

"Is there, like, an animal hospice you stroll up to for fresh victims?" Griffin drawls. He smiles when he catches my eye. Everyone laughs at Griffin's comment, which clearly doesn't sit well with Vencel. Griffin, on the other hand, grins, clearly pleased with himself.

"Funny guy! You're lucky Splanchomancy is a crime these days, my comedian friend." Vencel slams his butcher knife down blade first into the counter. It sticks.

"What is Splanchomancy?" Griffin asks.

Vencel smiles. "Splanchomancy is, you know, looking at the insides of human sacrifices. *Virgin* human sacrifices. You would be perfect for this. Igen?"

The room erupts in laughter, much to Griffin's chagrin, none laughing louder than Vencel at his own joke. Vencel's guffaws abruptly end as he scowls and shouts, "Enough! No more laughing. Joke is over." The class falls immediately silent.

Sebastian is pushing at the door when a knife whizzes by our heads, vibrating in the wood frame.

"I don't care who your father is. No more, Sebastian! Igen?"

"Igen, Vencel. Good lord. Igen." Sebastian slams the door shut behind us and leans back against it, rolling his head along the door to look at me. "That hulking Hungarian is an expert with knives. You were never in any danger. And he wasn't who I wanted you to meet, by the way."

I let out a shaky laugh. "What kinds of weapons will *they* have?"

His lip quirks. "Caffeine and gossip. Much more dangerous."

WE ENTER A ROOM SO THICK WITH SMOKE THAT FOR A moment I'm afraid it's on fire. Sebastian throws open a window, scattering some roosting pigeons.

"What was that?"

"Sounded like birds."

"You two sound like birds."

Three women's rasping voices sound in rapid succession, the last archly sarcastic.

"Don't be nasty, Felda."

The breeze helps thin the smoke to a filmy haze, and I spy three elderly women seated on plastic-encased colorful sofas. The women are arranged around a low table, a basin of sand in its center. There is a moat of tiny overturned coffee cups and discarded sunflower seed shells surrounding the sand, and an outlandishly large hookah pipe resting on the ground.

"It's me, ladies," Sebastian announces. Then, softly, just to me, "Double, double, toil and trouble."

"I heard that, you scamp. We are not witches!" A woman who looks like a Pomeranian chuckles, a puffy cloud of graying hair bopping around her narrow face. I recognize her voice as the one who lectured the woman she called Felda.

"He didn't say we were witches, Emina. He was reciting a poem," says a starving greyhound of a woman.

"No, he was quoting Shakespeare, Gelisa," Emina says. "Although with Shakespeare's use of iambic pentameter, and his mix of prose and verse, one could make the argument it is poetry!"

"What do you know about Shakespeare?" scoffs that third sarcastic voice, belonging to a woman who looks like a bulldog. Process of elimination suggests that this is Felda.

"I know plenty about Shakespeare, Felda, because I pick up a book now and again," Emina replies mildly. She picks up her tiny coffee cup and brings an eyeglass up to her eye to peer inside.

"They read Turkish coffee cups," Sebastian says in a low voice, as we take seats opposite them. Then, louder, "Sorry to interrupt..."

"You haven't interrupted anything. Except maybe their yapping," the sarcastic bulldog, Felda, says.

Gelisa snorts. "Yapping is what *you* do best, Felda."

"Please, both of you. Decorum. We have company," Emina lectures.

I throw a look at Sebastian. His lips are twitching, another crack in his poker face.

"Who's your lovely little friend, Sebastian?" Emina asks.

"This is Cassandra. She's one of the new Initiates."

"Clearly she's his new chicky, Emina," Gelisa says.

My cheeks go hot. "I am not—"

"Well, she seems sweet. Doesn't say much, though," Emina says.

"Maybe that's because she can't get a word in edgewise with you two blabbing," Felda snaps as she stares into her upside-down cup. She grabs the eyeglass from Emina. "I'm not getting a thing out of this cup." She picks up a hookah hose and attempts to blow a smoke ring.

"You have to speak up if you want to keep his attention, dear," Gelisa offers, and pats my hand. The dizzying speed with which they bicker and change subjects has me fighting to tamp down a hysterical giggling fit. My head throbs.

Gelisa picks up her cup. "My cup has a bird." Her brows are knitted together with extreme concentration as she looks down at the cup in her hand. She demands the eyeglass from Felda.

"*Is* she your girlfriend?" Emina smiles up at Sebastian.

"I'm not—" I begin again.

"She must be special if you're settling down, you scamp. No more mucking about with all those girls," Gelisa interjects.

"Or the boys. How he juggled them all, I'll never know," Felda says, pulling on the hookah again.

"Oh, that's lovely, both of you. What a thing to say in front of his new girlfriend!" Emina sighs. "'Nice to meet you. You're dating a tom-jones.' What's wrong with you two?"

"Well, you're the one who called him a tom-jones," Felda snaps.

"What's a tom-jones?" I ask, my curiosity getting the better of me.

"Word from long before your time, dear. Means he's a bit of a whore." Gelisa peers through her looking glass down at her cup. "My cup has two birds, actually."

"I didn't call him a tom-jones, Felda. I was saying that's what *you* two were saying."

"I never called him a tom-jones, Emina," Gelisa huffs.

"Can we not?" Sebastian sighs.

"You implied it, then made it worse by calling him an outright whore," Emina says. She shrinks in her seat, chastised, when Sebastian gives her an incredulous look.

Felda snatches the looking glass from Gelisa and looks at her cup again. "My cup actually has a bird too," Felda guffaws. "I'll be damned."

"Ladies, I brought Cassandra here for a reason." Sebastian looks mildly exasperated. "She had a pretty traumatic sleep scrying session. I thought, considering you three are omen reading experts—" The women sit up and preen. "—you might help her decipher what she saw. It was intense enough that I figured she wouldn't want to dissect it in front of the class."

"I always knew you had it in you to be a thoughtful boyfriend, Bastian." Emina leans over to cup his cheek lovingly.

"He's devoted, isn't he? How romantic. Reformed rakes make the best partners," Gelisa sighs.

"What do you remember from your dream?" Felda asks.

"I..." I look over at Sebastian and he nods encouragingly. The dream was an emotional Molotov cocktail, and remembering brings on an echo of that feeling, but the details pour out of me like a confession. They all wince when I mention eating. I finish up quickly, telling them what my faux dream mother said before my teeth fell out.

Emina, Gelisa, and Felda immediately stand and rest their hands on my head, probing.

When they release me, they sink back into their seats and their graying heads—one slick, one fuzzy, one shortly spiked—come together as they huddle to confer.

"You feel the vibration? And dragonfly is clearly—" I hear Gelisa say.

"The teeth... we all know that's—" Emina says.

When they conclude their whispered debate, they sit up as one. Emina rakes a small copper coffee pot through the hot sand and pours it out, pressing a cup on me.

"My dear, I think we've arrived at an interpretation. Keep in mind this isn't an exact science," Emina says.

"Death and deceit. They'll come from those close," Felda says.

"You couldn't soften the blow a little, Felda? Really?" Emina cries.

"What good would sugar-coating it do? Rip the Band-Aid off. Best way."

Emina ignores her. "There is one thing, though, that might help."

Gelisa pushes the cup I'm holding to my lips. "Drink!"

I slurp the coffee down, eyes wide as I wait for Emina to continue. It's strong and thick, with a slightly bitter, nutty taste. Gelisa whisks the cup away and turns it upside down on the saucer when I finish.

"There's something you want. Desperately. But the sacrifice is too great," Emina says.

"*Too* great," Gelisa echoes.

My heartbeat is a sledgehammer strike against my ribs. Colin's royal blue eyes, his lopsided teasing grin, flash through my mind.

"That's for her to decide," Felda scolds. She turns to me. "If you try, if you still want it, your dream's omens have a message for you: 'one key to see.'"

"What does that mean?" Sebastian asks.

"Not a clue," Felda says.

"You forgot to mention the red blessing," Gelisa scolds.

"Didn't forget nothing. You just mentioned it," Felda says.

"I was part of a group that helped save Ford..." I begin.

"Oh, yes, we heard about that," Emina says.

"And right before that, I had a few visions of red bless—"

"Must be it, then. Good to know," Felda interrupts.

"You know, scamp, I bet this girl solves that problem we talked about. Your father's people will have to take you seriously if you cut back on all that carousing," Gelisa whispers, quite audibly. Sebastian lips tighten.

Emina picks up her coffee cup and her looking glass. "My cup has a bird, too," she says with a puzzled expression.

For the first time since we entered, the room is silent. It stretches as they pass their cups and the eyeglass back and forth to each other. Felda grabs for my overturned cup.

"It's not ready yet, Felda!" Gelisa cries.

"Ready enough," Felda says.

"What are they doing?" I ask Sebastian.

"The coffee grinds. They coagulate on the bottom of your cup as you drink and drip down when you turn the cup over; they form symbols. They read the symbols."

"There's a lot to unpack in this cup, but no time. They're flocking!" Felda says, passing the cup to Emina. They all heave to their feet.

"It was nice..." Emina begins.

"It was a pleasure..." Gelisa over-talks her.

"We need to go," Felda offers bluntly. "Got to get this to Processing."

"Why don't you use the ICARUSS to send it?" Sebastian asks.

"We don't trust technology. Never have. And you shouldn't, either. It's a fat lot of tommyrot no self-respecting scryer would ever use. No offense to your father. We didn't even trust the pneumatic tubes," Felda says.

"Fair enough. Thanks for your help," Sebastian calls out to their rapidly retreating forms. They each wave a hand over their respective gray heads on their way out the door.

I count myself back from the edge, picking at my thumb. Sebastian bends to scoop a handful of sunflower seeds and leans back in his seat. "You alright?"

I rub at my eyes, trying to soothe the pain camped behind them. "Why are you being nice to me?"

I open my eyes, flushing when I take in his unmoved expression. "The dream was rough, so I'll let that slide. Do you know what they were referring to? The sacrifice being too great?"

"No."

He cocks an eyebrow, and I can see it in those peridot eyes the exact green of my summer birthstone: a wall is coming up, a draw-bridge, that's been missing for the last half hour.

"Thank you, by the way. For bringing me here. For introducing me," I say in a rush. I tell myself it's to soften my churlishness and *not* to draw the real him back out. "I liked them."

"They're sweethearts. Insane, but fantastic omen readers if you can pin them down long enough to get it out of them. They liked you, too," he offers stiffly.

It's so petty, but I can't stop myself from saying, "I think they got the wrong idea about me and you, though."

"Don't worry about that." He shakes up the remaining seeds in his palm.

"They won't spread...?"

"They'll tell everyone. Huge gossips."

"But you said not to worry!"

"Most people believe what they want anyway. Why worry? Plus, Vencel's entire class saw you holding my hand. The rumor was unavoidable." Sebastian shrugs. "The old girls don't mean any harm. They just can't help themselves. All that coffee has them jacked up." There's a note of gruff affection in his tone.

Regan had whispered that Sebastian looked "effing gorg" after spotting him in our dream Scrying class today. He was closing a far-flung window shade with a pole, and his face was illuminated by the sunbeam he was attempting to snuff out before our "Morphean

Drop" (fancy Luke Nox-speak for nap). His shirt rode up with his reach, exposing a hint of rippling belly and a golden dusting of hair at the base of his stomach, and Regan insisted that—although she was firmly Team Colin "in all caps"—I had to be dead not to feel a flutter of *something*. I brushed her off at the time, but looking at him now, I begrudgingly have to admit she's right. And if I'm being honest, competing with my upset over the dream and everything else going on is the *teensiest* bit of feverish glee that people might think someone like Sebastian could actually be interested in someone like me. Disastrous, OCD-pudding-brained me. It doesn't mean I want him and don't worship Colin. It's just... I frown, feeling disloyal.

Sebastian misinterprets my expression. "Your mom... she's not with us?"

I nod curtly. "She passed a couple of years ago."

Sebastian looks down. "Mine passed six years ago." His expression doesn't invite comment, so I don't offer one despite how enormous his confession feels. His next comment rips the wind from those sails. "You probably already knew that. But the point is, once you've mastered your thoughts, your dreams will find someone else to use as a messenger. Mine did."

I swallow and pick at my thumb again.

"What did you do to your hand?" he asks, nodding at my bandaged fingers.

"Accident with my ritual blade."

"It was fine the other day."

"When I saw you in your dad's office, you mean?" I decide to deflect, not wanting to discuss Mrs. O. "Your dad seems nice."

"He is."

"Were you guys always close? Or did you become closer when your mom passed?"

"You don't have to go back to class," Sebastian says suddenly. "Skip. Go read. Take a bath. Or we can hang out." He moves off his sofa with a squeak of plastic and holds out a hand.

I stand without assistance. He's close enough I can smell the crisp soap on his skin, his unique Sebastian scent. "I don't need a pity hang."

"Pity hang?" he repeats, his lips quirking.

"I can't skip class. I need to get back." *Pity hang?* I sound like I resent his lack of attention. Embarrassing.

"Careful, Cassie. You always do what you're supposed to?"

"You think you're going to *neg* me into coming?"

Sebastian laughs, really laughs, and it changes his whole face. He looks much younger, softer. "I guess not."

"Why *are* you being so nice to me? Doesn't seem like your thing."

He sobers, but a hint of smile lurks in his eyes. "You're not special, if that's what you're asking. I comforted that girl in your mirror scrying lab. I helped you to your dorm that first day. Being nice is more 'my thing' than you give me credit for."

"Yeah, nice people always start a sentence with, 'you're not special.'"

I spy Sebastian's dimple before he turns on his heel, insisting I follow him to a Coil shortcut. He claims it's to avoid a return trek through Vencel's class, but I wouldn't be shocked if it's to get rid of me quicker. He dangles the promise of Coil Walk tips when I balk, and I relent in the hopes of learning something to help my friends during the Agon. When my Coil-induced shivering has subsided, and my good hand is warm in his own, he says, "You're going to lead us to your class. But you can't rely on your eyes in here. This place is always churning, and time and space are warped. The route you take, the scenery, will be different from hour to hour or second to second. You need to follow your scryer gut to make it through."

I can just hear Griffin saying something about Magpie meat pies and scryer guts. "Is that what that blueprint thing was? My scryer gut telling me where to go?"

"You get a gold star."

I take in the placid English garden-like area around us. Stable. "Okay, so I just picture our class and—"

"I'm taking your sticker back. I just told you you can't rely on your eyes, and that includes past memories of what you've seen. When you're thrown in here for the Coil Walk and told to find the Laurel Plain, how are you supposed to tether yourself to somewhere you've never laid eyes on? You don't use your sight in here. You use your *sight*."

"Homonyms," I mutter. I miss Trivonometry. I miss Dad.

"What?"

"Nothing. How do I use my *sight* to get to a place I've never seen, then?"

"You concentrate on the *feeling* of being there. If your goal is the Laurel Plain, you'd feel what it is to belong. The feeling of victory. Control. The knowledge that you're one of the few in the world who can do what you do. *That's* how you chart your course. Your ICARUSS has a tether feature that'll help, but the blueprints should be your backup."

"Alright. What else do I need to know to get us to my class, then?"

"Lots, but experience is the best teacher." He stops. "Start with the feel of yourself in Nox's class. The mini airplane hangar look to it is one thing, but there's an airiness to the space, the way it echoes even though it's filled with rows of bunks. Now *will* yourself there. And follow where your feet take you. Simple."

"Yeah, easy." I roll my eyes.

He pulls me in front of him and reaches one arm around me, covering my eyes. "Come on. Try."

I freeze, startled. He's so close that I can feel the heat of his chest against my back. That taut tanned skin of his belly... I push it from my mind. I think about my classroom, Mr. Nox. I try to smell the lavender incense and hear the soothing music. I try, but all I can think is how Sebastian smells like summer nights. Like Ferris Wheels and outdoor concerts and a hint of wine. And I love Colin.

Holy crap. *Love*? I mean, I like him a lot, but—love is a heavy, *big* feeling and... I tuck the thoughts away to carefully dissect when I'm alone, when I can examine all the wires, the connections, like someone about to defuse a bomb.

"I can't concentrate," I say.

He steps ahead of me. "We'll try again some other time. In the meantime... don't get lost." He takes off running and my confusion melts into terror. I race after him, my heart in my throat.

What if you lose him? What else is in the Coil? No. Don't think...

He slows so I can keep him in sight, and when I reach him, I'm instantly furious. But laughter bubbles up through my relief, surprising me.

"Being nice is not your 'thing,'" I wheeze out. I bend over my knees, panting.

He dimples and winks. "Tough love."

"Ready to head back to class now, thanks."

"Boring," he drawls.

I roll my eyes and slide my hand back into his outstretched one, thinking I've held this person's hand way more than I've ever even touched the guy I like... love... *maybe* love. Sebastian's smile shifts, a small twist of his lips, deepening his dimple as he runs his thumb over my skin. My heartbeat skips like a stone across still waters as that pad brushes the sensitive skin of my wrist.

"Listen, Cassie, you should know... I'm not looking for anything serious."

I blink. "What?"

"I want to be upfront before... well, before anything," he says. "You're a pretty girl, but..."

"I hate candy canes."

It's his turn to look confused. "What?"

"I thought we were sharing random things about ourselves."

He smiles lazily. "What kind of monster hates candy canes?"

"The kind that has a boyfriend." I'd die if Colin heard me referring to him that way.

Sebastian purses his lips, his expression unreadable. "Do you? That's good, actually."

"Don't worry." I snort. "I'm not going to be one of those girls that falls in love with you."

"Happens more than you want to know." His cocky look makes me laugh in spite of myself, and hopefully deflates his gigantic ego. "How about you try to get us to your class again?"

"Fine. Whatever." I sigh. "I'm all yours, professor."

"No, you're not. You have a boyfriend." His lip twitches, and there's a lambent light in his eyes. "Close your eyes."

I close them promptly and listen to the whistling silence, the yawning quiet of the Coil.

Sebastian's voice sounds softly in my ear. His breath puffs on my neck, and goosebumps erupt up my arms. "Imagine you're where you need to go. The feel of your head on the pillow. The slide of the sheets."

I shiver.

"Come on," Sebastian whispers.

A spectral blueprint wavers, as if at the bottom of a crystalline pool viewed from above. I find a tether to the sleep lab. I feel the map inside me, everywhere, with every sense. I open my eyes and grasp Sebastian's solid arm. "I know where we have to go."

He cocks his head. "Where to, Ariadne?"

"This way." I wind through passage after passage, turning down corridors with confidence, the walls rippling and changing in our wake as I pull Sebastian by the hand. We're close, I feel it.

Sebastian tugs on my hand, hesitating. "Cassie, this is wrong," he says.

"What? But I..."

"The Coil is playing with you. You asked it to dance, but it's not about to let you lead. How do you think it sucks people in? You need to be careful. It won't give you anything without an effort. Your *will* needs to be stronger than what it throws at you."

I try to reclaim my concentration, but my trust in my instincts has been burned. *You're so gullible that sentient labyrinths dupe you without making an effort.*

No. I can do this. I bite at my nail. A blue cloud starts to gather again, crystalize. The cloud darkens, twists until I'm staring into the darkness of the hall in front of us.

I'm lost in the Coil. No one can find me. Dad—he's already lost Mom. Will Aunt Bree tell him? He'll never know what happened to me. My bones. Ten Agons from now, someone will stumble on them. I'm okay, I'm okay, I'm okay. I'm okay.

My mother steps out of the shadows. "You're safe now, Cassie." She greets me with open arms and a crumbling smile.

I scream and scream, falling to my knees, face to the floor.

"Who is that? Wait. It's okay." Bastian props me up by my elbow, forces me to remain where I am. "No, you can't go back! Stop."

"I saw my mom. Right there. The one from my dream." My chest rises and falls. I fight back the urge to screech at him.

"I did, too. It's the Coil. I didn't think... the Coil will use anything swimming in your head against you. Most of the boogiemen here are the ones we create. I'm sorry. I should have... I didn't realize you weren't ready."

I numbly let him lead me to my dorm instead of my class and sink against the door wearily when he's gone, picturing that monster wearing my sweet mom's face. The dry rot of my self-doubt creeps back. I'm kidding myself, thinking I'm special. That I can change anything. That I can save Colin.

18

The sky outside Pict's office window is blindingly bright, but the rain comes down in sheets.

"Fairy wedding," I say.

"What?" Pict barks.

"Sun shower."

"Congratulations, your powers of deduction astound. Now if only we could get your second sight to operate as well as your first." Pict climbs his ladder, reaching for a thin red text on a high shelf.

"This second sight helped save Ford, but whatever," I mutter.

"Your mumbling is tiresome. You were lucky in your efforts to save Sidney. It doesn't change the fact that you're not truly prepared." He shakes the book in his hand at me as he descends the ladder. "The Agon is coming up, and at this rate, we'll be lucky if you rank high enough to end up a chimneysweep, even with the individual competition exemption."

"You scry it in that book?" By now I'm pretty used to Pict's insults.

"I'm sure I'm mistaken and that passive aggressive tone masks a real question. The Agon's results are obscured. There are things even scryers can never know." Pict pushes back his jacket flaps and sits across from me. "Ms. Morai, you will not have scryers who have completed the Coil Walk in there with you, so the Coil's influence will be amplified. It will bring out the worst in all of you. Civilization is but a thin layer obscuring what people are truly capable of."

I won't be walking the Coil, but Pict doesn't know that. Worry for Regan, for Griffin, for Noah, whips through me.

Regan, her curls tangled and matted, dirty clothes hanging from her emaciated frame, lurches out of the Coil like Samara Trefoil. There's a hunted look in her eyes.

"There was a girl. Samara Trefoil. She was lost in the Coil," I say.

"She was missing for almost a year, but to her it felt like a great deal more time. Time doesn't operate in the Coil the way it does outside, which is why it provides an expedient method of navigating this building. Your Coil Walk will feel like a few days, but it will be less than a day out here. More would mean that something has gone wrong. It's exceedingly rare, but some do elude the rescue teams. Samara Trefoil survived on her rations, and when those ran out... Well, what one will do to survive is a fascinating study."

"But I thought you can't eat anything you dream up in the Coil. We can't eat anything we think up in the dorms."

"You can. But you'd starve once you leave Coil-connected spaces. There's a reason Ms. Trefoil is receiving extensive medical treatment as we speak, and a reason she is receiving that treatment in an area much like your dorms to keep her stable." He leans closer. "You need to take this seriously. I'm not trying to frighten you when

I say the worst that can happen to you and your friends isn't what happened to Samara Trefoil."

I feel a chill. "Okay, I got it." My leg starts moving on its own, bouncing. I bite at my fingernail. "Everything sucks, and I'm terrible at everything, and my friends are going into this thresher and, you know, maybe they'll all *die* by getting eaten by a Coil goblin or whatever." I give Pict a thumbs up and go back to biting my thumbnail. My chest rises and falls fast, so fast. The familiar tingle runs along my spine. *Oh God. Not in front of him.*

One.

Two.

This compulsion is not me.

"You'll watch your tone when you address me. What on Earth is wrong with you?"

Everything.

Three. Four.

I grab the book out of Pict's hands and knock it against my knees. Five times. "I'm okay. I'm okay. I'm okay, I'm okay, I'm okay, I'm okay." That was six times. It needs to be even. "I'm okay. I'm okay. I'm okay. *I'm okay.*"

"Why are you crying? Wh—" Pict cuts himself off and leans back in his chair.

I set the book down and bite at my painful too-short thumbnail.

"Have you been diagnosed?" Pict asks in a tone I've never heard from him before. No sneering. No sarcasm. No ridicule. It's just a normal tone, asking a normal question, and it almost sends me into hysterics.

"Yes," I choke out.

"What was it exactly?"

"It was…" I clear my throat. "…*is* intrusive thoughts, OCD, catastrophic thinking, anxiety…"

Pict steeples his hands on his stomach and bows his head. Then he gets up and pushes his rolling ladder along his bookcase, close to the windows. He peers up at the shelves, climbing almost to the top, then down one or two rungs until he finds what he was looking for. He returns to his seat.

"I read about this once," he says in a quiet voice. "At our first meeting, you mentioned your visions leading up to that point were scried without a medium. Was that true?"

My nail starts bleeding. I put it in my mouth and suck, the metallic taste a welcome sensory distraction from the fact that I had a breakdown in front of this man. "Yes."

Pict flips through the pages of his book. "It's because of your condition. You're so attuned to the *what-ifs* that you're especially sensitive to the *what-wills*. It makes for abilities that are incredibly powerful but *extraordinarily* difficult to control. Visions are sporadic, usually coming when emotions are already heightened. Perhaps on the heels of giving into an OCD ritual, or trying to fend one off. Typically, they're location-based, scrying something that will occur on that particular site, but not always. I would wager you haven't had as many lately because you're exercising your scrying muscle, giving your abilities a new outlet. Like a controlled release of steam. You'll be a danger to yourself and your team during your Coil Walk if you don't quiet your mind. Your perception becomes everyone's reality." He breathes in. "I will help you, but I need you to want to be helped."

My eyes well again. I blink them back. I won't walk the Coil, but if he can help me control… "I want to be normal."

"You'll never be that, Ms. Morai. You're dreadfully strange in a manner that completely predates your ailment."

"Was... was that a joke?" It's so improbable it startles me out of my anxiety death spiral.

Pict's lip twitches. "Perhaps. Answer my question. Do you want my assistance?"

"Can you fix me?"

"No." He pauses. "A 'fix' for what is wrong with you doesn't exist any more than 'normal' people do. But you have the power to help yourself. You can start by ceasing to think of yourself, of your mind, as broken in some way. You are not broken. You'll never be free of your demons, but you *can* learn to relegate them to a closet in your mind, where they belong. Learn to live with them in a way that allows you to move forward. Do you understand?"

"I've been to therapy."

"I'm not a therapist."

I give Pict a small smile, thinking of him in that role. He must take it as acceptance of his help because he nods his head. I concentrate on taking air into my lungs and letting it back out. "Okay. Yes. Thank you."

"Your therapist may have mentioned it, but scryers and non-scryers alike have found it helpful to keep a diary to track the objective event occurring during an episode—a visit to a store, an argument with your neighbor, et cetera—your thoughts about same, and what you are feeling in that moment. You need to understand your emotions if you are to control them. Then, before you act on an urge, you need to ask yourself who benefits from that act in the short term, and who benefits in the long term."

"DBT... yeah, my therapist mentioned we'd start using that if my

Exposure and Response Prevention therapy alone didn't..." I close my eyes. "Okay, I'll do it. But... can you start calling me Cassie... or Cassandra, even?" I don't know why I ask, but I desperately want to hear my name, my first name, from him.

Pict clears his throat, then says brusquely, "Absolutely not. As far as I am concerned, you don't have a first name. You hatched from an egg known as Ms. Morai. Now then, the Agon. True or false? One cannot travel backwards in the Coil."

"False. Technically, you can move backwards but there's a price, and it's different for each person."

"I may expire on the spot." It's an insult, but the heat is gone from his voice. "You know something, for once. Yes, we often tell people not to step backwards in the Coil, which some take to mean one physically *cannot* do so. Not so. Moving backwards is inadvisable because the Coil picks the poison, and most do not like the taste. The severity is entirely dependent on one's mental state. Physical pain, mental, some combination of the two... Some can march backwards a fair distance with relatively manageable consequences. Others cannot muster a single step without the Coil drawing them deeper. In the absence of knowing exactly what the Coil might demand, one is better off if they do not attempt to move backwards at all. Now, enthrall me with what you've learned of some of the Coil's native species. Begin with the Night Mara."

He's back to sniping, but his secret is out.

He's not the *complete* worst.

"I'M NOT SURE THIS IS A GOOD IDEA," I SAY. "SNEAKING OUT of Theban."

"It's the best idea," Regan replies simply. "Your aunt said she can't help Colin. This fortune teller lady said she can. What choice do you have?"

Madame Grey's Psychic Readings storefront shows no life except for the neon sign in the window. It's always on, day and night. Other than that... no employees rushing over to open the door. The faded red curtains don't move.

"How was Ford today?" I ask.

"He's still weak. Whatever he was drugged with hasn't worked its way through his system yet. But I was fussing over him, and he just kept saying, 'Ray-Gun, relax! I'm okay. I'll be fine.'" Regan pauses, her eyes misting. "He looked confused when I said we thought he was attacked by a woman. But then I swear I saw something in his eyes. Like he remembered... I don't know what. Probably Psycho du Lac coming at him with a knife."

"You're still on that du Lac kick? Bacchy said she had an alibi."

"Yeah, whatevs," Regan scoffs. "Like her husband wants it known his wife tried to murder her ex-boyfriend? Of course he gave her an alibi."

"Bacchy said she tried to visit Ford. Du Lac, I mean. The Magpies stopped her, and she ran away crying." *Did the curtains twitch?*

"That was crazy nice of you to use your favor to have the Magpies keep an eye on Sid, by the way. A Magpie favor is... If you asked for the crown jewels, they'd probably score them for you. Thank you. Seriously."

I shrug and look over at her, hearing the extra emotion surfing her voice, uncomfortable with the gratitude. I abruptly change the subject. "So, you weren't in your room last night when I stopped by..."

She smiles and flushes. "You know how I told you Noah and I were kind of messing around and... okay, so last night took a serious turn and... don't tell *anyone*, you're sworn to secrecy..."

"I only talk to you and Noah!"

"Okay, fine... I slept in his room. He changed it so it looked like we were having a nighttime picnic under the Eiffel Tower, and we..."

"Wait, did you sleep in his room or did you *sleep* in his room?" I ask.

Regan's cheeks have a distinctly rosy appearance. "Both."

I cover my grin with my hand, but it does nothing to suppress the scandalized laugh that tumbles through my fingers. Beneath the amusement a second emotion surfaces, just for a second. I feel left behind.

"Anyhow, I'm obsessed with him and he's amazing and every time I look at him, I want to bite his cheeks. Not to brag, but we're kind of the best couple ever. What about you? Heard from Colin?"

"Yeah, he emailed me yesterday." I bite back a smile, thinking of that four-word-long email. *Hey. I miss you.* I head off her questions. "Griffin's dating someone too, now."

Regan stiffens. "Yeah, Liz Dahn. Donkey Laugh Dahn."

"Not nice."

"*She's* not nice."

"If you have questions, I suggest you go inside and ask them," a man says from behind us. My heart beats like a snare drum in my throat as I turn.

The man is old and young, timeless and worn down at the same time. He's wearing an old-timey bowler hat and a stained checkered suit with a faded yellow bowtie. I resist the urge to shout "stranger danger" like a five year old.

"Who are you?" I force out. He crosses the street without answer. When he reaches Madame Grey's door, he props it open, waiting until we follow.

"Wait here," the man says when we enter. He swipes through the thick red bead doorway curtain and disappears. Regan's large gray eyes widen as she takes in the décor. I fight off my intrusive thoughts and the sudden stupid need to knock on the table. The compulsion surges through my bones as I count myself away from the edge. I don't have my Pict diary on me.

Madame Grey enters the room a moment later, the man trailing her. "Oscar said you were back, but I could scarcely believe it. And you brought a friend." She smiles at Regan. "Here to save that boy Colin, yes?"

"Okay, Madame Weirdo, why would you help? What's in it for you?" Regan demands hotly.

"Spirited," Madame Grey says, nodding approvingly and gesturing for us to sit. "I like her for you, Cassandra."

Narisa enters with some tea and sets it down. She gives me a kindly look and hands me a cup. "For your nerves," she whispers with a wink.

"We want to protect you, Cassie, and we want to help you save Colin. In return... there may come a time when we need you to help us," Madame Grey says.

"There we go," Regan says, satisfied. "What do you want?"

"Nothing right now," Madame Grey says mildly.

"What are you trying to protect me from? What do you think Theban Group is doing?" I ask.

Madame Grey looks at the man she called Oscar. He removes his bowler hat and taps it against his knee, then shrugs, communicating wordlessly. "We were once part of Theban Group. Oscar, Narisa, and myself. Others, as well. We left when development of the ICARUSS began. Jordan Welborne is lying to you girls. He's lying to everyone. He views the future as a blank canvas he can paint with whatever he wants it to be. Not with his 'money as influence' claptrap. Not by nudging future events along. By inventing them whole-cloth. We aim to stop him."

I sit back. "But he said we can't make really big changes."

"Lies."

"My aunt said the same." I frown.

"Either she doesn't know or she was lying, too," Madame Grey says.

Regan pulls out her ICARUSS. "There are rituals on here that—"

"He's given you the illusion of control. That device just makes info gathering more convenient for him. His algorithm's machine learning only works if it's fed a steady diet of current news and a heaping pile of what comes next, courtesy of all of you at Theban Group. Every vision, every omen you provide is ammunition for him," Madame Grey says. "There's a great deal that device won't provide answers for. Saving Colin included, or you wouldn't be here."

"So? Maybe the really big changes are off limits because of the company and the whole insurance deal or whatever," Regan says. "He probably has a good reason for blocking it."

"You'd make excuses for your jailor? We're not talking big changes. We're talking *invented* changes. Your entire future written by him," Madame Grey says.

I shake my head. "Even if that's true... he's helping people. Everyone at Theban is."

"What is life without freedom?" Madame Grey asks in disbelief. "A benevolent dictator is still a dictator, Cassandra. No person, no group, should have that much control over our lives."

Narisa nods earnestly. I look at Regan, and something in her expression says she agrees as well.

"So what, then? We scry something bad and we're supposed to accept it?" I ask with more force than I intend. I picture Colin lying in the street.

"This isn't about trying to change the things that we've scryed. Scryers have always done that. We're not advocating for denying our gifts. This is about Welborne acting as God. This is him stripping free will away from everyone," Madame Grey says.

"Not to mention the scryers Welborne has murdered," Oscar hisses. At my look he adds, "That mongrel is removing anyone who might get in his way. Making it look like accidents. Scryers dropping like flies all around the world."

That's not true.

"My daughter is dead because of that madman." Oscar slams his fist on the table.

Narisa's face crumbles, and tears streak down her heavily painted face, carving a path like water through a gully. She rushes out of the room. Oscar takes a step toward her, but stops.

"Do you see? What he's done to my wife?" Oscar looks again to where Narisa fled and turns back to me. "Our daughter bled out in my arms. She was our everything. Do you know what's left when your reason for *being* is gone?" He visibly tries to compose himself before leaning forward, his hands splayed on the table. "I have nothing to live for except taking down that miserable cur. If it spares even one other parent the tears we've shed, it'll have been worth it," Oscar says, stuffing his bowler hat on his head and turning to leave. My heart clutches in response to the kindred pain in Oscar's voice, even as my mind tries to reject the sincerity of his words.

Madame Grey puts a comforting hand on Oscar's arm. "Please, Oscar, stay. I'm sorry, Cassandra, he's emotional. We all are. We've lost people we care for in this." She shakes her head in disgust. "Welborne's turned our sanctuary into a cult."

She reaches for something in her pocket and sets it on the table. It's the clear glass-like oval eye she tried to give me last time. "We may need your help at some point in the future, but for now, as a token of good faith, please take this talisman with you and carry it at all times. Some know it as an evil eye, but this is a particularly powerful one. It will protect you. And we'll also tell you how to help Colin, no strings attached. Okay?"

I hesitantly accept the glass eye. It's cool and smooth to the touch, the iris the same shade as Colin's. I palm it and ask, "Can you really save him?" I think of Aunt Bree, of her insistence that there's no way to save someone destined to die. They say she was lying about other things...

Madame Grey doesn't even bat an eye. "Of course he can be saved. I wouldn't have suggested it if he couldn't. But I don't have what you need here." Regan opens her mouth, and Madame Grey holds up a hand. "I know where you can get it, though."

Oscar pulls out a paper and spreads it open in front of us. It's a photocopied page of text.

Madame Grey points at the paper. "During the course of my readings, I came across multiple references to a ritual called 'Halt the Harvest,' the only known ritual to have successfully averted a scried death. But I couldn't find the ritual itself. I started thinking it was a myth, to be honest. But then I found it. There is a book that contains the most arcane of scryer knowledge. Hand inscribed by monks in the fourteenth century. In relatively modern English, so you're in luck. It's called the *Galdr Leechbook*. Only a handful left in existence, and I know for a fact Linda Fenice has a copy in her office thanks to an article written about her last year in *Fortnight Foresight*."

I inhale sharply. I've been that close to saving Colin this whole time?

"*If* you can get the book, and *if* you can gather the ingredients for the ritual, you'll need to be careful. It's forbidden, so if you're caught... well. And the ritual is said to take three days to complete. Saving a life is complicated. Not for the faint of heart."

I nod eagerly, willing to do anything. I'd teleport myself to Fenice's office right now if I could. I shove the eye talisman into my pocket, and Regan and I stand. Madame Grey blows out a breath, as if in relief. "You're on the right side of history, I promise you. We'll be in contact when we need you. Just, please... keep that eye on your person at all times. You'll need it before all is said and done."

19

We emerge from Madame Grey's and I skitter to a halt. "'Tabloid rag,' my mom called it! I swear, I can't wait to tell her *Fortnight Foresight*... What's going on?" Regan asks as I yank her behind a tree.

Colin is at an ice cream stand. He's not alone. Greta, a cute girl from my school, is with him, pouting prettily. Colin grins and hands her a vanilla cone. She brightens and stares up at him, licking her cone, a flirtatious bent to her movements.

I cross my arms to hug my bag to my middle. The lonely little flame inside me winks out; the one I warm my hands on in the middle of the night whenever I think of Colin and a million breathless what-ifs.

The email he sent yesterday was unkind. Or it feels that way because I'm an idiot who read more into it. Read more into his feelings. Again. *Hey. I miss you.* He misses me as a friend. And after hanging out with Greta and probably other kids I know, who knows what they've told him about me? Will he even want to be my friend after they unload all of my baggage?

"That's Colin," I say in a flat voice, pointing him out.

Regan's jaw drops. "He's super cute! I approve, and..." She notices Greta. "Oh. *Ew.* You don't need to worry. He's so not into her. Deadass, that girl is a complete uggo. Also, who eats ice cream this early in the day?" Regan's expression is now one of outraged solidarity.

We head back to Theban Group, a pinch in my heart making it hard to breathe, and pause on the way only to pick up a gift for Theodore. Regan avoids mention of Colin and instead tries to distract me with the reasons she feels Donkey Laugh Dahn and Griffin are completely wrong for each other.

When we arrive, Theodore lifts one bushy white eyebrow, his sagging eyelid slowly following. He repeats the motion with the other. "Howdy, Cassie. Regan. No one came asking 'round here about you, 'cept your young man, Noah," he says to Regan. "I told him I hadn't seen ya."

"Thanks, Theodore," I say.

"Don't mention it. By the way, I knew blue would suit your eyes, Cassie." His Eeyore voice is soothing and slow. "For a second, I thought I was back home looking down at the water's edge, greens and blues and browns beside."

I flush. Theodore asked me last week why I always wear black, so today I tried to change it up. It's only a blue T-shirt, but somehow I feel more vulnerable wearing anything other than my usual armor.

"You'll be looking down at that water's edge soon enough, right? When's the big trip to Alaska? Next month?" Regan asks, propelling herself up onto his desk counter to sit.

"It surely is."

"What's your mom saying? Does she suspect?" I ask.

"Oh, she gave me guff just yesterday. 'I haven't seen you in fifteen years.' 'You're my only blood.' 'A good son would come and seen their momma before she keels over.'" He shakes his head. "That woman is healthy as an ox. She'll outlive me. But she's right, life passes you by while you're busy trying to make a living. I can't believe I haven't laid eyes on her in fifteen years. She's going to be bowled over when she sees this ugly mug."

I smile, the effort weighing on me. "I'm really happy for you. You'll have a bl ast."

His white whiskers shift, and although they cover his mouth, I can tell the shift is a smile. "Five, five, five today, ladies."

I set our gift down on the desk.

"What happened to your hand?" he asks me.

I flex my fingers. They still ache from Mrs. O's ritual. "Little accident. Don't worry. Not sure if you've ever had cupcakes from Tatiana's, but they're incredible. We picked you up some on our way in... for your *birthday*..."

Theodore's sleep-slackened features clear like the sun chasing away rain clouds. His eyes are wider than I've ever seen them. "I don't know what to say. How did you know?"

Bacchy's intel was right. Regan and I grin at each other.

"Don't worry about it. Just enjoy," I say.

"But we'll need a full report on which one ends up being your favorite," Regan piggybacks.

"That's mighty kind, girls. You got it." Theodore's whiskers shift-smile again, and he eagerly paws the bag open as we leave.

"How are you getting into Fenice's office?" Regan asks, when we're back in the Rotunda.

"Why do you need to get into Fenice's office?" Griffin asks from behind us.

We wheel around, my face surely reflecting my horror and Regan's a mask of fury.

"I didn't mean to eavesdrop, but I overheard." Griffin grins. "Because I was eavesdropping."

I grab him by the arm and drag him to a relatively quiet corner of the Rotunda away from the Magpie carts.

"Don't tell him!" Regan insists. "You were on the fence about telling Noah and he's way closer to you than *Griffin*."

"I'm not a snitch, Roland," Griffin retorts, looking offended. "And me and Cassie are tight...ish. So, what's the deal with Fenice's office?"

I make the decision to tell Griffin, hoping I won't regret it, and swear him to secrecy. I spare no details about Colin and his situation, or my need for what is in Ms. Fenice's office.

"Wouldn't it be easier to just find a new boyfriend?" he asks.

"What is your damage?" Regan asks.

"It's a joke!"

I spot Bacchy near the fountain and leave Griffin and Regan bickering to follow him to his cart. Bacchy dumps his pitcher of water into Betsy's new, larger aquarium. He smiles fondly at the turtle and pulls on his beard. "That's the last of it, Betsy. Ah, Cassie! Didn't see you there. How are you today?"

"I'm okay, Bacchy. Weird day. Hoping you can help me. I need to get my hands on a book..." I pull the translucent eye Madame Grey gave me from my pocket, holding it up.

"Oh, that's a nice evil eye amulet," Bacchy says, plucking it from me to inspect. "What are you looking to trade for? You still have a spot of credit with me even with the favor you cashed in, you know?"

"No, I was wondering—"

The explosion lifts me off my feet and throws me. A burst of pain follows. I grab at my hip. Screams erupt, but they're muted behind the ringing in my ears. I look around, dazed. There's a gaping hole where the fake elevator door entrance used to be. A dozen people in business suits are stepping through that hole and pulling weapons out of briefcases and jackets.

The stone in front of me pops, sending dust and bits of rock flying. I stare at it and cower against the side of the fountain when I realize what the pop was: gunfire. I can't see Regan and Griffin. Another explosion hits. I cover my head. More shots ring out. *You're okay, okay, okay...*

I stand and take off running, stopping when I see Bacchy on the ground, bleeding badly from a cut above his eye. I pull him up and he stands, confused, and immediately bolts, not even looking to see who helped him to his feet. The panicking crowds shove and shout. Someone pushes me, and I lose my footing. I go down hard on my hip—second time now. It stings. I whimper and roll to my knees. It's raining. Something stings my arm. Glass. It's raining glass from the dome.

"Go!" a woman, one of the attackers, shouts. "Move before the guards—"

Our guards return fire. The smell of gunpowder and smoke stings my nose. A man rolls a grenade, and it comes to a stop right in front of me. I take off running again. I cover my head when I hear the explosion, the screams. Another blast sounds a moment later, followed by a rumble of thunder.

Not thunder. The big mechanical zodiac wheel from atop the fountain rolls past me, freed of its moorings.

Theban guards pour into the Rotunda and I push past, trying to get through. I'm not the only one. We run headlong into a dead end, corralled by our own fear.

I need a place to hide. Protection. *Away.* We're too far away from the dorms. *Pict.* I need to get to Pict's office. If anyone would know what to do... I look around, desperate to get to him. *You're okay, okay, okay, okay, okay.*

An explosion goes off in front of me. The boy next to me screams as a hunk of rock barrels into his leg, breaking it.

"The Rotunda has been breached. I repeat, the Rotunda has been breached," a guard calls into his earpiece as he rushes past. "Get to the Coil. All scryers get to the Coil."

I run on, close behind a pack of older scryers, but hesitate to cross into the Coil with the others. Instead, I look around, recognizing the space around me. Ford's classroom and the Magpies who are guarding him are right down—

The corridor is empty. *Where are the Magpies?* There are legs in the doorway to Ford's classroom. I approach, dread compounding with each step. I push the door open slightly.

Ford's eyes are open, staring at the ceiling, seeing nothing. There's a small hole in his forehead; a stream of red has run from it, painting his nose. I scream, the sound culled from the depths of my gut. I scream again and again and stumble, falling backwards, then scrambling to my feet. I run to the elevators, shaking.

Think. Breathe.

I clamp my jaw shut to force myself to stop screaming.

I hear rumbling, and another explosion. Close.

The elevator doors open.

"Stop! Don't take another step!" someone shouts. Heavy footsteps sound behind me. I glance back, and my whole body goes cold—it's a woman, one of the business suit-clad attackers, and she's holding the scope of a long weapon up to her goggle-covered eye. That long black nozzle is trained on me. I raise my hands up, slowly, still facing the elevator.

She approaches, weapon pointed at my back. "Turn around slowly. Don't make any sudden—" I turn. "—Cassandra!" she says, lowering her weapon.

Her hair is at an angle on her head: a wig. White blonde hair peeks out from beneath it. She removes her goggles. Pale eyes, so pale at first glance it looks like they're devoid of irises.

I draw in a sharp breath.

Shouts sound, gunfire. Madame Grey falls back, firing. Two guards race through the doorway. A shot hits Madame Grey in the side of the chest, sending her reeling. I reach for her, even while I grapple with the fact that she's responsible for this. She retreats, seeking cover, returning fire.

I dive into the elevator and reach up to slap at the floor numbers on the panel. A man tumbles in before the doors close. As the elevator jerks upward, I fall back against the bar behind me, trying to get away from him, ready to kick out. But it's not one of them. It's Sebastian. His chest is heaving, his shirt torn and bloodied at the neck.

He looks up at me, his eyes a fierce hunter green before they soften with concern. "Cassie? Are you—you're bleeding!"

I look down. A gash on my arm I didn't even feel suddenly hurts like hell. I'm dripping blood on the floor. The doors open on a random floor, but I just stand there looking at my arm until they close again.

"I'm okay." I hold my hand to the cut. *I'm okay. I'm okay. I'm okay. I'm okay.*

"No, you're not okay. Here..." He reaches for me, but I pull at his collar, stopping him and exposing his neck and shoulder.

"You're bleeding, too," I say, my touch a butterfly's breath on the area above the wound. He's very still except for his heavy breathing. I use the collar of his shirt to wipe the blood away, exposing a long scratch. He seizes my hand in his and opens his mouth to speak when his ICARUSS chimes. He pulls it out of his pocket and glances at it. "Shit, I have to... Come with me." He stands and helps me up before pressing a button, and the elevator starts up again. It opens on a floor I've never seen.

"Sebastian," I say, my voice quavering. I'm not actually sure what will come out, there's so much information queuing at my brain's gate to get out. "Ford is dead."

"What are you talking about?" Sebastian stares intently into my eyes.

"I saw him. Shot. He was... his eyes were open. *His eyes were open!*" I shout it again. "His eyes were open. His eyes were open. His eyes were open." I clamp a hand over my mouth. Tears spilling over, my body quaking.

"Cassie." He grabs me and pulls me into his arms, holding me. "It's okay. You're just... shhhhh." I bury my face in his neck. I hear him curse under his breath as he runs his hand down my hair. His ICARUSS chime sounds again and he pulls away. "I'm so sorry, we have to go. This way. Hurry." He leads me down a dark corridor. A short walk later and he's pressing his ID onto a panel next to an unassuming doorway. The doors open to an octagon-shaped room that looks like NASA mission control on steroids.

I wipe at my eyes and my nose and gape at a wide, transparent glass cylinder that runs from the floor to the high arching ceiling. On it, news broadcasts from all over the world, in every conceivable language. Images of rockets being fired and overflowing hospitals flash. Most in the room are ignoring the news pillar, instead huddled behind a bank of clear, curving monitors on the far side of the room.

Sebastian pushes his way through the crowd. "There's a world to watch. Everybody, get back to your stations. You have jobs to do." The group disperses and hurries to their seats. Sebastian turns to a tall young man. "Sean, I need someone to help Cassie here." Then, to the room at large, "Who's on Bedlam watch?"

A young girl raises her hand. "I am. Darvis and Celia, too."

"Darvis, Celia, and Vex, come here."

I get the feeling he's forgotten about me, so I melt back a few steps. The boy named Sean commands me to sit and breaks out a first aid kit. I flinch as he washes my wound and watch as Sebastian settles in front of the monitors. Six different screens hop and skip through video snippets of what look like... yes, it's our city. I see the Middle Eastern restaurant down the block on one screen.

"What's the delay with these feeds?" he asks the girl named Vex.

"None. We're live. Real time. Bedlam split up as soon as they hit the street. We're still looking for the others, but we managed to track one. This is the feed from Commander Terner's body cam."

"Bring it up on the big screen," Sebastian says.

He stands and walks to the middle of the room, next to the glass pillar. The images on the cylinder change, depicting a man in a suit from behind—running fast, purposely pushing people so they become obstacles for his pursuers. We hear the huffing of Commander Terner's breath and the jostling of his body cam. The man ducks down an alley, out of the view for just a moment before Terner turns the corner after him.

Dead end.

Terner and the rest of his team approach the man slowly, weapons drawn, shouting for him to surrender. When the man in the suit realizes he is well and truly trapped, he turns around slowly, facing the camera, hatred burning in his eyes.

I press my hands to my face as everything inside me skates to a stop. It's Oscar.

"Down on the ground! Get down on the ground!" one of the guards shouts.

Oscar raises his hands slowly and sinks to his knees.

"Where are the others?" another guard asks.

Oscar smiles, taunting. "Why don't you tell me?"

"Where are they?" the guard shouts again.

"Patch me in to Terner. Now," Sebastian says.

"Commander Terner, Sebastian Welborne for you," a guy next to me says into an earpiece. Then he runs to hand off his earpiece to Sebastian, who pulls it on and holds the small microphone to his mouth.

"Commander Terner, turn on your speaker. I have something to say to the Bedlamite."

Terner presses something on his chest. "Ready for you, sir."

"This is Sebastian Welborne—" Sebastian says.

Oscar hoots, laughing out loud. "Welborne's little whelp? Too scared to come down yourself?"

"You're surrounded. Be reasonable and tell us where we can find the others."

"Why? You pigs at Theban know everything, right? Or you will, soon. But that's not the goal. It's not enough to *know* everything. Your daddy wants a world in chains, but he don't want a world that knows it."

"You don't know what you're talking about," Sebastian says evenly.

"You still think he's a hero." Oscar looks around him, but doesn't address the guards. He's talking to us in this room. "Hey! If you're watching this in there, all you stupid cogs in Welborne's machine, you're being used. He's taking out anyone who—"

"Shut your mouth!" one of the guards says, smacking the butt of his weapon into Oscar's face.

I blanch, my palms flying to cover my own.

Oscar cradles his jaw, but then looks back up at the guard, offering a red-wet smile. "Death comes quickly and respects no one."

My blood freezes in my veins. I remember those words, whispered alongside mention of the red blessing in Pict's office. *My* words.

Oscar spits a gob of blood onto the officer's feet. "Goodbye, Narisa. I'm going to our baby. I'm going to Mariela." Then he bites into the shoulder of his jacket.

Shouts from the officers erupt. Oscar's body starts to jerk and he falls to the ground, foaming at the mouth.

"No!" I shout. A wash of dread spreads over me as Oscar's struggles come to a stop, his eyes wide and blank in death. Like Ford's.

An officer kneels and looks up at the camera. "Beladyne pill in the lining of his lapel. I should've checked..." He kicks at Oscar's body.

"*Enough*," Sebastian snaps. "We don't desecrate bodies. Go search for the others."

"What about him?" The guard gestures toward Oscar's body.

"No use bringing him back here, he won't have anything useful on him. Just find the others."

From my chair, I can see a woman walking up to Sebastian with a clenched fist. "They jammed ICARUSS with this." Her hand opens: she's holding the evil eye that Madame Grey gave me.

Oh God. My knees nearly buckle. My fault. I suspected, but the confirmation is... Shame and regret war within me.

I am so stupid. How could I be so—?

"What is it?" Sebastian asks.

"We're not sure yet. Jammer sensor picked it up. Whatever's inside this thing took down our defenses the minute it crossed the Rotunda threshold. Blocked our ability to see this coming. Might be an inside job."

Sebastian takes it and looks it over. I avoid eye contact, as if my guilt is tattooed across the whites of my own eyes. I notice a glass room off to the side for the first time. Scrolling words and numbers are projected onto the back wall. The phrase "hollyhound crumble" jumps out at me, and I realize I'm staring at a ritual. It finishes scrolling, and a new one called "election outcomes" begins.

My chest hammers. I look down at my ICARUSS, quickly typing the same phrase into my phone's ritual search while Sebastian and the others debate the eye's meaning. "No such ritual," my ICARUSS reads. But I'm seeing it right now.

She may have lied about not wanting to hurt anyone, she may

have lied to use me, but Madame Grey didn't lie about this. Welborne isn't sharing all his rituals. There has to be a reason, though. Maybe...

"Let's take a walk, Cassie," Sebastian says. He's standing in front of me. I didn't notice him finishing his conversation, walking over. I let him pull me along, glancing back at that room.

"That man. The one who died. He was..." I stutter.

"He was one of the people who attacked us today. He won't be bothering anyone again."

"What was he talking about? The stuff about changing things? A world in chains?" I ask. Fearing I know the answer.

A muscle jumps in Sebastian's cheek. "Bedlam will say anything. Their whole goal is chaos. No rules. No oversight. No repercussions. You can't trust a word they say."

I learned that lesson too late. And what about the next lesson? Can I can trust Theban Group? Can I trust Sebastian?

20

It's been two days since the attack. Two days of going to sleep picturing Oscar's unseeing eyes and waking up having dreamt of Ford's dead stare.

My insides clench. In my mind's eye, I see Theodore's sweet Santa-whiskered face smiling over a birthday cupcake.

I killed my friend. I'm the reason Theodore's mother won't be seeing her son ever again. Fifteen years becomes forever. I choke on my misery.

I hate Madame Grey. I hate her with a rage that feels lit by a million suns. When I can't deal with my part in everything, my regret, my shame, my grief, I plumb the well of rage inside me and I *hate*.

The rotunda shows signs of rapid repairs, but you don't need the scars on the walls or the dry fountain to be reminded of what happened here. We'd stand in a somber shadow even without the tarp blotting out the sun and covering the remnants of the glass dome.

The surly guard at my side and I pass a group of watchful,

whispering girls my age. You'd think I'd be used to being looked at as a freak—I've been one at school for the past few years, after all—but I thought Theban would be different. I thought I could reinvent myself here. But here it's worse. Here I'm a murderer.

No one knows that yet, though. I'm being escorted by the guard to serve as a character witness for Bacchy, and the girls are only staring because everyone knows how close I am to him. I'm guilty by my association to Bacchy in their eyes. Ironic.

Regan rushes over, bringing our march to a halt. "I'm here for moral support," she tells the guard.

"If you're not a character witness, you can't come," the guard says, pushing me along. "*She's* moral support. You can't be moral support for moral support."

Regan makes a face and pauses to bark out an insult at the giggling girls.

"Regan, it's not worth it," I say, stilling her.

Regan shrugs. "Defending you and Bacchy is a good way of passing the time." What she means is, it's a good way of distracting herself. She looks down, and I take in the bandage on her forehead, the bags under her eyes, the sorrow in the curve of her neck. I heard the pain in her voice yesterday when she told me about Theodore. About Ford. About Noah.

Noah, at least, survived. He's been in the infirmary since the blast. He's missing an eye and has a nasty concussion, but the doctors expect he'll recover when he wakes up. Regan has been beside herself, only leaving his side once when I swore I'd stay with him.

"How is he today?" I ask Regan. I don't have to say who I mean. *I might as well have plucked out his eye with my bare hands.*

"Better! He's going to be so pirate-hot. Don't worry, I'm already bedazzling his eye patch." It's all false cheerfulness. I know Regan well enough by now to know the difference.

"That's as far as you go." The guard throws an arm up to block Regan's way.

"Tell Bacchy don't worry! It'll be okay. And you're going to do great, Cassie. Don't stress!" Regan's corkscrew curls hang limp around her ears, her eyes dishrag gray. I wonder if I look as bad. I can't sleep. Haven't really eaten. I'm being torn apart from the inside out. I give her an impulsive hug.

The guard leads me through the Coil, down a sharply sloping passage. My shivering continues long after we cross that threshold and intensifies the deeper we go. The sounds of our footfalls echo. The narrow path, which wouldn't look out of place in an archeological dig, zigzags as if taking us down a mountain pass, and it feels as if we're drilling down to the very bottom of the Coil.

You're okay, okay, okay, okay, okay. I pick and bite at my thumbnail, then force myself to stop. Who wins in the short term if I rip my thumb to shreds? Me, momentarily, since my OCD will be satisfied. Who wins in the long term if I don't? Me again, since I won't risk a wound that can become infected. My Dad and Mrs. O and everyone who love me will also win, since they'd be happy I haven't given in to an urge. Pict will be...

We reach a bridge stretching over black, yawning nothingness. A brown-hooded figure stands sentinel in front of it; he turns, leading me and the guard across and up to a pair of immense double doors that stretch high above my head.

"Follow him," the guard says to me, pointing at the hooded man.

I turn and face a dark anteroom. The hooded man moves through it into a larger space filled with flickering candlelight. I force my feet to do the same. "Cassandra Morai, of the clan Morai," the hooded man intones.

"They'll be ready for her in a moment," another cloaked figure answers. I recognize Ms. Fenice's voice. She pushes her hood off her head to give me a small sad smile and a hug before leading me toward the back wall, which is lined with wood chairs.

Up front, nine black-shrouded figures are seated on ornate thrones on a raised semi-circle dais. *The Grimoire Council.* I always thought they were nicknamed the "Grims" because of the Council's name, but seeing them perched on their seats like harbingers of death, all that's missing is a scythe in each of their hands.

"I cannot tell you where I got it," Bacchy says, his small, hunched figure kneeling in front of the platform.

Agatha Triggs, looking like she was laser-cut from a piece of sheet metal, is seated at a fold-out table and chairs next to Bacchy's kneeling form. She reaches into a metal urn and holds up a red stone.

"Well, I could tell you, but I mean I won't. Magpies never reveal the provenance of our trades. It's why people trust us." I walk farther along the back wall of the circular room, passing other observers, Fenice following. I want to see Bacchy's face. Reassure myself he's okay.

"Trust you?" One of the Grims leans forward. "Magpies are not known for being trustworthy."

Bacchy brings himself up rigid. "We certainly are. We've been atoning for Autolycus for centuries. If we're guilty for the sins of an ancestor, you bunch should be held to account for a fat lot more than that." Bacchy pulls at his pointed red beard, then mutters, "I suppose I shouldn't be yelling at my judges."

"So, he does have some sense," the Grim seated closest to my side of the room mutters. I can't see any of their faces, but I can tell this one is a woman from her voice. "Let's keep that going, shall we?"

"Alright, I *can* tell you the trader was as ignorant as me. Neither of us were—"

"So, you admit the person was a traitor?" the second-to-last Grim says, incredulous. "How can you defend—?"

"He said 'trad-er,' not 'trait-or,'" the Grim to his left corrects.

"They're one and the same," the second-to-last one sniffs.

"I wasn't involved in the attack. Neither of us was. We didn't know what that thing was. It was just something valuable to trade."

Triggs holds up a red stone, and the crowd gasps.

"Cripes," Bacchy mutters.

"Enough. If you have nothing further to say in your defense, we'll move on to the verdict," the old Grim who misheard says.

A woman rushes forward. She'd almost look like a photo-negative of an old English barrister with her white robe and black curled wig, except her wig's curls twist and jut out Medusa-like. "Not quite, your Excellency. Mr. Liddell is entitled to character statements. We have some people here who—"

"A waste of time! No one ever calls forth a neighbor he owes money to. I won't allow it. We vote now," the second-to-last Grim shouts. "All in favor of passing a sentence of Cateractus, say 'aye.'"

Bacchy and his advocate's protests are drowned out by a chorus of ayes.

"That sounded like a majority. The 'ayes' may claim his sight," the old Grim says, a smile evident in his voice.

"No!" I shout. I break away from Fenice and run to Bacchy's side. *You're okay. Okay. Okay. Okay. Okay.* I edge up to Triggs's table and tap my fingers against the surface five times, as discreetly as I can.

"Do you know what the sentence for interrupting a Grimoire Council Inquisition is?" the center Grim asks.

"I don't." I clench my fists, my catastrophic thinking coming up with dozens of punishments. *You're okay, okay, okay, okay, okay.* "But whatever it is, it's worth it if I can keep Bacchy from being punished for something *I* did."

The room explodes into confused shouts. Bacchy pitches to his feet, his earring dangling madly. "Cassie, don't—"

"No, it's true. I brought the evil eye in. Bacchy had no idea what it was."

"Neither of us—"

A guard's hand pushes on my shoulder until I drop to my knees. I catch a glimpse of Sebastian to the left of the dais. He whispers to an attendant, who turns and rushes from the room. His brow wrinkles and he shakes his head, mouthing something.

"What is your name?" another female Grim asks.

"Cassandra Morai."

Gasps again fill the room, and silence stretches.

"We must hear all. Start at the beginning, Ms. Morai."

I hug my arms around me and begin, haltingly telling them about Madame Grey. Oscar. The eye. Seeing them both again the day of the attack—Madame Grey in the building and Oscar dying. I leave out the parts about Colin, which takes a little on-the-spot editing but not too much.

"Even if you didn't know that the eye would take down our defenses, why did you think they gave it to you?" the third-to-last Grim asks.

Sebastian shakes his head. This time I make out what he mouths: *Don't answer.*

"I—"

"My niece is naïve, that's why. Bedlam filled her head with lies about what we're doing here, offered up a pretty little gift, and she took it. They manipulated her into acting as a Trojan Horse so they could take down our defenses, try and destroy the ICARUSS mainframe, and murder our ritual expert Sidney Ford." Aunt Bree walks into the room, her heels echoing like thunder claps. Her voice thickens and she clears her throat. "Because she's very, very stupid. Isn't that right, Cassandra?" To outsiders she looks calm. I can tell she's furious.

"Stupidity is no excuse. There are at least two dozen dead. At least four times that are gravely injured. Someone must be punished." The Grim in the center grips the arm of his chair so hard the wood creaks.

"Yes, *someone* should be. That someone is Bedlam. That's why we need this Council to lift all restrictions placed on Julian Welborne's work. We've been rejected multiple times now, and the situation has only grown worse. They strike and we hide. *Pathetic.* This Chamber now bears some responsibility for what occurred, but you *can* rectify that wrong." She lights a cigarette and holds her elbow up with her opposite hand before raising an eyebrow. "Well?"

The Council begins murmuring. Finally, the Grims sit back in their chairs. The female Grim on the left lifts a hand to silence the whispers. "Before we decide, we must verify your niece's story. Bring a new batch of stones."

"That isn't necessary," Aunt Bree says.

"I say it is," the Grim responds.

"I can easily verify it." Pict approaches, hastily throwing on a brown robe and pulling his book from his breast pocket.

"Martin Pict, what is your interest in this case?" one of the Grims asks.

"Cassandra Morai is my mentee," Pict says. His eyes shoot daggers at me.

"Then you are disqualified due to conflict of interest," the last Grim says.

Fenice grabs Pict by the elbow and leads him back to his seat. An assistant runs up to Triggs, holding a large drawstring bag and another urn. He hurriedly removes the old one as Triggs upends the bag's contents over the new urn's mouth. I flinch at the deafening sound of red and white stones striking the metal bottom.

"For the love of..." Pict grumbles. He crosses his arms.

The guard pulls me to my feet and forces me to the table. Triggs takes one of my fingers and pricks it deeply with her broach pin. I yelp as she squeezes my finger viciously over the urn until three fat droplets of blood fall.

She releases my hand, and I suck my fingertip, panicked about the sterility of the pin even while my mind recognizes I have bigger concerns. Why does it always have to be blood? *You're okay, okay, okay, okay, okay.*

"What is your full name?" Triggs asks briskly.

"Cassandra Morai."

Triggs draws a red stone from the urn and shakes her head. She sets it down on the table. "False. Your *full* name?"

"Oh. Cassandra Claire Morai."

She pulls a white stone from the urn and looks up at the Grims.

"Ms. Morai, did you plot with Bedlam to attack Theban Group?" the female Grim at the start of the dais asks.

"What the devil—" Pict says.

"No!" I shout.

White stone.

The female Grim quickly runs through questions to confirm my story. A white stone follows every answer.

"Are you responsible for the attack?" one of the quieter Grims asks.

"I already answered that—"

"No. You answered a question about actively plotting to attack Theban group. I'm asking about responsibility."

"No!"

Red stone. A wind whips up in my chest, swirling until it's a storm of sorrow and confusion and anger. I look to Pict. He's staring at the stone with revulsion.

"The stones expose truths you might not be aware of," one of the Grims say. "Why did you not share any of this with your aunt?"

"I don't know!"

Red stone.

"Because I don't trust her." The truth lands in the center of the room with a heavy thud and a white stone.

Aunt Bree clicks her tongue against her teeth. "And look how well that worked out for you." Her lips are pressed together in a tight line. To the Grims she says, "If we're through airing my family's dirty laundry, I trust we're done here. I'll deal with my niece. She was used by those who were smarter and more experienced." She flicks a dismissive glance in my direction. "She's a pawn."

The Grims share whispered debate amongst themselves for

several minutes, and then the one left of center raises a hand. "A confession means that Mr. Liddell is exonerated of the high crime for which he was charged. But I propose he be sentenced to stable duty for three months for obstructing our investigation. All in favor?"

A unanimous chorus of ayes sounds.

"Ms. Aubrey Morai, because of your years of service here at Theban Group, your standing with the company, and your family's history, *and* in light of your niece's tender age, we will spare her punishment. Your niece came here to confess when she found out that someone else was charged for her crime, which is commendable. Cassandra Morai is free to go with a warning. Further, tell Julian Welborne we reject your insulting claim that this Chamber bears any blame for what occurred. And this Council will *not* grant his request. If we reach for the darkest of rituals each time we face a hardship, where would we be?"

Aunt Bree protests, and while she and the Grims hold everyone's attention, Triggs holds up the red stone that proclaimed my responsibility for the attack. She shakes her head, her gaze cutting.

I didn't need a rock to tell me all the death and destruction of that day will rest on my shoulders forever.

AUNT BREE AND PICT LEAD THE WAY OUT OF THE chamber, followed closely by Fenice. Bacchy and I bring up the rear.

"She didn't know what she was doing. They disguised it," Fenice says.

"Yes, Linda. Hence my Trojan Horse comment," Aunt Bree says

with a humorless laugh. Pict looks at Aunt Bree like she's something he found at the bottom of his shoe.

"Didn't even know the Grim Council chamber had proper jail cells. In that room just behind the dais, they are. Wish I didn't find that out the hard way. And they're not the nice European kind of cells, either. Cold metal bars and... Well, anyway, I owe you," Bacchy whispers.

I tear my eyes from Pict and Bree. "Owe me? What are you talking about? This was all my fault." I look down, shamefaced. "You're being punished because of me. I'm so sorry."

"Hardly punishment. I don't mind animals. 'Cept the smell. And the noise. And the way some of them chew. Don't be sorry. Besides, the Magpie creed got me punished, not you. We don't divulge secrets about trades. That's where the phrase comes from, you know? Trade secrets."

That's not true, but the trivia nerd in me won't correct him. "I wasn't going to trade—"

"Don't know many who would've spoken up, by the by. Like the Grims said. To your credit! But that's not why I owe you. Deal's a deal and we failed Ford. Poor man." He shakes his head sorrowfully. "Our original trade still isn't even."

"Bacchy, forget it."

"Never. A Magpie without honor isn't a Magpie at all."

We emerge from the Coil. "I need a word with you before you go with Martin," Aunt Bree says to me. She practically shoves me into a small room and shuts the door before I can call out a goodbye to Bacchy.

"We could have prepared if you would have brought this to me, Cassandra. People would be alive. Your friend Theodore would be alive." Aunt Bree vibrates with fury. It's out of character for her.

"I know."

She holds up her hand, index finger extended and begins counting people off, extending a finger every time. "Theodore. Jacinta Mellor. Brick Griggson, Uther Ekert. *Sidney Ford.* Dead, dead, dead, dead, dead. Along with a dozen others."

"I know," I repeat.

"I spoke with Theodore's mother, you know. I was the one to tell her. Woman was utterly devastated. Did you know he died on his birthday?"

"He was going to see his mom soon." I try to swallow but an ache blossoms in the middle of my chest. Why did it have to be Aunt Bree to deliver that news?

"Heartbreaking. I'm sure those nice terrorists would've skipped him during their murderous rampage had they known it was his birthday or that he was about to visit Mommy. Poor Theodore. Happy birthday to him." Bree eyes her nails while she talks, avoiding eye contact.

I feel a tear threaten in the corner of my eye. I swipe at it.

"Those idiots on the Council don't realize it, but we're in a fight for survival. The ends justify the means, and they've cut off our means."

"Wha—what are you going to do?"

"Not me. *You.* You need to make this right." She pulls a paper and a small plastic bag from her jacket pocket. "The 'camp' promised your father you could go back home for a few days for your birthday. The timing is helpful since you wouldn't be able to pull this off on scryer property. You leave tomorrow." She hands me the paper and the baggie, which I realize holds a folded handkerchief. "You are not to tell another living soul about this. The handkerchief is stained with their leader's blood. We haven't been able to determine her real identity, but she took a bullet during the attack, and her blood is one of the ingredients you'll need. There is a Gloaming Moon eclipse tomorrow night—charge a mirror with it. You're going to need that as well."

"You want me to create a dark mirror and—"

Aunt Bree looks mildly surprised I know what the Gloaming Moon eclipse does, but recovers quickly. "Yes. Unless you don't want to atone for today? Conscience already recovered?"

"No! It's just—I can't hurt anyone. They deserve it, yeah. There were times when I want to. But I can't."

"Cassandra, you can't possibly be this dim. We're not the murderers here, they are. I wouldn't even need you if those ancient buzzards..." Aunt Bree bares her teeth, her red lips pulled back in a sneer. "The Grims don't have the stomach for war. The ritual won't cost anyone their lives. It's a trap designed to... even the odds, let's say."

I reluctantly take the paper and unfold it, scanning it quickly. "Where do I get a—"

"I don't know, and I don't care. You allowed them to strike at the heart of this organization. You figure it out. Now put those things away. We never had this conversation." She pulls open the door and turns back. "*Do* try not to get caught. If you end up back in front of the Council for this, I won't be swooping in to save you again."

21

I look around the Rotunda and chew my breakfast hand pie slowly. Even at the worst during school, I was never a hardcore social pariah. Not like this.

Griffin throws his hands behind his head and tips his chair back on two legs. "So, Cassie, you can't be a sleeper cell, get caught, and go back to being a sleeper cell, right? You only shoot your terrorist wad once, I'm guessing."

My face goes hot. "You're not funny. At all. People died. Please don't."

He sighs and looks up at the Rotunda dome and the morning sun. It's been repaired, but with nowhere near the craftsmanship it boasted before. This was a quick fix, something to signal normalcy as soon as possible. It lacks artistry.

"You have to laugh, Morai. The minute you let something become a third rail, you give it leverage. Can't let anything be sacred. In five years, this will all be a blip on the radar of your life."

I drop my pie and press my eyes. "Yeah, okay." I recognize he's trying to be helpful. Just in a very Griffin way.

"Silver lining? At least you don't have to worry about all that Red Blessing crap anymore. I mean, it sucks it happened, don't get me wrong. But we tried our best to stop it," Griffin says.

He's actually right. The agony of waiting for that hammer drop, picturing it, the gnawing fear that the Red Blessing could be someone I know... it was dry kindling for my kind of thinking. And that's over now. It sends an odd sort of relief flooding through me.

Regan makes her way over and takes a seat quietly, and my relief is replaced with an upspring of nauseousness and guilt. She's been grieving her mentor. She's worried about Noah. People we know are gone. I shake my head to clear away the memory of Ford's dead stare.

"Regan... I'm so sorry. I had no idea what the eye would do."

That elfin pointed chin of hers trembles before she firms her jaw. "Don't be stupid. I was with you. I don't blame you."

I've lost so many friends in the past two years, I didn't think I could care anymore. But it wasn't until she said those words that I realized how much I was worrying about losing this particular one. I blink away the sudden moisture in my eyes and look around.

"Okay. Um." I cough.

"Oh, come here." Regan pulls me into a bear hug.

"You guys are so Hallmark, it's cute," Griffin says. He's been a little more cautious with his words around Regan since the attack, but I guess he can't repress his baseline personality for that long.

Regan doesn't react, but she does let me go. "Tell us about the trial, Cassie. Literally everything."

I stumble a bit when I get to the part about the red stones and the blame they assigned to me, but I do tell them everything. Regan takes my hand and presses it between hers. I consider leaving out Aunt Bree's ritual to take down Bedlam, but I barrel ahead and tell them that, too. Weirdly, I hardly hesitate before sharing in front of Griffin. Once the decision to trust him was made, it was made forever, it seems. In for a penny.

"She said I can't tell anyone about the ritual since the Grims said it wasn't allowed," I whisper.

"I mean, if the Grims rejected it, then they did it for a reason..." Regan says.

"Screw that." Griffin slams his chair legs down with a thump so that he's seated normally. "An eye for an eye. Bedlam came into our house and blew our shit up. If whatever her aunt gave her will do some damage, I'm all for it. Give it to me, I'll do it."

"I can't. It has to be me. She gave it to me. She can't know I told you. You can't say a word to anyone."

"Second time you guys have suggested I'm a rat," he says, outraged. "Not only am I not telling anyone about any of this, I'm down to help find whatever's on the grocery list of ritual crap she has you hunting for. What about you, Regan?"

Regan blinks and frowns at Griffin. It takes me a minute to realize he's used her real name. "Of course I'm in."

"Bust out that ritual, Cassie. Let's see what we're working with," Griffin says.

"Not here. Too many people watching." I glance around. There's only one place I can think to bring them. "I have to go home for a few days. Do you guys maybe want to come to my house tonight? We can talk there. It's not far."

"Casa de Morai? Sure. I know the girl they have working the front desk late shift now. I have an astromancy lab, but we can break out after. Like nine o'clock?" Griffin says.

I look at Regan. She gives a short quick nod. "Nine o'clock."

DAD ISN'T HOME. I DON'T KNOW WHY I EXPECTED HIM TO be here, waiting. I wasn't due back for a couple of days, although I emailed before I left to let him know that I was able to get away early.

I lie in my bed, my real bed—not the Coil-generated illusion—and listen to 4D arguing with his girlfriend through the thin apartment walls.

The slow-burning ember of longing that lives deep inside me—ever present—catches suddenly, wildfiring through every other thought until the only thing left is her.

Mom.

I lean into the hurt and grab for my phone. I didn't have it with me at Theban Group, but now I scroll through old pictures, my heart squeezing when I reach one of her in the hospital. Withered away. A husk who used to have a sunshine smile and a laugh like fairy bells.

I blast through the few texts from her I have and move to voice-mails, rubbing salt in the wound. There are only two: one about chicken for dinner, and another asking where I am. It doesn't matter what she's saying though. Her voice... The sting at the back of my eyes grows.

I gather those little shards of multimedia she left behind and try to humpty dumpty her personality into existence, picturing how she would've reacted to all of this. I need more, though. *I'll never have more.*

I throw the phone down and cry with great big, ugly heaves. I need to get it all out. Purge before Dad gets home. Because that's what we do. We protect each other. We're "strong" for each other. We keep the poison to ourselves.

I wash my face and make dinner in the same way Dad makes lasagna—with a phone call and hidden delivery containers.

"Where's my girl?" Dad says as I set the last of the food on the table. I hear the door close behind him and race out into the hall, throwing myself into his arms. He pulls me close, laughing. "If I'd had more notice, I would've picked you up. They dropped you at the school?"

I nod and hide my sniffles against his chest. "I walk home from school all the time. Not a big deal." My voice sounds tear-thick.

Dad squeezes me tighter. "I missed you too, doll," he murmurs. "Tell me everything."

I fill him in on the scripted nonsense Aunt Bree's assistant fed me as Dad admires his plate of salmon. He wolfs it down, pausing only to ask the occasional question.

"You can slow down. It won't swim off your plate," I say.

"What?" he asks, fork in hand.

"The fish."

Dad laughs. He sets his fork down and leans back. He unbuttons the top button of his shirt and looks around, avoiding eye contact. "Listen, Cass, I'm hoping... that is, I wanted to let you know..."

I grip the table. *Oh God. One. Two. Three...*

"I... Eleanor..."

Four. "Dad, spit it out." My knuckles are white.

"I told Eleanor I would take her to a ballgame tonight. She's been down lately, something at work, I think... so I bought tickets. She's never been, if you can believe it. I didn't know you'd be home when I bought them..."

"Oh." So long as it's not a wedding, I don't care if he takes her to the moon. "That's fine. Yeah."

"Are you sure? It's your first night back! No... you know what, I'm going to call her and cancel. We'll go some other time."

"Dad. Go to the game. It's fine."

"How about this? Tomorrow night, Trivinometry. And this Saturday, all day, you and me. Dealer's choice. Whatever you want to do. Then we do up your birthday night in style."

"It's fine, Dad, really. Two of my friends wanted to stop by tonight, actually. I was going to ask if you were cool with it."

"Friends? Absolutely!" Dad sounds relieved. I rush him to get ready for his game and sit watching TV pensively while the shower is going. He emerges from the bathroom a short while later, dressed for his game and toweling off his hair. "How do I look?"

"Like a professor trying to fit in at a baseball game."

"Yukking it up at your father's expense?" Dad grins. "Alright. I'm ready. I'll never be *Jeffrey Morai, International Man of Mystery*, but hopefully Ellie approves."

That little pet name lands like a slap.

"You look great, Dad," I say quietly. "Really. Have fun."

He leans forward and takes my head in his hands, planting a kiss on my forehead. "Have I told you I have the best daughter in the world?"

"You'll have to introduce me to her when you get home. Go!"

Dad chuckles as he grabs his glasses and phone. "Your sarcasm is getting out of hand. Alright, I'm going. No wild parties with your *friends* while I'm gone, doll," he says, emphasizing the word "friends" with no small bit of wonder.

I look at the clock. Just a few more hours until the Gloaming Moon.

THE MOON HANGS PREGNANT AND LOW IN THE NIGHT
sky. It disappears for a moment behind thick, dark cloud cover. Do
clouds impact Magnitude Five Dark Mirror creation? Too bad
there's no shadow-arts help desk I can call into. I set my mirror on
the ledge of my rooftop as the moon breaks free of its cloud cage.

"You're back? Are you avoiding me or something? You didn't
answer my last email."

I jump at the sound of Colin's voice. He's crossing over the knee-
wall, his eyes nearly as black as his endearingly ruffled hair in the
dark. A fist seizes my lungs, squeezing.

"I just got back today. Why would I avoid you?"

"Then what is it?"

"Nothing," I say, turning to block him from seeing the mirror.
"I figured with Greta and all the new people you've met, you
wouldn't even notice I wasn't around." *What is wrong with you?*

"Greta? How did you... Of course I'd notice." He sounds
bewildered.

I close my eyes. Oscar's dead stare morphs into Ford's, then
Theodore's, then Colin's, with howitzer devastation. "I—it's not
you. Something bad happened. It was my fault."

"What happened? Use the wrong pasta for your macaroni art?
Push a counselor into a lake? Hey! Please don't cry." I feel an arm
go around me. He pulls me over to the knee-wall and sits. "It's okay.
Everyone makes mistakes. You want to talk about it?"

I shake my head.

"Then it's mud in the fire. Done with. Everything can be fixed
except death, okay?"

My heart spasms as I sob, emptying my heart and soul out into his shoulder. I let him hug me even though his hand is pressed against my Bedlam attack stitches. I need to finish this ritual for Aunt Bree, get back to Theban Group, and get what I need to save Colin.

If that wasn't a Madame Grey lie, too.

I lift my head off of his shoulder. "Thank you. Helped to get it out," I lie.

"Helps to talk sometimes," he suggests, giving me a half-smile.

"Oh yeah, Mr. Diplomat's rich son. What would you know about it?" I try and tease.

"No one's life is perfect, Cass." He blows out a breath slowly, his cheeks puffed out. "My mom spends most days stalking my Dad. He spends most days on top of his secretary. When they're together, they're either arguing or ignoring each other like a sad cliché."

"I'm sorry. Your mom seemed really happy."

"Trust me, lots of pharmaceuticals go into that look," Colin says. "Anyway, with us living like nomads, and them so wrapped up in each other, you learn to enjoy your own company, so it's not that bad. Actually, you want to talk about mess-ups? Maybe this will cheer you up. The Prime Minister of Romania's wife once hugged me and—I have no idea why I did this—I grabbed two honking fistfuls of her back meat when I hugged her back. Like a reflex. Just... *squish*. Stop laughing. It was awful. It was like there was a ledge, and I grabbed for it, and we both froze, and... yeah. Oh, and another time I confused a Russian diplomat's mistress with his wife and his wife with his mother and it was a whole thing. So my Dad doesn't exactly trot me out to meet his high-powered friends all that much."

"Thank you for trying to make me feel better by sharing that you're an awkward weirdo," I laugh. "And I'm sorry you thought I was avoiding you." *And I'm sorry that I was.*

"Is it selfish to admit I'm happy it was other stuff, and not because of me?"

"Very."

He grins. "I missed you. Everyone else I've met is so *nice*, it was going to my head. I needed a dose of mean. Someone to keep me in my place." I give him a faux outraged look, and he laughs. "Look at us, spilling our guts out. Free therapy by moonlight."

"About to be a lot less moonlight in a second. Gloaming Moon tonight."

"Gloaming Moon?" he asks.

"Sorry, that's what someone I know called it. It's a crazy rare lunar eclipse."

"You're seriously like a walking Wikipedia," he says. When I flush in embarrassment, he grabs at my hand. "No, Cass, it's awesome. I've never known anyone like that before."

I look down at his hand holding mine. "My mom was like that. My dad is a professor, but he used to say Mom could school him any day of the week."

"Did they get divorced? I've never seen her around, and you never talk—"

"She died two years ago," I say. "The big C."

"I'm so sorry, Cass. I had no idea."

I shrug, a weak dismissal of the most significant thing that's ever happened to me. "It's okay." I take the night air in deep. "You know, I used to hate when people said 'I'm sorry,' but now I realize it's because I was hoping for better words out of them. Magic words maybe. Something that'd change things."

"Here I am complaining because my dad cheats and you're sitting here..." He shakes his head.

I think back to what Regan said in Mr. du Lac's class. "Everyone has a monster they're grappling with. Mine doesn't take away from yours."

"Meh. Maybe," Colin says.

The earth's shadow starts passing over the moon's surface, casting it in an eerie rust color. I glance back at my mirror on the ledge.

"Holy hell, this is awesome," Colin says. "Come on." He hops off the knee-wall and grabs me by the waist, lifting me off. I fight off the frisson of pleasure that races through me at his lingering touch and follow him to his lounge chairs. We settle in next to each other exactly like that first night on this rooftop.

Not exactly like that first night, actually. That Cassie was terrified of him seeing my hands, or worse—kissing me. This Cassie is tired of hiding and wants nothing more than his mouth on mine. I reach for his hand, and his fingers curl to cradle my own.

We lie there, hand-in-hand, on those chairs for the one hundred and three minutes of the eclipse. But as much as his presence stirs up a fierce wanting in me, it also soothes. So much so that when I reluctantly get up to leave, I almost forget to grab my newly created Magnitude Five Dark Mirror.

Almost. After all, there's still magic to do.

22

My bedroom is small to begin with, but it feels even smaller with three people in it.

"Griffin, please don't touch that," I say. Right about now, I'm regretting inviting them over, to be honest. I just want to sit and replay my Colin-on-the-roof moment over and over in my mind.

Griffin puts down my *Wuthering Heights* snow globe and drops onto my desk chair. "Let's see the ritual, C-dawg."

Regan is sitting on my floor with her knees drawn up into the circle of her arms. She looks pale and small.

"You don't have to do this whole thing with me, you know," I say to her.

"Do what?" she asks.

"Pretend you're not crushed."

She looks away. "I'm not pretending anything. It's... When they said Noah would live, but he'd be a little banged up, I was so relieved. But then I found out about Sid and..." I hear the tears in her voice, crowding the exits to her tear ducts and begging to be released. "Roller coaster. I don't have family besides my mom.

So, like, Sid and you guys are what I've got. Or had. Those people are animals! Why would someone..." She shudders.

Griffin nudges her leg with his foot. "Hey. That's why we're here. If Cassie's aunt is right, we can take them down. For good. Right?"

Regan nods. "Okay. But... does it seem weird to anyone else that when we saved Sid that first time, it seemed like it was this whole production? The dagger, the mask... like a ritual. And then for them to just shoot him? And why did they want to kill him at all?"

I frown. "And if Bedlam got in the first time without help, why did they need me to bring in the eye the second time? Why not sneak in however they did before?"

Griffin sighs loudly. "You guys are really trying to make sense out of a bunch of murdering psychos? Look, Bedlam might be a bunch of liars, but they were telling the truth that they don't like the ICARUSS. And there wouldn't be an ICARUSS without Ford's work. They got caught the first time they tried to take him out and had to know he'd be guarded after that, no sneaking in and out like last time. So they figured they needed to go the bang-and-smash route the second. This isn't rocket surgery. It's what I'd do."

"Rocket surgery," I repeat, at the same time Regan says, "Because what you'd do is clearly the barometer for a healthy human mind."

"You called me family, by the way." Griffin grins.

"I meant Cassie."

"No returns. You're stuck with me."

"Can I exchange you for a sweater? Or a pair of socks?"

"No take backs, Egg."

"Egg! Where did that even come from?" Regan cries. "No wonder Donkey Laugh dumped you."

"Donkey Laugh! Who? Liz? She didn't dump me. We mutually decided I'm a terrible boyfriend."

I smile and pull Aunt Bree's ritual out from under my pillow. I've re-written it compulsively, as if good penmanship will make it all work out. I hand it over to Griffin.

"I've never heard of half of this stuff. What the hell is a Grisingturn Tuning Fork?" Griffin asks.

Regan snatches the paper from Griffin's hands. "Oh no. This is a mess with a capital M. You need a dark mirror! Nua said the eclipse—"

I smile again. "I took care of that. Gloaming Moon. Right before you got here. Let's make a list of the stuff we need, and we can run it by Bacchy."

Griffin eyes me suspiciously. "Why are you smiling? You never smile."

"That's not true. I smile," I say, my cheeks going hot.

"Not really. You do this." He gives a weird twist of the lips, Mona Lisa style.

"No, that looks like you're about to barf. It's more like this." Regan gives her own imitation. Neither version is flattering.

Griffin points at my face. "Yeah! That's your normal look, Cassie. That frowny thing you're doing now."

Regan nods.

"So, you two decide to get along to chop on me? Nice."

"You do seem legit... I dunno. Lighter. What's going on?" Regan asks.

"Maybe she got laid," Griffin says, grinning and spinning the desk chair around. His eyes widen as he rotates, and he slams his feet down to stop his spin. "You did!"

"Ew, no. What's wrong with you?" I say.

"Oh. Em. Gee. Play by play. *Now*. What happened?" Regan says.

I can see my reflection in my dresser mirror. I'm a guilty shade of hot pink. I glance at Griffin.

"It's just us gals here, Cassie," he says, and rests his chin on the back of his hands and bats his eyelashes. I laugh despite myself.

"I didn't 'get laid,' you creep. I saw Colin. While I was charging the mirror. We hung out. Alright?" I purse my lips to keep embarrassment and pure glee from showing.

"This dude?" Griffin pulls a photo booth strip of me and Colin from the corner of my mirror. "Oh man, he's a cutie." He looks up at Regan and me, who are staring at each other with wide eyes. "What? I can appreciate a nice-looking guy. I'm secure."

"I need to save him," I say, sobering. "I have to."

We strategize about how to get into Fenice's office over delivery. Griffin is getting pizza crumbs all over my bed when I hear the front door.

Rats crawl over me in the middle of the night, brought on by Griffin's habit of waving his food around when he talks.

"Can you not?" I gesture at the crumbs. Griffin slides to the floor, taking his paper plate with him.

"Hey, Cass." Dad knocks and pokes his head in. "Oh, sorry. Didn't know you had company here." He opens the door fully to reveal a delighted smile, probably thinking, 'My crazy daughter has friends again! Hooray!'

No. Not crazy. I need to be kinder to myself, Pict said.

"Dad, this is Griffin and Regan. Guys, this is my dad." I've warned them against telling my dad anything about Theban, so they

272

keep things nice and vague when Dad asks how we know each other. Regan's machine-gun chatter keeps Dad from asking too much more.

We move to the living room and share a few slices with Dad. He and Regan bond over their love of *The Hunger Games*, with Dad cornering her to explain the themes of the texts like a professor with a class of one. And Griffin makes Dad choke on his water with his sage advice for dealing with a particularly annoying colleague of his. "You have to weed-whack your way past the bullsh... er, crap. You know? Or just have *him* whacked."

"You guys want to come to Cassie's birthday dinner Saturday?" Dad asks.

Regan turns to me. "You didn't tell me it was your birthday!"

"I've been a little preoccupied lately," I say drily. "It's no big deal. I'm turning seventeen."

"We'd love to come, Mr. Morai!" Regan chirps.

Griffin agrees enthusiastically. "Hells yeah! Free food!" Regan kicks his leg. "And celebrating Cassie?"

"Yeah, yeah. Fine. I guess you guys can come." I smile faintly.

After we finish up and I close the door behind them, Dad's smile nearly knocks me on my back.

"They're really great, Cass. I approve. I invited Mrs. O to dinner, too, by the way. Saw her the other day," Dad says.

"Awesome."

"And, ah... I invited Colin," he says with a slight cough.

My eyes nearly pop out of my head. I concentrate on closing the pizza box as if it's the most complex piece of origami ever invented. I can't tell who's more awkward about this whole thing, but if hair blushed alongside skin, I'd be a Bacchy shade of red.

"Oh. Okay. Um. Fun. Should be fun."

23

I peer across the street at Madame Grey's storefront. The ancient tree in front of me should do a decent job of hiding me from view, but... I glance around nervously. The last time I tried to hide, it didn't work out well.

The neon sign is off.

What the hell am I doing? This pit stop on the way to Mrs. O's has become... what, exactly? A citizen's arrest?

A half-hour passes. No movement. This is so dumb.

What if they're in there? What are they plotting? What if they see me? What if...

Whatever. I will not think about it. Fears and compulsions only win if I let them. I force myself into the present. This moment. What my senses are taking in *now*, the way Pict coached.

I fully intend to continue on to Mrs. O's, but my legs somehow lead me to the front of the shop. My heart pounds my ribs with such intensity it should be visible to onlookers.

I throw the door open, and it bounces off the wall and nearly back into my face. The bells attached to the door jingle violently.

Dust, papers, an empty space. Only the window dressings, disclaimer on the wall, and the bead curtain hanging in the doorway remain. I kick at a random takeout menu on the ground and walk farther into the room, keeping an eye on the door to ensure it's still open. I kneel near a stack of papers.

"What are you doing here?" a voice says. I shriek.

Sebastian pushes through the bead curtain.

"Oh, thank God. You scared me," I say. "What are you doing here?"

He steps into the room, eyeing the papers. He kneels and picks one up, tosses it. "That's what I asked you. I'm trying to track down known Bedlamites. Checking this place again to see if I missed anything the first time."

"I—I came because everyone hates me. People got hurt because of me. I felt like I had to do something."

"Pretty reckless, considering you know what they're capable of."

"You're here alone, too."

He shrugs. "If I'm going to take over for my father one day, I need to prove myself to everyone. What's your excuse?"

"If they wanted to kill me, they would've, right?" I twist my lips into a humorless smile. "Like they did Theodore and the others."

He picks up another paper and skims it. "You and Theodore were close," he says. It doesn't sound like a question, but I answer anyway.

"Yeah." I clear my throat. "He was kind. And his poor mom—he was planning on visiting her before... Aunt Bree is the worst. I don't know why they had *her* call his mom."

"Come on. There's nothing here. Nothing important, anyway. I'll walk you home." Sebastian gestures toward the door. I abandon my decision to visit Mrs. O and lead the way.

We walk in silence for a bit, and I sneak a peek at him when he's not looking. God, he's just painfully handsome. His blonde hair glints gold in the fading light. He pins me with those gorgeous eyes.

"How's your arm?" he asks.

"I'm fine. How're you?"

"I've been better. I've also been worse."

"Do you blame me, too?" I ask in a small voice. I don't know why his opinion of me matters. It just does.

"No," he says, no hint of hesitation before his answer. "You were used. Anyone blaming you for this is an idiot."

"My aunt does. So do lots of other people." We reach my block and turn the corner.

"Like I said."

"Thank you. I'm a mess. I feel so…"

"Stop it." He turns toward me, gripping my upper arms firmly. "If I had brought that thing in, not knowing what would happen, would you have blamed me?"

"No, of course not!"

"So, you wouldn't blame me, but you'll beat yourself up for it?"

My voice cracks as I look up at him. "I feel so sad. All of the time now."

He pulls me into his arms and hugs me, resting his chin on top of my head. "I know. It's awful. But that isn't on you, okay?"

I nod my head, moving his chin with it. It's probably my imagination, but it almost feels like he busses my hair with his lips. "Good. Get some rest. And when are you coming back? You're not gone for good, right?"

"I'll be back in a few days." I say goodbye and turn to mount the stairs. Colin is sitting on his stoop, watching us.

"Hi, Colin." It almost feels like I got caught cheating. I purse my lips. That's ridiculous. We're not even dating.

"Hey, Cass. Roof in a few?" He says it loud, loud enough that Sebastian hears.

Sebastian smiles at Colin, his dimple in full effect. He turns that smile on me and lifts an eyebrow as if to say, *Did I get you in trouble with the boyfriend?*

"Yep," I respond. I wave at them both and bolt inside.

"WHO WAS THE MANNEQUIN COME TO LIFE?" COLIN asks. He's sitting on the ledge, legs hanging off of the building. *He flounders. I race to the ledge in time to see the look on his face as he topples over, dropping into the darkness below.*

"Come sit," I say, pointing at his lounge chairs. I hop over the knee-wall and force myself not to panic.

"You come sit here." He pats the spot next to him on the ledge.

It's too high. Too dangerous. You'll fall and... Screw it. I push up and swing my legs over, gripping the lip of the ledge behind me for dear life.

"So?" Colin asks.

"So," I repeat.

"Who's the blond guy? He looked like a Calvin Klein ad. What's his story?"

"He's a friend from camp," I say.

Colin makes a face. We're quiet for a bit before he asks, to my everlasting shock, "Are you guys going out?"

"What?"

"I asked if that's your... boyfriend, or whatever. You didn't introduce him."

"Sebastian is..."

"*Sebastian*? His name is Sebastian? Oh God."

"What's wrong with his name? I think it's a nice name. And he's sweet."

"If you say so." Colin snorts. "The only people named Sebastian are supervillains in comic books and crappily written love interests on fan fiction forums."

Colin is acting different. Off. I don't know what his problem is, but the fact he's giving me attitude when I'm busy trying to save his life is almost too much.

"Yeah, and the crab from *The Little Mermaid*, but of course you'd cherry pick the most dramatic options. Why are you being like this?" I ask.

"Like what?"

"Like *this*." I try to wave a hand in his direction but remember I need it to cling to my ledge perch.

"I don't know. Maybe because my friend avoids me, and when I finally see her, she's with some guy she's making eyes at and doesn't even bother introducing me to."

"We hashed out that whole avoiding thing. I haven't been avoiding you. And I wasn't making eyes at anyone." Why are we arguing?

"You were. Hugging in the middle of the sidewalk and kissing."

"He didn't kiss me!"

"He kissed the top of your head," Colin says.

So he did do it! "Oh my God, that isn't a kiss!"

"Still kissing," he says.

"So what? I don't get why—"

"You don't get why I'm all bent? For someone who knows so much about so many things, you don't know?" He inhales, his chest puffing up, before he blows it out, his shoulders falling. "You know what, it's fine. This is stupid. I—" He makes to move back onto the roof. I grab his sleeve, and he looks at me, his eyes big and blue as the ocean, the thoughts behind them changing like quicksilver. *Oh God, what if I pull his sleeve and that puts him off balance and he falls—*

"I like you, Cass. But it's fine. If you're happy with—"

"*What?*" I shout over him. I have no idea what is happening. My pulse races.

"I'm not repeating it."

"He's my *friend*. Sebastian is just a *friend*. We're not—" I swallow with an effort. "Tell me. Please."

He closes his eyes, and when he opens them, there's a look in them, an intense glint. "I like you. A lot. More than a lot. The day you left it felt like someone rammed a hot poker in my chest and would wiggle it around whenever I thought about you. Which was every three minutes. Because I think about you all the time when you're not around. And when you *are* around, I feel like... like when a painting—the colors, the shadows, the light—when it all comes together just right. No. That's dumb." His voice thickens and he swallows. "I'm bad at this. But—"

I launch myself at him, nearly sending us hurling off the ledge like lawn darts.

My courage deserts me when my lips are a breath from his. He cradles my face. His gaze, blue fire, is trained on my mouth, and his unguarded expression tells me everything he was struggling to say with words. My breath shudders out of me as he lowers his lips to mine, inch by agonizing inch. And when he finally presses them to mine, deepens the kiss, my blood hums through my veins, and I nearly weep at the sweet relief. Then he touches his tongue to mine and all thought flies right out of my head.

A second, a minute, a million years later, he lifts his head and beams down at me. I peek up at his handsome face and then away.

"Hi," I say, cringing, suddenly shy.

"Hi," he says, and hugs me close. "Was that your first kiss?"

"Y—yes. Why? It was obvious?" I stammer.

"Yeah."

I suck in a sharp breath.

He gives me a teasing grin. "I'm kid—"

"I guess I could always get some practice in with the Calvin Klein model—"

He has his hands cradling my face and his lips slanting on mine again before I can get Sebastian's name out. I close my eyes and smile against his mouth.

Later, when he lifts his head, I notice a thin streak of light threading through the black sky behind him, so bright it's visible even with the city glare. It's followed by another. I point the meteor shower out, try to get him to look, but he's more interested in me. He presses his lips to mine again, and I burrow further into his arms.

The heavens rain starlight down on us, and I can't help but stare at Colin as if he's retrieving them, one by one, just for me.

24

"Your turn," Dad says. He reaches for a Trivonometry card. "The word is 'amatory.' Good luck with this one."

"Amatory," I repeat. With a pang, I picture Noah, awkward and sweet, in his canary yellow shirt that first day of orientation. It sounds like what he'd call a "great-grandma word."

"Tick tock, tick tock." At my stern look, Dad smirks and mimes a zipper across his lips.

"It means... well, 'amor' I know... so something related to love?" I respond.

"Very impressive, Cass. Not enough to catch up, but still impressive." Dad grins.

I Frisbee a card at him and pick up my pint of ice cream.

"Um. Do we, by the way, have to have a talk?" Dad says out of the blue.

"A talk?"

"You know. *A talk.*" He sounds strangled. "It occurred to me we've never talked about *any of that stuff,* and you were really young so your mom wouldn't have before..."

"Oh my God! No. We don't need to..." I want to shrink and slip through the gaps in the sofa cushions.

"I mean, you want to respect yourself and—"

"Dad! I know. Everything I need to know, I know. We have cable. And the internet. And I haven't—don't worry. Please stop," I finish awkwardly, closing my eyes. One more word out of him might bring the Giuseppe's back up. *Cringe, cringe, cringe, cringe, cringe.*

"Okay. Good. I mean. Um. By the way, almost-birthday girl, everything is set for dinner tomorrow. I'm looking forward to it. Seventeen is a big deal!"

"Yeah, should be fun," I say, clinging to the topic change and shoving ice cream into my mouth. "You have to promise no singing Happy Birthday. It has to be completely low key."

"Absolutely. Low key. Just you, me, Mrs. O, Griffin, Regan, and your young man..."

Earlier, when Colin and I surfaced for air on the roof and I sat listening to his heart beat beneath my ear, he told me about my dad's invite. "He told me this really long story about the copyright history for the Happy Birthday song. I almost missed the part where he invited me," he said, wheeling a piece of my hair around his finger. Sounded about right.

"...at a nice dinner and..." Dad clears his throat, his expression a little unsure.

Please, no more sex talk.

"I was thinking," he continues. "If you were okay with it, maybe I could invite Ellie, too. You could meet her, and she's dying to meet you. We could all celebrate together."

I stare at Dad. All I hear is the roar of my blood rushing in my ears for a moment. Is that what this dinner is about? Meeting this woman? Instead of celebrating my seventeenth birthday with my mom, I'm supposed to sit across from her replacement all night, fake smile plastered to my face? *That's* my birthday gift? I begin shaking.

I set the spoon in my hand down carefully and concentrate on the rise and fall of my chest. I didn't even care to celebrate my birthday at all. It isn't a big deal, right?

"I don't want to pressure you, Cass. I just—"

"If you don't want to pressure me, then don't," I snap, stunning Dad and myself. My hands ball into fists. I look down and force them to relax. In through the nose. Out through the mouth.

"Cass, please. Your tone... We can discuss this rationally like two adults. No need to raise your voice."

"And there's no need to use your professor voice on me. Whatever. There's nothing to discuss." I blindly grab at my ice cream and napkins, and head to the kitchen. This apartment is too small. I need to be away. From him, from the roiling emotional magma bubbling—building—within me.

Dad follows. "There's plenty to discuss. I wasn't trying to force this on you. I only—"

I shove the ice cream into the freezer and close the door with a bang. "You figured you'd bring it up, and I'd cave because I want you to be happy. *And I do.* But you're attacking me because I don't want to meet her on my birthday. You're not only choosing her over Mom, now you're choosing her over *me*." I hate the hitch in my voice. I hate the stricken look on my father's face. I hate that I'm lashing out and that most of what's coming out of my mouth is hateful and false. But mostly I hate the fact that I can't stop now that I've started.

"Cass, I'm not attacking you! I would never choose anyone over you. You know that." He looks helpless. "And no one could *ever* replace your mother. That's not what this is. Ellie is..."

"Ellie!" I repeat. I make it sound like a curse.

"Your mother broke my heart, Cass! She did. And I know she broke yours, too..."

"Oh, you want me to let you in?" My eyes burn. Kept the poison to myself for too long. I can't stop from vomiting it up now. "To know how I feel? I look around at people and pick them off on the streets, like a psycho. Why is that old man allowed to live? Give me ten of his years for Mom. Why is that lady still around? Take ten from her. Why do they get to live and *my mom* had to go? I want to trade them like baseball cards. That's what I feel." There is a choking pressure in my chest and throat, like I've swallowed fire and ash.

"Cass, I'm so—" Dad reaches for me.

I jerk away. "She lied to me. She said no matter how bad things are, they'll get better, but that's a lie. Nothing, *nothing* will ever fix this. She's gone. Nothing will make that better. Nothing will bring her back. She's dead. My mom is *dead*. Gone."

I haul in a shuttering breath. "There's this ugly *thing* living inside me, and it claws up my insides whenever I think about her. But I feel guilty if I don't think of her, I'm scared not to, because I've forgotten so much already. I'll keep forgetting more, too. And when I do, those memories are gone forever because I can't ask her what *she* remembers. And I can't make new memories with her, either. I've got this draining well I can't fill because she isn't here. *She isn't here*." I'm speaking in fits of starts and stops. "Time doesn't heal anything. She's a hole *right here*, and she'll stay that way until the day I die too."

My vision is blurred. I can feel my eyes swelling. I'm an ugly crier. I push past Dad and drop to my knees onto the rug outside the kitchen door. I comb at the threads, straightening.

"No, Cass. Please. Stop that. You don't—"

"I need to! Let me go!" I scream, struggling against his hold as he tries to force me to my feet.

"Don't give in. Dr. Ward—"

"Dr. Ward has a mom. Did you know that? Her mom is ninety." I am manic. I am speaking too fast. I feel it. I can't stop it. "I don't. My mom is gone. I'll never get to see her again. I'll never hold her again. It's like she got off the bus, and I have to watch her get smaller and smaller as we drive off. And when we're far enough, I won't be able to see her at all. You only get one mom, and I only had mine for *fourteen* years."

Dad pulls me to him, running his hand over my hair. I want this conversation over. I don't want to hear what he has to say in response. Talking about this didn't help. I was right to keep the poison in. Why did I let it out? I pull away and head toward my bedroom.

"Oh, Cass. Honey..."

I wheel on him. "How can you *live* when she's dead? I don't mean 'live' like breathing in and out or... *existing*. I mean go out into the world and replace her—"

"*Stop*. I told you that nothing will ever replace her. *Never*. I see her everywhere. I see her in this house she and I made a home together, and I don't just mean in the photos we've got lying around. I see her making us pancakes in the morning. I see her holding you in her arms the day you were born; this little, squalling, red thing pressed against her chest. I see her whispering that you should punch Rob Riedel in the nose if he tries to look up your skirt again, and telling me her baby 'wouldn't start fights, but she was damn well going to finish them.' I see her playing Trivinometry with us, and her little victory dance. I see her for one breathless second at traffic lights in the faces of strangers, and I spin a conspiracy where she didn't die, because some part of my mind refuses to believe she could be gone. I see her every time I look at you. I close my eyes and I see her. She's everywhere. Everywhere. Because she's here." Dad covers his heart with his hand. Tears are coursing down his cheeks. "She always will be. And so will you. I promise you."

My tears begin anew. The poison is gone. The anger. All of it. All that's left is a yawning, aching emptiness, and two people peering into the void. Dad opens his arms, and I throw myself into his embrace. He holds me tight and rocks me back and forth.

When the shadows on the walls grow long, and the city settles into the quietest it's capable of becoming, Dad finally speaks.

"You know what I think of sometimes? She used to do that thing with her napkin..."

I hiccup out a laugh. "Where she'd fold it into a swan every time we went out because she worked as a banquet hall waitress that one summer."

Dad chuckles and squeezes me harder. "She refused to let that skill go to waste."

I reach up and wipe at my face. Dad goes into the kitchen and rips off a few paper towels. He hands me one. I blow my nose. It feels like sandpaper. People in mourning should always have tissues handy. "I remember when she decided to try that new place and got that haircut—"

"Oh God, not the bangs! She had acres of bangs," Dad groans. He grins down at me. "How about that incredible lullaby she always used to sing you? Even when you were way too old for it."

My lips twist. "She stole it from a movie, you know. She made me swear not to tell you she didn't come up with it herself."

Dad looks floored. "Are you kidding me? I thought she was so creative. I used to tell her we should try to get it copywritten and recorded!"

I giggle. "I know. She used to get a kick out of it."

Dad tenderly pushes my hair behind my ear. "You know, your mother was the love of my life, right up until you were born. We both agreed you snatched up the number one spot in our affections after that. We moved to number two on each other's lists."

I give Dad a lopsided smile and glance at the framed picture of her on the bookshelf, one I could draw from memory if I had Colin's talent. "I miss her," I say unnecessarily. To fill the silence, in the room and in me.

He sighs. "Me too, Cass. Me too."

I open my mouth to speak, close it. Open it again, whipping up a cyclone of mixed emotions behind my ribs. "Tomorrow. You can bring her. Eleanor." Her name scrapes by the tightness in my throat. "El—Ellie. I'll meet her."

"No. That wasn't well done of me at all. It's your birthday. It's not about me. It's not about anyone but you. There are three hundred sixty-four other days of the year when you can meet her, and I tried to hijack the one that should be yours."

"I want you to be happy. It's—"

"I am happy. You're the most important person in my world, Cassandra Morai. No one else comes close. I don't want you worrying about it."

Guilt churns in my stomach. "Really, Dad. It's alright. I—I don't want you to be alone. I'm sorry."

"Don't be sorry! Don't *ever* be sorry. I know it's not easy. I want you to know, Cass, it wasn't easy for me either. I felt guilt, confusion. But then I realized Ellie wasn't replacing your mom. You don't push someone out of your heart when someone else comes along. My heart swelled and made some room. Ellie seems like a good fit for the broken-down version of Jeff your mom left behind."

I wasn't the only one who felt that way. "Dad, I want to meet her. I... I'll adjust, I'm already adjusting, I promise. This talk... it helped. Really."

"We can talk about this some other time."

"No. I want to talk about it now. I want this, Dad. I swear it."

"Okay. You'll meet her soon, Cass, I promise. But she won't be coming to dinner tomorrow. That's final," he says. His eyes take on a faraway look, and he gives me a sad little half-smile. "You know, toward the end there, when it became clear your mom didn't have a lot of time left... she told me she wanted me to find someone when she was gone. I refused to hear it, but she insisted. She wanted me to find someone so long as, and I quote, 'She's not as cute as me. Or as funny.'"

My heart contracts painfully, thinking of Mom at the end. Skin stretched over bone, weak, but still joking. Still upbeat.

I lay my head on Dad's shoulder. "Is she? El... Eleanor. As cute? As funny?"

Dad heaves a big breath and rests his head against mine. "No. Your mom was a once-in-a-lifetime find. Only one person comes close. I'm proud to call her my daughter."

25

The crow is back. The bird I saw the day I met Colin rests on the knee-wall between our rooftops. I'm actually not sure it's the same one, but it looks familiar enough.

"Get out of here! Message received, dumb bird," I call.

I'm not afraid of it anymore. Our Omen Reading instructor said that a single crow was a sign I'd need to use my scrying abilities for something important. I've got Aunt Bree's ritual to do tonight, and Colin to save after that. I don't need a bird to tell me what I already know.

And yet, it remains. I look over again at Colin's roof door. He's late.

A piercing caw sounds. The crow now has a friend. Two black-as-night crows are watching me from the wall. I ignore the prickle of unease. It's nothing. But a few more settle on the knee-wall. Six crows, the sun glinting off their backs. I can see their prehistoric ancestors in those beady stares, and the hair on the back of my neck stands at attention.

"Holy Hitchcock! What are all those crows doing there?" Colin calls from his door, startling me. He carefully hops over the wall far from where the birds are perched and pulls me to him for a quick kiss. He tries to deepen it, but I can't... not with the crows watching. I pull away and give him a forced smile.

Six crows. Omen of impending death. A soul harvest. The red blessing was Ford, which means this can't be *that*... which means... Oh God. I feel it; a clock inside me has suddenly roared to life, Colin's clock. *It's* coming. I need that ritual. I pick at my thumb and ask Colin if we can go down to his room instead of hanging on the roof. If I sound panicky, he doesn't comment on it. *One, two, three... This compulsion is not me...*

We're nearly at Colin's roof door when Dad emerges from ours. The crows launch off the knee-wall in a flurry of squawks and flapping wings.

"Oh good. You're up here. I was going to see if you wanted Thai for lunch, Cass. I'm going to call it in, maybe in an hour or so? You in, Colin? Noodles?"

"I'm always game for noods." Colin grins.

Dad raises an eyebrow.

It's the first time I've seen Colin honest-to-God blush. "Noodles," he clarifies.

I nod at Dad and follow Colin to his room, silently counting.

"I DIDN'T REALIZE YOU'D BE GOING BACK. THIS SUCKS. I thought camp was over," Colin says, handing me a record.

"Yeah, I just came back for the weekend. For my birthday."

"Why don't you skip the rest of it? Stay here with me."

"I have to go back. It's only for one more week." *Less, actually, since I'm skipping the Coil Walk.*

"Calvin Klein going to be there too?" he asks nonchalantly.

"Are you jealous?"

He snorts. "No." He pauses. "Yes."

I lean over and kiss him, and run my hand over his head. He had a haircut this morning. His black hair is shorter than it's been since I've known him. I like it, but I miss running my fingers through it.

"What am I supposed to hold onto when we... you know... now that you cut your hair."

He laughs. "When we 'you know'?"

My face feels hot. "Yeah."

"You still can't say it. It's hilarious. Just say it! Kiss. When we kiss," he says.

"When we... make music," I say, looking at his records spread out in front of me.

"Nice euphemism. Sounds way worse than kissing. When we 'make music,' you can always hold onto my—why are you laughing, pervert? I was going to say ears."

"Well, thank God your ears jut out so mu—"

Before I can finish my taunt, I'm flat on my back with his lips pressed to mine. He slips his lips to my neck and kisses his way to my ear, spreading goosebumps with every touch. He bites at my lobe gently. "Your ears aren't so small either, you know."

"Yeah, but in comparison to yours, mine are dainty. So are the Easter Bunny's. So are Dumbo's."

I'm breathless from the tickle-attack he unleashes. And when he calls my eyes "gorgeous" and presses his open mouth to mine, I'm left breathless for a different reason.

We pull apart when angry, muffled shouting startles me.

Colin's chest heaves. I feel a thrill that I have that effect on him, but the shouting starts again. I look at the door with worry. "What is that?"

"What's what?" he asks. "Oh. I'm so used to it I don't even notice anymore. That is two-thirds of the prim and perfect Clay family and the daily airing of their grievances." Colin's face flushes a dull red.

"I only stay for our son. You wait until Colin's in college," Colin's mother shouts.

"Why wait? He's only a year away. Put us out of our misery! You think you're doing him a favor? You think you're doing *me* any favors?"

"Oh, please. Perfect wife, perfect life. You begged me to stay. Can't win an election if you're going through an ugly divorce, can you, Jon? And I swear to God, it'll be the ugliest—"

"What do you want from me, Katherine?"

"Let's go to the roof," Colin says, standing and reaching down to help me up. "Let me grab my hat." He walks over to his walk-in closet. I follow, pretending I'm not listening to the vicious hate-fest going on downstairs.

"I think your closet is bigger than my room," I say, talking to drown out the arguing. "Whoa. What's that?" I nod toward a bunch of canvases leaning against the wall near the door.

"No, don't touch—" Colin says.

I'm already thumbing through the canvases. "You painted these? They're amazing!"

"They're okay. Let's get out of here," he says, rubbing at the back of his neck, a supremely uncomfortable look on his face. I am about to take pity on him and leave the paintings alone when I see the last one in the bunch: a familiar face staring back at me.

I pull it up and look back at him. "You painted... me?"

The painted version of me is looking up from beneath her lashes with stunning kaleidoscope eyes. I look shy... pretty... vulnerable. I see myself the way he sees me, and I feel beautiful. Until I notice the hand pushing my light brown hair behind an ear. It is *my* hand. Scabbed. Rough. Damaged. I touch my hand to that painted hand.

"I painted that after that day we went to the Spite House," he says.

I look up at him. My eyes well. I'm not sure why.

"And I painted this one after the first time we 'made music.'" He reaches over and pulls a large painting out from another pile of leaning canvases. "I was up late for that one. And this one after I met Mrs. O." He pulls out another. "And this one the first day I met you." He's captured a haunted quality in that last one.

To see yourself the way someone you care about sees you... I feel exposed. Raw. I want to tell him about my OCD, about what's wrong with me, but I'm too much of a coward. Too scared of losing him.

"You don't like them," he says flatly.

"No, I do! They're... amazing. You're so talented. It's..." I look down at my hands.

"I see you, Cassie. I see all of you." He takes my hand in his and kisses it. I recoil. He runs his hand through his hair, forgetting it's shorter than it used to be, and drops it.

"See that suitcase on the bottom shelf?" he says. "It's filled with my stuff. Random things that are important to me. Hadn't occurred to me to take that stuff out and let it clutter up my room out there.

Because I've never done that. There was no point unpacking when we might have to move around again..." He pauses, visibly searching for what he wants to say. "My dad says we're staying here. He's running for Congress, but that's a whole other story. The point is... I swear I have one... the point is, you have your deal, and when you want to tell me about it, I'm here, but this is my deal: even knowing we're not moving, I didn't unpack because this place didn't feel like home. But you... *you* do."

I pull at his perfect ears and plant my lips on his. He smiles against my mouth a second before he runs his hand up my back. We don't leave that closet for a very long time.

26

Veranda Restaurant is all starched white tablecloths and bowtie-wearing waiters, but the dining room has a lively and festive feel to it instead of being stuffy.

I shush Dad, but his voice still carries even through the din. "When she was seven, she shoved a straw up her nose. It was wedged in there good and tight. We rushed her to the ER. She was screaming, and every time she would draw in a breath, the thing would whistle," Dad says. Mrs. O, Colin, Regan, and Griffin all laugh.

I feel myself getting hot. "Dad!"

He gives me an innocent look. "What?"

Colin slants me a crooked grin. "I didn't know you played an instrument, Cass."

"She plays the *tube*-ah," Griffin says. He and Colin exchange appreciative looks, admiring each other's lame wit.

"Terrible." Regan rolls her eyes.

"Okay, no more embarrassing stories," Dad says. He looks like

a man reborn. Me, his weirdo daughter, inviting friends around.
Hanging with a boy. His dream.

"Is that a swan?" Colin asks, looking at my napkin.

"Yeah," I say.

Dad winks at me and turns to Mrs. O. "Claudia, why don't you
tell us how you've been doing."

"Oh, you know me, Jeffrey. Plugging along. One foot in front of
the other," Mrs. O says.

"I don't want to bring the mood down, but... any news from the
city?" Dad asks.

"Oh! Yes! I heard from them yesterday." She smiles. To Regan
and Griffin she offers, "The city wanted to take my property, but
it's the strangest thing. The developer dropped out! The man from
the city called to say they won't be taking the place after all."

I grab for her hand, and she takes mine between both of hers,
giving it a squeeze.

It worked! The ritual worked! Regan gives me a toothy smile and
a little silent "yay." A parade erupts in my mind, bursts of color,
fanfare. *It worked!* I barely hear the others congratulating her. I
lean over and give her parchment thin skin an impulsive kiss.

"Amazing! How?" I ask.

"I don't know. He just abandoned the project altogether," she
says. She twists her lip a bit. "It's funny, though. I was almost sad
about it."

"Sad? Why would you be sad someone *isn't* yoinking your
place?" Griffin asks.

"I don't understand," I piggyback.

"The developer, a man who actually ended up being some kind
of wonderful—Paul Tautamo—I guess he caught wind of my

situation: how long I've been here, my family's history in the neighborhood. He offered me an apartment in the new building. Rent free for life. He said if I wanted to work, he'd give me a spot in the supermarket he was going to build, but that he'd understand if I wanted to spend the money the city gave me and enjoy retirement instead. Sweet man." Mrs. O sighs.

I freeze. "S—so you *wanted* the deal to go through?"

"It was tempting, is all." She pats my hand.

"But if you could've picked what'd happen, would you have picked his offer or—" I almost don't want her answer.

"I wouldn't have chosen at all," she responds, taking a long sip of her soft drink. "I would've let it be."

"What do you mean?" Regan asks.

Mrs. O's plump cheeks lift with her smile. "When I was a girl, there was a woman who would come into my father's shop. After I was blinded, I was angry, spitting mad. Uncontrollable. You have an idea of what your life is going to be like, and when something traumatic comes along and makes that idea impossible... Well, misery lives in the space between expectations and reality. She caught an argument between me and my father, God rest his soul, and pulled me aside to tell me a story. I can't do it justice, but it was something like:

"An old washerwoman named Yana served the royal family in the land of Ash. Day after day, after she'd finished the wash, she would stand at an enormous vat of boiling water alongside dozens of other women and harvest gray dye from slippery and spiky mollusks. In the evenings, Yana's young daughter Porto would rub her mother's gnarled, stained fingers while studying the ancient, forgotten art of Color.

"One day, Yana discovered she'd been replaced in the washing chamber by another.

"'You have lost your work, and I have none. How will we eat?' Yana's daughter Porto cried. 'This is a tragedy!'

"'Maybe no, maybe so. It'll all come clean in the wash,' Yana said.

"Yana showed her daughter how to make the trinkets of her youth, little beaded nothings, and they took them to market, praying they'd fetch enough for a loaf of bread. Their wares sold out immediately. In a drab world, Porto's knowledge of Color made their designs famous, and soon even the Queen commissioned a wondrous colorful headdress.

"'Look at all the gold we have!' Porto cried. 'How lucky we are, Mother!'

"'Maybe no, maybe so. It'll all come clean in the wash,' Yana said.

"Yana and Porto's beads were carved from the jagged shells found at the water's edge, and one day one such shell badly injured both of Porto's hands. Yana carefully washed and bandaged her daughter's wounds.

"'We'll never finish the Queen's headdress now, Mother! We are ruined!' Porto cried.

"'Maybe no, maybe so. It'll all come clean in the wash,' Yana said.

"Now it came to pass on the day the headdress was due to be delivered to the Queen a great coup occurred, and the Royal Family and all those inside the palace were murdered.

"'The poor Queen! But how lucky we are we were unable to deliver the headdress,' Porto called.

"'Maybe no, maybe so. It'll all come clean in the wash,' Yana said.

"The moral?" Mrs. O asks, like a patient schoolmarm.

"Yana only knew one phrase?" Griffin offers.

"That, and... you have to roll with what comes. Sometimes life falls apart to fall into place." Mrs. O sips her wine. "That's enough out of an old lady with her secondhand wisdom."

"You are a delight, and you know it," Dad says. "False modesty."

"You're right. I *am* a delight." Mrs. O raises her glass in silent toast. "Thank you for the reminder, Jeffrey."

"But what good came from you being blinded?" I interrupt. "I don't understand."

Dad gives me a quelling look, but Mrs. O responds. "I ended up going to a special school. I met my husband there. William was vision-impaired, too. But he saw me better than anyone, and I saw him. That man was the greatest happiness of my life." If remembering her love brings on that look, the full force of her loving must have been striking at the time.

Regan sighs.

Mrs. O shrugs and sucks in her bottom lip. "And my greatest sorrow was losing him. But that brought me to you, Cassie. I knew what you were going through. What do you do with all that love? Like being a pitcher with no catcher. I figured I could try and Sherpa you through that painful period. And guess what? You became my next greatest joy. You and your father, and now Colin here, you are my family. Everything happens for a reason."

I lean over and give her a fierce hug. Dad squeezes my shoulder when I sit back, his eyes suspiciously moist.

"Can I get a party started or what?" Mrs. O grins. "Too heavy for a birthday. Back to celebrating, please."

"Alright, that's a tough act to follow, so I won't even try... but I got you something, Cass." Colin hands me a wrapped gift box. "Open it."

I take the box and stare. I didn't expect a gift from him. Didn't really expect one from anyone but my father. I pull the lid off.

"Are those stuffed squirrels?" Regan asks.

"I don't understand girls at all, and even I know that's not the way to romance them, man." Griffin shakes his head.

"Squirrel fur..." I say, beaming at Colin.

"Slippers," Colin finishes, ducking his head and suddenly looking a little bashful. "They're not squirrel fur. Just squirrel-shaped. But I figured this was the next best thing."

They're perfect. So perfect. My very own Cinderella slippers. I cradle the two squirrel slippers to my chest and try to rip my eyes away from Colin's. There's a soft look in his blue eyes, and a small smile plays on his lips. His gaze slips past me, and I hear the first strains of "Happy Birthday" from the wait staff.

My eyes mist as I look at *my* family. At Mrs. O, belting out the tune enthusiastically. Griffin and Regan, their truce holding during the dinner, both singing for all they're worth. At Dad—my sweet, brave, selfless father—boisterously shouting it out at the top of his lungs despite his promise. And Colin, who is looking at me like I'm *his* birthday and Christmas gift all in one. I look down at the slippers in my hands.

For a second I concentrate on what I have right now—these people, *my* people—and not on what I've lost. I see what the world can be.

But only for a second. Because the clock within me is ticking, and I can't keep what I have unless I do something to save it.

"GRIFFIN TRIED TO READ YOUR JOURNAL. I DIDN'T LET him," Regan says.

We're back in my room post-birthday dinner. I grab the book and shove it into my desk drawer. When I glare at Griffin, he smiles.

"What? I was bored. You were up there on the roof with your boyfriend forever. Don't worry, I didn't even read two words before Snatchy McSnatcher here grabbed it from me," he says.

"Are you sure you want to spend the last few hours of your birthday working on a ritual?" Regan asks.

I nod and grab my pajamas. "I'll be right back. Have to say goodnight to Dad."

I've convinced Dad that all I want for my birthday is a sleepover with Griffin and Regan. He raised an eyebrow about a boy being part of that group, but since that boy isn't my boyfriend and Regan will be there, he didn't get all old-fashioned on me.

"Goodnight, Cass." Dad kisses my forehead and wraps his arms around me. "I know your friends are waiting so I won't keep you, but I wanted to say... well, how damn proud I am of the woman you're becoming. You're honest. You're caring. You laugh at my dad jokes. You're everything your mom and I always dreamed you'd be and more. I'm... I'm glad you're mine. That's all."

I almost miss Dad wiping his eyes since mine are suddenly swimming. I'm not honest. I've been lying to him about camp, about Theban, for an age now. I hug him tight and pray the image he has of me is never shattered.

"Oh! One more thing. Your present! I wanted to wait to give it to you." He pulls out a long thin box and holds it out to me.

"Dad, I told you I just wanted the sleepover. You didn't have to—*oh*." Inside the box is a beautiful gold fan-shaped necklace on a delicate gold chain. Each of the delicate wedges making up the fan houses a picture of my Mom and me. All but the last one, actually. That one is of the three of us.

"It's a locket! Antique from the Victorian era. See, you can close the fan up and it becomes a triangle, or you can open it up and the pictures, there's five of them... Do you like it?" Dad asks.

I blink back tears and throw my arms around his neck. "I love it." I kiss his scruffy cheek. "And I love you. I'm glad you're mine, too." He helps me put the necklace on.

"Beautiful. Like the person in the locket and the person wearing it." He winks. "Okay, enough mushy stuff. Get back to your friends."

I laugh and run back to my room, sobering when I see that Regan has already started getting the stuff together for Aunt Bree's ritual. "Okay, so Griffin made that disgusting paste from those beetles and the plants Bacchy got for us. I don't know how you're going to..." Regan shudders. "Anyway, I finished with the Sending Circle. I burned that sign Griffin grabbed from Madame Grey's wall yesterday, so we have the ash. You have the blood... I think we're good there," Regan says. "There's like five other things on here we still haven't prepped, but you can get started. The only other part that's going to suck is this..." She holds up a whip with five knotted ends.

"Hey, unless you're into it. Fifty shades of kicking Madame Grey's ass," Griffin says. He squints at the copy of the ritual in his hand and shakes his head. "Seventy-three lashes as part of the sacrifice. Pain-powered ritual."

"You'll only get one chance with the mirror, Cassie. Dark mirrors are one charge per ritual," Regan says. She hesitates. "Are we sure we trust your aunt on all of this...?"

I reach for the page with the ritual and the whip. "She wants to neutralize Bedlam, right? So do I. I can't... I need to make it right, Regan, and it needs to be tonight. Then I can concentrate on saving Colin tomorrow."

27

No two keyholes on Fenice's door are alike and, as Griffin put it, "even her locks have locks on them." How does she keep it all straight?

I wince as I lift my hand to knock, my shirt brushing against my sore back. The lashes I had to give myself for Aunt Bree's ritual aren't bleeding anymore, but the bandages don't do much for the pain. And they do nothing for my headache; I had to muffle the sounds of the whip and my groans somehow, and Griffin's attempts at DJ'ing incredibly loud techno sparked a migraine for both me and Regan. It also generated a banging broomstick warning from our downstairs neighbor 3C, an in-person visit from 4D, and a near heart attack when I couldn't remember locking the door and Dad rattled the door knob after 4D's visit.

"Dad, I promise it's not a sex thing, it's just a forbidden occult ritual!"

There is shuffling on the other side of the wooden door, then a brass butterfly's wing directly in front of my face slides away and is replaced with a magnified eyeball. The sounds of locks being turned sound until Fenice is standing in front of me, her bird's nest of hair extra poofy today. "Cassandra, hello. What brings you—"

"Pict," I interrupt, as tears spring to my eyes. Luckily, I feel like I'm betraying Pict since he's grown on me, which means that the tears come easy—I've always been able to cry when I feel guilty and ashamed.

"Oh, you poor—come right in. Don't you worry." She ushers me in and tosses a nasty glance over at Pict's door.

"Please don't tell him I came here. It'll make things worse," I say after she shuts the door and begins locking it behind us. I close my eyes so she can't see the lie reflected there. Technically it *would* make things much, much worse if she were to say anything.

"Of course not! Let me set you up with a nice cup of tea and you can tell me all about it."

Her office looks like a greenhouse, and not just because of all the live plants peppering the space. There are images of flowers on every conceivable surface. A room decorated entirely in floral prints should feel old and dated, but somehow Ms. Fenice's sanctuary is as refreshing as her presence.

She hurries over to a sideboard and comes back with a pair of chipped floral teacups. "Sit, please. I've been working on perfecting this particular blend for a while now. Sweet enough on its own, no sugar or honey required."

I accept the cup with a murmur of thanks, and Fenice seats herself across from me. "Now then, what did that brute do?"

"He's..." I can't force myself to lie.

"Let me guess. He's being a perfectionist, hypercritical, insulting ass? He's been that way most of the time I've known him, so it's no surprise."

"Most of the time? Why, he used to be different?" I ask.

"We're all a little different when we're younger and more idealistic. But Marty's story is not mine to tell." She shakes her head. "Present bad behavior isn't excused because of the past."

I want to ask so many follow-up questions, but I'm here for a reason. "I don't know. Maybe he's right about me."

"Nonsense! You are perfectly capable. You positively shine in class. And Magellan has warmed to you more than any of the others. He's a good judge."

I look over at Magellan, her raven. It's true that he doesn't peck at me as often as the others in class. Evidently, that's considered warming.

Fenice crosses to my sofa and takes my hands in hers. "Is this about the attack? We're scryers, Cassandra. Woulda shouldas are for other people. You can be a Marty, eaten up by the past and made bitter by it... or you can forgive—those around you, *yourself*, whomever—and move forward a little sadder and a lot wiser."

I wasn't thinking about the attack, but now... no, a pep talk doesn't get me off the hook.

"What did Marty say to upset you?"

"No, he's been... surprisingly supportive, actually. I—" *Say the words, coward. You lie every day of your life pretending to be normal. This is no different.* "It's not about the attack. I... I damaged a book of his. Something called the *Galdr Leechbook*, I think?"

Fenice's eyebrows disappear somewhere in her nest of frizzed curls. "Marty had a copy? How..."

She leaps up, rushing to one of the trunks lining the room, and throws it open. She paws through text after text, setting them on the ground, before rushing to another and doing the same. She mutters the entire time, mostly things that sound curse word-adjacent—things like "clucking dingdong."

I set down my cup and watch her repeat the same in yet another trunk. "That lousy, thieving... once a crook... I should have known..." Then she crows and holds up a book in triumph. It's a dull green with gold leaf lettering. She returns, clutching the text to her chest.

My pulse thumps so hard I feel it throughout my entire body.

"That's the same book I damaged! Did you think Mr. Pict stole your copy?" I ask.

"The thought crossed my mind, yes," Fenice says, setting the book down on the table. "I don't know where Marty got a copy, but I'm glad he didn't swipe mine. There are only a handful left in the world."

"He isn't someone who would steal."

"You'd be surprised what people are capable of when they feel they don't have a choice. Always remember, Cassandra: trust should be earned, not freely given."

"Even if he wanted to... your door is..."

"Oh, that." Fenice gives a devilish grin. "The best security system is the one that deters folks from even bothering to try."

"Is it true there's a ritual in that book to stop a scried death?" I ask, trying to sound casual. "I didn't get to look at Pict's."

Fenice flips through the book carefully. "Yes... ah, here it is: 'Halt the Harvest.' This book is incredible... a collection of the most powerful, and therefore forbidden, rituals we scryers have ever developed."

I reach over. "Can I see—"

"I'm sorry, Cassandra." Fenice closes it and hugs it to her chest protectively again. "I can't afford to let anything happen to it, and you just told me you damaged Marty's copy."

"But if I can—"

"I have to protect these texts." She gives me a pained look. "You understand, don't you?"

I reluctantly nod, wishing I could wrench the thing from her. I debate telling her about saving Colin, but something tells me she won't be on board with me doing a forbidden ritual, as nice as she is. I need another way.

———————

"HEARD OF THE BOOK, AYE," BACCHY SAYS, DRINKING HIS ginger cider and looking around the Rotunda. "Exceptionally rare. If you saw it in Linda Fenice's office, chances are that's the only copy we'll ever come close to in our lifetimes. Marko's your man."

"Marko? The pickpocket?" I ask. "He lifted my wallet my first day at Theban."

"That Magpie is a master thief. Reformed, though. But back in the day he was a legend. He could steal the hair off your head and sell it back to you as a wig, and you'd be none the wiser. If anyone can help you, it'd be him."

We thank Bacchy, and Regan looks past his retreating form with a blinding smile.

"Yikes," Griffin mumbles, his eyes sliding away. I turn and see Noah haltingly making his way toward us. Regan pushes away from the table and rushes over to him.

I stand and wring my hands, trying to avoid staring at the eye-patch covering his left eye. "Noah, I..."

"You didn't tell me *she'd* be here," Noah says, hate burning in his one eye, startling me.

"Noah! Cassie is a victim in this, too." Regan rests a gentle hand on his arm.

"A victim with two eyes, at least," Noah spits.

I hang my head. "I'm so sorry—"

"I don't want to hear anything you have to say. You got all those people killed. You did this." He points to his eye.

One, two, three. This compulsion is not me.

"Noah, please," Regan says.

He wrenches his arm away from Regan's touch. "There's nothing you can say, Regan. I'm going into the Coil in a couple of days with a limp and one eye. I'm not bringing a murderer in with me, too. You should've told me she was going to be here."

Four, five, six. I control it. It doesn't control me.

"She's your friend, Noah. She's my *best friend*. You don't know the whole story. Sit down and—"

Seven, eight, nine. I am strong.

"I love you, Regan. You know I do. But this... I need to get out of here." Tears swim in Noah's eye, and his entire body vibrates with emotion. "I can't be around this vile—"

"Nah, man," Griffin says. "You can't talk about Cassie like that." He doesn't raise his voice, and his tone has that special Griffin joking quality, but there is an iron undercurrent to his words. "We all feel bad about what happened to you, but it wasn't her fault."

Ten. If he'd cracked a chair over me, I don't think the blow would've hurt more. My friend, the one who gave me my first ginger cider and laughed alongside me in class, is gone. It feels like a death. The ache in my core is unadulterated mourning.

Noah turns and limps off without another word. Regan hurries after him. Their exchange looks heated.

"Well, the honeymoon is over," Griffin says, openly staring at the two of them arguing. "This is like the telenovelas my grandma used to watch. All that's missing is an evil twin."

It makes me sad to watch them. Noah adored Regan before the blast. I think he still does. But he's been replaced by a simmering pot of a boy, a quiet cauldron of rage. And when Regan said he didn't "know the whole story..." well, my best guess would be that she hasn't told Noah she was there when I got that amulet.

My attention is diverted by the man passing behind them. Marko waltzes gracefully around the hall like a cross between a ballet dancer and a street magician, lifting things off of people and handing them back with his apologies. He bumps into Regan and bows, presenting her with her own pack of gum. I see her eyes go wide, and she whips her head toward me. I nod and leave Griffin, trailing Marko across the hall. It's hard. He dances with shadows.

"Marko?"

"I didn't touch it. If it missing, it not my fault," he says, his gaze shielded behind his heavy lashes.

"I'm not missing anything. I'm hoping you can help me out."

He narrows his eyes. "What kind of help?"

"After you give that guy back his watch, I'll tell you."

He laughs and jogs off. He lifted that watch so fast I almost missed it. "Your eye, it's very good! You are... empty wallet with cartoons on it. Yes?"

"You remember that?" I ask, incredulous.

"Every liberation, I remember. What you need from Marko?"

Marko rats me out. I'm hauled in front of the Grims—

I push the thoughts out of my head. I whisper, "I need you to borrow a book from Linda Fenice. It's in her office."

"Sorry, I cannot help you." He pivots and walks away.

"Wait! *Please!*"

He turns, maybe sensing the desperation oozing out of every one of my pores. "Marko move to this country to put past behind him. Marko is retired."

"I just watched you jack like fifteen things!" I say, following him as he begins walking away again.

"That is impulse. I give everything back."

"But we'd be giving this back, too! I need to take a look at something inside the book."

"Book inside office, you say. Liberate and return something borrowed from your pocket? Okay. Grims no like, but they no punish Marko. Liberate something from locked office? No. Grims punish. Marko on *probation*. I no break in."

"What if I break in? And you just get me the keys?"

"Stubborn girl. Marko say no." He sits at one of the café tables and accepts an espresso from a server.

"What would it take? There has to be something you want."

His broom-bristle lashes fall over his eyes in bliss as he sips his coffee. "Marko want nothing. Good coffee. Bed to put head. Nothing more." He looks past me, and something flickers in his eyes. I turn and see Nua, our mirror scrying instructor, turning a mirror this way and that at one of the Magpie carts. Marko averts his gaze and takes another sip of his coffee when I turn back to him.

"You like Ms. Nua."

"No."

"You're lying!"

Marko sets his cup down and circles his dark fingers around the delicate porcelain. "No lie. 'Like' is too weak a word. No passion.

Listening to rain at night, Marko like. Plums. Good cheese. Thessely Nua..." He says her name like a prayer for salvation. "Marko *love.*"

Nua's nose scrunches up, and her little pointed chin becomes even more pronounced as she laughs with the mirror-selling Magpie. Marko melts into his seat, naked longing in every line of his being.

"Have you asked her out?"

"Crazy girl. No."

"Why don't you talk to her?" I ask.

"Talk to her? Marko has talked! Many times. Always she forgets. 'Nice to meet you,' she says. Over and over." He releases a sigh with a kind of despondent gusto. "Marko can steal anything. Except Thessaly's heart."

"What if..." I offer, desperate for his help. "What if I can find a way to make sure she remembers you? Would you help me get the keys to Fenice's office, then?"

Marko peers at me. "Marko no steal, but... if you do this thing you say with Thessaly, Marko show you how to liberate Linda Fenice's keys yourself."

Not what I was looking for, but better than nothing. "You'll teach me to do what you do?"

"Get out of here!" He roars out a laugh and slaps the table. "She's so funny, this girl!" he says to no one and everyone. "Ten years, I train at the Seven Bells under a virtuoso. Another twenty years of practice before I become a master. Larceny is artistry. I cannot teach this in one day." He stands and throws down a few coins for his coffee. I stand with him.

"But you said you'll show me—"

"The basics, I show you. Maybe it help. Maybe no. But we try." He smiles at a girl passing by and bows extravagantly. She smiles in response before she notices me and rushes off. "There is a rhythm. Identify mark. Choose right time. Exact right distraction. Then speed and scrying. Ohm yes, the scrying. You didn't know. Up here, I picture what I want." He taps his temple and gives a snaggle-toothed grin. "And presto, I make it come to me." He twirls a purple barrette between his fingers lightning quick.

"You don't use the ICARUSS for that? The scrying?" I ask. The passing girl's hair no longer sports one of her two purple barrettes.

Marko flips it to me. "Never! Welborne, he act like scryers are helpless before his little silver machine. 'Oh! Thank you, Welborne! We change things now!'" He laughs. "Bah, Seven Bells students can do that forever. Other scryers, too. Your instincts—that is all you need."

Marko's face lights up as Thessaly Nua approaches, but he slumps when she walks past without an ounce of recognition. He watches her go.

"You help Marko. Marko help you," he says.

I pull a little pad and pen from my bag. "Fine. Tell me everything you know about Thessaly Nua."

NUA WALKS BRISKLY ACROSS THE ROTUNDA, BOOKS clutched to her chest and her brown skirt flowing behind her.

"Do you think this will work?" I ask.

"If Griffin does his part, it should... I hope," Regan says. She clears her throat, her voice more hesitant than I've ever heard it. "Do you want to talk about Noah—"

"No," I say firmly. At that moment, Griffin bumps into Nua,

sending her books flying. He helps her gather them up, apologizing loudly, and hands them over. She looks befuddled when she notices the sheet of paper Griffin deposited on top of her books. She looks for Griffin, but he's already raced past us with a thumbs up.

Regan and I trail Nua as she unfolds the paper addressed to her and hesitantly follows the instructions written there. She reaches Scryer Services and presses the button by the door. The slot in the door opens and a sheet of paper is slipped through the slot before she can say a word.

Ms. Nua reads the paper and walks on, down the hall. I quietly slip a meat pie through the Scryer Services door slot and whisper my thanks. The slot slides shut.

We keep our distance, watching as Nua juggles her books and bends to pick up another folded note. There is now a note every few feet. She reads each scrap of paper before shoving them into her sweater pocket.

Regan sighs quietly. "This is so romantic."

I shush her. We're not so far now, the gray stone walls and weathered tapestries about to give way to the mirrored hall of the Momentorium. Nua picks up the last note and the small blue flower resting on top of it. She enters the Momentorium and gasps. Even I, who helped set it all up, am momentarily overcome.

The red carpet that runs the length of the Momentorium is now a lush blanket of blue flowers. Candles rest on each of the display cases, their light bouncing off the hundreds of mirrors hanging on the walls and ceilings, casting the room in a brilliant and warm glow. At the other end of the Momentorium stands Marko, his dark hair clubbed back and his fingers nervously tugging at his borrowed suit.

"What is all of this?" Nua breathes.

Marko takes a step. "These flowers," he says, his voice is soft but carrying. "They are not like the rose, big and bold. They are maybe not something you would look at two times if you pass them by. They are humble and small, but they carry an important message. They are Forget-Me-Nots." He takes another step toward Nua, his hands outstretched. "Just as I can forget you not."

"Oh." Ms. Nua doesn't even notice Regan taking her bag and books and setting them on one of the display cases. Regan gives Nua a little push that sets her walking.

"You do not remember Marko, but I remember you, Thessaly. Everything you ever say, Marko remember."

"Is that what these notes are?" Nua pulls out a few scraps of paper from her pocket.

"Yes. With each step that brought you here, I wanted you to see what Marko remembers. I remember your favorite color is the purple found in the sky when the sun rises. You say this during All Hands meeting four years ago. I remember you have three sisters and three brothers and you, you are in the middle. You say you feel forgotten in your big family when you were little girl. You say this seven years ago when young boy go missing in the Coil. I remember you say you like jazz. You say this ten years ago during Orientation party for initiates. I remember you say your cat Clementine, she was sick last year."

"Clem died," Nua says, taking another step toward Marko, transfixed.

"I am sorry for your loss. Marko remembers you do not like mayonnaise."

"It's so gross." Nua whispers the words.

"Marko remembers many things. Many conversations. Little

details. They stay here." He points to his head. "Because Thessaly Nua... she stays here." He taps his chest.

I grin, hearing him recite the line I gave him.

Marko is now standing directly in front of Ms. Nua, almost in the center of the room. He kneels to scoop up a handful of little blue blossoms. "About you, I remember everything. Before today, you do not remember Marko. But maybe now, in this place of remembered things, you forget me not?"

Nua fans herself. "I think I'll remember this all my days."

"Marko kiss you now?" Marko asks, looking uncertain.

"Oh, please do."

Marko sweeps Nua into a passionate embrace and then spins her around, her skirt billowing out around them and kicking up a flurry of flowers. When he sets her on her feet, she looks dazed and clings to him, dizzy from the kiss or the spin or both. He gives us a joyful look and nods when he catches my eye.

I'll be getting my lesson in thieving, I guess. But first, they deserve some privacy.

"YOU MADE FUN OF MY ROMANCE NOVELS," REGAN SAYS as we wait at the café.

"I didn't!" I insist.

Regan sips her tea and beams. "You did. In your mind. I could totally read it in your eyes. I am *really* good at picking up on vibes, I'm telling you. But if it wasn't for me, those two wouldn't be together. That whole thing with Marko was *exactly* what the Duke of Longburn did to win Edwina Devlin in *The Duke Must Live.*

Well... I mean, the characters in the book didn't talk about dead cats or mayo, and they ended up making love right on all those flowers, so it wasn't *identical*. But close—"

Regan trails off as Marko approaches, whistling. He grabs for Regan's hand and my own and kisses them both before sitting down, looking like he inherited the sun.

"After your plan with flowers and notes in Momentorium, Marko walk Thessaly to her class. We have dinner tonight, she say. She say she can never forget Marko after today. You are genius. More happiness cannot fit in my body. I explode."

"I'm really happy for you, Marko," I say. I mean it, too. But his happiness makes me all the more desperate to save Colin. The clock within me has been roaring. "Can you show me what we talked about? How to... liberate things? I need to get those keys."

Marko grins. "These keys, you mean?" He flashes a hefty janitor-worthy set of keys.

"But, what... how?" I ask, completely confused as he takes my hands and presses the keys to my palm. "You said you couldn't."

"I pass Linda Fenice on the way here. I seize opportunity. You say you will return the keys? And the book? Good. Maybe the Grims no find out. Or if they find out, maybe they go easy on Marko. You make Marko happiest man today. Marko make you happy, too. My gift to you."

"Marko, you're my hero!" I leap to my feet and press a quick hug on him before rushing off, pulling Regan along.

28

There are one hundred and thirty-seven locks on Ms. Fenice's door.

"Even if we figure out which key goes where, there are three combination locks, and this thing looks like a biometric thumb reader. What the hell is she protecting in there? Her doily collection?" Griffin gives the door a small kick.

"Stop!" I look back at Pict's pink door across the hall. "Someone might hear."

"Give me the keys." Regan holds out her hand and thumbs through the iron ring. "This one looks like a super old skeleton key. This keyhole here looks like the oldest one. Maybe..." She tries to fit it to the lock. It goes in easily but doesn't turn. "Ugh. This is hopeless. Where's Bacchy?"

"He's on his way," Griffin says.

I take back the keys and try fitting them to locks with no success. I drop to sit on the ground and inspect the eight little acorn tumblers along the bottom of the door, spinning them to a random series of numbers.

"What are you going to do?" Regan asks me.

I lean my head against the door and bang it twice. Then three more times for good measure.

"Made some headway, have you?" Bacchy booms. We all shush him at the same time, and he glances around. "Sorry," he whispers. "Did you get it? Headway? She banged her head and—"

"There's no way we're getting in," I whisper-wail.

"Let me see." He takes the keys and inserts them willy-nilly. "This one looks like it'll take your hand off." Bacchy gestures to the bird beak lock. "And this dragonfly—"

I scramble to my feet. "Dragonfly?" I stand and peer at the brass dragonfly lock, a keyhole resting between its shiny eyes. I grab the keys and start sticking them, methodically, into that keyhole.

"What is it?" Griffin asks.

"You think this has something to do with your dream?" Regan asks, catching on immediately.

"Felda, Emina, and Gelisa said there was an undercurrent to the dream. 'One key to see.' And the other day when I asked Fenice about her locks, she said something about the best security system being a good deterrent."

"Deterrent... You think these are all dummy locks?" Griffin asks.

"Clever," Bacchy says, stroking his beard.

I run through ten more keys. Please let this not be my trivia-obsessed brain looking for patterns. *Please!*

A click sounds, followed by a thunderous rolling clank. I try the handle, and the door swings open.

"You did it!" Regan shouts, before clamping her hands over her mouth. We jump up and down and mouth cheers to each other silently.

"Best not get caught before you finish the thing," Bacchy says from inside the door. I rush in after him, but we need a lookout.

Regan volunteers. "My mentor is down the hall. I have an excuse if I'm caught. Go!"

"It smells like the inside of my grandma's purse exploded in here," Griffin says when I close the door behind us. "Looks like it, too."

"Not every flower smells sweet," Bacchy says.

"Who said that?" Griffin asks absently.

"I did. Just now. Cassie, I think your friend might be cracked," Bacchy says.

"No, man... I mean it sounded like you were quoting a book—never mind."

I open the chest I watched Fenice place the book in before I left.

"I wouldn't do that—" I hear Bacchy say a second before I hear the crash. Griffin bends to scoop up the jar of seeds he knocked over.

"It's not here." I rifle through the contents of the chest, pulling books out frantically. "It has to be here!"

We rummage through more chests and come up empty.

"Guys, hurry it up! Classes are going to let out soon," Regan hisses from the door. The door clicks closed behind her, the sound echoing like a starting pistol.

"Where can it be?" I ask, panic creeping into my tone.

"This closet is filled with dried leaves and flowers or whatever. No books here," Griffin says from the sideboard.

"Only book here is a ritual recipe book. Not what we're looking for," Bacchy says.

I look over at Fenice's desk. And sitting right smack on top of the light oak surface is a fat book. A dull green book. My heart thunders.

There's no way.

I hurry to the desk.

It is!

"I found it!" I call out. My hands shake as I thumb through the text. "*Halt the Harvest*! This is the ritual!" Relief courses through me as I offer up silent thanks to the universe. "'Stave off the foreseen reaping of a soul,'" I read. I turn the page. "Oh no. Oh no."

"What? What is it?" Griffin asks as they rush over. He spins the book toward him. "Shit."

"What's the problem?" Bacchy asks. "Cripes, grab the pages and let's be on our way!"

"Bacchy, man... it's..." Griffin shakes his head. "Had to be a Magnitude Five Dark Mirror. Cripes is right."

Bacchy reads over Griffin's shoulder. He shrugs. "I don't see what the problem is. You said you have a dark mirror for the ritual your aunt gave you. Saving your young beau's life is more important than that Bedlam mission of hers."

I open Fenice's drawer and close it five times. When I look up, Bacchy and Griffin are staring at me. "It's okay. It's okay. Okay. Okay. Okay."

"What? What is it?" Bacchy asks.

"Cassie used that mirror a few days ago. When she *did* the Bedlam ritual," Griffin says.

"Heart of the Coil," Bacchy says. "It's the only way."

"What's that mean?" Griffin asks.

"Guys! Someone's coming!" Regan calls from the door. "Hurry!"

Damn it! Damn, damn, damn, damn! No time to copy it all down now. I rip the pages out, feeling a brief and fiery burst of guilt for book desecration, and we set the room to rights. I pull the door closed behind me and shove the key into the dragonfly lock. The mechanism clanks closed, and our Aeromancy instructor runs past us a moment later, looking as windswept as always.

"What's the Heart of the Coil?" Griffin asks Bacchy.

Bacchy pulls at his pointy beard. "Only two things are dark enough, powerful enough, to create a Magnitude Five Dark Mirror. A mirror charged with a Gloaming Moon eclipse... or one charged in the darkest place a scryer can venture short of death: the Heart of the Coil."

"This Heart of the Coil thing is good news, then!" Griffin says. "Right? You don't have to wait seven years for an eclipse to charge your mirror. We can just pop into the Coil and charge that sucker now."

"Can't. The Coil is wound tight. Got to wait until the Coil Walk, when it unfurls," Bacchy offers. "Then there's the finding of the thing. Only person I know for sure has been there, at least from what they say, is Samara Trefoil."

"Okay... so we talk to the nutjob, figure out how she got there, and we find the Heart when we do our Coil Walk. We can take a little detour on our way to Laurel Plain," Griffin says.

Regan looks contemplative. "Yeah, but what if the Heart is what *made* Samara a nutjob?"

Bacchy whistles. "It's a tall order, but it's probably the only thing available to you, Cassie. I've asked around—if anyone has a Mag Five, they aren't telling."

"I can't walk the Coil," I say, shock melting away and rapidly replaced with desperation.

"What are you talking about? Of course you—you can't stay at Theban without walking the Coil!" Regan says.

"I wasn't planning on staying. I was going to save Colin and leave," I say. Regan looks wounded. "It's not what I *want* to do. My OCD. My catastrophic thinking. All of it. It would be dangerous for you in there with me! Look what happened with Samara Trefoil. Pict said—"

"Do you want to save Colin? Yes or no?" Regan demands.

"Of course I do!"

"Then you need to stop worrying about us. We're a team. We'll be going into this thing with our eyes open," she says. "Right?"

Griffin hesitates. But when Regan narrows her eyes, he says, "Right! No, I'm all in. For sure. I was just thinking... there's no way we can tell Noah. I know he's your... whatever, but you can't tell him."

"That's not fair to Noah," I say, my voice quavering, "or anyone."

"If you love Colin, then you don't have a choice," Regan says. "Griffin and I will take care of getting the stuff we'll need for the Coil Walk. You concentrate on performing *as much* of this ritual as possible, and save the part that needs the dark mirror for when you're in the Coil."

"Happy to help with whatever you need," Bacchy says.

Pict approaches. "What is this motley crew doing outside my door, Ms. Morai?"

"They were... we were training! For the Coil Walk."

"*Delightful.* With these shining specimens of scryerhood by your side, you'll race right through to the Laurel Plain in no time."

"Martin Pict!" Bacchy says. "We need to find you a nice lady friend. Or a man friend? Either way. Improve your temperament a bunch. Take it from me. Don't have one now. I'm miserable! Had one before. Much happier. Course, I was always soused at the time so who knows if I was really happier or just didn't know I was unhappy. Could have been—"

"If you'll excuse me, I have work to do. I'm sure you can continue that conversation with yourself elsewhere?" Pict lets himself into the office. "Ms. Morai, inside. Your workbook awaits."

29

The light in Samara Trefoil's room is blinding, the furnishings sparse. The walls occasionally quiver, but the space around us does not change. Regan, Bacchy, and I approach the slight figure lying on the cot. We heard her feeding tubes had been removed, but she's still hooked up to some manner of monitor and IV.

"Melusine said we only have a few minutes. Make them count," Bacchy whispers.

"Samara," Regan calls. "Sorry to bother you... we're hoping you can help us."

Samara explodes from under her covers and scrambles onto all fours, yanking the machinery attached to her tubing. Her hair hangs in her face. The filth has been washed away, but her eyes seem to look inward as much as out, to her past as much as this present.

"No sneaking," she hisses.

"Easy, now. We're all friends here," Bacchy says. "Just want to ask you a little question before your nurse gets here. That's all."

I feel a pang of guilt, slipping in to ask someone so unwell to dredge up their worst memories. "Samara... I'm so sorry to bother

you, but I need to know. Did you really find the Heart of the Coil?"
I ask softly.

She scrambles backwards. "No names, no games. Don't play
with your food."

"What does—" Regan starts to ask.

Lucidity flashes in Samara's eyes. She brushes her hair from her
face and eyes us warily. "Who are you? Why do you want to know
about the Heart? No one should ever—"

"I need to find it. It's the only way I can save someone."

"*Save* someone?" she scoffs. I watch the sanity slip from her gaze
again, like blinds being pulled, her eyes going unfocused. "I'll play.
I'll play."

We glance at one another, and I try again. "How can I find the
Heart?" A thought occurs. "What did it feel like? Being there?"

"Step back, step back!" she shouts. We leap back practically as
one. She resumes her whispering, "Backwards. Then forward. Dark,
so dark. Dark likes dark. Deep and deeper. Despair there. Despair
here. Inside there. Inside here." She knocks on her head violently,
then whisper-sings, "Heart finds you." It's all we get out of her before
a memory resurfaces. "I'll play! I'll play!" she sobs. She shrieks,
tearing the tubing at her arms.

"Easy now, love," Bacchy says. "You'll hurt your—"

Samara leaps at Bacchy, knocking him over. Regan and I cry out
as she tries to race from the room, but Griffin is there to block her
way, grabbing her around the waist.

"I need to go back," she wails. "It's calling to me."

We help get Bacchy back on his feet. I can't tear my eyes away
from that slight figure as Griffin deposits her onto her cot. She
crumbles onto her blankets immediately.

"Let's away before you're caught," Bacchy says. "Poor girl. Melusine is going to have my head for this."

SOMEONE HAD THE IDEA TO DECORATE THE COIL WALK entrance with balloons and glittery pep rally signs. The crowd at our back cheers. Another group waves as they enter the Coil.

"Strap on your water bladder, Cassie. Here..." Regan reaches behind me and attaches a vest-like contraption filled with drinking water.

"Too bad we can't bring an extra real bladder to hold all that liquid in. Not sure what we're supposed to do if nature calls," Griffin says.

"Probably like real camping. But let's hope we're through to Laurel Plain before we have to find out," Noah says. His eye patch is dark across his face.

"We can replace 'does a bear crap in the woods' with 'does a scryer shit in the Coil?'" Griffin says, leaning down to fill his cargo pants with supplies.

"You guys are gross," Regan says.

"Guys? Don't lump me in with him." Noah leans down and gives Regan a gentle kiss, a brush of his lips. Angry Noah is lying dormant at the moment.

Griffin straightens. "I need more jerky. I'll be right back." He stomps off through the clusters of Coil Walk teams.

Regan runs her hand over Noah's close-cropped hair and reaches down to help him put on his pack.

Bacchy approaches and shoves the cups I asked him for into

my hands before enfolding me in a bear hug, nearly upending the contents. "Be well, Cassie of the Cuff." He rushes off, complaining of dust in his eyes before I can thank him.

I turn to Noah and press one of the cups into his hand before I lose my nerve. "Cheers." I clink my cup against his. "Ginger cider for the road. Didn't want you 'groaking' mine."

He looks up at me for a breathless moment before handing it off to a crestfallen Regan, resuming his careful inspection of his pack straps. Griffin returns and I hand my cup off to him, deflated.

Pict paces nearby. His jaw moves as he grits his teeth. He finally does what I know he's been waiting to do all along: bursts into a flurry of last-minute guidance. "Ms. Morai, I must make it clear that despite your strides toward improving your mental health, you should *not* risk moving backwards in the Coil. You don't know what the cost of doing so will be. Moving side to side isn't prohibited, but I'd rather you not risk that, either. At most, you can pivot around on a planted foot. Control your thoughts every second of every minute. I cannot stress that enough. Use the methods we discussed. You don't want to be a danger to the others. You'll be tired. It will be less than a day out here, but it'll feel like more in there. Pace yourself. It's a marathon, not a sprint. Ration your food and stay hydrated. Sleep when you can, but always have someone keep watch. Pour out a salt circle whenever you stop. Also, remember, you absolutely do not want to employ dream scrying—did you follow my instructions? Each of you have the Somnum Sand I told you to get? Spread it wherever you plan on sleeping, and it'll prevent dreams—"

I nod. Counting as he speaks.

"Are you listening to me, Ms. Morai, because—"

"Yes! I've got it! I know all of this," I cut him off. "It's sweet you're worried about me, though."

Pict narrows his eyes. "Don't die, don't get anyone else killed, and don't embarrass me."

"You once told me my dying would embarrass you, so isn't that redundant?"

Pict walks away, and I grin at his back. My momentary amusement doesn't last. *You'll be a danger to yourself and others.*

We approach the pre-Coil Walk checkpoint. Agatha Triggs pulls my bag toward her and begins pawing through my supplies. She pulls out my mirror and runs her hands over it, examining it. There's nothing remarkable about the mirror, but it almost feels like anyone handling it will know where I plan on taking it and what I plan to do with it after.

"All clear. Take your position on the starting block," she says.

I join the others from my group. Griffin reaches into a pocket and pulls out a protein bar.

"Shouldn't you save that for the Coil?" I ask.

"I'm hungry now."

"Cassie." I noticed Sebastian earlier, standing near the entrance, answering questions from some of the initiates. He approaches now, his face blanked of emotion. "Remember to use your gut. Think about how it'll feel to make it through to the Laurel Plain. I'll be there waiting. You can do this."

I heave in a breath. "If anything happens..."

"Nothing will."

"No, but if something does..." I search the room, but my aunt isn't here. Shocker. "Don't let Aunt Bree be the one to tell my dad. Please?"

He stares at me for a long while before giving a short nod. "I called his mom, by the way. Theodore's."

"What?"

"I—you said that your aunt called her. I figured after a call from Aubrey Morai, the poor woman deserved a follow-up from someone with a little bit of—"

"A soul?" I ask.

"I was going to say empathy." He glances up at one of the sparkling signs taped to the stone archway.

"How was the call?" I ask, though I know the answer.

"She cried. Of course," Sebastian says. "She said it wasn't natural to lose a child. I can't imagine... I told her what you said, about Theodore planning a trip out to see her. She worried about his life before he... went. If he was happy. I told her he was popular here. Told her about your cupcakes for his birthday. Bacchy told me about them, when they found a few at Theodore's desk after... Anyway, she wanted me to thank you for being his friend and taking care of him on his birthday. She said that it brought her comfort."

A tear slips silently from the corner of my eye, followed by another. Sebastian catches the third. He looks down at his finger.

"I didn't want to make you cry right before you went in. I just thought you'd want to know."

"No, of course I do. I'm glad you called her. You're not what your reputation says you are."

He takes a step back. "Reputations are usually earned. But if you're taking it upon yourself to reform me, you'll have to make it out of this thing alive." There it is: the dimple.

A guard approaches and ushers us forward. The crowd quiets.

"Next group! Start your Walk!" the guard calls out. His

announcement is greeted with a shout of approval from the spectators.

My breath catches. Regan takes my hand. "We're going to do great. Ready, Freddy?"

I can't tell if she's trying to reassure me or herself, but I give her hand a squeeze. Griffin takes up my other hand and Regan grabs Noah's.

We step into the Coil.

The sounds of the rally behind us wink out the second we cross, and that feeling of having an ice cube sliding down my back follows. We're swallowed by the darkness.

"Do you hear that?" Regan whispers. "Sounds like a heartbeat?"

The Coil feels different. Wilder. Like a sludgy stream roaring to life after a dam is removed. I break our human chain, my eyes acclimating. "We need to start moving. We don't want the next group to catch up."

It feels as if my lungs are filled with cotton, every breath a fight. I can't tell if I'm hearing my heart or that strange rhythmic Coil beat around us. We pad forward through a ramshackle landscape like a quarry, stepping over piles of stone, our shoes scratching along gravel. The walls ripple and the rock walls give way to enormous hunter green hedgerows stretching for miles. I run my hands over the small leaves and look up. It feels as if we're outdoors, but above us the sky is black and unknowable. There's a dark wonder there, on the edges of my fear. This place shouldn't exist. I shouldn't be here. But the reality is, *shoulds* don't matter anymore.

Noah holds up a hand. "We have to plot a course," he says.

"I'll do it on my ICARUSS," I offer. I'll try and get us as close to Laurel Plain as I can before I break off in search of the Heart.

"We should have two people do it," Noah says. He doesn't spare a look at me, his expression pinched. "That way, if we get conflicting directions, we'll know the Coil is messing with us."

"But we can verify with omens," Regan says. "It's exhausting being the one with the tether. We'd be wearing out two people."

Under normal circumstances, Regan would probably balk at me being the one with the tether for exactly that reason. A weakened Cassie is one who'd probably struggle more with her thoughts. But she knows why I need to set our course.

"I'll do it. I'll be the second," Griffin volunteers, shutting down debate.

"Alright, whatever. Give me a second," I say, clutching my ICARUSS and thinking of our destination. The flapping wings on the screen appear, waiting on my energy to generate the machine-enabled tether. I set my other hand on top of the device and picture the cheering crowds waiting for us at the Laurel Plain. *Sebastian nods approvingly. He's impressed. Pict is smiling! But most importantly, I'm proud of myself. I did it. I beat the Coil. I beat OCD.* I glance down at my ICARUSS, and the wings burst into an electronic map. "This way!"

Griffin verifies my direction, and we follow along for what feels like hours, mostly silent, a thick carpet of dried fallen leaves crunching under our feet. Every time the space around us pulses or quivers, I find myself holding my breath, but our surroundings don't change.

"Let's play a game," Griffin says after a while.

"Griffin, this isn't the time or place," Noah says.

"No, this is good. It'll help us relax," Regan says, glancing at me. I know what she's thinking. "What's the game?"

"How about Bang, Marry, Murder? Martin Pict, Luke Nox, or Jordan Welborne?"

"Different game, please," I say. "I don't want to talk about murder. Or banging."

"Not a smart game in here, either," Noah says. "Coil won't react to positive or light-hearted thoughts, but a game involving murder?"

"If you murder anyone but Pict out of that lineup, you're crazy," Griffin says. "Fine. Let's play... Deal Breaker."

Regan frowns. "Never heard of it."

"It's this game where you picture the person you think is perfect for you. Someone you have a crush on, or a celebrity, or whatever. You don't have to tell who it is. Then we mention terrible qualities, and you say if it's a deal breaker. Here, let's start it. Egg, picture the perfect guy—doesn't have to be the one you're with now." Griffin glances at Noah.

"Okay," Regan says. "And?"

"Would you stay with that person if they hated that movie you're always talking about... what's the name... *The Notebook*?"

"Deal breaker," Regan says, without hesitation.

Noah smiles at her. "Not sure who you have in mind, but for the record I like the movie."

"Of course you do," Griffin says. "So, Noah, picture your perfect girl. Now tell me if it's a deal breaker if she..." Griffin searches for something grotesque enough. "If she had feet for hands?"

"That's so dumb," Noah says.

"Answer the question," Regan says.

"Like when you make out, she'd gently cradle your face with her foot-hands," Griffin supplies.

They go on like that for a while, bickering when Noah proclaims perpetual barf breath a deal breaker and Regan takes it as a sign he wouldn't stand by her if she ever fell ill.

We pause so I can verify ICARUSS's path to Laurel Plain by reading some omens. I throw down my rune stones, examining the messages while Griffin goads Regan.

Their game and the arguing would be funny if we weren't in a place where Pict warned me I'm a liability. *You need to not picture insane things, and everything will be fine.*

The hedges give way to an expanse of cracked white earth, like salt flats I've seen on TV. The others trudge on, still debating absurd deal-breaker defects. I carefully set my foot down, then hop to another crack-less patch.

No. Fight it.

I force my foot down on one of the cracks. Then another. Then another. The cracks in the ground are a little wider here. Easier to misstep. *The earth opens up, I fall through the cracks. Stop! You're okay. You're okay. Okay. Okay...*

A rumble sounds.

"What was that?" I ask.

"Probably my stomach," Griffin complains. "I'm starving. We've been in here for days."

"It's been four hours," Noah says. "You literally ate just before the Coil Walk."

The rumble starts again, this time with enough force that we all throw our arms out for balance. "Was that an earthquake?" Regan asks.

In answer to her question, the ground begins to quake, specks and pebbles dancing across the surface. The cracks in the dry white ground below us begin to widen, deepen.

"Run!" Noah shouts.

We race across, leaping over expanding gulfs. *I did this. I did this. I did this. I did this. I did this.* The thought pounds through my head as I run. *Liability.*

Up ahead the salt flats shimmer, rippling, changing, like an oasis. In the distance there's now a dirt path bracketed by a rough wooden fence. It looks out of place, as if someone ripped a piece of a page out of a picture book, revealing the next image.

"Get to the path!" Griffin yells.

The space beyond the path shoots up like a gunshot, a distant purple mountain range.

I leap over an expanding fissure, barely getting my feet under me before it widens further. Regan jumps behind me and falls short, catching hold of the edge of a crack. She struggles to pull herself up, clawing at the ground.

"Regan!" I scream. Noah and Griffin are farther ahead, unaware. I hesitate, frightened of moving backwards, even for her, then drop down, kicking back a leg. "Grab on!"

Regan clutches at my foot, and I pull with all my might to draw my knee up, unable to pull her forward.

"Your pack! You're too heavy!" I shout. "Get rid of your pack!"

Regan quickly shrugs off her straps, releasing my foot for a breathless second each time.

I pull my leg forward, reaching for the crack in front of me for leverage. "Come on! Pull!"

Regan screams as she lifts herself up, kicking a leg up over the edge. She rolls onto the ground and jumps to her feet. We don't have time to dissect that near miss.

Regan and I jump along, seeking out the smallest leaps. We reach

Griffin and Noah at the dirt path and pant, turning to watch as the entire salt flat crumbles apart leaving a gaping void.

"What the fuck!" Griffin shouts. He catches my expression. I see the moment he realizes it was me. He winces. "It's fine. We're alright."

I try to regulate my breathing.

"My mentor said the Coil feeds off our energy. We need to calm down. Think good thoughts. Or even better—think no thoughts," Noah says in a voice that shakes. "Come on. Let's find a place for a fire and try to read some omens."

Regan explains what happened to her pack to a horrified Noah and Griffin as we set off down the path. No one mentions what could have happened if I hadn't been close enough to help. And no one accuses me of being responsible for it in the first place.

The mountains and the dirt road melt away after a bit, and we walk for hours through spaces that vibrate and change periodically, taking small, silent breaks to add or remove layers of clothing with the weather or to pass around food and water. I can't turn off my thoughts, so I try and redirect them like a Judo master. *Blue skies, green fields, butterflies. Happy thoughts.*

The Coil here is awash in scuttling sounds, a collection of bump-in-the-night terrors. I don't dwell on them, although there are a few times I expect to see another group of Coil Walkers, or something infinitely worse.

Griffin throws out an arm, halting our trek. "There's a drop here," he says, pointing down in front of him toward a small slope. I look out to a grassy clearing, a large field ringed by a dense ridge of tree trunks. It's lit by a dim glow—like a full moon's light. A few butterflies flitter by.

"Does this place look familiar?" Regan asks.

"Button Field. Is this Button Field?" Griffin responds.

"It does look like it," Noah says. "Makes sense, if the Coil draws on us." He hops down and reaches up to help Regan. I reach out a hand to him and end up having to slide down on my own when he walks away. Griffin jumps and lands beside me as I dust off my pants and wrestle with my hurt.

"This looks like an okay place to camp for the night," Noah says. "No rippling, so it seems stable. Don't know if we'll find better if we keep moving."

We pick a spot along the left edge of the park, close to where we sat in the real field. We pour out a large protective salt circle, handing the container off to one another to avoid accidently moving backwards. After it's completed, it's sweet relief to be able to move around freely within it. Our dreams are the only way the Coil can reach us in a salt circle, so I spread Somnum Sand on the ground liberally before unrolling my sleeping bag.

"I had the cutest sleeping bag," Regan says. "It had, like, a princess body print from the neck down. It was a Sleeping Beauty sleeping bag. I'm bummed it's gone."

Noah cracks a small smile. "If there's a princess that needs kissing, you can always snuggle with me in my bag. It's big enough for two people."

"No. No way," Griffin says. He slams his bag down. "They told me we might run into some creepy crap in the Coil, but they didn't say anything about you two feeling each other up all night. I'd rather be eaten by whatever was making that noise earlier."

Noah shakes his head, the spark in his eye extinguished. "You have issues."

"You don't want me to get started on your issues, man," Griffin mutters. He fishes out his Somnum Sand and throws a handful down before climbing into his threadbare sleeping bag next to mine. He turns away, resting on his side.

"Can Cassie and I share your double bag, and you take hers?" Regan asks Noah. He nods. "Is that cool with you?" Regan asks me.

"Of course." I throw down some more Somnum Sand, and Noah spreads his bag out on top of it for us, then sets about making a small fire to ward off the chill. The three of us gather around it to warm ourselves and to read the flames and smoke. Regan settles next to me and glances at Noah.

For a spell, the only sounds are the crackling of the wood and a softly whistling breeze winding through the trees. I lean closer to the fire. I've never been camping. It's just a split second, but I forget I'm not really on a little trip with friends instead of in a scryer test labyrinth hell. I can almost see why this stuff appeals.

"Would you ever tell Colin about this whole thing? Like being a scryer, or whatever?" Regan whispers suddenly.

I pause, glancing at Noah, who is pretending not to listen. Colin's name brings with it a pang of longing. "I don't know. He'd probably think I'm crazy. And I've had enough of people looking at me like that to last forever."

"But it's such a huge part of who you are. I mean, my thing with Noah is really nice because he knows the whole me, you know?"

"Yeah."

I don't want to tell her that with grief, there's no way to let someone know the whole you anyway. There's always a piece of yourself that you hide away so you don't bring others down. The only ones who understand are those who've experienced it. But as Regan moves over to cuddle with Noah, I recall I don't have a monopoly on grief. Better not to dwell on Ford in here, though.

I watch Noah and Regan across the dancing flames and feel like I've wandered into someone else's dream. It's all too absurd. And after the thing with the salt flats... I need to break off soon. It's the right thing to do.

"We're on the right track," Regan says, pointing to a spark pattern in the campfire.

"The smoke touched the ground," I say. "I don't like it. Bad omen."

Regan gives me a look, clearly thinking about my condition. "I didn't see any smoke touch the ground. You sure?"

I narrow my eyes at her.

"Fine! Okay! Someone should keep watch. We can take turns," Regan says. Noah nods. "Hey, Griffin. We're going to take turns keeping watch."

"I heard. I'm literally right here. Just because I'm not facing you doesn't mean I can't hear you."

Regan rolls her eyes and mouths, "He's the worst."

I smile, ducking my face into my collar. Regan does the same, but I see the laughter lurking in her gray eyes.

I avert my gaze. She makes a tiny sound. I try to avoid it, but my eyes migrate back to hers. The second it happens, I choke off a giggle. Regan's body shakes, and her eyes well in repressed mirth. The more we try to hold it back, the harder it is... until the levee breaks and we give in to the snorts and laugher. Even Noah chuckles, smiling as he pokes at the fire.

Griffin abruptly struggles out of his sleeping bag and stands, grabbing his gear and storming off toward the center of the field.

"Griffin! We weren't laughing at you!" I call out. He doesn't listen, instead reaching into his pack and then pouring out a rough salt circle. He flings down a fistful of the black Somnum Sand before dropping his stuff and climbing into his sleeping bag again.

"We have to stay together! It's not safe to sleep out there by yourself," I say, sobering now.

A loud snore greets my words.

"Faker!" Regan calls out. More snores sound.

"He'll be okay," Noah says when Regan looks to him in concern. "I'll take the first watch."

Regan and I settle into the soft confines of the bag on the hard ground, and I glance again at Griffin's lonely form in the center of the field. I fight the heaviness in my lids. *A creature creeps along the edge behind us. I close my eyes, never hearing it approach. Its fangs, stained red, sink into my throat. I gurgle out a cry for help...*

Oh my God. Stop. Stop. Stop. Stop. Stop. Colin. Healthy. Alive. I save him. Happy thoughts. Happy thoughts. Happy. Happy. Happy.

It's a long while before I finally give in to sleep's pull.

A PIERCING CRY SHATTERS THE QUIET. I TRY TO SIT UP, but there's something holding me down. "Cassie! Noah! Wake up!" Regan says. There is a frantic edge to her voice.

I turn my head. Regan's eyes are flint pools of terror. She thrashes her head from side to side.

"I can't move!" Noah shouts. "What's happening?"

"I heard something. I woke up. Couldn't move." Regan struggles against her invisible restraints. There is a howling, like the sounds of a muffled slaughter carried on a ghostly wind.

"What was that?" I whisper.

"That's what woke me up," Regan hisses. She's dripping sweat, her face is a damp mask of fear.

The crushing pressure on my chest is unbearable now. The more I silently strain, the tighter it holds me. "I can't breathe!" I bite out, on a rising tide of claustrophobic panic though I'm in a wide-open space. An acrid smell fills my nose, and sweat drips down my brow.

The sound. That horrible howl.

"That was behind us," Noah whispers. The shadow of a large man-like creature falls on the ridge next to me. I whimper. Happy thoughts. Happy thoughts. Happy...

It's not a shadow of a creature. It *is* the creature. The shadow circles us. Regan's pained shrieks mingle with Noah's yells. I can't see what's happening to Noah, but I can see the shadow creature leaning over him, and Regan's reaction. I scream until my throat burns. When Noah's shouts quiet and the shadow moves to Regan, I squeeze my eyes tight. I can't watch. I can't.

Regan goes silent, too.

The shadow is now hovering over me. I feel the heat of it, its breath on my face, hear the airy yowl loud in my ears.

"Oh God. Oh God. Oh—" I whisper.

Something gritty, like sandpaper, is pressed hard into my eye. I screech and try to turn my head away. It grabs hold of me and does the same to my other eye. I try to buck. I can move! I push up and roll away. It jumps on me again and holds me down.

"Cassie!" the creature shouts, sounding like a million death rattles. "Stop!"

It forces me back down onto the ground, straddling my chest. I try to fight it off, but it grabs my wrists.

"Cassie! Open your eyes. Come on!" Griffin shouts. He roughly wipes away the grit on my eyes. I blink through it and find him on top of me.

"Griffin!" I scream. "Get off of me! Help! That thing is—"

There are fireflies circling Griffin's head. Not fireflies—sparks. I hear crackling and bursts. There's an inferno nearby. My face burns and my clothes drip with sweat. "Regan! Noah!"

"I'm going to let go. Okay? But you can't move backwards. You're on the edge of the salt circle," Griffin says. He releases me, and I rub at my face, my hand coming away with black sand. "Somnum Sand?"

Griffin helps me sit up. Noah is holding Regan just beyond Griffin's back. "Yeah." He drops back on his haunches. "Shitballs, that was insane."

I edge away from him and look around. The smoke in the air around us makes it hard to see and breathe. My sleeping bag—or rather, the one Noah let me and Regan use—has been yanked away and is smoldering near the dying campfire. My original sleeping bag is engulfed in flames.

"What happened to us?" I ask, trembling.

"I woke up because I heard another team cross the field," Griffin says. "They tried to be quiet so we wouldn't hear them, but I'm a light sleeper. I pretended to be asleep, but the second they climbed up the other ridge, I turned to get your attention and..." Griffin pauses, a queer look crossing his face.

"What? What is it?" Regan asks.

"The place was all smoky. I could barely see you. And the

campfire flames were, like, I don't know, they were reaching out like arms or whatever, like they were looking for something to burn. Noah's bag was already on fire down by his feet, and your bag was starting to catch, it looked like. And you guys had these spider *things*, size of cats, with these long ass spindly legs and... God, they looked like friggin' nightmares... sitting on your chests. I thought you were dead at first. And I—I grabbed my stuff, my knife, and ran over and—cut one of them! Look." Griffin points to a trail of fresh blood leading up toward the ridge of trees.

"Not nightmares. Night Mara," I say, shuddering. "I read about them in a book Pict gave me."

"But we used Somnum Sand," Regan counters. "They can only get to you if..."

Noah leans down and rifles through my pack. He picks up my container of sand. "Give me your sand, Griffin."

Griffin hands it over, and Noah pours some from both of our containers out onto his hand.

"Fake," Noah says with disgust.

"What?" I ask, startled.

"Look at Griffin's. The grains are finer. Yours looks like someone crushed up some black rocks or something." Noah chucks my bottle of sand into the fire.

"But wouldn't your sand have to be fake, too? I saw one of those things surfing your chest, too, man," Griffin says.

"Cassie'd already thrown down some when we switched sleeping bags. I figured I was covered," Noah says.

"But Bacchy got it for us. For all of us. He would never—"

"Bacchy wouldn't. But someone sabotaged your stuff, Cassie," Griffin says.

"I don't know who would..." I trail off. Lots of people would, now that they know about my role in the Bedlam attack.

"Who else handled your pack?" Regan asks.

"You almost got us killed. Again," Noah says to me. "Bedlam attack not enough for you?"

Griffin turns on Noah. "Weren't you supposed to keep watch?"

Their argument heats up, culminating with Griffin accusing Noah of being "more concerned about getting into Egg's pants than our survival."

"Now we're down to fifty percent of our supplies!" Griffin continues. Noah's pack. I realize for the first time that his bag of supplies is part of the bonfire that is my old sleeping bag.

"Maybe if you hadn't pitched a fit and gone to sleep in the middle of the field!" Noah shouts.

"Then he wouldn't have been able to help us, right? *Enough.* Both of you. We get it." Regan rubs at her temples. "No looking back. Let's figure out what we do now."

30

We sit cross-legged on the cracked tile floor of what looks like the Taj Mahal's shabbier cousin and work through our strictly rationed food and water. With Regan and Noah's supplies gone, we're left with my stuff and whatever Griffin packed—something he's been moaning about on and off all morning since it's curtailed his snacking.

Regan rests her head on my shoulder and eyes Griffin. "I guess heroes and herpes really are only a letter apart," she murmurs. I shake my head with a little huff of laughter and continue gnawing the tough piece of jerky in my hand.

Regan sits up, a thought occurring. "Hey, Griffin, how come nothing happened to you? When you came back to help us, I mean? You had to move backwards in the Coil."

"I wouldn't say nothing." Griffin holds up his palms, where a star-shaped burn viciously mars the skin of each.

"Oh my God!" Regan shouts.

"Yeah. Stings like crazy. Starting to bubble now. Didn't exactly feel great in the moment, but I guess adrenaline…" Griffin shakes his head.

"So that's it?" I ask, hopeful. "Just physical pain?" Physical I can deal with. But the mental… there's nothing scarier to me than my mind.

"No. I—I saw some stuff too, I guess."

"What did you see?" I ask.

"Just stuff. Random stuff. It's fine," he says.

"But do you think—"

"Cassie, holy shit, what difference does it make whether I saw Pict in a Speedo or something worse?" Griffin blows out his cheeks. "I'm okay. I won't be… I won't be stepping backwards again if I can help it, and I don't think anyone else should chance it, either. Okay? Is that enough for you? Can we talk about something else?"

"Thank you, by the way," I say, as I look down at the gnarled jerky in my hand. "I didn't say it before. You saved us."

"You guys would've done the same for me," Griffin says, leaning against a marble pillar. "Well, maybe not Egg. She hates me. But you two."

"I don't hate you," Regan says softly.

"Wow. Whispering nothing-sweets with your boyfriend right there." Griffin shakes his head and tips his canteen to his lips. The sound of pouring water is audible.

"You're dogging it. Save some water for us," Noah says.

Griffin pulls the canteen away from his lips. "It's a sip. Relax." The sound of running water continues. Griffin frowns and looks at his canteen.

I stand and follow the sound, the others right behind me.

An ocean. There is an ocean beyond this doorway.

Regan steps down onto the wet sand, and the crisp air catches her curls, sending them tumbling over an eye. "You've got to be kidding me."

The peaceful sounds of gulls and crashing waves are at odds with the fact this is an eerie dreamscape determined to kill us. A relatively stable dreamscape, at least, since there is no rippling. I wipe a hand over my face wearily and pull my ICARUSS out of my pocket. "Okay, so this thing is saying we need to go straight." I let out a humorless laugh and point toward the horizon. "Because of course it does."

"I can't swim," Griffin says. "No one told me we needed to know the frigging doggy paddle for the Coil Walk."

"Boat!" Noah says.

Sure enough, a little way down the beach near the water's edge there is a small row boat, white paint chipping off the sides. A boy is pushing it toward the ocean while his two companions watch.

"Dill!" Griffin calls out. We race over and Dill, Griffin's friend with the absurdly patchy mustache, pauses in his efforts with the boat to watch our approach with sunken eyes. Joe and Helen, from our mirror scrying class, shuffle listlessly and stare at the pack slung over my shoulder. Dill licks at his pale, chapped lips.

"You guys are still in here, too? Do you have water?"

Regan reaches behind me and fishes out our canteen. She hands it over to Helen, and her group tosses it to one another, drinking greedily.

"Didn't you guys have Tessa on your team?" Regan asks.

"Tessa disappeared," Dill says. "Ran backwards to get away from..." He blanches, remembering something he does not share, and falls quiet. I close my eyes, spent. I think of Tessa, with her sunflower hair and her warm smile full of metal, confiding in me about her nightmares. About messing up.

"We heard her screaming. Sounded like she was somewhere a ways back. We waited but she didn't show, and we started wondering if it wasn't just the Coil messing... and—I mean, she disappeared in front of our eyes! Same could've happened to anyone who tried to go back for her," Joe says, ending on an angrily defensive note.

"Moving back doesn't always do that," I say. "Pict told me it probably depends on the person and their mental state. So one person can take a few steps and disappear, and another person can run clear across a field and..." I gesture toward Griffin, who holds up his hands to show off the blistering burns on his palms.

"Too late now. We've got to get out of here." Helen brushes her long braid over her shoulder. She gives Joe and Dill a loaded look. "And there isn't room for seven people in this boat."

I now know what animals must experience when they sense a threat: a crackling heaviness has descended on our group, fog-like, at Helen's softly spoken words. Every cell within me is suddenly on high alert.

"You would've let Leo DiCaprio drown, too, huh, Rose? No room on that door?" Griffin drawls, raising an eyebrow. His joke does little to defuse the tension.

"Everyone, let's just relax... We can figure this out," Noah says, taking a small step closer. Dill grabs for an oar and holds it out threateningly.

"Dill! Dude! What are you doing?" Griffin cries.

"Here's what I know," Dill says, ignoring Griffin, his desperate stare boring a hole through Noah. "We saw what happened to Tessa, and you see Griff's hands are a mess. Moving backwards isn't pretty, no matter what. And one tiny boat means that one group rides out and the other has to double back to find another way through. As far as I can tell, *we're* the group in the boat. You can accept that, or..."

Griffin shuffles forward, pausing abruptly when Joe drops into a wrestler's crouch an arm's length from him. Griffin watches Joe but addresses Dill, his tone hushed. "Dill, you're my boy. You're really pulling this? You don't know for sure we won't fit."

"Don't come any closer or we'll have to retaliate," Joe barks.

"I grew up around boats my whole life, you moron," Helen interjects. "That thing is about ten feet by five feet. That means three, maybe four can ride safely, and that's if it's seaworthy to begin with. We're not chancing it."

"You'll be fine. You're with the princess," Dill says, gesturing to me. "Her aunt practically runs this place."

Joe and Griffin continue to size each other up, their heights and weights making them a pretty even matchup, though Griffin is weakened by his tether to the Laurel Plain and his injuries. Dill and Noah are similarly engaged, although there's the buffer of a boat and an oar between them. Helen's eyes dart between me and Regan. The standoff is a silent one, with no sudden shifts on anyone's part. But every micro-movement is aggressive, every muscle twitch a threat.

"Okay, this is mental," Regan mutters, her chest rising and falling rapidly. "No one wants to fight, right? And risk moving backwards? Let's talk this out."

Dill's expression wavers, indecision flickering in his eyes. Suddenly there is a blur of motion, and Joe is clutching Griffin's hand in a strong grip, his thumb digging into the pale gray burn on Griffin's palm.

Griffin grasps Joe's forearm with his free hand and cries out, sinking, nearly to his knees. "I wasn't attacking you, you fucking idiot!" Griffin shouts. Theirs is a kind of mid-air arm wrestling; they vibrate with the effort, a test of strength and, in Griffin's case, painful endurance.

"Joe, stop!" Regan screams. She moves to intervene, and Helen blocks her approach with an arm. "Dill, he's your friend! Do something!"

Noah grabs at Dill's outstretched paddle and holds it firm when Dill tries to pull it away. "Listen to me, Dill. If you guys don't stop and someone ends up moving backwards, getting hurt, that'll be on whoever caused it. Can you live with that?" They stare at each other fiercely for a few beats until Noah gently releases the oar and raises his hands. Dill glances over at Joe and Griffin, his thoughts warring across his face.

Griffin has a hand on the ground, the other still in Joe's vise grip, when, without warning, he throws sand up into Joe's eyes. Joe screams, immediately releasing him, but has the presence of mind to avoid stepping back as his hands come up to his face.

Dill tosses the oar into the boat and grabs the boat's edge, pushing it into the surf and catching Noah off guard. He hurdles a small wave and then jumps in, fumbling with the oar. Noah runs into the water after him, grabbing at the boat with both hands, pulling it back with all his might and catching the crest of a small wave. The boat edges backwards, past Noah, toward the shore, like a bull waved on by a matador. It beaches itself.

It's empty. Dill is gone.

I hear a noise, and it takes me a moment to realize that it's Helen's guttural wail. She grabs for Regan wildly and falls, carried by her own momentum. Her broken screams and incoherent pleas trigger a horrifying realization—Helen's moved backwards, retraced her own steps. She writhes in agony, lost in what sounds like anguished memories and a terrible physical pain, as shock ripples through me. Regan blanches and looks over at me helplessly. "I didn't... She..."

"You're *dead!*" Joe shouts, bloodshot eyes taking in his team's plight. He pulls a small knife from his pocket and crouches in front of Griffin once more, still precise with his movements, but now radiating a savage brutality.

"Cassie!" Regan calls out. "Bring me your pack!"

I run the few steps to her, breathing heavily, though I've not exerted myself at all. Regan grabs my pack and paws through it, pulling out a few containers of herbs, then digging a desperate hole in the sand.

"Get in the boat! Hurry, please!" Noah shouts. He throws his hands out, bracing and trying to balance as a wave crashes into him. He fights to remain standing, to give no ground, and manages it. But only just.

I look back at Regan. "Noah can't last long out there." But she doesn't look up from her hole in the sand. She drops a mix of herbs in it and moves her lips, chanting.

Joe is solid as a tree stump, the only one armed with a real weapon, fueled with rage and hate. His eyes never leave Griffin, who looks bone tired as he climbs wearily to his feet, his heavy pack still on his back, his face pale even with his darkly tanned skin. He clutches his palm.

351

Joe shifts, lunges to strike—and his foot slips in the loose sand. He stumbles, arms flailing, and lands heavily on his side. I send up a silent thank you that it was just to the side. When he doesn't immediately leap up, Griffin risks a step closer, then nudges him with a foot.

"Out cold. But breathing," Griffin calls out. "Head hit a rock."

"Really?" I ask, bewildered.

"Hurry!" Noah cries.

"Should we try to bring them...?" I say, looking from Helen to Joe with horror, uncertainty.

"No time! Noah is—come on," Regan says.

We run to the boat, Griffin helping me push it farther into the water as Regan scrambles into the thing. We leap inside, and Noah tries to grab for Griffin's outstretched hand as we pass. He's thrown off balance.

"No! Noah!" Regan cries.

Noah teeters for one moment. I blink the briny water out of my eyes and clutch the side of the boat, reaching with my right hand as far as it'll extend. Noah's hand latches onto mine and we pull at him, nearly capsizing. He lands at our feet with a crash, breathing heavily, his clothes plastered to him.

Regan cradles Noah as we paddle toward the horizon. I stare back at the two figures lying on the beach.

We're okay. We're okay. Okay. Okay. Okay.

31

I step backwards. The wooden sliver in my finger from this oar erupts into an untreatable infection. They have to amputate.

"So, I was a little busy, but did I hallucinate Dill just... disappearing?" Griffin asks, shattering the quiet. He looks troubled. I know they're close friends.

"Guess they weren't kidding about not going backwards," I say quietly, rowing.

Griffin curls his fingers into fists and winces, immediately opening them again and looking down at his burns. He turns to me. "Thanks. For whatever you did. The ritual. I hope you didn't have to give up too much."

"That wasn't me," I say. I look to Regan.

"Egg?" Griffin asks, the surprise on his face evident.

She shrugs. "Button Field Billiards. Only cost me a minute off the end of my life."

A blink-and-you'd-miss-it spasm of emotion crosses Griffin's face, too fast to read with any accuracy. "Thank you," he says simply.

Noah stares off across the water. "I hope Dill is okay," he says.

"I just pulled at the boat to keep it from... I didn't mean to... I didn't know that even in the boat it would—"

"Woah, yeah, that's crazy," Griffin says. "Reminds me of this time a girl brought an evil eye into Theban and didn't realize what she was doing. It's weird, though. Because here you've maybe killed one of our classmates and she's treating you with nothing but sympathy, but you—"

I rest a hand on his knee, stilling his defense. Noah's eye has teared up, and his jaw tenses as he turns away. The last thing we need is for Noah to dwell on this, to give the Coil something else to feed on. The fact that it hasn't yet is no small miracle, and speaks more to how easy it is to prey on me than anything else.

"Is the sun just resting on the horizon?" Noah asks, finally. "It hasn't moved for a while."

The sun here isn't like the one outside the Coil. Looking at it isn't unbearable—it has more of a nightlight glow to it. Right now, it perfectly bisects the horizon, sitting like a postcard sunset in a sky that looks like Colin's painter's palette. And Noah's right. It hasn't moved. But it has gotten bigger.

I look down at my ICARUSS. "I don't see any land, but the ICARUSS is saying it's not far off."

I look out at the vibrant reflective streak of light we're following across the water, trailing it to its source and trying to work out what about it feels so wrong.

Actually, the sun *hasn't* gotten bigger. It only looks that way because it's getting closer with each press of our oars on the water. It looms huge in front of us. We hear a scraping sound.

Griffin peers down into the water. "What now? Shrieking eels?"

Noah presses an oar down into the water and knocks. It's shallow here, and the ground beneath the water is like cement. The horizon doesn't remain in the far-off distance the way it normally would, an illusion of sky and sea meeting. The Coil horizon is apparently a very real place: a thin boardwalk running in both directions as far as I can see.

Noah jumps onto that horizon-boardwalk and bends to hold the boat so the rest of us can hop up next to him. We approach the glowing Coil sun looming above us like a Ferris Wheel.

"This thing looks like a billboard of the sun," Griffin says. He hesitantly reaches out a hand toward it.

"Don't touch it!" Regan calls out. "Oh my God, do you not have enough burns to deal with, you moron?"

Griffin taps it with his fingertips. "It's not hot."

"Where are you going? Watch your step," I say.

He circles *behind* it, careful not to step back as he edges around. "This thing is two-dimensional!" he shouts. "Move out of the way."

We join him in back of the thin faux sun. Griffin hefts a foot up and kicks at it. The sun tips, wobbles, and goes down slowly, partially crashing into the water.

"That is some weird crap," Griffin says.

"Look!" Regan says. The boardwalk behind the sun opens to an expanse where, suspended in the air, sit all the colors of the sunset we saw from our boat. We roam into that color field, running our hands through translucent clouds of purples and golds and blues and yellows. The colors stream through our fingers, swirling together in midair.

Regan blows out a breath, and the colors in front of her spin and curl, like something out of a Van Gogh painting.

Griffin sucks in a breath through his mouth, taking in a heaping helping of orange, and blows the breath out of his nose, sending it out like a bull. "Sick!" He grins at me. His smile is full of childish delight. "So, the sun was two-dimensional, but the sunset is 3D. This place is so off."

I walk alongside the group, watching, waiting for what comes next, praying it's OCD anxiety and nothing more. A breeze blows my long bangs into my eyes. I wipe them away and glance at my ICARUSS before digging in my bag for omen-reading materials.

"Use the mirror. Or the runes. Quicker than a fire," Noah says. He's corralled a puff of blue air in-between his hands. The more he brings his hands together, the darker the blue of the puff becomes, packing the color together like a floating snowball.

I give him a small smile, a kernel of hope sprouting inside me. He spoke to me. Willingly. Without anger. Maybe the thing with Dill—hell, maybe even Griffin's words, though I never thought those would be a game changer—have put a dent in his hatred for me.

The wind blows again, this time hard enough to temporarily halt our progress.

What if it blows so hard someone accidentally takes a step back?

I sit cross-legged, throw the runes down, and inspect them. Nothing interesting. I look up, across the color field, and the wind picks up once more. I taste dirt. It's in my mouth and stings my eyes. It begins to blow into my face so violently it's choking off my air supply, burning my face. Can you suffocate in the wind? I gasp, then gag on the dust. I can't see the others. It's a dust storm. A dust storm made up of all the colors of the rainbow.

"What's wrong? What is it?" Regan asks me.

I blink, and the sensation and the scene in front of me is gone. Like with Colin. Like Mom. But somehow the clock within me knows this vision is a lot more immediate than theirs were. I *feel* it.

"We need to move. *Now*," I shout. I grab my bag and take off running, the rest of them following close behind. They don't need to be told twice.

"What did you see?" Regan calls as we run.

"A storm. The colors. Wind."

And then it begins, a wind so fierce it almost drives us backwards. We push forward, leaning against those powerful gusts. The colors whip and bite, becoming a dust cloud so thick that we can't see in front of us. We press on.

"Keep going! Don't let it push you back!" I shout, my words carried off by the gale the second they cross my lips.

I can't even see my hand in front of me now. I reach out, fighting against the almost solid color wall now, and I feel something. I grab onto it, thinking it's one of the others, but it turns in my hand and a crack in the color squall appears. I pull harder, dropping my bag to yank on it. The crack widens. A doorway!

"Door! Grab my hand!" I hold onto that door handle with all my might and reach back, desperately feeling for anything, anyone to pull forward. A hand grabs mine, and I pull, faint from the lack of air. Regan comes staggering forward, passing through the door—then sprawling and skidding down the corridor, suddenly free from the driving wind.

I reach back again, screaming Noah and Griffin's names. A hand closes on mine—I pull hard and Griffin tumbles through the doorway, crashing down next to Regan, his pack spilling over beyond him. His face is covered in color, and he slaps at it, gasping for air. I shout for Noah, relieved when his hand meets mine... until I feel him pulling on me harder than the others—harder than the wind. He pulls himself up next to me and grabs my other hand, the one holding the door handle. He digs his nails into my fingers, and it's a second before I process he's trying to pry my hand off the door.

"No! What are you doing?" I scream, pushing at him while I desperately cling to the handle. Regan and Griffin jump to their feet, their troubled faces barely visible through the doorway as I push at Noah.

"You did this!" Noah shouts.

"Noah, stop!" I shout, lowering my center of gravity and trying to press toward the doorway. He manages to get my fingers off the handle, but I grab hold of the doorframe with both hands, fighting the wind, fighting him. I kick back.

"Noah, what the hell are you doing?" Griffin shouts.

"You think I don't know? About the Heart? The dark mirror? You think I'm stupid? You'll drag Regan down with you," Noah shouts at me. "You drag everyone down with you." The door is wide open now, and Noah holds onto the doorframe next to me. He grabs at the neck of my shirt, and one of my hands comes off the doorway involuntarily, trying to keep my collar from choking me.

I slap at him. I can't hold on anymore. He's right. *Just let go. Let go. Let go. Let go. Let—*

Griffin screams as he moves back toward us, his palms licked by a white-hot fire, cooking his burnt flesh further. He hurls himself at Noah with a growl. The blow doesn't dislodge Noah, but it does knock my already weak grip loose.

I fall back, swallowed by the storm.

32

I wheeze, trying to catch my breath, dropping to all fours and coughing until I gag up the contents of my stomach. All around me is a bombed-out desolation.

I stagger to my feet, slapping at my skin and scraping my nails down my arms. I need this colored dust off of me. I can't. I can't. I can't. Can't. Can't.

Count. *Count.*

One. Two. Three.

This compulsion is not me.

Four.

It's everywhere. I can't breathe.

I hear Noah's voice in my head: *You drag everyone down with you.*

He's right. I'm an infection.

It felt as if I were yanked here by an invisible thread fish-hooked into my belly button. The center of my stomach aches.

Five. Six.

Oh God. I moved backwards. What did it do to me? I frantically feel my body, searching for wounds. I can't find any. I wheel around. I'm alone. *Alone.*

I could quiet my mind when I had the others to distract me. But now I'm alone. *Alone. Alone.*

I feel my pocket, looking for my ICARUSS. It's not there.

It's okay. Okay. Okay. Okay. Okay. You were planning on breaking off anyway. Find the Heart. Use the blueprints.

You don't have the mirror. You don't have the mirror. You don't have the mirror. You don't have the mirror. You don't have the mirror.

I clutch at my sore middle and a wracking sob spills out of me, followed by another, and then another. This isn't how this was supposed to go. I *need* that mirror. I *need* to save Colin. That clock is ticking in my ear, deafening. But even if I find the Heart now, I have nothing to charge. It's over. It's over. It's over. Over. Over.

You drag everyone down with you.

I scream up at the tops of the pockmarked buildings, the sound tearing up my dry throat. It echoes louder and louder upon every return until I'm forced to cover my ears.

You are not what Noah says.

One. Two. Three. Four...

I count myself back and run a soothing hand over the stinging scratches I've inflicted on myself. I concentrate on my breathing the way Pict and I practiced.

Water. I need water.

I find a Y-shaped stick that might do for water witching and concentrate, trying to find a drop, a drip, in this war-torn hell. I'm not as good as Regan, but I follow the pull of the stick toward a blackened shell of a building. As I approach, the space around me ripples.

Ahead, surrounded by thick vegetation, there is now a tumble-down temple, the path leading to it a dilapidated flat wooden bridge with no rails. Bridge. That means water. My wand gives a violent tug and I race on, ignoring the biting insects and the suffocating humidity.

I reach the low bridge, slowing as I notice the algae-green stagnant waters beneath it. *Flesh-eating bacteria... lurking. Stop.* I fight my desperate disappointment. I can't drink that.

But if I can clear the algae... I reach the center of the bridge and kneel at the edge, reaching down to splash at the carpet of green with my stick again and again, clearing enough of it away so that I can see my reflection in the dark water below. I pull my little unicorn horn-shaped pendulum from around my neck, untangling its black cord from the locket Dad gave me, and lie down on my stomach. I clear the encroaching algae with my stick again and center myself, linking myself to that dangling onyx horn. I breathe out my fear, breathe out the notion I'm alone in the Coil with only my mind for company, breathe out images of myself replacing Samara Trefoil in that blinding room. I ask a few control questions—my name, age—to determine a yes response from a no, then scry the question building within me like a bleed on the brain.

Will I save Colin?

The pendulum is still. No response.

Can I still save Colin?

Yes.

My breath shudders out of me. Oh God.

Do I need the Heart to save him?

Yes.

Will I find the Heart?

The pendulum is still.

Samara's voice echoes in my mind: *Heart finds you.*

There is a thrashing in the brush back the way I came. I jump to my feet and run into the dark structure of the temple.

The walls inside ripple, and I'm at the bottom of a shadowed valley covered in red snow. I scoop up a handful of the snow and start when I realize it's as warm as an exhale in my hand. I drop it, brushing at my skin anxiously, and walk on, not brave enough to experiment with putting what looks all too much like bloody snow in my mouth, though I'm desperate for water.

I close my eyes and try to get a blueprint tether to the Heart going. I concentrate on the relief that will course through me as I reach the Heart, when I find whatever it is I need to save Colin there; the joy of knowing that Colin with his black hair and melting blue eyes, Colin with the teasing quips and searing kisses, will live.

A wraithlike blueprint hovers. I have the tether, but I'm not sure I trust it. Sebastian's smooth voice sounds in my mind: *The Coil is playing with you. You asked it to dance, but it's not about to let you lead.*

This tether is different than the one to the Laurel Plain. It comes with a heavier, oppressive, but slippery feeling, like climbing up the damp walls of an ever-tightening well.

I look up at the sheer canyon walls and swallow, dropping to clear away the red snow to reveal the dirt below. I hate geomancy, but scrying with the dirt is the only thing available to me right now, and I need to see if I'm on the right path. I chew at my thumb before stopping, remembering my therapy.

A voice halts my efforts. I squint and can just make out someone kneeling in the snow up ahead.

I approach slowly, cautious after my experience with Dill and his team.

Dill. Maybe...

"Hey..." I say.

The man turns and stares up at me with a pale face topped by a flop of brown hair. A familiar scar stretches from his eye to his chin. I choke on my scream, my breath sawing in and out of my lungs. There is a small, gory hole in the center of his forehead, above his dead eyes.

Sidney Ford holds up two handfuls of red snow. "Go on. Take it. It's a blessing. But not for me."

My swallowed scream comes out a whimper instead. He stands and I step back, frozen with horror when I realize what I've done. Nothing happens, though. No pain, no fishhook deeper into the Coil. I shriek, slapping at Ford's outstretched hands, and run past him, plunging headlong into the shadows ahead.

Something grabs at my leg and I kick at it, crying out as I fall, skinning my chin.

"Run. Run," Dill moans.

"Dill?" I whisper, scrambling to my knees next to him. "Oh, thank God. Dill?"

"No names. Don't name your food," he says. His eyes are nearly black in the murky light. Empty. Wiped of everything but fear. Samara's eyes.

He grabs at my hair on both sides of my head and pulls my face painfully toward his. "Run before the Heart finds you."

I yank myself away, shaking, the terror in his voice freezing the blood in my veins more than the words. "But I need to find the Heart. I need it, Dill. You found it? Where is it?"

"It's a lie. A lie. The Heart is a lie," he sobs as he staggers to his feet. "Heart finds you. Don't let the Heart find you."

"Come with me. I'll take you..." I set a hand on his arm. I have no idea where I can take him, but I can't leave him like this. And having him with me, even in this state, is better than...

He violently thrashes, and I drop my hand, startled. He races into the shadows, leaving me alone. How is he moving backwards? Why was I able to when Ford—

I look back, and a figure approaches.

My mother's crooning voice fills the canyon, the lyrics to her plagiarized lullaby bouncing off the hills:

> *Set out at dawn, first hint of light /*
> *Not west, nor east, straight on 'til night.*
> *Walk on, walk on, and sing this song /*
> *For some, day's short, for others, long.*
> *The Young Hound frets and paces so /*
> *Will his children thrive and grow?*
> *Worry nips at his four heels /*
> *Throughout his solitary meals.*
> *The Grizzled Wolf laments and wails /*
> *For distant ships and distant sails.*
> *Some imagined, some are real /*
> *He weeps for all he once did feel.*
> *The Lion rises, meets the sun /*
> *Much to do 'fore day is done.*
> *He's missed by Wolf at eastern bay /*
> *unnoticed by Hound's western gaze.*

FORETOLD

Set out at dawn, first hint of light /
Not west, nor east, straight on 'til night.
Walk on, walk on, and sing this song /
For some, day's short, for others, long.

It isn't the dream version, or the Coil version of my mom I saw with Sebastian. It's *her*. Her cheeks are flushed with good health, her eyes bright and happy and filled with love. She's wearing her favorite yellow sundress. And her voice is her own, clear and sweet as spring's first bloom.

I've missed that voice. I barely remember it unless I listen to my voicemail. To hear her clear as day, singing *that* song, to know that this has all been living in my head, unreachable except through this horrible place... this is the cruelest of all. To use her, the *real* her, with no Coil-nightmare artifice. To draw on my memories, some I didn't realize were still rattling around my head.

I moan, my eyes stinging. She's not real. She's gone forever. "Not her. Please. Not her. Use anything but her. Please no more. No more. No more. No more. No more." Stopping and sinking onto my haunches, I clutch at my ears and tightly press my eyes shut, shutting her dear face out, my face wet with tears.

Please. Not my mom. Get out of my head. Get out of my head. Out of my head. Out of my head. Out of my head.

The Heart is a lie.

I was so stupid to think I could fix things. Fix *me*. I've never done anything worthwhile in my life. Even Mrs. O said she would've been happier with the developer taking over her place. I can't save Colin. The Coil is toying with me. Has been toying with me.

"Get out of my head!" I scream.

I open my eyes and drop my hands from my ears.

It's sunny. Birds chirp. I'm squatting on a road leading up to a bucolic farmhouse a dozen paces ahead.

I pick up a rock and heave it at the house with all my might, shattering a window. It doesn't make me feel better, so I pick up another and let it fly. It hits the door. More follow. The last one I throw goes wide, missing the house.

My arm aches, my mouth is a desert, and I'm standing on wet spaghetti strands instead of legs. I drop to the ground. Even the tether to the Heart I distrusted is gone. There's nothing I can do for Colin now. I'll be lucky if I don't die in here myself. I rub at my chest, at the hope-sized hole throbbing inside me. Maybe I didn't escape a physical punishment after all.

I hear footsteps behind me and I freeze, visions of Ford and my false Coil-mother blasting through my mind's eye.

A little boy giggles as he passes. He stops in the lane and peers down at me with bright eyes too big for his pale cherubic face. He looks about five or six years old and is wearing what looks like a faded school uniform, complete with little white knee socks and shiny black laced shoes. His hair is a brown shock topped by a cap. "Come on. Or do you want to destroy my house some more?"

"I—I'm sorry?" I stammer, as I struggle to my feet. "I didn't mean—wait, you live here?"

"Let's go," the boy says. He turns so that he's shuffling back-wards toward the place, facing me as I follow. "You're sad."

"I am," I agree.

He smiles.

You're not meant to save Colin. You don't belong at Theban. I look up at the blue Coil sky. A flock of black birds fly overhead.

Six crows.

"I need to get out of here. I need to go home and accept however much time I have with Colin, and... and..." I say, swiping at my eyes. "Maybe I can buy some time. If I tell him about the vision."

We've reached the boy's front door. "If you're abandoning hope, you can come inside with me. The way to Laurel Plain is through my home."

"Do—do you have any mirrors in there?"

"No mirrors."

I look down the road stretching past the house. What if there's something just around the bend that can help Colin? I can't lose him, lose *me* again.

I look back at the boy. His smile is angelic.

Go to Colin. Be with him for as long as you have together.

"Okay," I say. It comes out rough, anguish wrapping its arms around that one little word and weighing it down.

The boy gestures for me to open his door, a simple white rectangle of wood and a rusting black knob. I'm going to lose Colin. I failed.

One, two, three. This compulsion is not me.

Four, five, six. I control it. It doesn't control me.

My heart aches. I twist the knob. Five times.

The door opens and the boy scampers inside. I follow.

I HOLD MY HANDS OUT IN FRONT OF ME, FEELING MY WAY through the darkness.

"Are you there?"

It smells like flowers, but not any one particular flower. It smells like dozens and dozens of them, their fragrances blending. It smells like a funeral.

"Hello?"

"Vali, what have you dragged home?" a deep, ringing voice asks. I hear the boy giggle. "I want it."

I feel the cold wash of dread. *One. Two. Three. Four.*

A click, and a small gas lamp is lit. It spotlights a seated man in profile, a beard of soot-black bristles coating his chin and climbing up the side of his face to meet his hairline. It's a regal face, reflecting the light off his firm brow and cheek, but weary enough to make me think he's older than he looks. The rest of him is embraced by shadows. The little boy climbs onto the man's lap.

"Who are you? Where am I?" I whisper.

"It's sad and afraid, Asterion," the boy says. "Can I eat it now?"

"Not yet, pet, you just ate. You'll make yourself sick," the man says soothingly.

Just ate? He can't mean... *Dill? This isn't real. This isn't real. This isn't real—*

"Why does it keep repeating itself?" the boy asks.

"Y—you can hear my thoughts?"

"It has an illness, pet," the man says. He shifts slightly, and I shrink back in on myself, seeing for the first time just how hulking and powerful his frame is. Although he does not turn his face toward me, his one visible dark iris, set in a soupy bloodshot umber, passes over me in a searching scrape; an eye at odds with his kingly, bearded face.

"Oh good. Like the other? Or does this illness spoil her for eating?" the boy sings out.

"Oh God." *Take a step back. Take your chances deeper in the Coil—away from...*

"No use. You tried earlier. No place deeper than the Heart. Only way out is the way you came," the man says.

"I'm... I'm in the—" I'm in the Heart. I'm in the Heart. The Heart. The Heart. The Heart. I draw in choppy breaths. Every muscle aches, tight with the need to run. I'm not scared. I'm pass-out-from-fear-terrified.

"Heart of the Heart. You're consumed with *what-weres*, *what-ifs*, and *what-wills*. Real and imagined. It's a delicious anima," the man says. "My pet and I have eaten, and still, I'm tempted."

"I—I want to go," I whisper, taking a step back toward the door.

"If I can't eat, I want to play!" the boy pleads. "This one likes games, too."

"What do I always tell you? You mustn't play with your food."

"If I can't eat it, then it's not my food. Yet," the boy pouts.

I back up another step, carefully, slowly. Samara Trefoil and the hunted look in her eyes, Dill and the emptiness I sensed in him, these *things* are responsible.

"It knows the others!" the boy says with joy, leaping off the man's lap.

"I don't want to play. I want to go home."

"It doesn't want to go home. It wants to save a boy. It wants a mirror," the boy says to the man.

"A great sacrifice is needed," the man says. "What have you to give for this boy's life?"

"Presents!" The boy claps.

"I—I thought..." Dill said the Heart was a lie. But if... if it isn't?

"I don't know. Minutes off my life? A year?"

The boy shakes his head.

"I... Tell me what you want." I tug at my necklace, afraid to hope, afraid to succeed.

"Bring that to me, pet," the man says to the boy.

The boy scampers over. I rear back. He smiles at me with teeth that are now sharp as needles and points to the necklace my Dad bought me for my birthday. I unlatch my necklace with shaking hands, pooling it in the boy's awaiting palm. He holds it up for the man's inspection.

"Open it," the man says. The boy obeys and flicks the fan-like locket open. I flinch, hating the idea of these creatures staring at my memories. "You do not want us to view these images? But we've seen one of these before, you know. The thing you call mother. You have, too, in this place. Not very long ago," the man says to me. He reaches out a yellow, curling fingernail and traces one of the wedges of the locket. "You painted with your pain. Thank you."

I hug my arms to my middle, hold my breath.

"This is precious to you," the man says, tapping at the five fanned panels of the locket. It is not a question. He brings each panel to his eye, lingering on the final photo of the three of us together. "You would give it to us?"

"Yes," I respond.

"This loss is an acceptable trade," the man says. The boy closes the locket and runs off into the dark.

"My locket is..." How is a necklace enough to save a life? That can't be enough. "I can save Colin by sacrificing *that*?"

The man stands and dips his head in acknowledgment. "You will have a tool to save the thing you love. We have accepted your sacrifice."

The man lifts the lantern.

I smother a shriek. The part of him he'd hidden away, the left side of his body... the bulging black eye of a bull, coarse hair covering the side of his face leading to a curved horn, hooves instead of a hand and foot.

He smiles, I think: a grotesque twist of lips and snout. "My appearance offends you. But *I* am not the one who wanders about inside *your* home. Your kind crawl and burrow and build nests in my walls, and then you're offended to find me here, still lingering on after all these years. But you have only yourselves to blame for that. Nightmares linger long after the night has gone when you feed them."

The man—bull—*thing* sets his lantern on top of a hearth and opens a small case with his human hand, passing something small to the boy. The boy sets a small, flat stone down in front of me.

I stare at them, trembling at their proximity until I hear a hissing. Something slithers along my foot. I leap back, chest heaving. Serpents slide in from around the room, congregating around the stone. Seven snakes in all. In unison, they all bare their fangs and bite down on the stone. *I'm in a room full of snakes. A dark room full of snakes.*

"Their venom is potent. Mustn't stand too close," the man says.

I edge back, and one of the snakes snaps at me before sinking its teeth into that stone disc again. A depression appears in the center of the stone, the snake venom eating away at it like acid. A hole appears, grows, and when the stone has a perfect circle housed in its center, the snakes disperse, slithering off to whence they came.

The man bends, setting a second hoof on the ground as he picks up the stone. He straightens and extends it out, pinched between two thick, yellow fingernails.

"This is an adderstone glass. To use one is a blessing. You may use it now to finish your ritual and save the thing you care for," the man says. "Use it as you would the mirror. Look through and create the reality you require."

I take it from him. The hole has a rose-colored transparent film, thin as a bubble's skin stretched over it. This is the last piece of my ritual: visualizing the soul whose harvest I want stopped in a Mag Five Mirror.

Save Colin. Save Colin. Save Colin. Save Colin. Save Colin.

I hold it up to my eye and peer through. I picture Colin, and he appears in the center of the adderstone. He's alive. He's older. It's years from now. He's living a life full of laughter and... he has children of his own. He doesn't die in the street in front of Mrs. O's shop and the school. *He lives. He lives. He lives. He lives. He lives.* I say it, and I see it, and I believe it.

I look up from the stone. The boy holds his hand out. I place the stone in his palm.

"The boy will live," the man says. "And you will stay."

"Stay... here? No! But—" My pulse is a battering ram. My throat works as I swallow. Samara's sobs sound in my mind's ear in a sharp voice like broken glass. *I'll play. I'll play.*

"What if—I... I'll play to..."

"Yes!" the boy says eagerly. "A game!"

"No games, pet."

"But I want to!" the boy whines, stamping his foot. "If it loses, we can still feed on it."

My heart jerks. "I'll play. I'll play." *I'll play. Play. Play.*

The boy cries out, a thirsty, grating sound. He rushes to the man's side and pulls on his sleeve. "A question game, I think," the boy coos.

The man—at least the human half of his face—appears resigned and amused. "Very well." He turns to face me more fully, and I can't stop my shudder. "You'll play with my pet. If you are victorious, you may go. But if you lose..." He smiles.

Is this where Samara failed? Where Dill failed? Or was it the fear that drove out all the light in their eyes?

The boy smiles, his fangs reflecting the light, and approaches slowly. I shake, a marrow-deep cold settling in me as I watch him.

"What is dead before the dawn, lives for the day, and dies after dusk?" he asks in a sing-song voice.

I lick at my dry lips, tasting the color storm. There is a warning tingle at the base of my neck. *Trivinometry. Treat it like any game of Trivinometry, Cassie.* One where my life is on the line. For once, that's not my catastrophic thinking exaggerating, either: riddles have always been my least liked part of Trivinometry.

I repeat the riddle in a whisper. "Is the answer... light?"

"That's right, but it asked me," the boy tells the man. "That's not fair. This is my question game. It didn't answer, it asked."

"Ask it another."

The boy takes another step forward. "I am a glimmer, a ray, an undying spring. I am lost, abandoned, a shattered thing. I am raised, and dashed, a lifeline to some. When all others fled, there was only one. What am I?"

I repeat the riddle to myself. I dissect it. Trying different answers on in my mind and discarding them.

"It's having trouble with this one," the boy says. "I hope it's wrong! I'm getting hungry again." He sings out the riddle as if it were a lullaby, to the same melody as my mother's.

"H—hope." I nearly say it in a questioning voice, but I manage to spit it out firmly. That might be Pict's best lesson to me. If I make it out of here alive, or with my mind intact, I'll have to let him know he would approve of this ghoul.

The boy pouts.

"Last question, pet," the man says.

"Fine," the boy barks. "What is always coming, but never here?"

"Never here. Always coming... always coming... never... never here. It's tomorrow!"

The boy scowls. "She's been here too long and doesn't smell fresh anymore, anyway," he says. I can see the hunger for me fade from those too-big eyes, along with his interest.

"Go now," the man says. The front door swings open. I back up toward the door, keeping my eyes on them both. The boy follows, his teeth are no longer razor sharp. He once again looks like a mop-haired child with big doe eyes. I'm almost at the door. I don't dare ask the question, even to myself, but he answers it anyway.

"Your fear was a good snack. I would have liked eating you. But you have to go."

I shudder and step through the door. I'm slapped in the face with the sunshine and cheering crowds.

33

I squint and stumble, eyes attempting to adjust to the light, my mouth dry as the sand beneath my feet. My heart is still thumping against my chest like a war hammer. The music is disorienting.

Mountains. A range of blue-gray mountains loom over me. An impressive ancient amphitheater and its red-brown pillars in front of me. People, laughing, dancing.

The Laurel Plain?

I look back the way I came. From here, it looks like a dark tunnel burrowed into a mountainside. A calling wind breezes from it. Like any entrance to the Coil.

I look up. This amphitheater, this whole space, is carved out of the mountain. A hand lands on my shoulder, and I shriek. Another pulls at my hand. Two girls I recognize as prefects from class. They're speaking to me. Kindly but urgently, asking me to follow. They lead me up the rough limestone steps to the shadow of the amphitheater pillars. From up here, I can see down into the valley of the mountain range where glittering azure waters are snaking their way along bends and curves.

"Cassandra Morai!" an announcer shouts. A cheer goes up—and an almost equal number of boos, I notice. The band begins to play louder, though I didn't think it was possible. One of the prefects sets a laurel wreath on my head. Another sets a blanket about my shoulders and hands me a water bottle. I greedily gulp it down, so quickly it almost comes back up.

All around us there are bonfires, and Magpies with carts, and music... the whole thing feels like part music festival and part human sacrifice in one.

"Cassie!" Regan shouts. I shrug off my blanket and rush to the edge of the platform. She pushes through the vendors and crowds and rushes up the stairs to launch herself at me. We cling to each other. She's showered and changed her clothes since last I saw her. "I was so scared. We weren't sure what happened to you after you disappeared. And when you took so long to get out..." Her eyes dart around nervously.

"Regan! I did it! I saved Colin. And... what is this place? This is the Laurel Plain?"

"Yes. It's the Coil version of Mount Parnassus. Temple of Apollo... it's not a ruin here..." She trails off, peering at someone in the crowd. "We need to go. Now."

The crowd's chants pound in tempo with the ache in my head. They're chanting something in Latin. "What's going on? What are they saying?"

Regan pulls me along, down the stairs over the objections of the prefects. "Initiating you into the order. We made it to the Laurel Plain. We're Oracles now. Come on."

"Where is Griffin—"

"Infirmary. Him and... and Noah... they got into it when we got back because of what Noah did. Don't worry, Griffin's okay. They were finally treating his hands when I saw him. The place is mobbed. Only six people have made it here on their own so far, and we're two of them. The search parties have pulled out most of the others, but some are in bad shape. Another search team just went in looking for you and the other three still inside."

"How long were we in there?" She's pulling me toward another mining tunnel cut into the mountain.

"For me, it felt like a couple of days in there, but out here it was only about twenty-three hours. For you, though... we went in on Thursday. It's Monday."

"*Monday?*" We duck around a stone pillar. "I'm going home today." I try and swallow. "Water. I need more—"

"When I say go, we run. Ready—"

A guard steps in front of us, almost knocking Regan down. "Ms. Morai. You're going to need to come with us." He grabs my arm away from Regan and shoves me toward the mineshaft entrance Regan was leading me to.

Regan follows, pleading. "Let her go. Please! This is a mistake."

"Where are we going?" I ask. He tightens his grip. I pull back, dragging my feet until we stop. I can't move.

One. Two. Three. Four.

This compulsion isn't—

"Move or I'll make you move." The guard shakes my shoulder. "I'm not telling you again."

Five.

He grabs me and throws me over his shoulder. I fight and twist as I hang.

"Put her down!" Regan shouts.

"If you keep following, you'll end up in a cell with her."

"Good!" Regan spits out.

The space around us is a dirt tunnel, propped up by wooden beams embedded in the walls and ceiling every few feet. Lanterns hang from nail pegs, enough of them to banish most but not all of the darkness. It's not enough. The ceiling is high, but I feel the tunnel closing in around me. *The shaft caves in. I can't breathe. The dirt in my lungs...*

"Regan, get my aunt! *Please.*"

Regan wrings her hands. "Your aunt knows, Cassie. That's how I found out. I heard them telling her they're bringing you to the Grims for trial. I didn't hear what it was for, but I heard her say she won't protect you anymore."

I make a sound suspiciously like a whimper in the back of my throat. Regan grabs for my hands.

"Cassie, we'll straighten this out. I'll find... someone. Someone who can help. Don't worry."

The guard unceremoniously dumps me on the ground. "You're heavy. Walk." He turns to Regan. "I'm going to count to three. If you're still here, you—"

Regan leans down to help me up and gives me a quick hug before running off to fetch help.

It's then that I feel it. The clock. It's still there. A spasm squeezes my heart and I gasp, clutching at my chest. The clock within me thunders with resonance, fiercer, deeper than ever. It's grief. *Grief to come.* It's close. Oh God. Colin. *It didn't work.*

I did the ritual. I made the sacrifice. That thing in the Heart said it was enough. Why didn't it work?

"Please. Let me go. There's a life that—"

The guard yanks me so hard I feel my arm strain against its socket.

I numbly march on, down a twisting path that eventually brings us to the bridge to the Grim's Council chamber. The guard leads me straight past the anteroom and into the empty Council chamber itself. Then he shepherds me through a doorway behind the dais to a strange room tiled with round, polished tree-ring slabs. There are three metal jail cells along the wall.

"Get in there." The guard pushes me into a cell, closing the door behind me and locking it. He pockets the pinky-sized key. "This room is lined in *jet*. It'll block any ritual you or any of your friends try. Somebody will be by later with food and water."

"Wait!" I shout, a manic edge to my voice. "Why am I being held?"

The guard closes the door to the chamber behind him. A jail within a jail.

34

I t's been hours since the guard closed me in here. Hours that I've paced the perimeter of this cell, looking for any hint of a way out. I know, because I've been counting ever since he locked me in here.

Colin. Colin. Colin. Colin. Colin.

Colin with his sapphire eyes and his crooked smile. Colin with the paintings of me and the unpacked mementos of his life. With his slow, sweet kisses. What if something has already... I close my eyes. Nothing has happened to him. Somehow I'd know it. He's still alive. But I need to get to him. *Now.* I need to try whatever I can to save him.

I still feel death approaching, stalking, but it's not as strong as it was before we entered this room. Is it the jet in the walls? If so, jet must only dull scryer abilities instead of blocking them completely.

I'm supposed to be home by now. I bite at my lip, wondering if Dad will worry. I can handle anything except scaring him like that. Or losing Colin.

A person can live three days without water. What about Coil-days? *I die of thirst, covered in color storm dirt. Dad—*

"I'll bring the food in and be on my way," a familiar voice rasps from outside the wood-tiled door. It's Emina, carrying a large tray. I rush to the bars when I see her Pomeranian face and gray cotton candy hair. She shakes her head, a warning in her eyes. "Well, this nice young lady doesn't look capable of that awful crime. And I've *certainly* never seen her before in my life."

"Less yapping, more delivering." The guard follows on Emina's heels, peeking at the tray with interest.

Emina swats him away. "People used to respect the elderly, you know. This is for the prisoner. I have a tray out there for you."

The guard pulls open a metal flap in the middle of the cell door, large enough for Emina to hand me the tray. He lets the flap drop with a clatter as soon as her hands are clear.

I look down at the tray: steaming meat pies, water, some of the red beet-poppers Bacchy loves so much, and a small Turkish coffee cup and bright hammered-copper Turkish coffee pot. I don't have an appetite for any of it, except the water. I crouch to set the tray down, grabbing at the cup of water and sucking it down so quickly I cough.

"You'll want to drink that coffee while it's hot, dear," Emina says with special emphasis. She points at the inky depths. "Learned the recipe in the Seven Bells under a virtuoso."

I look up, my pulse quickening. She winks and follows the guard out of the room.

I DON'T KNOW IF MARKO JACKED THE KEY HIMSELF OR IF he showed Emina how to do it, but I could kiss the both of them. I wipe the coffee off the key and reach through the bars, opening the lock to my cell door.

I creep to the wood-tiled door to the Council chamber and open it a crack. There is no one in the chamber. I don't see any other way out but the way I came in.

The awful foreboding feeling hits me square in the chest again the second I'm clear of the room. It stuns me silent; death beating a drum.

I hug the wall with my back as I gingerly make my way toward the doors leading to the anteroom, as if I'd somehow be able to camouflage myself against the stone if someone entered. One of the doors is closed, but the other is open, as are the massive doors leading out to the bridge. I have a clear view straight through. I screw up my nerve, ready to run—until I spy the guard seated outside at a small table, reading a tarot spread.

I flatten myself back against the wall, breathing hard. How am I supposed to get past him?

"Mac! What are you doing down here?" Sebastian calls out as he strides into the anteroom. "They pulled the last of the initiates from the Coil. Laurel Plain is wild right now."

"I'm watching the prisoner," Mac says.

"Prisoner? Didn't realize we had one."

"Yeah. A girl. Cassandra Morai."

"They sent *you* to guard one little girl, locked in a cell, in a room carpeted in jet, in the middle of the Grimoire Council's secure chambers?" The way Sebastian asks the question, it sounds as if Mac is too important for a simple job.

Mac scratches his neck and shakes his head. "Dumb. But orders are orders."

"Well, I'll leave you to it... but... oh, tarot? New deck my father's people developed, is it? What do you think?"

"Shite." Mac doesn't hesitate to respond.

"Ah, but there's a trick to it. Here, let me show you."

I peek out the door to see Sebastian shuffling the cards. His blond head is bent as he sets the cards down.

"Give me one of your hands. Now close your eyes and keep them closed, Mac. I need you to concentrate; think about something you desperately want to happen. What you need to make happen. Think long and hard and don't open your eyes until I tell you to."

I nearly gasp when Sebastian pins me with his green gaze. He mouths *"Go now."*

I slip past the table, glancing at the guard whose eyes are screwed tightly shut. I run, as soundlessly as I can, as Sebastian adds more instructions for Mac. I race across the bridge, hiding just beyond a bend while I think about my next move. I can't leave through the Rotunda. Someone will see me.

A hand slips over my mouth, smothering my scream.

"It's me. Are you okay?" Sebastian asks, looking so golden and clean it reminds me of how filthy I am from the Coil. He removes his hand.

I nod. "How did you know I was here?"

"Bacchy found me," he says. His anger radiates through his coiled shoulders. "I didn't know you'd been arrested. I should have been told. I'm going to find out why I wasn't."

"Do you know why I was arrested? They wouldn't tell me—"

"Let's just get you out of here." He takes me down the path the guard used to bring me here, and then through a doorway to our right. The space around us shivers but does not ripple. Stable. It occurs to me that the Coil feels smoother now. Not as malevolent.

"You were arrested because they say you created and used a Magnitude Five Dark Mirror in a forbidden ritual targeting Bedlam."

I clamp my lips together and clench my teeth.

"Where'd you get the ritual?" he asks.

"It doesn't matter. How am I going to get out of here if the guards all know I'm supposed to be in a cell?"

Sebastian shakes his head. "Don't change the subject."

"I can't tell you anything about it."

"Why not? Bacchy did. He told me everything." He actually looks hurt, as if my decision not to confide in him was a test. "Including the *second* forbidden ritual you're working on."

"If you know, then you don't need to hear it again. Can you answer me? How am I supposed to get out? Where are you taking me?"

He pauses, raising a finger to his lip, and looks around a corner. He pulls me along, down a hall of gleaming white floors and navy walls. I hear a sound, and before I can react, Sebastian has pushed me against the wall, his strong arms wrapped tight around me.

It knocks the wind out of me. I look up in confusion and gasp a second before his firm lips come down on mine, molding to my own. His hand reaches up and fists in my hair, gently tugging until I tip my face up to his. I can't think, my heart is beating out of my chest, until I hear a throat cleared. Whoever it is rapidly moves away.

Sebastian stops his kissing but keeps his lips on mine, shielding me, until the sound passes. Even knowing why I had those skillful lips on my own, I feel guilty. Colin. Colin. Colin. Colin. Colin.

Sebastian lifts his head slowly and looks down at me, his green eyes black in the dim light. I blink and struggle to catch my breath.

"This is the executive entrance. Your aunt commissioned it, and no one except Oracles know about it. That's how I'm getting you out." He turns and leads me down a hall to our left and throws open a door, peering outside. He holds it open over my head and gestures for me to step out into the mid-afternoon light. I realize we're nowhere near Theban Group's main entrance; this one has let us out onto a street at least a dozen blocks away. I turn back to Sebastian, a *thank you* on my lips.

Instead, I ask, "Why are you helping me?"

He doesn't answer, just stares down at me, his gaze probing, penetrating. Finally, he says, "The boyfriend? I hope he's worth it."

"He is," I say softly. "Thank you."

"Then good luck. I'll do my best to cover for you here. Do what you need to do." Sebastian leaves a beat. "You know this isn't a permanent fix, right? This isn't over."

"I know."

He looks away and nods, pulling the door closed, and I am left standing between a nail salon and a bank.

I run toward home. Toward Colin.

35

P lease be okay. *Please be okay. Please be okay. Please be okay.
Please be okay.*

I'm dripping sweat and almost delirious with worry by the time
I round the corner to my block.

Firetrucks, ambulances. No. No. No. No. No.

I stumble forward, trance-like. My home is engulfed in flames;
they lick greedily up the front of the building from what used to be
my living room.

I look around, dazed. I don't see Colin. I don't see my father,
either. I see Mrs. Clay, Colin's mom. She's talking to one of the
firefighters. I push through, forcing my way past the police and the
taped-off area.

"Colin! Is he okay? Where is he?" I shout.

"Cassie! There you are! You look like a mess. Are you okay?
We were all worried sick! Your apartment caught fire and we didn't
know what to think... Colin is fine! He ran over to Mrs. Otero's to
see if she'd heard from you."

My heart bounds into my throat and lodges there. I take off

running, past my frightened neighbors, past the fire crew, as fast as I can in the direction of Mrs. O's shop. To the place I watched Colin die.

IT'S HAPPENING. IT'S HAPPENING. HE CAN'T BE DEAD. Whatever is about to happen, is about to happen now.

I scan the street before tearing across to Mrs. O's bodega, pushing her shop door open and setting the bell jangling like mad.

"Cass!" Colin runs to me, grabbing me in a bear hug.

Mrs. O rounds the counter and opens her arms. "Oh, thank goodness. I can't tell you how worried I was when your father came by."

I pull Colin along, unwilling to let go of him, unwilling to let him out of my sight. *He's alive. He's alive. Alive. Alive. Alive.* I let Mrs. O hug me, and I throw an arm around her too, still holding Colin's hand.

"You're okay," I tell Colin.

"Of course I am. You're the one... Cassie, your apartment is on fire. We thought you were inside. Your Dad said you might have let yourself in... that you were due back from camp hours ago. He looked like he was about to crawl out of his skin until the firefighters told him there was no one inside. The camp wasn't answering his calls..."

"Mrs. O, I need your phone. I need to call his cell. Colin, don't go outside for any reason. I need to talk to you," I say, my Colin anxiety warring with my guilt and misery over Dad.

"You don't have to call him. He left maybe two minutes before you got here, little one. He's right across the street in the school parking lot, hoping your bus finally shows up. He didn't know what else to do since no one was answering his phone calls and your guidance counselor isn't in," Mrs. O says.

I run to the door. "Colin, *please* stay inside. Okay? Don't move. For *any* reason. I'll be right back. *Please.*"

I hurry to the curb and start pounding the crosswalk button five times with my knuckle. Oh my God, our house is on fire and his mentally effed-up daughter has been missing for hours and he's gotta be crawling out of his skin by now—

"Cass!" Dad's voice cuts through the busy block's noise.

I spot him across the street. His eyes glint with relief. He looks worried and haggard. I did that to him.

He wipes at his eyes and steps into the street.

36

No one talks about the day after the worst day of your life.

You hear about *the day*—the worst day, a waking nightmare where everyone you know is now an actor playing a sad version of themselves.

You hear about the general *after*—that vague period when time no longer exists and the days and weeks and months meld together in a fog of tears, anger, and discarded tissues jamming up pockets.

But no one talks about the *specific day after* the worst day of your life. When you wake up having forgotten... remember... then wish you'd never woken up at all.

Flashes of soul-searing recollection are hurriedly folded away by a hulking and protective disbelief. You feel like you're sleepwalking, numbly tripping through a bramble patch, those dull stings and aches dogging every step as you go through the motions of brushing your teeth, maybe washing your face, probably not brushing your hair.

"Cassie, I'm sorry to bother you, honey, but people are going to start coming and—you should get dressed, okay?" Colin's mom says.

She's been kind. I slept in her guest room last night. My home, both the place and the person who made it feel that way, are gone.

I cry, I brush my teeth, I put on clothes—new, with tags, since I no longer own anything. They're nicer than anything I owned before. I wouldn't care if they were rags.

There's a knock at the door. It opens a crack, and I expect to see Mrs. Clay again. My heart gives a dull twist when I see Colin's face.

"Cass, can I come in?" He looks miserable. He looks nervous, too. I make the observation in a clinical way, detached, like an anthropologist making a guess based on dusty bones. This numb haze doesn't allow me to process any more than that.

I've changed. So has he, for me anyway; he just doesn't know it yet. I nod.

"How are you feeling?" he asks, and then runs a hand down his face. "Dumb question. Ignore that." I don't respond, and he abandons his anxious attempts to draw me out, instead leading me to the drawing room in the front of his home. The room I used to daydream about whenever I passed is identical to what I imagined. My scryer instincts were right about the place, but wrong about the feelings.

Colin's mom brings me a cup of tea and ushers him out of the drawing room over his protests, the politician's wife correctly reading my need to be away from him. I sit on the window seat and stare at the yellow police tape guarding the charred ruins of what used to be my home. I guess I was right about the sprinklers.

I see 2A, the old couple James and Chris, who have a cat named Madame Déficit because they spend all their money pampering her. They're staring up at the half-blackened shell of the building, Chris calling out to Madame every so often. I hope she wasn't inside when the fire... I stare down at my cup of long-forgotten tea and try to scry, hoping to find Madame for them, failing miserably. My mind was never clean to begin with.

There's a knock on the door.

"Cassie, someone here to see you," Mrs. Clay says. She opens the door wider, and Aunt Bree steps in. Mrs. Clay closes the door behind her.

Aunt Bree looks haunted, with circles under her eyes no amount of concealer can contain. Her black skirt and jacket emphasize them.

"Congratulations. You killed my brother," she says.

I flinch. I clutch my tea cup and saucer.

"No response? Well. I'll do the talking for both of us, then." Aunt Bree throws her handbag down on the fancy little sofa and sits. She folds her legs and tips her head, her unkind smile a red slash across her pale face. "You were supposed to do the ritual I gave you so Bedlam didn't trouble us again."

"I did," I croak out.

"Ah, but you didn't *just* do that ritual, did you? That stunt with the Heart of the Coil. Your friend Noah didn't know why you needed the Heart, or if you made it there. I do. You did something to save that boy out there in the hall." She tips her head toward the parlor door, and her lip curls in disgust.

"How do you know?"

"Because he was supposed to die!" She bites it out before taking in a breath and forcing herself to visibly relax.

"Wh—what are you talking about?" I stammer. It feels as if everything is muted, like it's coming at me from the bottom of a lake: sounds, thoughts. I can't understand what she's saying.

"I laid out, very carefully, small changes that needed to happen in the world in order to accomplish certain objectives. Dominoes that needed to fall. That boy's death was one. I needed to set his father on a certain path. The ritual that you performed to hurt the Bedlam witch was another. They both needed to happen in order to—"

"You told me the Bedlam ritual wouldn't hurt anyone!"

"Oh, Cassandra, you can't be that naïve. I blame your mother's genetics for how stupid you are. Jeffrey was smart. Your mother's side... well, they've been Darwin'ed out of existence, haven't they? You're the last of them. Thank God."

I launch off my seat and fling my cup of cold tea in her face, wishing it was piping hot. Wishing I could hurt her. She sits for a moment, shocked, before reaching up to wipe at the tea clinging to her lashes.

"Cute. The fact remains that whatever you did to save your little boyfriend killed your father." She holds a hand to her cheek and shakes her head in disbelief. "My brother *is going to be put in the ground*. Agatha even swapped your Somnum Sand as a precaution, to run out the clock, and I told her she was being overly cautious. If you had just done what you were supposed to—"

"I guess I'm not a very good pawn, am I, Bree?" I drop the cup and saucer onto the rug and clench my fists. "Get out. Leave."

She stands, presses a hand to her tea-wet hair, and grabs for her handbag. "This isn't over, Cassandra."

"Get out," I scream again, louder.

She walks to the door. "You know, when Jeffrey and I were little, he promised me he would always protect me. I promised him the same. If I'd foreseen today, I would have strangled you in your crib."

37

There was a funeral. There was a burial. People were there. Dad's body is next to Mom's now. They had to move her headstone to make room for him. I didn't like that.

I sit in Mrs. O's little apartment, alone even with her in the room. I'd rather be here than Colin's, though. I can't look at him knowing I traded him for my father. I did this. For him.

Mrs. O's sofas are covered in plastic. She tried to give me her bed, or at least share it, but I refused, so this crinkling and uncomfortable sofa is my new home. I get dressed and brush my teeth. I wash my face. I wash my hands. And wash my hands. And wash my hands. And wash my hands. And wash my hands.

"Little one, someone's here to see you. Please come out," Mrs. O says, opening the bathroom door and firmly turning off the faucet.

I find Colin standing near my makeshift bed, staring at me soulfully. I sit on the sofa with a crunch of plastic, and he approaches, cautious, and sits next to me.

"Hey, Cass... I wanted to stop by and see..." He runs a hand through his thick black hair. "I have something for you." He pulls out a small colorful square, no more than three inches side to side. I accept it and stare down at the paper-covered square. "God. I'm an idiot and wrapped it. I shouldn't have wrapped... Habit, I guess..."

I pull at the paper and tug the square from it, wishing him away from me. Wishing myself away from here. It's a tiny canvas. I turn it over and my heart stills.

He's painted my dad.

I close my eyes, tears painting my cheeks.

"You don't have any pictures," Colin says hurriedly, "and I thought... I mean, I didn't have anything but memory to go from, but mine's pretty photographic. I think it's pretty close, right?"

I shake, violently, as if the pain within is a sort of internal turbulence that might rip the shell of my being apart.

Colin envelops me in his arms, squeezing tightly as I tremble, then tips my face to his, kissing away my tears. I wrench away and rush back to the bathroom, setting the canvas on top of Mrs. O's vanity mirror. I turn on the faucet and wash my hands.

Mrs. O knocks a short while later. I leave the bathroom to find Colin gone and Regan sitting on my sofa, with Griffin, both of his hands heavily bandaged, standing next to her. He looks pale, haunted, the shadows beneath his eyes dark as bruises. I haven't seen him since the Coil. Since he tried to save me. I launch myself at him, squeezing tightly. Regan stands and hugs the both of us. We stay that way a long while.

"You look awful," I mumble into Griffin's shoulder.

"You don't look so hot yourself," he says, pulling away with a sad smile. "But we can trade beauty tips another time. We're here about you now."

"You're okay?" I ask.

Griffin nods dismissively.

"What about...?" I can't bring myself to say Noah's name. And yet... he tried to hurt me, but a part of me can't quite hate him. He was trying to protect Regan. He was right to try and stop me. He was probably right about more than that. *You bring everyone down with you.*

"Yeah, chucklefuck is fine," Griffin says.

Regan grimaces and gives him a quelling look. She sits next to me and covers my hands with one of her own. "Cassie, we're so sorry," she says. "Your dad was—"

Was. Past tense. They aren't the right words. The magic words that will make everything better.

I jerk my hands away. "Don't be sorry. You didn't kill him. I did."

"Cassie—"

"No, it's true. Saving Colin is what killed my dad. Aunt Bree said so." I hang my head, fighting the urge to say more. But needing to, as if in confession. "I knew. I knew the locket wasn't enough. But I wanted to believe it. Ford said the sacrifice gets picked for you if... but I didn't want to press. I *knew* the locket couldn't be enough. I—" *Oh God.* "Ford. He was kneeling in the red snow. 'It's a blessing, but not for me.' The adderstone. 'To use one is a blessing,' that thing said. The red blessing... the whole time it was..."

I cup my hands over my mouth. I can't bring myself to say it. But that doesn't matter; it echoes loudly enough in my head. *My dad. Dad. Dad. Dad. Dad.*

Regan and Griffin look at each other uncertainly, not understanding my words, unaware a new landslide of destructive anguish is rolling through me. Then Regan wraps her arms around me, and

Griffin does the same. I don't know where their tears begin and my own end.

And for the first time in a long while, what-ifs don't consume me. But only because what-was is clawing at my door.

EPILOGUE

It's chilly for September. A miserably rainy and cold first day of school. I train my eyes on Mrs. O's bodega awning to avoid looking at the place *it* happened.

If only you could've scryed it. The errant thought rises, zombie-like, for the millionth time. *You could've warned... could've stopped...*

Idiot, it was because of you.

"Cassie!" Colin calls out.

I don't turn. Something within the salted earth that is my heart stirs, but I pull my hood more securely over my head and burrow into my jacket, pretending I didn't hear. I rush across the street. The moment the bells to Mrs. O's shop door jangle, I kick myself for not going straight to her apartment instead. Colin can follow me here.

"I don't know," a familiar rasping female voice says from somewhere in the back of the shop. "It's an old lady hobby."

"Newsflash: you're an old lady," an archly sarcastic voice says from somewhere near the candy aisle. It takes me a moment to place them, as out of place as they are; like the confusion of seeing someone from school during an out-of-state vacation.

"Why do you never take my advice?" Mrs. O calls from the office. "Trust me."

"You never take mine either," Emina says.

"I have some plastic-covered sofas upstairs that would beg to differ," Mrs. O says dryly.

"Newsflash for *you*, Felda: you're the eldest of us," Gelisa says.

"Yep, I'm ancient. And you're dim as the day is long. Best part of getting old is saying what you want and not giving one red damn about what people think," Felda says. "No internal censor hitting the buzzer every time you open your yap to say something unpopular."

Mrs. O laughs and approaches from her office, shaking her head. She stops and tips her head toward the door. "Cassandra?"

I watch as Emina's Pomeranian fluff of hair emerges first, followed by gaunt Gelisa and then stout Felda from their respective corners of the store. "What's going on here?" I ask. I'm a mess, and today at school didn't help, so my sluggish brain works overtime to try and make sense of this tableau.

I accept hugs from Emina, Gelisa, and Felda, and nod curtly to accept their condolences. All the while, I keep my eyes trained on Mrs. O, who looks more uncomfortable than I've ever seen her.

"What are you doing here?" I ask.

Emina puts her arm around Mrs. O's shoulder and squeezes, as if in comfort. "It's time, Claudia."

Mrs. O nods and gestures that we all should follow her to her office. She gets a stepladder, and Emina volunteers to fetch what she needs from the shelf above her desk as we crowd the entrance.

"Box labeled 'tampons,' dear," Mrs. O says. Emina finds it, a brown box about the size of my arm in length and half that in height, heavily taped.

Felda hoots. "Lot of tampons."

Mrs. O smiles slightly. "It went unlabeled for years, but I had an insistent helper this summer who demanded he be allowed to dust and organize. Couldn't have him poking around that particular box."

Mrs. O hands me the boxcutter and I look up at them all, uncertain. I slice through the tape, pull open the flaps, and reach in to pull out a large wooden box nearly as big as the cardboard one that housed it. I sit down in Mrs. O's chair and set the box down on my lap, tracing a finger over the carving on the lid: a snake swallowing its own tail, its body forming a figure-eight.

"Your mother gave that to me before she passed. It was in her family for generations. You're the last of them."

I suck in a breath. I'm holding something from my mother? "Why didn't she give it to my dad?"

"But your home burned down, didn't it?" Gelisa says, in a tone that makes it sound like my question is an absurd one. Emina frowns at her and waves her hand, discouraging further interruption.

I wrinkle my brow, my nerve-endings sputtering and then firing fully, like an old car finally coming alive for the first time in a long while. I lift the lid and rear up, grabbing for the box before it can topple off my lap. *This can't be.*

"What's going on in here?" Colin says from the doorway.

My head snaps up, and I jerk the green and gold book out of the box and to my chest.

The Galdr Leechbook. My mother's copy.

THE
SCRYERS
BOOK TWO

HINDSIGHT

Coming 2022

ACKNOWLEDGEMENTS

I will undoubtedly forget to thank someone, and I'm sorry in advance. Please know I'll be rewriting this page in my mind long after this book is published, and my anxiety over it will be punishment enough.

First and foremost, thank you to my agent/soul friend Jon Michael Darga of Aevitas Creative Management. From the moment we met at Rebecca Heyman's The Work Conference afterparty, I knew you were the creative partner of my dreams. I so appreciate your expert eye, your smooth brain, and your friendship.

To Rick Lewis of Uproar Books, thank you for believing in this story and in me. I am so happy this book found a home at Uproar. You understood the story I was trying to tell on a level I scant could've imagined, and I am in awe of your editorial feedback. Thank you for making this book so much better and for putting it out into the world.

Thank you to my husband Emirson for your support and boundless patience as I spouted off about the people in my head. I have interrupted countless Netflix shows with random plot point questions, and I couldn't have done this without you cheering me on. You're my champion, and I love you.

Thank you to my sister Valerie Biberaj for pushing me to put pen to paper, for being the best sounding board on the planet, and for forcing me outside of my comfort zone when I needed it most. We can call it square for all those dodgeball rescues. Your talent is only rivaled by how kickass a sister you are.

I wish I could say the same about my baby sister Ariana Durollari. Thanks for nothing.

I'm kidding. Ari, I will always cherish the "book cover" you made me. There is no one else I'd rather roadtrip with.

Thank you to my mom Rita and my dad Alan for your sacrifices, for your lessons, and for instilling in me a love of learning and reading and writing and just... creating. Because of you, I've never been bored a second of my life. I love you both. You always told us we could accomplish almost anything we set our minds to. I never became a Kim Zmeskal-esque gold medal Olympian (I never even learned to do a proper cartwheel), but I'm convinced it's because I didn't want it enough.

Thank you to my grandmother Bedrije ("Betty"), for being the picture of perseverance and grace in the face of unimaginable strife and grief. If I become half the woman you are, I will still cast a long shadow.

Thank you to the brilliant Rebecca Faith Heyman of Rebecca Faith Editorial. What would I have done without you? Wait, I know... probably nothing. You have been one part Sherpa, one part doula, and one part friend, and I will never write a book I don't darken your door with before I even think of sending it to Jon and beyond.

Thank you to the two best beta readers on the planet—Adriana Ward and Catherine Thorsen (Carta Editorial Services). I can't even count how many rounds you guys went with me, sometimes reading the same bits over and over. If not for your enthusiasm, I fear mine might have been dulled. If not for your brilliant minds, I fear this story would not be what it is today.

To Richard Franke, my high school honors and AP English teacher, thank you for scaring me into reading the stuff I ended up loving. Thank you for giving me A's on my report cards and "not working to capacity" on my progress reports. And thank you for being the best teacher I ever had. I credit your influence as one of the most important in my academic life, and I wish I were smarter/more talented so that statement would carry more weight. Please never read a word I've written outside of this acknowledgement because otherwise I'll never stop worrying about what you thought of it. I still owe you a cherry red Ferrari.

To Mark Carnes, the most wonderful mentor and professor and boss. Thank you for helping me put myself into the skin of others. If not for you bringing history and literature to life for me, for helping me live it, for helping me see the world in a more creative way, I don't think I would enjoy writing as much as I do.

Thank you to my mother-in-law Nancy for always offering up help and childcare and love and excitement for everything I do.

Thank you to my friends ("The Kalis")—Nick, Matt, Jason, Michelle, Laurence, Mediha, Lenny, Hany, and the guest appearances by Orges and Frenchie and so on: I'm so lucky to have such a group of accomplished, smart, funny, amazing friends. Being around you makes me want to do/be better.

Thank you to my friend Nell for always seeing my silly and

raising me another. From darts to footed PJs to kicking trees over Euro currency design to ridic mom stories—you're the best.

And thank you to Aferdita and Dorisa Emini for being the very first readers of the very first draft. I'm proud to know you.

This story started to slowly reveal itself to me in the aftermath of a loss, like the remains of an ancient iceman being exposed inch by inch in melting snow. Thank you to Cassie for helping me through that time.

If you are suffering from anxiety or OCD, you are not alone. Here are two wonderful resources with tons of great content for young and old alike: the International OCD Foundation (iocdf.org) and the Anxiety and Depression Association of America (adaa.org).

Violet Lumani was raised in a family of superstitious omen-watchers, absorbing the stories and myths her family brought to America with them. She holds a BA from Barnard College of Columbia University and an MBA from UCONN and lives in Connecticut with her husband, two kids, and forever-dieting chihuahua named Kiwi.

Also from Uproar Books:

ASPERFELL by Jamie Thomas (Gothic Fantasy)

Named one of *Booklist*'s Top Ten Debut Speculative Fiction novels of 2020, Asperfell is a must-read for fans of Jane Austen who always wished she'd dabbled in blood magic.

SAND DANCER by Trudie Skies (Young Adult Fantasy)

In a desert kingdom where fire magic is a sin, a half-starved peasant girl must disguise herself as a nobleman's son to learn the ways of the sword and find her father's killer.

ALWAYS GREENER by J.R.H. Lawless (Dark Comedy)

In the corporate dystopian world of 2072, the world's most popular reality show starts a competition for world's worst life, and now everyone is out to prove just how bad they've got it.

THE WAY OUT by Armond Boudreaux (Sci-Fi Thriller)

When a virus necessitates the use artificial wombs for all pregnancies, two fearless women discover the terrifying truth behind this world-changing technology.

WORLDS OF LIGHT AND DARKNESS (Sci-Fi Anthology)

The best speculative fiction from *DreamForge* and *Space & Time* magazines, including stories by Jane Lindskold, John Jos. Miller, Scott Edelman, Jonathan Maberry, and more.

For more information, visit uproarbooks.com